L EVELAND

WAYWARD SONS #1

BODY COUNT

Cover by: Miblart

Copy and Developmental editing by: Aspen Tree EAS

Proofread by: Abrianna Denae Proofreading

Also by
L Eveland

Wayward Sons

Body Count

Skin Deep

Monsters in My Bed

Kissed by the Krampus

Scales and Song

Hearts and Halos

Lassos and Lace

Bounty and Bone

Kindred Spirits

Culinary Creatures

Brimstone and Bolognese

Brimstone

Beefcakes

Bluz

Brewtiful's

<u>Flame and Shadow</u>

A Dream of Flame and Shadow

A Glint of Steel and Roses

Contents

For everyone who likes their men like they like their coffee:
dark AF with a hint of sweetness, addictive as hell, and always there to pick you up after a long night of bad decisions.

No. Matter. What.

SPECIAL *Thanks*

SPECIAL THANKS TO MY superfans who helped make this happen: Alexa Fichtel, Katie Poff, Jocelyn Adams, Jolie, Catherine Hale, Kim Franke, Charee Beatty, Caitlin Colby, Taylor Kennedy, Sarah Khawaja, Sheryl K Bishop, D.R. Perry, S. Leigh Sparks, Lacey Sutton, Kyleen Valleaux.

If you'd like to get special perks and read the next book in the series before anyone else, you can join us here: https://reamstories.com/leveland

Content *Warnings*

THE PLOT OF THIS book deals heavily with human trafficking of children and forced prostitution. While no sexual assaults appear on the page, one of the main characters is an adult victim of child sex trafficking. Reader discretion is advised as this may be triggering to some.

This book contains CNC (consensual non-consent) and resistance play.

Body Count is about a possessive narcissistic sociopath, the man who comes to love him, and their extended family of serial and spree killers. River and Theo don't always practice safe sex or risk aware consensual kink (RACK). No safe words are used. This is not meant to be a realistic or healthy depiction of a BDSM relationship, or any relationship for that matter.

Seriously. River is a walking red flag.

A full breakdown of content warnings, kinks, and tropes in Body Count can be found on the next page.

To learn more about human trafficking in the USA, and how to report it, please visit humantraffickinghotline.org or the National Center for Missing and Exploited Children at missingkids.org

Content
Warnings

Sex trafficking, including child victims
Murder, blood, violence, dismemberment
Childhood abuse and neglect (referenced in the past)
Alcohol consumption
Torture of antagonists
Minor character death
Gun violence/gunshot wounds
Dissociation and dissociative episodes
PTSD and c-PTSD
Dubious consent
Drug overdose
Emotional abuse
Imprisonment
Organized crime (Mafia)
Mental illness, including non-compliance with medical treatment
BDSM themes
Edge play/Resistance play
Power imbalance

Discussion of STIs, including HIV

Brief instance of suicidal ideation

Implied cannibalism

Kidnapping

Carjacking

Cremation of human remains

Sexually explicit scenes

Delusional thinking/Delusions

Physical restraints in a psychiatric institution

Discussion of suicide/assisted suicide

Inferred animal death/abuse

<u>Kinks included</u>

CNC/consensual non-consent

Resistance play

Edging

Primal play

Biting/marking

Blood play

Praise kink

<u>Tropes</u>

Insta-love

Rescued by a sociopath

Touch him and die

Possessive boyfriends

Vengeance as a love language

One
River

"You know that's the preferred drink of psychopaths." The bartender set my gin and tonic down in front of me hard enough that it sloshed over the lip of the cloudy glass, darkening the half rotten wooden bar like a shadow.

He meant it to be a light-hearted opener to a conversation, but I wasn't in the mood for a chat. If I had wanted to talk, I wouldn't have set up in the corner of his shitty dive bar.

The silence between us grew as he leaned on the bar for an awkwardly long time waiting for me to reply. Instead, I picked up the drink and frowned at the sad looking lime wedge he'd jammed onto the rim. No way I was putting that anywhere near my mouth.

"Gin and tonic and black coffee," he continued, more to hear himself talk than anything. He struck me as the sort.

I forced my face to maintain a neutral and interested expression, using the bartender's silence as a cue to nod politely. Just like Mom had taught me to do.

His demeanor instantly relaxed when I moved back into the pointless dance of social interaction.

While he went on about the favorite drink orders of famous psychopaths and some study done in Austria, I scanned the bar, taking in the worn décor, the thin layer of grime on everything, the neon. The place really was a disgusting dive.

Why am I here?

I'd left work frustrated and without a destination in mind. The further I drove, the more intense my aggravation became, until it was an itch under my skin that I couldn't scratch.

I needed to hurt someone, or maybe fuck someone. Maybe both. Maybe neither. When I saw the dive bar sign from the freeway, I'd felt that tug at my subconscious, the one that said this was where I was supposed to be. Yet as I looked around, I couldn't for the life of me figure out *why*.

The crack of billiard balls drew my attention to two pool tables in the far corner. Only one of them was occupied. The men playing were older, typical dive bar types with their blue jean cutoffs and greasy hair. They didn't interest me.

But the redheaded young man with the sad blue eyes did. He stood behind the two older men in a worn V-neck t-shirt that was two sizes too big, his pale, skinny arms folded over his chest. His hair was a tad too long and shaggy, his face too thin. The strip of black leather around his pale neck stood out like a sore thumb. The O-ring in the front sat perfectly over his Adam's apple. He was staring straight back as if he could see through me.

We stared at each other from across the bar, a strange electric feeling crawling over my skin.

The moment was over when the bigger man stepped back, cue stick in hand, and threw a possessive arm around the redhead's waist. The redhead looked away and down, cheeks coloring, but not with embarrassment. The way his jaw flexed, the way he stiffened and pulled away until the older man's hand tightened to hold him in place—there was anger there. Resentment. Maybe even hate.

Are you why I'm here, little finch?

I tapped my fingers on my glass. Living people rarely interested me beyond whatever immediate purpose they served. I found the dead much more interesting to be around. They couldn't lie and had no ulterior motives. What you saw was what you got with the dead.

Living people were another story entirely. Always lying, scheming, looking for ways to hurt one another. I had learned long ago how to walk like them, talk like them, to disappear in crowds of them. I had the same organs, the same five liters of blood inside of me, but I would never be like them.

Yet sometimes I liked to pretend. I liked to observe, to put things in motion to see how they'd play out.

Shepherd called it playing with my food.

But I didn't want to play with the little redhead across the bar, at least not in the normal way I liked to play with people. I wanted to *possess* him. I wanted to take him and put him up on a shelf like the little porcelain doll he was, place him where no one else could reach him. Maybe he would fall from that great height and shatter, and maybe I would put him back together. I needed to know which way it would go.

Still watching the redhead intently, I brought the gin and tonic to my mouth.

"What do you know about the trio at the pool table?" I asked the bartender, whom I'd cut off mid-sentence.

He turned his head as if he hadn't noticed them. "Who, Rick and them? Regulars, I guess. Never seen the redhead before. Rick's always coming in here with a new boyfriend, always younger than the last."

He shook his head. "You think he's under twenty-one? I didn't card him since he ain't drinking."

"Do they ever drink?"

"Who?"

"The boyfriends." I glanced back at the bartender.

Consciously, he didn't know anything about me, but subconsciously, he knew. I could see it in the way he distanced himself, the sweat shimmering on his forehead. His lizard brain knew he was talking to a predator even if he didn't.

He shrugged, probably trying to ignore the part of his brain screaming that he should run. "Not when I'm in here."

I turned back to watching the trio at the pool table. Rick, who was apparently the one who'd put his hands all over the redhead, was at the table taking his shot. The redhead had slinked back to the corner as far away from Rick as he could get without being accused of trying to escape. He gripped his elbow and stared low and away, giving off the air of a beaten dog. There were dark circles around his wrist. Bruises. They were difficult to make out in the low light, but I knew what I was looking at. There were more of them in faded yellow around the leather band he wore on his neck.

A normal person would be angry on the redhead's behalf when they realized what I had. They'd be disgusted. They'd also turn away and pretend they saw nothing wrong. Doing something would cause a scene, and normal people didn't want that.

I, on the other hand, knew that some people were more useful as fertilizer for my mushroom garden than taking up oxygen.

I left my seat at the bar, approaching the pool table with my hands in my pockets.

The redhead stiffened when he saw me coming over. His eyes danced to Rick as he shrank further into the corner, almost as if he could slip through the cracks.

Rick didn't look up until I put my hand down on top of the eight ball. He scowled at me, leaning on his cue stick, his black mustache twitching. "Fuck off, Chinaman."

I stared at him a moment too long, allowing myself the pleasure of fantasizing about shoving the billiard ball down his throat and breaking the cue stick across his skull. "I'm not Chinese, you racist fuck."

The other man came forward a half step, leaning on his cue stick. "Look, man, we're in the middle of a game."

I pushed the eight ball into the corner pocket. "Looks like your game's over."

Rick surged forward until his friend put a hand on his chest, holding him back. "What the fuck do you want?"

My eyes slid to the redhead in the corner. I tipped my head toward him. "Him."

The redhead's eyes widened and he shrank slightly, glancing at Rick.

"He's spoken for," Rick snarled.

I examined the end of the cue stick before seizing the chalk. "How much did you pay for him?"

"What the fuck are you talking about, asshole?" Rick demanded.

My eyes flicked up to his briefly before I met the other man's eyes. He was drenched in sweat and looked ready to bolt. "You aren't made of money, given the venue. He looks like a good lay, but I don't imagine he's worth your life. I'm willing to buy him from you. Name your price."

The second man swallowed and looked at Rick. "What the fuck, Rick?"

"I don't know what the fuck he's talking about," Rick insisted and waved his cue stick at me. "You better fuck off before I break you in half."

"The way I see it, this ends one of two ways," I said calmly. "One, you take the money for Red. You walk away and never come back here. You leave him with me, and everybody wins. Or two…" I set the chalk down and met Rick's eyes again. "You die. Slowly. I take him. I win."

"I don't know who the fuck you think you are…" Rick made the mistake of taking a step toward me. It would have been his last if his friend hadn't grabbed his shoulder.

"The kid ain't worth that much, Rick," mumbled the other guy.

He was right, at least statistically speaking, unless they were planning to kill him and harvest his organs. Then a thousand dollars would be a steal. But for a quick fuck and dump? They'd be smart to take the money and go.

"It ain't about that," Rick growled. "This fucker can't tell us what to do."

"You should listen to your friend," I advised. "Just take the money and go."

"Fuck you!" Rick spat and swung the pool stick at my head.

I ducked, easily avoiding the swing, and jammed the end of my cue stick into his throat from down low. Rick made a gagging sound and dropped his cue stick, stumbling back to grip his throat. I stood, pulling the stick back and eying Rick's friend, half expecting him to step in.

The second man threw his hands up and backed away. "Fuck this. I don't want none of this!" he shouted and ran for the door.

Rick was still recovering, making wet wheezing sounds as I closed on him. He was lucky we were in a public place, or I'd have finished the job without a second thought. I was being generous as it was.

"Come on," I said, and grabbed the redhead by the arm.

The redhead stared at Rick, wide-eyed as I pulled him toward the door. "Is he going to be okay?"

"Probably. He got off lucky with a bruised windpipe," I said, taking his hand. His fingers were small and delicate, his palms silky. I immediately wanted to bite them.

"But..."

"Forget about him," I said. "You belong to me now. We're leaving." I pulled him toward the exit, drawing looks from everyone in the bar. The bartender was on the phone, probably calling the cops after what he'd just seen.

"My name's Theo," he said, following numbly behind me. He didn't even try to pull away or escape. "But you can call me whatever you want."

"Theo's your name, isn't it?"

"Yes," he replied quietly as I pulled him through the front door.

"Then that's what I'll call you."

"What should I call you?" Theo asked after following me for a moment.

I looked back at him stumbling along behind me wide-eyed, almost as if he were drugged. Maybe he was.

"River," I said.

"River," he repeated, as if trying it out.

I liked the way he said my name far more than I expected to. I wanted him to say it again just so I could watch the shape his lips made when he did. Instead, I pushed open the door and gestured for him to follow me out.

The air outside was chilly enough that I could see my breath, but he didn't have a jacket. His pale cheeks and the tip of his nose were already flushed pink from the cold. He rubbed his bare arms, breathing fast.

Theo jumped when the door behind us crashed open just as we reached my car.

"Motherfucker," Rick spat in a hoarse voice, staggering around the side of the building.

I rolled my eyes. He was an idiot to chase me down.

I shrugged off my jacket and placed it over his shoulders. "Stay here, Theo," I told him and turned around to face Rick, putting myself between him and Theo. I stared him down with a bored sigh as he staggered toward us. "Well, come on. It's cold and I've got places to be."

There was the telltale *shick* of a switchblade coming out. "Fuck you!" Rick snarled and charged me.

Idiot.

He was half drunk, unsteady on his feet. I was in my element and clear headed, even if I was unarmed. I didn't need a weapon to kill him.

I let him grab my shoulder with his off hand, seizing the opportunity to twist his wrist. There was a loud snap as I broke it, and he let out a squeak before jabbing limply with the knife. I caught his hand with ease and twisted, stepping in to push the blade back toward him. Rick had enough strength and balance for a brief struggle before his eyes widened and the blade sank into his body. I pushed in, throwing all of my body weight into it and jamming the knife in to the hilt while he stared at me, grimacing in pain. I'd hit his liver, which meant he was a dead man. He just didn't know it yet.

Rick released the knife and tried to grab onto me, but he lost consciousness before he could get a good grip.

"Fuck, you're heavy," I mumbled and let him fall to the pavement.

Theo immediately turned and vomited.

I sighed and shook out my keys to open the trunk. Inside, I quickly got to work, ripping open one of the cheap shower curtains I kept back there for emergencies and spreading it over the upholstery.

While I struggled with getting Rick into the trunk, Theo spat and coughed, continuing to vomit loudly near the front of the car. Shit, I hoped he didn't get any on my coat. That thing was dry clean only. At least I didn't have to worry about getting blood on it. I had surprisingly little blood on me by the time I managed to wrestle Rick into the trunk. Leaving the knife in place had limited the bleeding, which would make clean up much easier.

I shut the trunk and leaned on it before glancing behind me to scan the rooftops for cameras. Should've done that first, but then I hadn't intended to kill Rick out in the parking lot. Thankfully, I didn't spot any.

Theo coughed again and spat, wiping the back of his hand across his mouth.

"Get in the car," I told him.

He twisted to stare at me, eyes wide with terror. His chest rose and fell with fast, heavy breaths. "You...you killed him."

Theo flinched and shrank as I stepped up to him, lowering his eyes to the ground.

I reached to pull up the collar on the coat. "Get in the car, Theo. We have to go."

His jaw trembled, but he didn't resist as I pulled open the passenger side door. Theo sank numbly into the seat. He sat stiffly, as if he were waiting for another command, so I told him to buckle up before walking around to get in the driver's side. I turned the key, and the heater came to life, blasting stale, hot air into the enclosed space.

I put my hands on the steering wheel and looked over at him. The car smelled like panic sweat, like terrified prey.

"Are you going to run away from me, Theo? Because if you run, I'll have to chase you, and if I chase you, I will catch you."

His wide eyes swung to me. "What?"

I reached across the space, cupping his cheek. "Don't run from me," I told him. "Ever."

He licked his lips and shook his head. "I won't."

My shoulders relaxed at his promise. Why would he want to run from me? I'd saved him. Besides, where was he going to go? There was nowhere he could run to that I wouldn't find him, not now that he was mine.

I put the car in reverse and backed out of the parking lot.

Two
Theo

I sat still in the passenger seat of River's car, trying not to look at him too much. It wasn't easy. He wasn't like the other men that Father made me work for. He was much prettier, so beautiful he didn't seem real. His hair was cut nice, long enough to run fingers through without being unkempt, and he had an angular jaw with sharp cheekbones.

I didn't want to piss him off or make him think I was trying to memorize his face so I could identify him later. Fuck, what if there was no later? He'd killed Rick, tossed his body in the trunk like he was nothing, and now I was trapped in a car with him. The lights had dimmed, and the traffic had thinned out. There were fewer and fewer exits appearing along the highway, which meant we were leaving the city.

I rubbed my sweaty palms on my knees. *Where is he taking me? Probably out into a field somewhere to kill me. I'll be buried in a shallow grave right next to Rick by dawn if I don't do something.*

But what could I do? I couldn't escape. Throwing myself out of the moving car would likely be just as fatal, and if I tried, he'd almost certainly catch me and hurt me. Maybe once we stopped, I could make a run for it, but I wouldn't know where to go. I didn't even know where we were, let alone how to get back to Master.

Fuck, was that really where I wanted to go? Back to that awful tiny room? Back to a life of getting beaten and used by men like Rick? Was that better than dying?

I hugged myself, fighting off the shiver of fear that went through me. The move brought the collar of River's coat closer, and I inhaled deeply. It smelled clean, like the laundry when it came back once a month. Maybe vaguely like shaving cream? I couldn't tell. All I knew was that it didn't smell like anyone I'd ever known or anywhere I'd ever been, and that made it comforting.

"How old are you, Theo?" River suddenly asked.

I looked over at him, heart pounding. Why did he want to know? The only time anyone asked me that was when they thought I was underage. Some guys were careful not to fuck underage boys. "I'm twenty."

He sucked in a deep breath and let it out slowly, his shoulders sinking as if he were relieved.

I watched the yellow dashed line in the center of the road fly past. "Are you going to kill me?"

He was quiet for a minute as we drove on. A field rose off to our right, but the grass was so high that I couldn't see anything. "I hope not."

My heart jumped, beating faster.

River glanced over at me briefly. "I don't want to, no."

I tried to swallow the nerves threatening to squeeze off my air. "So is this... Do you want me to blow you or like a hand job or..."

I trailed off when River shot me an angry look, my heart rate soaring. Sweat dampened the back of my neck.

"I didn't want you for sex," he said, turning back to the road.

I frowned and blinked rapidly as bright headlights filled the car briefly. "What else would you want from me? I'm not... That's what I'm for."

"What you're for?" He gave me a funny look.

I shrugged. "I don't know how to do anything else, so if you don't want to kill me or fuck me... What should I do for you?"

Maybe he was one of those guys who just wanted someone to talk to. I hadn't had many clients like that, but there had been a few. Those were the easiest jobs, the best ones, where all I had to do was whatever they said and listen. It had been a long time since I'd had such an easy job.

"I'm not sure how to answer that in a way that would make sense to you." He glanced over at me. "The important thing is that you'll be safe if you stay with me. I won't let anyone else hurt you."

Anyone else. He seemed very careful with how he worded things, as if he spent a lot of time thinking about it. Did that mean he thought he might hurt me? Everything he said implied it was a possibility.

"He might come after me, you know," I said.

"Who?"

"Master. I belong to him."

He looked over at me with that intense gaze again, and I thought I felt my heart stop. "I own you now."

I shook my head. "He won't let me go. I'm his property. He'll think I ran from him, or that you stole me."

Hadn't he? I didn't think it would matter if Master caught me—whether I'd run or was taken. The punishment would be the same either way.

"I don't want you to worry about that," River said. "If he comes for you, I'll kill him, too."

I stared at him, unsure of what to make of that. He talked about killing people like most people talked to me about sports, like it was an everyday thing.

I flinched when the turn signal clicked on.

River looked over at me, his expression blank. All the anger that had been in his voice a moment ago was suspiciously absent, as if he were somehow able to flip a switch and turn his emotions *off*. I wished I could. Everything would be easier if I could do that.

The car turned down another road, the faint glow of a small town ahead. It hit me suddenly that I had no idea where I was or how to get back home. All my things were there. Everyone I knew, all my clothes... My whole life was back there. Without Master, who would make sure I had food to eat? How would I know what clothes to put on or what to do every day?

What if I never went back? Who would take care of me then?

I knew I shouldn't want to go back to that awful place, but it was like my mind was fractured. I didn't want to go back, but I didn't know anything else. Everything outside was new and terrifying. Uncertain.

"I'm going to take care of you," River said, as if he could hear my thoughts. "You don't have to worry, Theo."

The car rolled into a sleepy, small town that looked like a painting out of one of the picture books strange men sometimes read to me when I was younger. There were empty shops, their windows darkened. Houses with manicured lawns and comfy looking porches. Sidewalks with chalk pictures on them. We drove by a house with a bright red bicycle out front, the color so vivid I wished I could touch it just to make sure it was real.

He drove through the small town and out into the country for a while before the car slowed and River turned on the turn signal again.

The car turned into a gravel driveway leading up to a huge brick house with a round tower on the front that reminded me of a castle.

I leaned forward, eyes widening as I strained to pick out details in the dark. Panic surged up my throat and my breathing got fast when he shut the door behind him. Should I get out? Was I supposed to stay? He hadn't told me what to do. What if he left me there? That was almost as terrifying as taking me inside to kill me.

My door opened, and he held it, holding out a hand. "Come on."

I undid my seatbelt and put my hand in his. My heart calmed immediately when his fingers closed around mine. I stood, and he moved like he was going to pull his hand away, but I tightened my grip on him.

"Is it okay if I hold on to you?" I blurted.

He tipped his head as if the question was strange. Maybe it was. Normal people probably didn't go around holding hands with strangers they just met, but I didn't know what else to do. I felt better when we were touching.

River nodded and squeezed my hand. "It's okay. I like how your hands feel in mine. They're soft."

"I use a lot of lotion." I didn't know why I said that. He hadn't asked why they were soft.

He didn't acknowledge my nervous babbling, instead turning to walk toward the house.

I followed River up the stairs, a step behind him, and onto a large porch. It was bare except for a worn welcome mat. His keys jingled as he shook them out, jamming one into the door. He unlocked it and held it open for me.

My heart jumped up into my throat again at the idea of walking into a darkened house with a killer behind me, but I didn't dare hesitate more than a moment, afraid he'd change his mind.

The hardwood floor creaked under my weight as I stepped into a dark entryway. It wasn't a large room, but I could make out some stairs ahead and a big window on the landing where the stairs curved the other way. I flinched when the door swung shut behind me. River walked past, tossing his keys casually into a glass dish sitting on a desk. He clicked on a small lamp before coming back to help me out of the coat.

"You live here by yourself?" I asked, and then immediately added, "It's nice." I didn't want him to think I was trying to get information from him, and men liked it when I told them they had nice things.

He gave me a strange look, as if what I'd said didn't make any sense. "You live here with me now, Theo."

I flinched, blinked, looked around at all the nice things, all the space. It was too big, too open, and everything looked so expensive. I didn't belong in this room, let alone this house.

River's hands slid down my arms and closed around my fingers. "Come," he said, pulling me toward the stairs.

I tried to slow my breathing and get my heart rate under control, but I couldn't. I was in full panic mode. He'd said he didn't want me for sex, so why was he taking me upstairs? What could possibly be up there except for his bedroom? And if he took me in there, what was there to do with me but fuck me?

He guided me up the creaky stairs to a hallway with wood paneling. There were four doors in the hall, and he took me to the first one on the right, pushing it open. I was almost relieved to see it was a bathroom and not a bedroom.

River let go of my hand to step into the bathroom, where he opened the medicine cabinet to retrieve a toothbrush that was still in plastic packaging. He ripped it open with his teeth and held the toothbrush out to me.

I flushed and took it. He was right though; my breath probably smelled awful after throwing up so much.

River's eyes raked over me as I bent over the sink to brush my teeth. I tried not to notice the way he was looking at me, taking me in as if he could see through my clothes. I didn't know what men saw in me. I was too skinny and pale, and my hair was a wild mess of reddish curls. Master had a pair of clippers he used to shave it down twice a year, but otherwise he didn't let anyone cut our hair. Growing it out made my face softer and I looked younger, especially since I wasn't allowed to have facial or body hair. Men liked clean shaven and thin boys with nice complexions, so that's what he made me into.

River reached to turn on the bath. "How hot do you like it?"

"Um." I chewed on my lip and looked over at him, unsure of how to answer.

"I'll set it how I like it and we can go from there." River adjusted the water until steam started to fill the bathroom before opening the cabinet again. My breath caught when he brought out a pair of scissors. "Hold still," he demanded and grabbed the leather collar around my neck, pulling it away from my skin.

I let out an involuntary whimper, turning my head away. As he pulled on the front of the collar, the back dug into the fading bruises on my neck—a memento from a man at a truck stop last week who thought the collar should be used as a handle. I'd blacked out briefly from the way he'd used it to choke me, and when I came to, I couldn't speak for days.

The leather suddenly fell away, the painful pressure against the fading bruises releasing. I opened my eyes and drew in a sharp breath of relief.

"There. That's better." River unceremoniously pitched the collar in the trash and turned back to getting the bath ready.

My fingers closed around my neck, sliding over the strange, naked flesh. Without my collar, I felt exposed and vulnerable. Completely unprotected. We were never supposed to take our collars off; we weren't even supposed to touch them without Master's permission. The only time they ever came off was on the rare occasion they needed to be cleaned or resized. I couldn't remember the last time I'd felt bare skin on my neck.

I don't belong to Master anymore, I thought, tears threatening. River had told me that I belonged to him now, but it hadn't really sank in yet that I wouldn't be going back there. This wasn't another job that would be over tomorrow. I wasn't going to wake up in my cell tomorrow, aching and alone. Whatever River wanted with me, he wasn't letting me go back.

At first, the realization sent waves of grief through me. That life was all I'd ever known. Without it, there was no certainty, no safety. No one to take care of me. I was alone in the world for the first time in my life.

Except I wasn't. River had promised to take care of me.

I wrapped my arms tightly around myself and glanced up at him while he fiddled with the knob to turn the shower on instead of the tub. Did he expect me to do for him all the things I'd done for Master? He'd said he didn't want me for sex, but maybe I should try anyway, show him that I could please him. I could do anything he wanted, as often as he wanted me to. I had to prove to him that I could be good, that he hadn't gone through all this trouble for nothing.

He stood and looked back at me, lips turning into a frown. "Why are you crying?"

I pushed the tears away. "I'm sorry. I'll stop. I didn't mean to."

River yanked the towel free and drew it across my cheeks. "I don't like it when you cry."

"I won't do it again," I promised. "I'll be good."

He hesitated. "I didn't mean it like that. I'm not going to punish you, Theo. I just..."

He let out a frustrated growl when I blinked and more tears fell involuntarily. I reached to wipe them away, but River grabbed my hand and held it. I tensed when he leaned in and pressed his lips to my cheek, first one and then the other, kissing away the tears. It was such a strangely intimate gesture, and it might've been sweet if I wasn't so utterly terrified and confused.

"I'm the only one who gets to make you cry, Theo," he said, holding my face in his hands. "No more tears for dead men, okay?"

I nodded slowly, even though I wasn't crying for Rick.

"Good." River stepped back. "Now take off your clothes."

Three
River

THEO MET MY EYES briefly and then looked away. His thin fingers gripped the bottom hem of his t-shirt, and he pulled it over his head without so much as a word of protest.

I frowned, watching him carefully fold the t-shirt and set it aside like something precious. I had expected him to be thin and pale, but he wasn't all skin and bones under there. His chest and stomach were like the rest of him. Delicate. Beautiful. Perfect. Oh, he could stand to put on a few more pounds, maybe some muscle, but he was beautiful as he was too. I wanted to lick him, to bite him and watch the bruises bloom. They'd show up well on such pale skin.

But I didn't dare. He was still flinching at every little sound, every sudden movement. I didn't want to break him, not yet.

And now he was chewing on his bottom lip, pressing hard enough with his teeth to turn the skin white.

I seized his rounded chin with two fingers. "Don't bite your lip."

He looked at me with his sad eyes. "Sorry."

"You don't have to apologize. Just stop doing it."

I ran the pad of my thumb over his pale lips. They were the color of white strawberries, and I was desperate to find out if he tasted like that, too. "I want to kiss you."

The knot in his throat bobbed. "So do it."

I focused on his eyes, his posture. Everything about him said he didn't want me to. Mom said consent was important. She'd drilled that into us, making sure we understood that was one boundary we were never to cross. If any of us ever did, she'd hunt us down herself and make sure we never hurt anyone ever again.

"You haven't said you want me to yet," I pointed out.

He blinked as if he'd been asleep and was just waking up, eyes coming into focus.

"Do you want me to kiss you, Theo?" I whispered, already leaning in.

"No." He jerked as soon as he said it, almost as if he'd been slapped. His hands flew to his mouth. "I'm sorry. I didn't mean that."

I smiled and stood up straighter, trying to visualize the personal space bubble Mom was always trying to get me to imagine. "Yes, you did. And it's okay. You'll never upset me by telling the truth, Theo. If you don't want me to kiss you, then I won't."

He lowered his hands slowly. "But...you *own* me."

"You are mine," I confirmed. "Still, as much as I might not like it, you do get a say in what happens to your body. Within reason."

His lips turned down in a frown. "And what does that mean?"

I closed my hands around his. "It means that you're done sleeping with other people. You're not going to let anyone hit you, and you're going to take care of yourself. That means eating every day, drinking plenty of water, and sleeping in a bed. My bed."

He turned his head, eyeing the shower.

I turned his face back to me. "We don't have to have sex, but you're going to stay with me now. I want you close to me."

"Because I'm yours?"

I smiled. "Now you get it."

"I'm not sure I do, but if you say so."

I grabbed the back of my shirt and pulled it over my head.

His eyes widened. "What are you doing?"

"We're taking a shower together. I thought I made that clear."

"I..." His eyes dipped below my face, and he bit his lip again.

I smirked and lowered my arms, letting him take all of me in. I wasn't as built as War was, or as tall as Xavier and Xander, but I took care of my body, and I was proud of it. While I wanted to take his hands and put them on me, I expected he'd only do it because I told him to, not because he wanted to. I wanted him to want me.

I wished he'd let me kiss him though, because now I was craving bubblegum; his nipples were exactly the same color as bubblegum. Thinking about sucking on them, imagining the sounds he'd make if I did, was making my cock hard.

"Has anyone ever told you your nipples are the same color as bubblegum?"

He blinked. "Huh?"

"Your nipples. They're the color of this bubblegum I used to buy for pennies when I was a kid."

His face flushed, and he lifted a hand as if he meant to cover them, but stopped short. "Um. No. Nobody's ever said that."

"I hope your cock's not the same color, because then all I'll be able to think about is putting it in my mouth when I see it." I unbuttoned my jeans and kicked them off.

Theo froze with his fingers over the worn brass button on his jeans. "You'd *want* to suck my dick?"

Was that so unbelievable?

I shrugged. "Sure. Why not? And technically, since I own you now, it's my dick. I'm allowing you to have bodily autonomy."

"I don't know what autonomy means."

"Independence," I defined. "A state of self-governance. In other words, I own your dick, but I won't suck it without your permission, no matter how much I want to. Well? Go on. Get undressed. Can't shower with your pants on."

He took a deep breath and pulled his pants and underwear off in one go.

I grinned at the sight of his half-hard cock. "Uh-oh. I'm in trouble."

Color spread across his cheeks as he looked down. "They're not the same color, are they?"

"Yes, they are. Look, mine matches too." I pulled down my boxers, grabbed my hard dick, and pointed. "Though I'm a little darker than you. What color would you call that?"

"Oh my god," he choked out, flushing bright pink to his ears.

"Never heard of that color. I was going to say brown sugar."

"You're ridiculous," he said, and for the first time, I saw his smile. It was sweet, warming the whole room. He had a face made for smiles. I didn't want him to smile for anybody but me, and kissing him felt like a way to claim it, to mark my territory.

"Are you sure I can't kiss you?"

His smile faded, and he lifted his eyebrows, gaze dropping back between my legs. "That baseball bat you're swinging suggests you want to do more than kiss me."

"I do," I admitted with a shrug. "But not tonight."

"Why not?" He almost sounded disappointed.

"Because I'll never force you against your will, and you're still afraid of me." I took his hands and guided him toward the tub. "I don't want to break you."

"You won't break me. People have been rough with me before. I'm used to it."

I gripped his chin, dropping my voice an octave. "I'm not any of those other guys, Theo."

"I know."

"No, you don't. I need you to understand," I said slowly. "I'm not like other people."

He looked down at my hands and then back up at me. "You mean because you kill people?"

"Yes," I answered and stepped into the shower, ushering him in with me.

I put him in the water first and grabbed the loofah, watching the way the water flowed in little rivers over his skin. Theo had a light dusting of freckles along his shoulders, and while I soaped him up, I tried to count all of them. I made it to sixty-three before his shoulders relaxed even slightly.

As much as I enjoyed touching him, it was stressing him out. His muscles were stiff and his expression fixed in one of worry. He reminded me of a zoo animal who'd just discovered the door to his enclosure was open. He could've run, but he'd been so beaten down, resistance didn't even occur to him.

Theo didn't fight me when I lifted his arms to wash under them, but he didn't help me either. His complete lack of any sense of fight or flight was confusing. I wanted him to do one or the other because at least then I'd know where we stood. Without those familiar roles to fall into, everything was awkward.

I'd never been responsible for another human before. Mom had never even trusted me to watch Xander and Xavier. Of course, they were older when they came to live with us, and they were only five years younger than me, but still. I hadn't even been allowed to have a pet. I had no idea what I was doing, and yet here I was, suddenly responsible for his every need.

I liked how dependent he was on me, maybe too much. Come Monday, I was going to have to go back to work, which would probably mean spending several hours apart, which I didn't know if he could handle. Theo was still alternating between being terrified of me and clinging to me.

He flushed bright red when I washed between his legs.

"You don't have to be embarrassed," I said quietly.

"I'm not," he lied. "I can clean myself."

"I like taking care of you." I gestured for him to turn around.

Theo turned slowly. He didn't react much as I soaped up his back, but as I went lower, he shied away more and more.

I sighed and hung the loofah back on the side of the shower. He started to twist to see what I was doing, but stopped when I commanded, "Stay." I pressed my thumbs into his shoulders and slowly started working firm circles in the muscles to get him to relax. "Tell me if it hurts."

He nodded and leaned his head forward against the shower wall, letting the hot water come down over his neck and shoulders while I massaged him. His upper body was incredibly tense, but I had to be mindful of all the bruises scattered over him. Some of them were days or weeks old, yellow and faded with age, while others still looked fresh and dark. The biggest one ran across his shoulder toward his spine in a thick line like he'd been hit with something long and thin. Without thinking, I leaned forward to plant a gentle kiss on the injury.

Theo flinched away.

Fuck, I shouldn't have done that. "Did I hurt you?" I asked.

"No," he said, shaking his head. "Just surprised me is all. I was zoning out."

"Are you okay with me kissing you now?" I moved my hands slightly lower, pressing in to rub with my thumbs.

Theo closed his eyes and tipped his head up. I was cheating, buttering him up with a back rub to bring down his defenses, but if it worked, it worked.

I saw his resolve waver and then slip. He turned and dipped his chin toward his chest. "If you want."

"Thank fuck," I murmured and gently pressed my lips to his.

Four
Theo

I SHOULDN'T HAVE SAID yes, but I felt like I owed him already. I wanted him to be happy, because happy men were less dangerous. They hit me less. River was less likely to hurt me if I got him off and kept him happy. Besides, who was I to say no to him? Nobody, that's who.

Steam filled the bathroom around us as the soft, full lips of the world's most beautiful killer met mine in a brief press. It was so quick, I was left disappointed. That was it? All this worrying and anxiety over a kiss and that was it? How was I supposed to judge anything if he was going to kiss me like that?

I turned around in the shower, daring to meet his eyes. He had beautiful, dark eyes, and they were looking at me with such intensity that it was hard to breathe. River wanted more. It was written all over him, from the heavy way he was breathing to the way his hard cock stood straight out, flushed and full. He wanted me, so why didn't he just take me?

"You can kiss me more than that," I said, licking my lips. "If you want."

"Yeah?" he said, nostrils flaring.

I nodded. "Yeah."

River gripped me by the chin and pulled my lips back to his.

I'd kissed a lot of men and never enjoyed it. It had always felt like a violation or an invasion, and I'd never chosen to do it except when clients asked for it. I hadn't expected to enjoy kissing River, either, and yet, it was an almost spiritual experience, the slow way he traced his tongue over the seam of my lips, tasting me, savoring me. When I parted my lips for him, he groaned and tangled his tongue in mine. I waited for him to yank me closer, for this kiss to turn into him grinding his cock against me, but he didn't.

What was I supposed to do with that? I didn't know how to be anything other than a sex object to anybody. That's what felt safe. He owned me, and he wanted me. Shouldn't he have me?

I shifted how I was standing, moving in against him to close my hand around his hard cock.

River pulled back. "What are you doing?" He sounded angry.

Panic threatened to make my throat swell shut. "I thought… I was…"

"You're tempting me to make a very bad decision, little finch."

I blinked at the nickname. "Finch?"

"Because male house finches have a bright red head. Like you."

And because birds are kept in cages, I thought. He was right. It was an appropriate nickname.

He smoothed his thumbs along my temples and kissed the top of my head. "No sex until you've been medically cleared. You need to come? You can jerk off, but that's it. Understand me?"

"Yes, sir."

He shook his head. "Not sir. River."

I swallowed. "River."

"Good boy." River leaned in and I almost lost my balance trying to lean away from him.

The water suddenly stopped. It took me a minute to realize he'd been reaching to turn off the water and not trying to kiss me again.

After our shower, River wrapped us both in towels and we went back down the hall to his room where he gave me a pair of sweats to put on, yanking on a near-identical pair himself. They didn't fit me right, but I didn't argue. River told me to get comfortable and plopped into bed with a book that had mushrooms on the cover, propped up against a pile of pillows.

I stood there, unsure how to follow his directions. I didn't know if I could be comfortable in a strange bed with a stranger, but that was clearly where he wanted me to be.

I pulled the blanket back carefully, making sure I didn't disturb him while he was reading his book. When he didn't look up, I slid into the bed and laid there stiffly, staring up at the ceiling. The bed was easily big enough for both of us, but it felt like I was taking up too much space. We were too close. I wanted to be away from him, but not so far away that he'd think I was trying to escape.

Should I lay with my back to him? Will that make him angry? Maybe I should face him instead, so he doesn't think I'm trying to ignore him. But he might not want me to look at him. It felt like such an impossible decision, deciding which way to lay in the bed. It was stupid. *I* was stupid, but I was also panicking. Why hadn't he told me which way to lay?

This would all be easier if he'd just fuck me, and then I'd know what he wants. I knew how to deal with that, how to cope with being used and thrown away. This...I didn't know what to do with what was happening to me.

Eventually, I decided it would be safer to turn away. I curled up on my side, arms folded over my chest and legs drawn up. Half of me was hanging over the edge of the bed, but I couldn't bring myself to move. If I jostled around too much, I'd interrupt his reading.

"Theo?"

I held my breath. What had I done wrong? I'd tried so hard not to disturb him.

He sighed and the lights went out. There was the dull thud of a book hitting the floor before an arm curled around my middle and dragged me across the bed. River pulled me tight against him, almost like a giant teddy bear, nestling his head over mine.

"You're safe here," he promised. "This is the safest place, Theo. They're never going to hurt you again."

My throat felt tight, and when I blinked, the corners of my eyes were damp. "How do you know?" I whispered into the dark.

"Because I won't let them." He squeezed me harder, and we lay there in silence for a while, the only sound his steady breathing.

"Why me?" I whispered in the dark. "Why'd you save me?"

"Because I wanted you for myself."

There was something refreshing about the honesty, even if it wasn't the answer I'd been hoping for.

"You don't like my answer?"

I shifted slightly against him, surprised at how warm he was. "I don't understand your answer. People don't do whatever they want because they want to."

"I do," he said with a shrug. "I saw you, I wanted you, so I took you and I brought you here."

"Why did you want me? What for? I know you said not sex, but...I don't know what else I can do for you."

River sighed and nestled his chin over my head. "You seemed so fragile. I wanted to protect you, put you somewhere safe and keep you there to see what you'd become. There's a part of me that hopes you'll stay up there, well away from me like a smart boy. If you don't, I might break you. I like to play rough with my toys, Theo. I know it doesn't make sense, this conflicting need to break you and keep you safe, but that's what I feel when I look at you." He was quiet for a minute before asking, "Does that make you afraid of me, Theo?"

"Yes," I answered. "But..."

"But what?"

My chest and neck flushed hot. "But I'm more afraid of what will happen to me if there's no one to take care of me."

"I won't abandon you," he promised, running his thumb over my bottom lip. "And I won't let anyone hurt you. I promised you that already, little finch."

"I know, but other people have said the same."

"I told you I'm not like everyone else. But you need me to prove it, don't you? That's all right. I can do that."

River began to hum and put his hand over mine, massaging firmly until I opened my fingers from the fist they'd formed involuntarily. When my hands relaxed, he moved to my wrists, slowly working his way up my arm. I didn't know the name of the song he was humming, but it was a simple melody and oddly comforting. Maybe it was a lullaby. If it was, it was one I'd never heard before.

By the time he started massaging my chest, it was a struggle to keep my eyes open. I was so sore, so tired, and the bed was so soft and warm. With the soft song he was humming for me, it was impossible to be afraid of him.

Not that it mattered if I was. I couldn't fight him. I couldn't fight anyone. Whatever was going to happen, I told myself it would happen whether I was awake or not. There was no reason to fight so hard against something I needed so badly.

River pressed a gentle kiss to the top of my head. "Sleep, little finch. I'll watch over you."

With River humming softly against my head, I finally gave in and closed my eyes.

Five
River

I HELD THEO UNTIL I was certain he was in a deep sleep; his body was slack against mine and he was snoring lightly. Then I held him a while longer, watching the minutes tick by on the alarm clock next to the bed.

Tomorrow was Saturday, and War was in town. I could take Theo over to Mom's to get him a clean bill of health and then...

Then what?

I'd promised him I could wait, and I wanted to make good on that promise, but I didn't know how long I could wait for him. I wanted him now, and I was used to getting what I wanted, when I wanted it, but I couldn't have him, which left me with a conundrum.

Lying there with my body wrapped around him felt good. It felt right, even if I was burning for more, especially now that he smelled like my soap and my sheets. If I stayed there, though, I didn't know if I could control myself, and I *had* to. Mom had raised me to know better, to fight those urges even if I didn't want to.

My fingers started twitching with the need to feel more of him, skin burning with the urge to feel him against more of me. What did his skin taste like? What sounds did he make when he came? Did he whimper and cry? Fuck, I hoped so.

Shit, I shouldn't be here with him. I didn't trust myself.

When the clock down the hall struck four, I quietly got up. I made sure he stayed asleep as I exited the bedroom. I avoided all the creaky spots on my way down the stairs and went into the basement to retrieve a few things, sliding out the basement exit and around the house.

My breath came out in small white clouds, coloring the October night, and dry leaves crunched under my feet. I shifted the tools under my arm to grab my keys so I could open the trunk.

The first signs of rigor mortis were just starting to set in for Rick. His skin had gone all waxy, and when I unwrapped his arm, it fell stiffly over the lip of the trunk. His major muscle groups still seemed pretty flexible, though, which would make my task a lot easier.

I put my tools down near his still wrapped head, grabbing the thick block of wood first and placing it under his wrist.

If there was a school for serial killers, the first thing they'd teach the students would be not to take trophies. That's how they caught all the famous ones. It was stupid and petty. I'd never understood why anyone bothered. Reliving the crime had never held any appeal for me. Murder was a task I completed, not something I usually enjoyed. It was perfunctory, impersonal, and impassionate.

Until Rick.

I hadn't enjoyed killing him. In fact, it was a huge inconvenience. Tomorrow, I'd have to leave Theo to go put his body through the cremator, and tomorrow was supposed to be my day off. I detested going into work on my day off.

I'd had all night to think about him putting his hands all over Theo, about what he intended to do with him. He'd tried to take Theo away from me. Putting a switchblade in his liver was too good a death for him after he tried to take what was mine. Couldn't do much about that. Bastard was already dead, and I didn't even believe in an afterlife. He wouldn't face any punishment.

The only thing I could do was ensure he wasn't whole when he went to the fire tomorrow.

He didn't bleed much when I used the cleaver to cut off his hand. I wrapped the rest of him back up and took my prize back into the house wrapped in a plastic grocery bag, heading up to the attic to check on my mushrooms. I was experimenting with a new type of fertilizer that was supposed to work better for oyster mushrooms, but so far, I hadn't seen a difference. The small shelving unit I'd turned into a makeshift greenhouse had six bags, all of them showing at least two good-sized clusters. The CO_2 levels were good, so I misted them and moved onto checking my batch of lion's mane mushrooms.

The lion's manes were a bit more finicky than the oysters, but they were worth the extra work. Their distinctive tendril shape was quite beautiful, and the taste was akin to crab when cooked. They looked good, so I gave them some water and moved on to my final task: planting my *Lactarius indigo*. I'd been saving them for a special experiment, and Rick was going to give me a helping hand.

Six
Theo

I WOKE UP WITH a start, eyes darting around in the dark only to settle on where River sat in an armchair next to the bed, wide awake. I stared at him, trying to will my heart to stop pounding. "Were you…watching me sleep?"

He leaned forward, resting his elbows on his knees. "I like watching you sleep. It relaxes me."

Coming from anyone else, that might have creeped me out, but coming from River, it lined up with everything I knew about him so far.

I sat up and looked down at the unfamiliar clothes, taking in the unfamiliar bedroom. *This is my home now. River's going to take care of me.*

The thought shouldn't have been as comforting as it was. I'd watched him kill a man the night before.

The scene replayed in my mind for the millionth time, but I didn't react as strongly to the memory as I had the night before. Maybe sleeping in a warm, comfortable bed had done me some good. Maybe I was getting numb to it.

I stretched. "Didn't you sleep?"

He shook his head. "I'll be fine, little finch. I've gone plenty of nights without sleep before. Besides, as much as I want to snuggle up with you, I've still got to take care of Rick before the sun starts to heat up the car."

Rick. Fuck. That's right. He's in the trunk of River's car.

Ice cold fear shot through me. What if River got caught? What if the police took him away? Who would take care of me then? I didn't want to go back to work for Master, or back to my tiny room, even if it was familiar.

It was probably a good thing he'd killed Rick, then. Rick probably would've gone straight to Master to tell him what I'd done. At least this way, it might take him a while to realize I was gone.

I looked at River. "Does it make me a bad person that I'm glad he's dead?"

River got up from the chair. The bed dipped slightly as he sat on the mattress near my feet. "I might be the wrong person to ask, but I don't think so. Some people are a plague on society. The only way they'll ever be useful is as fertilizer."

I agreed with him. Would a good person think that? Probably not, but I couldn't help it. It's what I thought. Rick was dead, which meant he wasn't hurting anyone else, and I didn't think a single person would miss him.

River shifted forward to plant a gentle kiss on top of my head. "Come on. Get up and brush your teeth. I'm taking you to my mom's house for breakfast."

Panic bubbled up my throat like acid reflux. "Your mom's house?"

"Yep," he said, bouncing up from the bed. "On Saturdays, Tatty makes *syrniki*."

I didn't know what *syrniki* was, but I had to pee, and I was starving. All I'd had to eat the night before was a cheese sandwich before I went to work, and I'd been too wound to even think about eating after.

River's clothes were all too big for me, but he found a hoodie for me to wear and a pair of sweats that stayed on once I tightened the string enough.

"I'll buy you new clothes and shoes tomorrow," he promised while I knelt to tie my worn tennis shoes.

"You don't have to do that. I can keep wearing these." I stood.

"I want to." He pulled open the door.

Though the sun was up, the morning felt much colder than the night. Fog clung to the green field across the road. I was thankful for the hoodie. I didn't know how River could stand to be out in the chilly air without a coat, but he seemed fine in his turtleneck and jeans.

My eyes rolled over him in the morning light, taking in the way his clothes clung to his body. He was stunning, much more attractive than anyone I'd ever seen. What had I done to be worthy of attention from someone like that? It didn't feel like I'd done anything, and yet he'd decided he wanted me. Eventually, he was going to realize how undeserving I was. I needed to work harder to make sure he liked me so that when he did realize, he wouldn't abandon me.

I expected the car to smell awful since there was a corpse in the trunk, but it smelled the same as it had the night before. "What are you going to do with him?" I asked River as he started the car.

"I work at the mortuary with my dad. Rick's going in the cremator," River said. "Don't worry. I know what I'm doing. When I'm done with him, no one will ever find him."

It wasn't a far drive to his mom's house. Apparently, she lived in the small town we'd passed through the night before. Driving by all the picturesque little houses in the foggy morning sun felt like a dream.

The sleepy little town didn't feel real. None of this did. Maybe I was asleep, and when I woke up, it would all be gone, but I hoped not.

River turned down a side street and quickly pulled into a small parking lot filled with cars ranging from a Land Rover to a hearse. Next to the parking lot was a building that would have passed for a house, but the back end of it was all wrong. Instead of a yard, it had a ramp that led up to doors that almost looked industrial in nature. There was also a huge stone chimney, bigger than any I'd ever seen on a house.

The house next door was much more quaint and cozy looking. It was a big, two-story house with window boxes and a flower garden out front, the kind of house a family lived in.

"Your mom lives here?" I asked as River opened the door for me.

"Her and the triplets," he said. "Well, two of them, anyway, and sometimes Tatty."

I frowned at him. "Who's Tatty?"

"She's mom's girlfriend."

Her girlfriend? But I'd also heard River mention his dad. Were they not married? How did that work? I shook my head, hoping I'd figure it all out as I went.

We were about to head for the front door when a man in a matching pullover and sweats came jogging around the corner and into the driveway.

"Perfect timing." River turned away from the house, jamming his hands into his pockets and approached the man, who'd stopped with two fingers to his pulse while he stared at his watch.

The man barely gave River a glance as he approached, instead choosing to level a murderous glare at me until I shrank behind River.

He removed an earbud from his ear, letting some upbeat pop song bleed into the air. "I didn't know you had a boyfriend." He jerked his cleft chin toward me. "Who is he?"

"This is Theo," River said, pulling me out from behind him slightly. "Theo, this is Warrick, my much older brother."

His brother? I scanned Warrick's curly blond hair, sun bronzed skin, and tall but lean build. He looked absolutely nothing like River.

"I'm not that much older than you, you little shit," Warrick growled before I could reply.

"Um. It's nice to meet you. Sir," I offered.

"Doctor," he corrected with an obvious hint of irritation. "Why are you here, River?"

"I could ask you the same thing," River said with a shrug. "Shouldn't you be in Miami drinking mimosas on the beach with your rich patients?"

War rolled his eyes and marched past us. "Forced vacation." He jogged up the stairs onto the porch and pulled open the front door, going through it without bothering to wait for us.

I frowned. "He seems...nice."

River snorted. "He's an abrasive asshole, but he's mostly harmless," River said, his hand closing around mine.

River led me up the stairs, squeezing my hand tight. My palms were sweaty, and my heart was pounding hard in my chest. Warrick hadn't seemed very friendly. What if the rest of them hated me? That would be bad, right? River probably wanted his family to like me if he was going to keep me around.

"It's me," River called, stepping through the door, "plus one."

Going through that front door was like walking into another world. The lights were warm and inviting and the air smelled like fried dough and warm butter. We stood in a hallway with a small door off to our right. Another door to the left opened into an eat-in kitchen that looked like I imagined houses in TV and movies looked. Homey. Quaint. Happy and lived in.

A plump faced, middle-aged woman appeared in the doorway to the kitchen, a frilly pink apron over her t-shirt and jeans. Her gray hair was pulled back in a loose bun. Beaded strings hung from her glasses, giving her a grandmotherly look. She eyed me, drying her hands on a dish towel.

She doesn't look like River either. Was he adopted?

"River!" she said with a big smile. "War said he saw you pull in. Who's your friend?"

"He's not my friend," River replied, but he didn't offer any further explanation than that. "His name is Theo. Theo, this is Annie Laskin."

I nodded politely. "I'm very pleased to meet you, ma'am."

She smiled warmly and tipped her head to the side. "Well, aren't you polite? Come, come in. Have something to eat, dear."

I looked at River who nodded and escorted me into the kitchen, where another woman was at the stove, flipping what looked like thick pancakes. With her long, blond hair, flowing robe, and perfect feminine features, she looked like a movie star.

"River, darling!" the second woman exclaimed, all smiles. "It's good to see you!"

"Good to see you too, Tatty." River pulled out a chair at the kitchen table and held it for me. "Theo, this is Tatiana."

"Call me Tatty, love," Tatty said, all smiles. "God, aren't you *adorable*? How'd you two meet?"

"Theo's his boyfriend," Warrick supplied, coming in through a secondary entrance in the kitchen.

Tatty's eyebrows shot up. "Boyfriend?" She twisted so that War could plant a kiss on her cheek.

When they were right next to each other, the similarities between Tatty and Warrick were striking. She was a good bit older than him, though. Maybe his mother? An aunt?

"He's not my boyfriend," River protested and sank into the chair next to me.

"Then why's he wearing your hoodie?" Warrick leaned against the counter, arms folded.

River shrugged. "What else was he supposed to wear? His clothes were dirty and he didn't have any more."

My face flushed hot and I looked away under Warrick's scrutinizing eyes.

Annie walked over and put a hand on Warrick's arm. "War, dear, why don't you go check on Xander? See if he's feeling any better?"

"He's hungover, not sick," War protested, but he pushed off the counter and left the kitchen anyway.

A plate of fluffy pancakes appeared in front of me on the table and Annie slid into the seat on the other side of me. "Theo, how did you come to meet my son?" she asked, her tone more serious than before.

I opened my mouth to speak, but nothing would come out. How was I supposed to explain everything that'd happened last night?

"Last night," River said, closing his hand around mine. "At a bar. A couple of assholes had bought him for the night. I didn't like the way they were handling him, so I stepped in. One of them ran. The other one was stupid. Followed me out into the parking lot and attacked me with a switchblade. He's currently cooling off wrapped in a shower curtain in the trunk of my car."

My eyes widened at River's matter-of-fact explanation to his mother, and I stared at her, my heart pounding, waiting for her to freak out. That's what a normal mother would do, right? She should've been upset, beside herself that her son had murdered a man and brought a prostitute home to meet her.

Instead, Annie sighed and sat back in her chair, crossing her arms. "Well, at least you're cleaning up your messes."

"I made sure there were no cameras," River volunteered. "No one saw. I'm going to take care of the rest right after this."

Her eyes fell on me, scanning me up and down with more attention than before, almost like she was looking through me to see the filthy things I'd done. I turned away, my face burning. I didn't belong in that kitchen any more than I'd belonged among all the nice things in River's house.

Tatty patted my shoulder. "Poor *rybka*. You don't need to be ashamed. We're here to help you, not judge."

"Tatty, can you start the kettle?" Annie said before turning back to River. "You should go take care of what you need to sooner rather than later, River dear."

River frowned and looked at me. "But I was going to have breakfast with Theo first."

Annie gave River a scolding look. "Young man, you know we have a procedure in this house."

River sighed, rolled his eyes, and stood. "All right. Fine."

I blinked when he tipped my chin up and blushed furiously when he planted a quick kiss on my lips.

"Stay here. I'll be right back," he promised.

I suddenly felt sick. River and I hadn't been apart since last night, and the idea of being left alone in a strange house with people I didn't know... It terrified me. "W-wait! Where are you going?"

"I have to go take care of Rick," River said and combed his fingers through my wild hair. "Don't worry. You're safe here. I'll be gone three and a half hours tops. I promise."

The floor creaked as he walked out of the kitchen.

My heart jumped into my throat, and I had to fight against the urge to get up and follow him. All I could think about was what would happen to me if he didn't come back. Logically, I knew he was going next door to deal with Rick's body, but I couldn't shake the fear that took hold in me when I watched him walk out that door.

"Theo, dear, you haven't touched your *syrniki*." Tatty pouted and set a mason jar full of homemade jam in front of me. She opened the lid and spooned a generous helping onto the pancakes before sitting on the opposite side of me. "Eat up, love."

"Yes, ma'am," I said and picked up the fork.

Despite the sick feeling churning in my gut after watching River leave, the first bite was so good, I could barely slow myself down. The *syrniki* were unlike any pancake I'd ever had before, sweet and savory with a complexity that I couldn't quite nail down.

Tatty and Annie watched me eat a few bites before Annie asked, "Are you happy with River, Theo?"

I hesitated, a big bite of *syrniki* still in my mouth, glancing between the two women. How was I supposed to answer that?

"The truth now," Tattie prompted. "We know he can be impulsive and difficult."

I swallowed. "He's not really. I mean, he's different, and sometimes it's a lot to take in, but... He saved me and he's been nice to me so far."

Annie and Tatty exchanged a look.

"Theo," Annie started gently, "we'd like to help you. It would help us to know what you need if you'd tell us exactly what your situation was before this."

I flushed hot, feeling my ears reddening. They'd said I didn't have to be embarrassed, that they wouldn't judge me, but that was before.

Once I told them what I was, they'd never look at me the same again. That was better than lying to them, though. Safer.

"I…" I blew out a breath and put the fork down, folding my hands in my lap. "I'm a prostitute. Or, I was. I don't know what I am now." I looked away, only to jump when the tea kettle screeched.

Tatty pushed up from the table and went to shut it off, pulling three matching teacups down from the cabinet.

"It doesn't sound like that life was your choice," Annie said.

I shook my head, staring at the floor. "It's how it's always been. Master, he owns us. We're expensive. Our food, shelter, clothes… It all costs him money, so we work for it. And when we're not working, we stay in our rooms."

I looked up at her, watching her brows pinch together.

"It's not as bad as it sounds," I said quickly. "He feeds us, gives us medical care, and we get to go out with all kinds of people."

"It's all right, sweetheart. You don't have to justify it," Tatty said, returning to the table. She placed a steaming cup of light brown tea in front of me. "How long have you been working for this Master?"

I glanced up at her and then quickly away, shame making my insides raw. I knew what I was supposed to say, what Master had coached me to say, but it wasn't the truth. "As far back as I can remember. Since… Since I was little."

Tatty spat a string of words in a language I didn't know. I didn't need to speak it to understand she sounded upset.

Annie put her hand on my wrist and offered a sympathetic smile. "Well, that's over. You're not going back to that life, Theo. We're going to make sure of it."

I took in a deep breath and let it out in shaky bursts. "Thank you."

"River's a good boy," Tatty said, putting more *syrniki* on my plate and topping them with jam. "If he says he'll take care of you, then he will."

"But if you're ever uncomfortable, sweetie, you can come to us," Annie promised, patting my hand.

"Yes, River knows who runs things around here," Tatty said, picking up her tea. "You have nothing to worry about, Theo dear. Me and Annie have got your back. Whatever you need, love."

My insides suddenly felt warm. Was this what it was like to have a family? The words were nice, but maybe that's all they were. People said a lot of things, not all of them true. Only time would tell if they were telling the truth or not.

Seven
River

I STARED AT THE cremator, wishing it'd go faster. There wasn't any rushing it though. It took up to three hours at nearly two thousand degrees Fahrenheit to break a body down to bone fragments. Then I'd have to put him in the cremulator to reduce him to fine ash, which I could dump anywhere I wanted.

"You know you can't keep him, right?" War said from the doorway behind me.

I twisted to scowl at him. "Who says?"

"He's not a pet, River."

I shrugged. "Where else has he got to go? He won't make it on his own."

"You're right about that," War said with a sigh. He uncrossed his arms and paced further into the crematory room. "I just came from eavesdropping on an interesting conversation. Apparently, your boy toy's been a lifelong sex slave for some creep he calls Master."

I turned away from War to stare at his reflection in the polished marble around the cremator door. Some of that I already knew. The rest, I had surmised based on the way he acted. People didn't become that beaten down over a period of weeks or months. It took years to condition the fight or flight out of somebody the way it'd been done to Theo. A lifetime, apparently.

My rage only grew as I imagined a much younger Theo being manhandled by men like Rick and the horrible things they'd made him do. It made me want to murder Rick all over again, except much slower this time. With more screaming and begging for mercy.

"Honestly, I was surprised to see you take an interest," said War. "I always thought you were sex repulsed like Xavier."

I snorted and turned my back on the cremator. The less I had to look at Rick, even through marble and iron, the better. "I have sex. Just because I don't whip my dick out five days a week like the rest of you perverts doesn't mean I'm a virgin. I still probably get laid more than you do."

It was a low blow, one I knew would piss him off, but he'd come in there to intentionally piss me off. Turnabout was fair play.

War's eye twitched and he went back to crossing his arms. "My sex life is none of your business. Besides, Xander and Shepherd are the deviants. Not me."

That much was probably true. I'd only ever seen War date the most boring, vanilla guys. Clean cut doctors, lawyers, and country club types. I didn't even think he knew what a kink was.

As for me, I didn't understand the appeal most of the time. I understood pleasure, and I enjoyed getting off as much as the next guy, but not as much with other people.

Other people weren't even the problem. It was what to do with them afterward. It upset them when I told them to leave when we were done. They wanted to cuddle and touch and compliment. They wanted connections I couldn't provide. Even when I hooked up with people through apps specifically for casual fucking, people wanted to hang out after. They'd offer to buy me a coffee, or start trying to give me feedback. Most post-coital interactions could be replaced with comment cards, which made them pointless since I didn't give a shit about feedback from people I mostly saw as holes to come in.

"So, what are you going to do with him?" War asked.

I shrugged. "Why do you care what I do?"

"Frankly, I don't give a fuck what you do, not unless it puts this family in danger."

Here we go, I thought and rolled my eyes to the ceiling. Just what I needed. Another Saturday lecture from my adoptive brother. War really liked to remind the rest of us that we weren't his *real* family. Not that he was related to Mom or Dad either, not directly. He was Tatty's son from her marriage to Nikita Volkov, who was Dad's lover. The four of them were one big happy polycule, but there was only one kid between them, and they'd spoiled War half to death. He thought because he was the oldest, and their only biological son, that he shit gold and the rest of us should eat it.

"This whole situation is a ticking time bomb," War continued. "You think a bunch of human traffickers are going to let you take their merchandise and kill their customers without impunity?"

"Theo is not merchandise," I growled.

"To them he is, and these kinds of people protect their assets." War closed on me and drove a finger into my chest. "Did it even occur to you who you might be fucking with? You don't know if he belonged to the Greeks, a cartel, or some gang. You and your stupid dick could've thrust this family into a fucking gang war, River!"

I swatted his hand away. "Please, I'm pretty sure we can handle a couple of gangbangers."

"And if he's a Greek asset? Then what?"

I shrugged. "Then Nikita and Tatty smooth things over, I kiss some ass, and everything turns out fine. You worry too much, War."

"And you don't worry enough. People could die because of what you've done, River. Innocent people."

Ugh, that was the trouble with people like War. Always so hung up on morality. There was no such thing as an innocent person. What he really meant was an uninvolved person, but I didn't bother pointing that out. It'd be a waste of breath with him. He cared way too much about collateral damage.

All I cared about was Theo. He was mine, had been mine since I first spotted him across the bar. The only thing that mattered was keeping him safe and near me. War wouldn't understand that.

"Everything is going to be fine, War," I assured him. "Nobody even knows I have him."

"Whoever this Master guy is has probably noticed," War pointed out.

"Well that won't matter once I track him down and kill him, will it?"

"Jesus Christ. You're even crazier than the rest of us. Does Theo even want you to kill the people who hurt him?"

I shrugged. "Why wouldn't he?"

"Because he's not a sociopath."

I rolled my eyes again. "That's technically an offensive term, you know. It's called anti-social personality disorder."

"You do realize, River, that most people don't consider murder a romantic gesture?" War asked.

"Most people are boring." The timer finally went off on the cremator and the countdown began for when the door would open. I walked over to grab the scraper from where it rested against the wall, leaning on it and turning back to War. "So, are you going to help me or not?"

War studied me for a long beat before answering, "No. I'll clear him medically for you, but I'm flying out back to Miami soon. I promised Ken I'd watch him at the Miami Open."

I wrinkled my nose. "You're still dating that ascot-wearing tool?"

"Ken is a world-class golfer. He's been in the PGA tour twice."

I snorted. "He's an ascot wearing tool. Guy's so vanilla, he's allergic to chocolate. No way he's got good dick game."

"There's more to making a relationship work than being good in bed," War protested.

I leaned on the scraper and lifted an eyebrow in doubt.

War deflated with a sigh. "Okay, so he's boring. So what? Some of us like boring. I want a normal life, River. A family. If that means a boring job, in a boring city, with a boring husband, then so be it."

"You *have* a family," I spat back. "I'm your fucking family. Theo could be too if you'd let him."

"At least sleeping with Ken is never going to start a turf war between the Russians and the Greeks." He grabbed the end of the scraper and held it. "Nobody's going to die because of my choices."

"You take that oath to do no harm way too seriously, Barbie girl." I yanked the scraper handle away. "You forget the second part of that is take no shit."

"That's not how the Hippocratic oath goes, River."

"Whatever." I waved him off. "Rollerblade back to Ken and your dreamhouse in Miami. Go live your plastic life. I don't need your help."

"Don't be an asshole, River."

I ignored him, turning my back to him and waiting for the crematory door to open. Eventually, War had enough of being ignored and left. Good riddance. I didn't need him. I had three other brothers and a whole fucking army of Russian mobsters to go to. If nothing else, I would find and kill Theo's former Master on my own. Fuck War. Fuck anyone who tried to stand in my way.

Eight
Theo

I FLINCHED AS WAR pressed the needle into my finger and cringed as he squeezed it to get the blood to well to the surface. He pressed my finger firmly into a tiny strip and held it there. He hadn't told me what the test was for, but I knew an HIV test when I saw one. I'd certainly had enough of them.

I turned away, but the sickness churning in my gut had nothing to do with the blood. I hated doing this, being so exposed, being handled this way, treated like I was infected. Like I was *filthy*. Master told us we did important work, and that had made it bearable, even if I didn't like it, but the people I had to service… Even if my screenings were clean, I never felt it. It was as if they'd infected me somewhere deeper, down in my soul.

The constant battery of tests, the monthly exams I'd had to endure? Those were even worse. The doctor never looked at me, never addressed me by name, treated me as less than human as he went down his checklist of questions. *Any rash, fever? Does it hurt when you urinate? How does this feel? What about this? Bend over. Give me your finger.*

I shook my head. I couldn't sink into that, not now. River had promised me this would be the only time I'd have to go through this, and I wanted so badly to believe him. I didn't know if I could do this again.

When War was satisfied, he pushed my hand away, handling me as if I were a mannequin and not a human being.

"You could be nicer, War," River commented.

"There's a reason I don't work in family med. Aside from the money being crap, most people who want new noses and liposuction don't give a shit if I'm nice to them as long as I make them look good." He set the test aside and picked up a pad of paper, scribbling something on it.

"I want you to start taking a multivitamin," War said as he wrote. "And some vitamin D. You also need to be careful to put on sunscreen when you go out in the sun, even if it's not a sunny day. You're at a higher risk for skin cancer with pale skin like that." He tore the page off and held it out to me.

River snatched it before I could take it.

War looked over at River. "You want anything?"

River shrugged. "Xander would want me to ask for something."

"Xander can get his party drugs somewhere else. You can put your shirt back on, Theo," War said, and he laid the test flat before crossing his arms.

I did as I was told, stealing a glance at River as he pocketed the scripts his brother had given him.

"You know," War said at length, "you should take him to see Shepherd."

River's lip curled. "What? Why?"

War eyed him, his face an expressionless mask. "He is a board-certified psychiatrist, River. After everything he's been through..." War's eyes swung to me as if he'd just remembered I was still in the room. "Someone who's trained to treat extended psychological trauma should see you, and Shepherd's specialty... Well, he knows a lot about what you might be going through, Theo. He might have some insight the rest of us don't."

River wrapped an arm around me possessively. "Shepherd is the last person he should see."

"It was just a suggestion," War said with a shrug. He glanced down at the test, picking it up to glance at it briefly before holding it out to me. "Congratulations. You're negative."

I flushed, the sick feeling returning. I should've been used to the humiliation by now, but I wasn't. Even though the test had come back negative, it was embarrassing to have to take it at all. They probably didn't test their other random sexual encounters. This was something they only did to me because of what I was. Because I was a dirty whore.

I swallowed my humiliation, refusing to meet his eyes, and pitched the strip into the trash.

War peeled off his gloves and went straight to the sink to clean his hands. "If you have any trouble sleeping, come back. I can give you some Ativan." He pumped more soap onto his hands and went back to washing. "You have any upset stomach? Tatty said you didn't eat much."

I frowned. "I ate two of those pancake things."

"I'll feed him," River promised.

"Wyoming, Wisconsin, West Virginia, Washington," War mumbled, pumping soap from the dispenser onto his hands a third time.

River rolled his eyes and grabbed my arm. "Come on. He's going to be at it awhile." He escorted me from the bathroom, slowly closing the door behind him.

"Is he okay?" I asked, glancing back at the bathroom door as River led me away.

"Yeah, that's normal for him. It's a thing he needs to do sometimes." River shrugged. "Are you hungry? There's a restaurant downtown. They've got cheeseburgers and stuff."

I put a hand over my stomach and looked over at River. "Are you hungry?"

"Starving," he admitted. "I had to skip breakfast, remember?"

"Oh. I'm sorry. Yeah, I guess we should eat then."

"We'll go right there after this." River shrugged again and paused in front of another door down the hall. He lifted a fist and pounded on the door so hard it rattled in its frame.

The door jerked open a moment later, revealing a half-dressed young man with messy dark hair and bruised eyes. He had more bruises all over his torso, his arms, his neck, his fingers... He looked like he'd been hit by a bus but somehow managed to keep his designer sunglasses on.

"Did War give you any Vicodin?" the man asked, hanging on the door like he might fall over without its support.

"No," River answered.

The man made a disgusted sound and started to swing the door shut, but River forced it open. The two stared at each other for a moment before the newcomer lowered his sunglasses, revealing bloodshot eyes. He scanned me from head to toe. "This is your new toy?"

"Theo, this is Xander," River said, gesturing to the obviously hungover man. "Xander, this is Theo."

"I'm very—"

Xander cut me off with a snort and pushed open the door. "Fine. Come in. But leave the lights off. My fucking head is killing me."

"I told you not to drink that last tequila," came another voice from in the room.

I didn't see the second man until we were already in the room. He was sitting in front of a trio of computer monitors, the only light in the room. One of them looked like it was running some scan while another clearly contained grainy security footage from somewhere that definitely wasn't the house. A game loading screen was on the third monitor, the image of a masked killer with a machete.

The second man looked exactly like the first, minus all the bruises...and with the addition of a headset that he pulled down when we entered.

"That's Xavier," River said, pointing to the one in front of the monitors. "These are my youngest brothers."

"What do you want?" Xander slouched in a second computer chair near his brother's.

"Theo needs to borrow some clothes," River said. "He's closer to your size than mine."

"Bro, just go to Walmart." Xander grabbed a big can from somewhere behind him and popped it open, chugging loudly. "And get me some pain killers while you're there. No cap, this headache is ass."

"Don't be a dick, Xander." Xavier got up and walked over to a closet on the far side of the room.

"Nothing with your stupid horror movie stuff on it," River insisted.

"Well, that's going to severely limit our options," Xavier said, giving me another once over before going back to digging in the closet.

"So what's up with you, bro?" Xander asked and slurped loudly from his energy drink. "Are you two like fucking or something?"

"He doesn't have to answer your questions," River said firmly.

"Chill, bro. I'm just trying to feel out the situationship here." Xander chugged from his drink again and then lifted another, wiggling it. "Want one?"

"No thanks," I said quickly and then glanced at River to make sure I'd said the right thing. River was too busy glaring at Xander as if he wanted to stab him.

Xander sighed. "What? I was trying to be polite. Trust me, I am *not* interested in your boy toy."

Xavier chuckled from the closet. "Since when have you ever seen Xander fuck anyone less than twice his age?"

"I can't help it if I've got daddy issues." Xander shrugged and drank from his can.

Xavier came back with a stack of black T-shirts and a couple pairs of sweats. "These are mid but should do for now."

"By the way, I haven't forgotten you owe me, River," Xander cut in.

"No, I don't. Remember, I had to cover for you with Mom that one time last month," River said.

He scrunched up his face. "What one time?"

Xavier snickered. "He means that time you had an orgy in her van."

"It wasn't an orgy," Xander insisted. "There were only like five people. Besides, I can't help it if literally everyone thinks I'm hot. But fine. I guess we're even." He waved us off. "Take your clothes, peasants, and leave me to mourn the loss of my innocence." He spun the chair around.

River snorted. "I don't think you know the meaning of the word innocence," he said, and he led me from the room.

The stairs creaked as we made our way down. River was slower moving than before, reminding me that he still hadn't slept. I felt guilty for being the reason he'd lost a night's sleep, but I was tired too.

Maybe more tired than hungry, but I didn't want River to change his plans for me.

"Not staying for lunch?" Annie came out of the kitchen, catching us between the stairs and the front door.

River shook his head. "I'm kind of tired. I was going to take Theo to lunch at the diner downtown and go home."

My heart jumped. Home? Was that what River's house was now?

"It's Saturday, dear," said Annie, wiping her hands over her shirt. "The diner only opens for breakfast and dinner on Saturdays."

Saturday? I almost smiled. Saturdays were my favorite days. It was the one day a week we were allowed out to socialize. Master let us all curl up in his room with him and watch movies. Sometimes, he'd even read to us. We'd sit in a big pile like a family. While we weren't allowed to talk, I'd found some solace every week from laying my head on David's shoulder, or from the way Ben squeezed my hand. It was nice to be able to touch people without the expectation that it would turn into sex.

But those days are behind me now, I thought, my heart sinking. I'll never see them again. I'd never get to secretly trade bubblegum or candy with David when Master wasn't looking, or feel one of the younger boys squeeze my hand during a scary part of the movie. No more laughter when Master read to us in silly voices.

"Damn," River was saying. "I forgot."

"Why don't I make you boys some ham and cheese sandwiches to go?" Annie offered. "Then you should go take a nap, River. You look exhausted."

River squeezed my hand and looked over at him. "You want a sandwich?"

I wasn't sure if I did or not, but I nodded because I knew he was hungry.

Annie made us four ham and cheese sandwiches, and we drove back to River's to eat them. Before lunch, he gave me a quick tour of the house. The night before, I hadn't gotten a good look around River's gigantic Victorian style house. There were two floors plus an attic, and I felt like I'd get lost wandering around on the first floor.

"What's the difference between a parlor and a sitting room?" I asked as I followed him into the formal dining room, which had a long table and six chairs.

River shrugged. "Parlors are like old fashioned living rooms, I guess, and sitting rooms are for... Well, they're for sitting."

I pulled my hand free. "Why do you live in this big house by yourself?"

He paused and turned back around, cocking his head to one side. "I don't. You live here with me."

"I mean before that. You were all alone in this big house. Didn't you ever get lonely?"

River looked longingly through the opposite door toward the kitchen. "Human relationships require a certain amount of...*vulnerability* to work. Loneliness would require me to crave that level of vulnerability with someone, and I just don't."

I fidgeted with my fingers. "That doesn't mean you don't wish you could."

He closed his hands over mine and lifted them to his lips. "I have my family, and my mushrooms, and now I have you. I don't need anyone else."

For the next week, things were different. I slept a lot. At night, I slept in the big bed upstairs next to River. Every morning, he took me back to the big house where Annie, Tatty and his brothers lived, and he went to work at the funeral home next door.

Annie and Tatty were kind to me while he was away, always bringing me food and tea or sometimes chatting with me while they watched soap operas and medical dramas. River's brothers came and went whenever they pleased, almost never talking to me. Sometimes, I heard Xavier or War talking about me in the next room, always in hushed tones, but they avoided me. It was just as well. It seemed all I wanted to do was sleep because every time I curled up on the couch to stare at the TV, I was drifting off. I'd wake up and find someone had put a knitted blanket over me or placed a sandwich on the coffee table in front of me.

Then, in the evenings, we'd go back to River's house to shower, eat, and go to bed. Sometimes, he'd read his books. Once or twice, he'd offered to read them to me, but they were science textbooks and magazines, and I didn't understand a lot of it and just wound up zoning out or falling asleep anyway. For some reason, it was like I hadn't slept for years, and my body decided to make up for lost time.

When I wasn't asleep or just trying to make it through the basic functions of being human, I spent a lot of time in my head. Not remembering. That was too hard. I didn't want to think about everything I'd been through and my life before. It was easier to pretend like all of that had happened to some other Theo, and I was a new Theo living on this side of something that had cut my life into a *before* and *after*. Before Theo belonged to Master. He lived in a little house with all the other boys and let people do whatever they wanted to him. He ate what he was told, slept where he was told to sleep, let people use him however they wanted.

After Theo could be anything, anyone. After Theo started to have opinions about foods like grilled ham and cheese. He was tired of it. *I* was tired of having it every day for lunch, but I was too afraid to say anything. That was Before Theo. Even when I tried to forget him, he'd come creeping back into the After times, reminding me that I should be good and do as I was told. Before Theo made After Theo eat the same sandwiches on the fifth and sixth day, even though I didn't really want to.

Sometimes, I wondered about what people from Before Theo's life were doing. I wondered if they'd even noticed I was gone. Part of me wished Master would show up just so that I'd know he cared. The other part of me was terrified he would.

I missed parts of my old life. Not the abuse. Not the constant gnawing hunger, or the uncertainty of never knowing what would happen to me next, but I did miss the other boys from the house. I missed my roommate, David, and the small rituals of the Before. Things like our weekly movie nights. I missed cuddling up with the other boys in the house and feeling safe with them, the light shoulder bumps, the innocent touches that didn't lead to anything but laughter or warmth. I was used to getting a lot of that, but ever since River had saved me, he was the only one who touched me, and it didn't feel like enough, especially since I slept through it half the time.

And when he did touch me, I still flinched a lot. I kept expecting him to demand I have sex with him. I knew he wanted to. Whenever I woke up in the middle of the night, or we showered together, he was always hard, always looking at me with hunger in his eyes, even if he didn't act on it. I wanted to please him so he wouldn't get bored of me and send me back, and I wanted to touch him, to be close to him, but I was scared. Some of the men who bought me seemed nice until they had sex with us. Then they turned into sadists who only wanted to hurt us. I didn't want that to happen with River. I wanted to make him happy, to ensure that he wouldn't leave me, to make him like me, but the only way I knew how to do that was through sex, and that was too much.

My thoughts felt like jigsaw pieces from two different puzzles, and I was trying to jam them together to make a complete picture. It didn't work. How could I both crave and be repulsed by touch? How could I have wants and needs but be terrified to communicate them, especially when these people had shown me nothing but kindness and patience so far?

My mind said it could be a trap, that things could change at any time. I kept waiting for that other shoe to drop, waiting for River to lose his patience with me, or for Annie to get irritated with me eating her food without earning my keep.

After a week, it never happened.

The next Saturday, River had to do a half day of work to get ready for the upcoming holiday when the funeral home would be closed. He dropped me off with Annie and Tatty like normal, and I curled up on the couch like normal, but I wasn't tired. I stared at the screen, watching doctors and nurses dramatically save patients and fall in and out of love with their co-workers in the space of single episodes.

I hate this, I realized. *I miss happy, animated songs, and superheroes saving the day. Why can't I watch that?*

Because I haven't asked to watch that. How will anyone know what I want if I don't tell someone?

I glanced toward the kitchen where Annie was washing the dishes while Tatty sat at the table with War, having tea. Asking them to change it felt like too much. I didn't want to walk in there when all three of them were there.

My eyes dropped to the remote sitting on the coffee table in front of me. *I could change it myself.* Then I wouldn't be bothering anyone.

But what if they get mad at me? Then I can tell them it was an accident and change it right back.

I looked back at the kitchen, then at the remote, then back at the kitchen.

Where the sudden surge of bravery came from, I didn't know, but I sat up, grabbed the remote, and pushed the arrow key, flipping through channels until I found an animated show about rescue dogs.

"Theo?"

I froze, my breath caught in my lungs.

"If it's bothering you, I can turn it off," Annie said.

"I can..." I swallowed. "Could I watch something else maybe? Just for a little while. I'll put it right back. I promise."

Annie smiled sweetly and adjusted her glasses on her nose. "Watch whatever you like, sweetheart," she said and went back into the kitchen.

I spent the rest of the morning watching the rescue dogs show. It was clearly made for little kids, but I didn't mind that. It was more interesting than the hospital drama, at least.

River came back much earlier that day, before Annie even brought my sandwich out, so she sent some with us in a bag. When he took me back to his house, he asked me the same question he always did, the one I never had an answer for. "What do you want to do now?"

I squirmed in place for a minute, shifting from foot to foot while he hung up our coats. Usually, I just let him pick, and he'd suggest food or a nap while he read his books. This time, I said something. "Could we watch a movie together or something?"

River tilted his head, looking at me strangely.

"It's just that we used to watch movies on Saturdays," I explained quickly. "Musicals and superhero movies and stuff. I kind of...miss it."

River considered me in silence for a minute. I was about to tell him never mind when he shrugged like it was no big deal and said, "Okay."

He led me away to the sitting room. There wasn't a TV in there, so I wasn't sure how we were supposed to watch a movie until he opened a streaming app on his laptop.

"What kind of movies do you like? Action? Mystery? Romance?"

I bit my lip while he scrolled through the options, unsure of how to answer him until I saw a familiar poster for an animated superhero movie. "That one!" I said excitedly and pointed, only to immediately blush. "I mean...I've seen that one before. It's good."

River laughed and selected the movie. "Okay, *Spiderman* it is." He put his arms around me and pulled me into his lap, kissing my cheek. "This okay?"

I nodded and picked up one of the sandwiches, offering it to him while I ate mine. River didn't pay too much attention to the film, quickly growing distracted by something on his phone. I didn't mind. I was happy he'd agreed to indulge my silly request.

I knew the way I'd been raised was supremely messed up, and maybe I shouldn't want to keep any of the traditions from that time, but to call it all bad would be untrue. There had been plenty of happy times, even if my life wasn't normal. We had pizza parties, and birthday cakes, and dinners together. Even some of the regular clients weren't that bad. They'd show up with candy or pop and let me listen to music.

But they weren't as kind as River. Not as caring.

I turned my head to look at him and smiled when I saw he'd nodded off to sleep leaning on his arm. He was snoring lightly, his mouth open. Hard to imagine that it'd been just a week since I'd watched him stab a man to death. He looked so sweet and innocent when he was asleep. So *normal*. While I knew I should still be terrified of him, I couldn't bring myself to feel that way after spending most of the week with him. He'd been nicer to me than anyone in a long time, maybe ever.

"Hey," I whispered, gently nudging him.

River's eyes snapped open. "What? I'm awake."

I chuckled. "You sure you wouldn't be more comfortable in a bed? You're going to have a sore neck sleeping like that."

"I wasn't asleep," he insisted as he lowered his arm around my shoulders. "I was watching this with you."

You were watching the back of your eyelids, I thought with a smile, but I didn't say it, instead settling against his chest to finish watching the movie.

Except within a few minutes, River was snoring again, this time louder.

He woke when I shifted against him, arm tightening around me. "I said I'm awake. Hold still and watch the movie."

I sighed and did as I was told.

River fell back asleep, but at least he didn't snore. Listening to his steady breathing and heartbeat had my eyelids feeling heavy, and I eventually drifted off to sleep with him. When I woke up again, the movie was over and the shadows were long. River was still sleeping, but my back was killing me. I desperately needed to change positions to alleviate the pressure.

Carefully, I sat up and looked back at River, half expecting him to shout at me. He didn't. He only shifted positions slightly, mumbling something incomprehensible before he was back out, sleeping with his lips slightly parted.

God, he really is beautiful, I thought. *Why does someone like him want anything to do with me?*

He'd been so good to me, but I'd been nothing but trouble for him so far. He'd lost so much sleep because of me, and I'd wasted so much of his time.

I should pay him back for all the kindness he's shown me, but how? I don't have anything. Even the clothes on my back are his.

The only thing I had was my body, but did he even want that? He'd said he didn't want me for sex, but then why was he kissing me and holding me so often? Maybe he did want me, but he was afraid I didn't want him? But that didn't make sense. No one had ever cared about that before. Why would he?

Do I want him, though?

It wasn't like I'd never experienced sexual attraction before. I had, but the whole thing was so intrinsically tied to all the bad things that'd happened to me, so I didn't usually like to experience it. My body responded like any other to the right touch, even if I didn't want it to.

But I had responded to River's touch, and I hadn't minded it. Actually, I'd enjoyed the kisses we sometimes shared a lot more than I expected to, and I liked all the small touches we'd been exchanging. I liked it when he kissed my head and when he held me. The little gestures of affection didn't leave me feeling like I had to reciprocate or that they were a downpayment on sex he expected to get later. River gave that to me freely, and I wanted more of it.

But did I want more than the casual affection we'd shared so far? Did I want more than a kiss?

It was a strange thing to consider whether what I wanted even mattered. It never had before, and I wasn't sure what I wanted, except I knew I didn't want him to leave me or grow bored with me. He needed to get something out of our interactions. It wasn't fair otherwise.

And there was only one way to know for sure if this was what I wanted, too. I had to decide.

I bent over him. His body was so warm, and he smelled so nice. "River?" I whispered.

He didn't respond.

I leaned in, lips hovering over his. His breath tickled my chin. I licked my lips and, after a moment's hesitation, closed the distance, pressing a kiss to his lips.

He didn't wake right away, but when his eyes fluttered open, my heart skipped a beat. What if he got angry? What if I'd made the wrong choice? What if—

My worry vanished when he put a hand lightly on the back of my head and his lips parted. His tongue darted over my lips and he groaned low and deep when I let him inside for a taste. The kiss deepened and I panicked for a moment as I felt his cock harden against me, but he didn't make a move to do anything about it, even though I would have let him. Didn't he know? How could he own me and not use me?

We stayed on the couch in the darkened sitting room, just kissing and kissing and kissing until I couldn't stand it. I needed to touch more of him, if only to confirm that this was all real and not some fever dream.

Slowly, carefully, in case he changed his mind, I slid my hands under the bottom hem of his turtleneck and over the hard muscle of his stomach. He didn't object, so I moved my hands up, feeling more of him, running my palms over his chest.

River retreated from the kiss to sit up enough that he could peel his shirt off and drop it to the floor. He caught my lips briefly before saying, "I want to touch you too, Theo. If that's okay?"

I nodded and River helped me pull the borrowed hoodie over my head. I chewed on my lip as he ran his hands over my pale, skinny chest.

"Don't do that." River ran his thumb over my bottom lip. "Don't bite your pretty lips, Theo."

I frowned. "Nothing about me is pretty, River."

"Yes, it is. Everything about you is so pretty and delicate. You're like one of those collectable porcelain dolls Tatty keeps around. I know I'm not supposed to touch you, but it's all I can think about all the time. I want it so bad, it's driving me crazy."

"You can touch me," I said quietly. "However you want. I belong to you, remember?"

He shook his head. "Don't tell me that."

"But it's true. You said—"

"Forget what I said. I just want to keep kissing you, Theo." He pulled my lips back to his, and I was surprised to find I liked the way he did that.

River held me against him, letting me guide the pace and heat of the kiss. His hands slid down my shoulders and over my back, little more than chaste, teasing touches until I was the one rubbing my cock against him through my sweatpants. I couldn't help it. It felt so good—the way he held me, the way he touched me—and I wanted to make him feel just as good. The only way I knew how to do that was through sex.

I closed my hand around his cock, still trapped in his jeans, but River caught my hand. "Please, River," I whispered against his lips. "I want to make you come."

He considered me for a minute. I waited for him to release my hand, but he held onto it. "Only if you let me make you come first."

"What?" I frowned and sat back from him. No one had ever countered my offer like that. Nobody said no. Nobody. "Don't you want me, River?" I asked in a small voice.

"Can't you feel how hard I am for you, little finch?" he asked and kissed me again. "I definitely want you. I want you more than I've ever wanted anybody. But right now, I want to make you come. Has anyone done that for you, Theo?"

I sighed and looked away, an icy ball forming in my lower stomach. "The kind of people who rented me didn't care about whether I enjoyed it or not, River."

River's hand closed around me through the borrowed sweatpants, and he started giving me a few lazy pulls. "Well, I care."

"Why?" I asked, trying to bring my breathing back under control.

"Because I want to be the only one to make you come, little finch. I told you already. You're mine to take care of, every part of you, and that includes your needy cock. You only come for me now, understand?"

I shuddered and nodded.

"Do you want me to make you come now, Theo?" River asked and sat up to nip at my neck.

"Yes," I breathed with barely a thought. What he was doing to me felt so good, even through my clothes, and I did want it. Maybe it was selfish, but dammit... I wanted him to take care of me. I wanted him to want me, and if that's what it took to stay with River, I'd done worse things for worse men.

"Are you sure?" River's tongue traced a hot, wet line across the hollow of my throat.

I swallowed. "Yes."

River kissed his way down my neck and collarbone before dropping his head and carefully pulling down the sweats, freeing my cock. I flushed, embarrassed by how obvious it was that I was enjoying the attention. I didn't often get hard for other men without a lot of effort, but when River kissed me, it was like my body had been programmed to respond. I was harder than I'd ever been in my life.

"Look at how hard you are for me," River crooned before spitting in his palm.

I gasped when he started stroking me in earnest, but River swallowed the sound with another kiss. He crushed our bodies together, practically devouring me with hungry kisses while he worked me with a fist.

"Does that feel good, little finch?" he asked, teasing the head of my cock. "You want it tighter? Faster?"

I dug my fingernails into his shoulders. "Please..."

His velvety chuckle sent goosebumps racing over my arms. "I've got you. You let me take care of you. You're so fucking sexy right now, Theo."

I didn't feel sexy. My body was desperate, my nerves raw, but my head had started to go somewhere else, drifting off to the same safe place I always went whenever I had sex. My body worked on automatic, starting to thrust into River's slick palm in search of relief. It was like I was outside of my body, though, looking over my own shoulder, watching a fictionalized version of myself fuck into River's hand. I wasn't the one moaning and panting, even though I felt the sparks of pleasure racing over my skin and the pressure building at the base of my spine.

It was my ears that heard River whisper in awe, "That's it. Make yourself come for me," but the words came to me through a distant filter, garbled slightly and muffled.

None of that stopped me from chasing my own orgasm.

"I'm close," I whispered, desperately hoping he wouldn't pull his hand away and leave me unsatisfied like so many others had done. They thought it was funny, leaving me hard and desperate, robbing me of release.

But River didn't even try. He tightened his grip on my cock and used his other hand to gently massage my balls. "Come, Theo."

I exploded with a shout. My hips shot forward, my cum streaking over River's stomach in messy lines. Before the pleasure had even begun to fade, I was mortified, terrified, some tiny voice in my brain screaming that I shouldn't have done that. It was against the rules, he was going to be angry at me, and I'd ruined everything.

River let out a low, rumbling sound of approval. "Good boy," he said and lifted his cum-coated hand to his mouth.

My eyes widened and another small shudder of pleasure went through me as I watched him lick my release from his fingers.

My whole body was trembling, my head floating back and forth between terror, guilt, and bliss as River seized my lips in a kiss, pushing his tongue into my mouth. I moaned at the taste of myself on his lips, savoring it like a love letter. It was probably as close as I'd ever get.

"Fuck, Theo. You taste so damn good. Don't you think?" He grinned at me.

I didn't know how to answer, so I kissed him again and palmed his erection through his pants. When I reached to free him, he grabbed my hand.

"I want to make you come too," I whispered hoarsely. "You said after..."

"I didn't say when after," he replied smugly and released my hand before sitting up. "And right now, I want ice cream."

I frowned as he kissed my cheek and gently pulled my pants up over my hips. "But what about..."

"We can cross that bridge later. After ice cream." He walked into the kitchen and left me sitting on the sofa, more confused than ever. "You want chocolate fudge or salted caramel?"

I sighed and got up from the sofa to stand on wobbly legs. "Caramel," I shouted and went to join him in the kitchen.

Nine

River

I WATCHED THEO LICK the back of his spoon, wishing it was me. Part of me wanted to immediately haul him upstairs and bury myself in him. He'd probably let me, especially after his earlier performance.

For the last week, he'd been absent, as if he were sleepwalking through life. Barely responsive. Now he seemed to be waking up, coming alive. Maybe he'd talk to me about before so I could start hunting down the people who'd hurt him.

I put my spoon down in my empty bowl. "What was it like? Your life before this?"

Theo froze, taking on that terrified rabbit look that made me want to scoop him up and snarl at whatever he was so terrified of. He was mine, and it pissed me the hell off that anyone would make him that scared. I was supposed to protect what was mine, but I couldn't do anything to protect Theo against the assault of memory he was battling.

"It wasn't all bad," Theo said at length. "I mean, yes, a lot of bad shit happened to me. I was pimped out to fuck whoever Master said I had to, and some of them beat me. But in between, life was pretty boring, honestly."

"Where did you live?" I tried not to sound too invested, although the information was essential. Once I tracked down this Master guy, I was going to kill him, nice and slow. I didn't want Theo to know what I was planning, though, since he'd reacted so strongly when I'd killed Rick.

Theo shrugged. "A house. All of us lived together. We had our own bedrooms, right next to each other, but we didn't work in the house. We lived there."

"Where at?"

Theo lifted his eyes to mine with a sigh. "I don't know."

"Well, were there any landmarks nearby?" I pressed. "Buildings you saw when you went outside? Or what school did you go to?" That would at least give me a neighborhood to start searching.

His face flushed and he looked away. "I didn't go to school."

My fingers curled against the tabletop. "What?"

"Yeah, so, we didn't go to school," Theo said, gripping his arm. "I know I'm stupid—"

"You're not," I cut in and then almost snarled when I saw him flinch at the rough tone of my voice. "You're not stupid, Theo. It's not your fault. If you didn't go to school, though, what did you do?"

He blinked up at me with his big, sad eyes. "Whatever Master said to do."

"What about your parents?" I was almost afraid to ask, but if he had family, I needed to know.

Theo shook his head. "It was only Master. I don't know anything about my mother. Master said she..." His hand tightened around his arm and he stared at the floor. "She didn't want me. That's where we all came from. Our mothers were addicts and prostitutes who didn't want us, so they sold us to him."

I stood up so fast that Theo scooted away, looking up at me with wide, terrified eyes. I knew I was scaring him, but I couldn't help it. I was so goddamn pissed off. How could anyone tell a kid that? No wonder he was so fucking scared that I didn't want him.

He flinched when I reached to touch his face, but I made sure my touch was gentle. I didn't want him afraid of me. Not now. "I'm not mad at you, Theo. I'm pissed off this happened to you. Nobody should tell a kid they weren't wanted."

He shrugged as if it didn't matter. "It was probably true. It happens right? We were lucky he was there or else we'd probably all have been left in dumpsters or public toilet stalls to drown."

"Jesus, Theo." I shook my head. How could he be so casual about that, saying it like it'd been said to him a thousand times? It probably had.

Master would have pounded into his skull exactly how lucky he was to have someone to take care of him, how scary the world outside was. He would have wanted Theo to be terrified and totally dependent on him for everything. My stomach turned over as I realized I only knew that because it's what I would've done if I didn't have Mom and War and everyone else to steer me right.

I sank back into my seat. "I don't care if it's true. That's not the kind of shit you tell a kid. It's a manipulation tactic, Theo, used to break you down and make you believe he's your savior. He wasn't. This asshole took advantage of you."

"I know that," Theo said quietly. "In my head, I know. But he also took care of me when no one else wanted me. My feelings are all mixed up, River. Don't get me wrong. I never loved Master. I hated him and the things he made me do, but I..."

I took his hand and squeezed it when I saw him tearing up.

Theo blinked and a tear fell. He pushed it away. "It's good to tell someone. All this time, it's been bottled up in there. I've been so confused. I wanted to get out, but I didn't want to hurt Master. I knew that was a thought he'd put in my head, but I couldn't help it. Now that I'm away from all that, it's like a fog is slowly lifting and I can see things the way they are for the first time."

I nodded. That was a fog I was intimately familiar with from the other side. Sometimes, I got so wrapped up in what I wanted, or how I saw the world, that I needed someone to pull me out of it. Mom and Dad did their best with me, but the older I got, the more difficult it became for them, since I wasn't around them all the time anymore. I needed someone to remind me how to be human, and Theo had done that in his own way. We hadn't been together long, but my head was clearer when we were together, that itch under my skin more bearable.

"What about you?" he asked in a practiced, polite tone. "Annie's not your real mom, right?"

"My mother died when I was four," I told him. "She was a heroin addict."

Theo's eyes widened. "I'm sorry."

I shook my head. "Why? It's not your fault. You had nothing to do with it."

"I just said all that and..." Theo licked his lips. "I guess we have something in common there. How did you wind up with Annie?"

"After Mom died, I didn't have any family," I said. "They tried to find my dad, but Mom was here illegally from Korea. I went to the hospital. Then into a group home. They kicked me out of there after I attacked an orderly who was touching the other kids inappropriately. I bounced around a few foster homes, and I got placed with Annie and my dad, Yuri, over Christmas. It was supposed to be a temporary placement. They'd already adopted Shepherd and were raising War, but by New Year's Eve, they'd asked me if I wanted to stay with them forever. I said yes and they adopted me."

Our stories weren't that different. I was lucky, in a way. Someone found me and I got tossed into an uncaring system that chewed me up and spat me out the other side into a good home with people who knew how to handle someone like me. Theo hadn't been found. He was an invisible child who grew up to be an invisible teen and then an invisible adult. He would've died that way eventually if I hadn't stepped in, I was sure of it.

"I was lucky," I added. "Annie and Yuri have been good to me."

"I'm glad," Theo said with a small sigh, staring at the tabletop. "It's good to know there are good people out there, you know?"

There was an awkward silence between us that I didn't like. I wasn't used to the tight feeling in my chest, the strange pull to do something, make it better, do something for someone else.

What was there left to do for Theo? I'd provided him clothes, food, shelter, entertainment, given him an orgasm... He needed another distraction so he wouldn't be sad. If he was happy, maybe that feeling in my chest would go away.

"Do you want to see my mushrooms?" I asked.

Theo blinked, obviously confused by the turn in conversation. "What?"

"My mushroom garden," I said as I stood and collected his bowl. "It's up in the attic. I grow them. You want to see?"

His lips twitched back, almost as if he wanted to smile. "Sure."

Ten
Theo

THE ATTIC SMELLED DAMP like a forest floor. River had some makeshift greenhouses set up, and he walked me through everything, showing me several different species of mushrooms.

I followed him around the room, only half understanding what he excitedly explained to me about the fungi he was growing. He seemed intensely interested in the subject, and I tried to at least pretend I was too. I was good at pretending to like things, but this was different. I didn't do it because I had to. It was genuinely adorable the way his face lit up when he talked about his experimental growing techniques or a new species he was trying to cultivate.

After the mushrooms, it was late and we were both tired. We washed our hands in the little work sink upstairs and went down to get ready for bed.

While we were side by side, brushing our teeth, it hit me again, the wave of emotion alongside the thought that this could be forever. I didn't have to go back to Master. This was real, and it was my life now.

I was free of one monster, but had I climbed into bed with another?

I wasn't exactly free to do as I pleased with River either, was I? I couldn't leave. I couldn't eat what I wanted, or sleep where I wanted, even if he'd given me more options than Master ever had. But it wasn't freedom. Not really. For me to be free, the option to leave had to exist.

Would he let me go if I asked? Did I even want that?

"What?" River asked, looking over at me.

I frowned and put the toothbrush back, turning off the water. "Nothing."

By the time we made it to bed, I was a nervous wreck again. I laid stiffly in the bed next to him while he read one of his books, staring up at the ceiling. I couldn't ask him if I was allowed to leave, because I knew that'd upset him. He'd been angry in the kitchen before, and that had been terrifying, even if it wasn't directed at me.

River lowered the book. "What's wrong, little finch?"

I looked over at him. "Nothing. Just tired."

He wasn't buying it. I could tell from the look on his face as he scanned my body. Familiar hunger flashed in his eyes as his gaze settled between my legs. I suddenly felt way too naked and wished I'd put on a shirt.

"Do you need to come again?" River asked. "Might help you sleep."

"No," I said and turned over, giving him my back.

River sighed and reached over to turn off the light, plunging the room into darkness. A moment later, his strong arm slid around my ribs and he pulled me back against him. "Do you regret what we did earlier?"

"What? No."

Why would I? It had felt good, and I'd needed it, even if it was awkward and confusing. It'd helped clear my head enough to talk, at least for a while. I was glad it was River and not someone I was being forced to do it with, but there were still so many raw emotions tied up in all of that, things I was still trying to process. I had wanted it, but I felt guilty for wanting it, and even more so that I hadn't been able to give him anything in return.

I rolled onto my back and found myself looking up at him as his body leaned over mine. "Why didn't you let me finish you earlier? Didn't you want me to?"

"Theo, I'd fuck you into next week right now if you were anybody else. Of course I wanted you. I still do. Stop asking me that."

"Why not me?"

He was quiet for a minute.

My hand trembled as I reached into the dark to touch his cheekbones. "I want you to treat me like you would anybody else you'd have in your bed."

"But you're not anybody else," River said, putting his hand over mine.

"And you're not the men who hurt me," I pointed out before letting my hand drop back to the mattress with a sigh. "I just want things to be normal."

"Nothing about either of us is ever going to be *normal*," River said with a small snort.

That was true. My life was too fucked up, too different, and River... Well, he was built differently. It was one of the things I liked about him the most. He was honest to a fault, even when most people wouldn't be, and he'd been trying so hard to take care of me. Sometimes, he scared me with how intense he could be, but so far that intensity had never been directed at me. He hadn't hit me, hadn't hurt me, hadn't done anything but care for me.

And yet I was still trapped there.

"River, can I ask you something? It might make you mad..."

He sat up. "I won't be mad at you."

"Promise?"

He darted down to quickly kiss my cheek before replying, "Promise."

I took a deep breath. "If I wanted to leave, would you let me?"

River was quiet for a long time, letting my heart race in my chest without a reply. When he spoke, his voice was soft, almost childlike. "You don't want to be with me?"

My chest *ached*. He sounded broken, like he was seconds away from tears himself. All I wanted to do was put my arms around him and reassure him that I wouldn't leave him, that I'd never wanted to, but that wouldn't be the truth.

I sat up, putting us almost nose to nose. "It's not that. I don't know what I want. I've been trapped my whole life, River. You wanted to prove you were different from Master and the other men? They never gave me the chance to leave. It wasn't even an option. Wouldn't it mean so much more if I chose to stay here rather than being forced to do it?"

"I'm not forcing you to do anything," River said, his tone suddenly cold. "I'm taking care of you."

I sighed and laid back down, mumbling, "Never mind."

"Theo..."

"I'm not going anywhere, River," I told him. "Where would I even go?"

He didn't seem placated by that, but he laid down next to me again. This time, he didn't put his arm around me, and the ache in my chest worsened. I'd hurt him with that question. I knew it was risky to bring up, and I'd screwed up.

I never should've asked that, I thought and curled up tight.

I WOKE UP SHAKING and sweaty, my throat sore and my heart pounding so hard, it felt like my whole chest was bruised. I was sitting up in bed but still curled tight, my fists clenched and arms drawn in against my chest. River's arms were around me and his head was on my shoulder. He'd half pulled me into his lap. I was panting like I'd come from running miles, but I hadn't moved an inch, and my cheeks were wet with tears.

"It's okay," River was whispering gently as he held me. "You're okay."

I wanted to ask him what was going on, find out what'd happened, but I couldn't get the words out. I was still sobbing.

Was it a nightmare? I couldn't remember, and my head was so heavy. I didn't remember anything at all, but there was a lingering dread in the pit of my stomach, like something terrible had happened.

River squeezed me and lifted his head, looking at me with furrowed brows while I tried to catch my breath. "Are you coming around?"

I tried to say something but coughed on the tightness in my throat and chest.

"Here." River let me go and reappeared a moment later with a glass of water.

I didn't know where he'd gotten it from. Maybe he'd left. Time felt odd, like it was jumping around, and I couldn't breathe. Why couldn't I breathe?

When River held the glass to my lips, though, I drank eagerly. The cold water was enough to shock me out of some of my panic, though it did little for my pounding heart and throbbing head.

"I'm sorry," I managed, chin trembling. "I don't know what happened. I didn't mean… I'm sorry."

"It's okay," River said, rubbing my shoulder. "It's a night terror, but it's over now. Take a minute and try to breathe. You'll feel a lot better."

I was feeling better already, and when he handed me the cool glass of water to hold, the chilly glass grounded me more. "Night terror?" I repeated.

River nodded. "Xander used to have them a lot when Mom first adopted him and Xavier. He'd wake up the whole house screaming like he was being murdered. Xavier was the only one who could get him out of it." He looked at me and drew a hand through his hair before plopping back onto the bed. "You're safe here. I won't let anything happen to you."

I considered the water trembling in my grip before lifting my eyes to his. "Even though I asked about leaving?"

River took a deep breath. "I don't want you to leave, but I guess… If that's what you decide you want, I…" He sighed and looked away. "I don't know how to answer that. I know I should tell you that you can leave if you want, but the truth is, I don't think I can let you go. All I can think when I look at you is that you're mine. The idea of you ever being with someone else, it makes me want to…" He clenched his fists briefly before forcing himself to relax. River shifted on the bed to face me. "What did I do wrong?"

"Nothing," I said quickly and put the glass on the bedside table. "You didn't do anything."

"Then why would you want to leave me?" he asked again in that quiet voice.

I sighed and leaned my head against his shoulder. "I don't know what I want, River. Right now, I'm tired. My chest hurts, and I kind of have to pee. Can I just go to the bathroom and back to sleep? You can forget I ever brought that up, and we can go back to how things were before."

I didn't know if that was possible, and I didn't know how to communicate exactly what I was feeling. It wasn't that I wanted to leave him. Every time we were apart, I was scared he wouldn't come back, but when we were together, I was scared I couldn't leave. It was incredibly confusing, and I didn't know what to do with any of that.

River nodded. "Okay. You want me to go to the bathroom with you?"

Yes, my brain answered. The thought of facing that big empty house alone in the dark was daunting, especially after whatever had just happened.

But if I was going to have enough space to figure things out, that meant creating it where I could. I needed to learn how to think and function without River so I could make decisions with a clear head. It was silly, but I thought I could start by creating some physical distance between us in small doses until I got used to doing some things on my own.

I shook my head. "I know where it is."

"Okay," River said and scooted back to sit cross-legged on the bed.

I got out of bed and went to the bedroom door, where I paused to look back at him. He was staring back at me, his expression flat and unreadable. "I'll be right back," I promised, but that didn't seem to change his demeanor any.

On my way down the hall, I gave a casual glance at the front door. *I could leave*, I thought. *I could walk out the front door and keep walking. That would be the true test, wouldn't it?* If River came after me and dragged me back, it meant he was no different from Master. It meant I was a prisoner. But if he didn't, what then? I couldn't just come back. I'd have to keep walking, and I didn't want to be alone.

I finished in the bathroom and went straight back to the bedroom without even looking at the front door this time. River relaxed almost as soon as I came through the door. He scooted back to make room in the bed for me, and I slid under the covers with him. When he didn't make a move to put his arm around me like he normally did, I scooted closer and closed my hand around his.

"I'm not going anywhere," I told him, squeezing his hand.

His head rolled toward me. "Can I kiss you again?"

"God, yes," I replied, relieved that he'd want to after everything I'd said earlier.

River surged across the space between us, and I braced for a rough, claiming kiss. Instead, what I got was a long, slow, and deep kiss. One that made me forget about the night terrors and the world beyond the front door, if only for a minute. As long as the taste of River was on my lips, I couldn't think about anything else but him, and I liked it that way, just as I liked knowing he still wanted me. Despite everything I was, everywhere I'd been, River still wanted *me*, and he proved it again and again.

I felt like an ass, asking if he'd let me leave. Deep down, I knew I didn't want to be anywhere but with him.

River pulled back when I reached for his hip to pull his body against mine. "You need your sleep, little finch, and so do I."

A lightning flash of fear shot through me. What if I had another night terror?

River kissed the end of my nose. "If you have another night terror, I'll be right here. And I'll be here even if you don't. I'm not going anywhere either."

That was more comforting than anything he'd said all night. I scooted closer, letting my head rest against his chest. "Can I sleep like this?"

"Yeah, I like having you this close," he said and dropped another kiss on top of my head. "Sleep well, little finch."

"Night," I offered sleepily as I closed my eyes.

Eleven
River

We slept in, and after a late breakfast the next morning, I decided I should take Theo shopping.

The drive from Millcreek to Ewing's Crossing took us down a winding road through the Hocking Hills that was mostly abandoned. It was fall, so the leaves had started to change, and Theo stared at them falling in our path, glued to the windows as we drove through the country.

I brought us around the sharpest curve on the road, doing about sixty, steering from muscle memory. My brain was stuck on what he'd told me last night and the things I wanted to do to his Master when I finally found him. Cutting off his hands wouldn't be good enough. Even with a tourniquet, he'd eventually bleed out, not to mention he'd probably pass out from the pain. No, cutting those off would have to happen toward the end. I wanted him to suffer first.

I built the scene in my mind, put the gurney in the basement, strapped him to it. Alcohol wipe. Hold still, this will sting. Hang the saline fluid and set the steady drip. Ketamine to render him immobile and to dull the pain without killing it completely. Cut shirt from the abdomen. No need for iodine or alcohol. He won't live long enough to die of infection. Feel up the side, count the ribs. Have to find the right place so I don't puncture a lung or hit the liver. Insert trocar and—

"I never figured you for a rap guy," Theo said.

"Huh?" I tucked the fantasy into a box for later and filed it away before looking over at him.

"The music." He nodded to the car dash. "You like rap?"

I realized for the first time that he was talking about the album playing. "Not really," I said, reaching to shut it off. "It's background noise to me."

Theo's eyes lingered on me, almost like he was waiting for something. When I didn't say anything, he turned away, shoulders slumping like he was disappointed. What did he want from me?

Ask about him. I could practically hear Mom's voice in my head. *Ask him what he likes.*

For a minute, I was a kid again, standing in the kitchen after school. The memory was so vivid, I could feel the paper I was clutching in my fist, the weight of my backpack. The teacher had sent home yet another note saying she was worried I didn't have any friends. It wasn't that I didn't want friends. I did, even if most of the other kids annoyed me. Despite my irritation with people, I was still human. I wanted to fit in.

"The other kids don't like me," I said in my squeaky, pre-pubescent voice.

"Have you tried talking to them?" Mom asked patiently from where she sat at the table.

I shrugged. "They don't want to talk about anything interesting. All they care about is movies and video games or the girls they like."

Mom sighed and lowered her teacup. "River, sometimes, when you want to get close to someone, you have to pretend to be interested in the things they like."

"Why?" I demanded.

"Because while those things may seem boring to you, they're major parts of other people's lives. Just because they don't share the same hobbies and interests as you doesn't mean they don't want to talk about what interests them. If you listen to them talk about their interests, they're more likely to listen to you talk about yours."

The memory faded and I was back in the car, feeling that gentle tug in my chest, the one that said I should *do* something.

"What kind of music do you like?" I asked Theo.

"You don't have to do that, you know."

"Do what?"

"Pretend." He shifted in his seat to lean on the window. "You don't care what music I like. It's kind of obvious when you're forcing yourself to pretend to be interested in me."

Taking my eyes briefly off the winding road, I looked over at Theo and frowned when I saw him slumped over and staring forward blankly. "I am interested."

"Just not in my music preferences," Theo pointed out.

"I want to talk to you, Theo, but I don't know how."

He gripped his elbows and squirmed. Maybe it was hard for him to talk about music for some reason, but I couldn't figure out why. "I mostly only heard whatever was on the radio when I was working, so I don't know much about it."

"I can find something you like."

He shrugged. "I think I'd rather talk."

"Okay," I said, gripping the steering wheel around another tight turn. "What did you want to talk about?"

"I don't know," he said with another shrug. "How about your brothers? You don't seem very close with them."

I sighed. "It's not that. I've always been the odd one out, being the middle child. I was too young to be friendly with War and Shepherd, and Xander and Xavier didn't show up until I was already an adult."

He looked over at me. "You said they were triplets. Where's the third one? Is he in college or something?"

I chewed on the inside of my cheek, deciding how much to tell him. Xander and Xavier's drama wasn't my problem, and I didn't consider Xion to be my brother, especially not after the shit he pulled.

"Xion's in a state-appointed forensic psychiatric facility," I answered at length.

"Shit. What happened? I mean...if you want to talk about it."

I sighed. "It's not my story, but he used to live with us until he had a psychotic break and attacked Xander and Xander's puppy."

"But Xander doesn't have a...." He trailed off, eyes widening as he realized exactly what'd happened to Xander's dog. "Oh."

"Yeah. Xander's lucky to be alive. He was in the ICU for twelve days."

We fell silent again.

"You never answered me about the landmarks," I said after a moment. "Around the house where you were being kept? Did you ever see anything out the windows or..."

Now it was Theo's turn to sigh.

"I know you don't want to talk about it, Theo, but..."

"Actually, it doesn't bother me," he said, though his body language said that wasn't entirely true. He scraped his palms over his thighs. "There was only one window and it was high up. Master kept it covered with a garbage bag, so I never saw the outside. Whenever we had a job, he made us wear blindfolds so we couldn't see. I have no idea where the house is, River. If I did, I would tell you."

A window high up meant he was likely being kept underground, which didn't tell me much. Most old houses in the Midwest had basements. Without a neighborhood or some other information, I was no better off than before.

Am I sure it was a house? I'd assumed that based on what he'd told me, but Theo also seemed impressed with the size of my house. The old Victorian was decently sized, but it wasn't a mansion by any means, even if he acted like it was. *If this basement was big enough for their movie nights, and for all of them to be held in separate rooms, it had to be huge. Bigger than any house basement I'd ever seen, unless they were all crammed into tiny rooms.*

I glanced over at him as we hit the Ewing's Crossing city limits. Quaint little one-story houses sprang up on either side of us with toys and broken-down cars in the yards. "What were the walls made of? Do you remember any distinct sounds like traffic or bells?"

Theo turned to stare out his window. "Not really. Whenever we left, there was a sound, but it's hard to describe."

"Try," I urged.

He closed his eyes and let out a slow breath. "It was...an echo. Voices carried. My shoes made scraping sounds. There was always a double chirp when they unlocked the doors, and that echoed. The place felt like a crypt."

A parking garage maybe? If that was true, it definitely narrowed it down. There were plenty of parking garages scattered around Columbus, but if he was being held close to one, that gave me a starting point at least.

"Sometimes," Theo continued, his expression growing distant, "the client's cars were already there. Other times, they drove me to where I was supposed to work. The places were nicer when I was younger and...more personal. Like houses. One time, I stayed in this place for three days. I had my own room, as much pizza, root beer, and ice cream as I wanted, a whole room full of toys..."

My fingers tightened around the steering wheel as visions of murder danced through my head. He was pointedly ignoring everything else that had happened to him in that room. Maybe he was intentionally blocking it out. It was horrific, the things I imagined had been done to him. Nobody deserved that.

And that was coming from a monster like me.

I took Theo to a fast-food joint, where he stared at the menu with a frown while the impatient clerk glared at us in irritation. I'd already ordered my food, but Theo seemed stuck. Maybe he'd never eaten at a Burger King before.

"How about some chicken nuggets?" I suggested. "Unless you want a barbecue bacon cheeseburger. They're pretty good here."

He let out a relieved breath. "Yeah, a barbecue bacon cheeseburger would be great."

"Make it a meal," I added.

The cashier barely looked up. "Fries or onion rings?"

Theo looked at me. "Onion rings?"

"They're ok," I said with a shrug.

I was starting to notice a pattern with him. When I asked him what he wanted to eat, or what he wanted to wear, he didn't have an answer, but if I asked, "Red shirt or blue shirt," he didn't struggle so much.

Too many options at once, and Theo seemed to shut down. He could make some decisions, but it seemed easier for him if there were only a few specific things to choose from. He struggled with open-ended questions and long lists of options. I couldn't tell if that was due to his trauma or some other underlying issue.

The more time I spent with Theo, the more I wondered if War was right and I should take him up to see Shepherd. Having a psychiatrist look at him probably wouldn't be a bad thing, but Shepherd and I didn't always get along.

I took Theo into a big box store to go shopping. While he pushed the cart, I grabbed lube and condoms from the shelves, some strawberry scented shampoo, shaving cream, a new set of clippers, and the best razors they had. Then we went over to the clothing section and I helped Theo pick out some clothes. He seemed hesitant at first, objecting to me spending so much money on him.

I didn't see it that way. While I would've gladly let him wear my clothes so he'd smell like me, they didn't fit. I didn't like seeing him in Xander and Xavier's shirts, and it was starting to get under my skin. He wasn't theirs; he was *mine*. The only viable solution was to get him his own clothes so he'd stop reminding me of them every time I looked at him. Besides, I liked providing him with what he needed, and I enjoyed spending money on him. Better than letting it sit in my account and do nothing.

After clothes shopping, we went to the electronics store where I picked up a burner phone for him. I activated it on the way out and tossed it to him.

He frowned at it, holding it all wrong. "What's this for?"

"So you can call me or text me. My number's already in it."

"But you're right here with me."

"Right now I am," I said, taking his hand. "But I can't always be with you, Theo. I might have to go do something for work."

Theo lifted the phone and stared at the screen as we walked. "You should take it back."

"What?" I said, coming to a stop. "Why? Theo, I told you, I like spending my money—"

"It's not that. I can't use this phone to text you."

I blinked at him and looked down at the phone, then back at him. "Why not?"

His face flushed, and he lowered his head to mumble, "I can't read."

There was that distant tug at the edge of my subconscious again. His body language said he was ashamed, but that didn't make any sense. It wasn't his fault. He'd told me he didn't go to school, so it only made sense he didn't learn to read. I hadn't even considered that when I bought the phone, but now...

"You can text without words," I told him, quickly grabbing the phone away from him. I fiddled with it for a few seconds, adding an app. Then I held up the phone. "Push this button and it'll transcribe talk to text. And if you want to call me instead, you can push the phone icon."

Theo's chin quivered like he was going to cry. What had I done wrong?

He flung his arms around me so suddenly, I almost dropped the phone. "Thank you, River."

"It's just a phone." I chuckled and dropped my arms around him to pull him in tighter. His hair smelled like my shampoo, and every time I realized that, it made me want to make him smell even more like me.

Theo let me go and stepped back. "It's not the phone. It's everything. This whole trip. This whole weekend." He sighed. "I'm not good at explaining, but it means a lot to me."

"I told you I'd take care of you," I said and took his hand again as we walked toward the car.

He smiled, and it was good to see the way it lit up his face. "Maybe we could get some ice cream on the way back?"

"Actually, I was thinking we'd go see Shepherd."

"Your other brother?" Theo tilted his head to one side. "Are you close?"

I sighed and shook my head. "Not really, but..." How should I put this so a normal person wouldn't find it offensive?

"Because he'll have special insight into me as a psychiatrist," Theo supplied. "War said that last week."

Damn War and his shitty bedside manner. At least I knew how to pretend well enough to blend in most of the time. War didn't even have an excuse. He was just a grade-A asshole.

I opened the trunk and dumped the rest of our bags inside before leaning on it. "I won't make you go if you don't want to, but War might be right. Shepherd's specialty is sexual psychology and trauma, and he's kind of got this thing about consent and punishing people who don't respect it. He might be able to help you remember some things that help, or have suggestions that could help you cope better, but..." I sighed.

"But?" Theo gestured for me to continue. "I can sense there's some tension."

I sighed again. "I can deal with Shepherd, but we don't know if it's actually Shepherd we'll be talking to. If we walk in there and it's Bryce and not Shepherd, we might as well not bother. I actually like Dex, but Keres..."

"I don't understand," Theo said, shaking his head.

"Like the rest of us, Shepherd isn't what you'd call neurotypical. He has DID. He's four people, one body, and three out of the four are a handful. Shepherd is in the driver's seat most of the time, and I know him well enough to know if something is off. If you want to go up there, that is." I lifted my phone. "But I need to know now so I can call him and tell him we're coming. Shepherd doesn't like surprises."

Theo carefully tucked the phone into his pocket. "If you think it will help, then let's go see him."

Twelve
Theo

My stomach dropped into my pelvis as the high-rise elevator ascended. River had pressed the button for one of the top floors, which was apparently where Shepherd lived.

And I thought River's house was nice. I stared at my reflection in the polished chrome of the elevator car. There had been a man at the door and a front desk downstairs. What kind of apartment place had a front desk person?

"This place is...nice." I offered, trying not to fidget too much.

River snorted and folded his arms over his chest. "It's pretentious, is what it is. I don't get why Shep can't live in a *normal* house like the rest of us. Probably compensating for something."

The elevator slowly came to a stop and the doors slid open to reveal a carpeted hallway. River led me out and to the right where he pressed the buzzer next to a door.

"Are you sure we're not underdressed?" I looked down at my borrowed clothes. "Maybe I should've changed into my new clothes."

"You'll be fine," River assured me. "It's just Shepherd."

River hit the buzzer again, and the door opened. The man that answered wasn't much older than me and had sandy brown hair and black-rimmed glasses and a cleft chin. He reminded me of Clark Kent from the old Superman movies Master let us watch.

He pushed his glasses up his nose. "You must be River and Theo."

"And you must be Shepherd's new house pet," River said and pushed past him.

I gave the man an apologetic glance as River dragged me into the apartment.

"I'm his research assistant," said the man at the door, stumbling to get out of our way.

"Sure." River didn't sound like he believed him.

I was too busy gawking at the décor. Everything was sleek, modern, and flawless. A huge television stood over an unlit gas fireplace surrounded by furniture so nice it looked like no one had ever used it. Even the floors were spotless. It felt like I'd walked onto a television set and not into someplace where someone lived.

"Wow. This place is nice," I pointed out, much to River's irritation.

"Thank you," said a man from the hallway.

Something in me immediately wanted to turn around and run away as quickly as I could as soon as I heard him speak. He stepped around the corner, adjusting the cufflinks on his immaculately tailored suit. He wore a pair of leather gloves, but otherwise, he wouldn't have looked out of place at a corporate office. Dark green eyes scanned the room as if the very air in it was beneath him. Maybe it was. This guy belonged on a runway modeling Italian suits, not talking to us.

The man smiled at me. "It's always nice to meet someone who appreciates the finer things. Maybe some of your good taste will rub off on my darling little brother."

"Shepherd," River said in greeting, his tone tense.

The corners of Shepherd's lips pulled back into a predatory smile. "River. I was surprised when you called, but you're always welcome here. You and your...friend."

River's arm tightened around mine as Shepherd eyed me up and down.

"Is this family business or personal?" Shepherd asked.

"Personal," River ground out through his teeth.

"You've caught me at an awkward time, I'm afraid. Gavin and I were about to head out for this evening's research." He crossed his arms over his chest. "But maybe if you ask me nicely, I could be convinced to change my plans."

River was snorting like an angry bull next to me. I half expected him to launch himself at Shepherd and start swinging. Instead, through clenched teeth, he mumbled, "Please, Shepherd, can we speak to you in private about a personal matter?"

"What was that?" Shepherd cupped a hand behind his ear. "I'm not sure I heard you clearly, little brother."

"Twenty minutes," River spat. "It's all we want, you bag of dicks with a god-complex. I'll even pay you for your time."

Shepherd regarded us with an amused expression. "You're *family*, River. I would never dream of charging you outside of business hours. If you're having performance issues, I'd love to hear about them." He waved to his assistant, who'd met us at the door.

Gavin nodded and picked up the phone.

"If you'll be so kind as to step into my office?" Shepherd took a step back and gestured down the hall.

The office Shepherd ushered us into was neat and tidy. Bookshelves lined one wall while a cherry wood desk sat in the middle. Behind it, huge floor to ceiling windows showed lights on the freeway beyond, but it was the artwork on the interior wall that caught my attention.

While the rest of the décor in the apartment was all black and white, the paintings were all portraits in vivid yellows, bright greens, and deep reds.

"They say he was only epileptic, but I disagree."

I jumped at the sound of Shepherd right behind me. He smirked when I glanced back at him.

"Who?" I asked.

"Van Gogh." He took a step forward to stand next to me, admiring the paintings on the wall with his hands folded behind his back. "He did suffer from seizures, famously so, but to stop there would be doing a brilliant mind a disservice. The near feverish pace with which he produced his art, the utter devotion to it, paired with extended episodes of delusion, depression, and several well-documented moments of sometimes violent psychosis? The man was very likely schizophrenic. But no one wants to admit that, because there is still such a stigma attached to psychiatric disorders. Epilepsy is more acceptable. Schizophrenia simply isn't sexy enough."

"Did he paint these?" I asked, nodding to the paintings.

Shepherd chuckled. "No, unfortunately. A real Van Gogh would go for over a million dollars. These are my poor attempts at capturing his likeness and style."

I didn't think they were poor attempts at all. Even though I had never seen a real Van Gogh painting, Shepherd seemed to have matched the moody, distorted self-image the man must've had.

Shepherd went to the seat behind his desk. "Please, sit."

River sat stiffly in one of the chairs across from him and I sank into the other, sitting on the edge. My knee started bouncing up and down on its own. I forced it to still.

I felt naked under Shepherd's intense stare, almost as if he were shining a black light on me and he could see all the dirty places on my skin other people had touched.

"Well?" River suddenly blurted, and I flinched.

Shepherd sighed and lowered his hands, leaning forward against his desk. "Patience was never your strongest asset, was it, River?"

"I didn't bring him up here for you to stare at," River growled.

"Why *did* you bring him here?" Shepherd's mouth quirked up in a slight smirk when River struggled with the question. "You don't know, do you? You only know that your toy is broken, and you need your big brother to help you fix it."

River glared at Shepherd.

He knows, I realized. *Shepherd knows what I am.* My face heated. "How much did he tell you?"

Shepherd's eyes slid to me again. "River said nothing. Nothing useful anyway. If you want someone to blame for what I know, blame War. I spoke with him this morning and he filled me in on some of it."

"War doesn't know shit," River mumbled and crossed his arms.

Shepherd ignored River's outburst to focus on me. "What is it you think War told me?"

I glanced over at River before lowering my eyes. "That I'm a whore. That people bought me, used me. And that River saved me."

"You were a prostitute."

"It's the same thing," I pointed out with a shrug.

"Is it?" Shepherd studied me with a blank expression, folding his hands on the surface of the desk. "Perhaps they mean the same thing, but they have different connotations. Whore is a derogatory term. Choosing to use that word in place of another is very telling."

I swallowed. "It is?"

"You could have said you were a victim of human trafficking. They all mean the same thing," Shepherd said.

I chewed my lip and tried the phrase out in my own mind once. Theo, human trafficking victim. "No," I said, shaking my head. "That's even worse."

"How so?" Shepherd urged.

"Because I don't want anyone to see me as a victim."

"But that's what you are, Theo. You didn't have a choice. Powerful men preyed upon you, took away your freedom. To be a victim is not a negative thing. It puts the blame where it belongs, shifting it from you to the perpetrators of your abuse." Shepherd leaned back in his chair. "What about the word *survivor*? How does that word feel to you?"

I licked my lips, thinking. "It feels like a lie. I haven't *survived* anything."

"And why not?"

"Because surviving would mean I've come out the other side stronger." I shook my head again. "I'm not. I'm terrified all the time that I'm going to wake up and find this is all a dream. And when I go to sleep, all I dream about is being chased and dragged back there. I can't even go to the bathroom on my own without wishing River was next to me. I know it was awful, but sometimes I wish—" I broke off, eyes widening as I realized what I'd been about to say.

"Yes?" Shepherd's eyes sparkled. "Sometimes you wish what? Finish the thought, Theo."

River was watching me, his eyebrows drawn together in concern.

I turned away and mumbled, "Sometimes I wish I could go back. At least then I wouldn't be afraid anymore."

I didn't actually want to go back. I couldn't anyway. Master would punish me, maybe even kill me for running away. I just wanted things to go back to the way they were. I wanted my life to have some level of normalcy and predictability, even if what I knew was coming was bad. Anything was better than this exhausting gauntlet of waiting for him to find me, waiting for River to grow tired of me, waiting, waiting, waiting.

"I'm tired of waiting for bad things to happen to me," I whispered, closing my eyes.

"What about good things?" Shepherd prompted. "Tell me something good that's happened to you since you met River."

I started to answer.

"And you can't say meeting River." He smirked.

Dammit. How did he know exactly what I was going to say? I looked over at River, trying to pick something specific. "River bought me a phone today."

And when he kissed me last night, I wanted him back. I hadn't thought myself capable of wanting someone else, and that I did was confusing. Did I really want to be with him, or was it some survival mechanism kicking into overdrive? Maybe I only wanted him because he was nice to me. Was that how easy I was? Ready to come for the first man who didn't use me up and throw me away?

"What else are you thinking about, Theo?" Shepherd asked, bringing me back.

"Nothing," I said quickly, skin flushing hot.

Shepherd glanced back and forth between me and River. "There's no reason to be ashamed, Theo. I'm a scholar of human sexuality. I have literally coached couples through intercourse. I co-own a BDSM club. There is nothing you can tell me that I haven't heard before."

I blushed harder and squirmed in the chair.

"You thinking about the hand job I gave you last night?" River asked in a smug tone.

I sank further into my chair.

Shepherd sighed and pinched the bridge of his nose. "River, it's imperative that Theo be allowed to speak for himself."

I nearly jumped out of my skin when someone knocked on the door.

"Come," Shepherd called.

The door cracked open and Gavin stuck his head in. "Food's here. I hope you guys like pad Thai."

"Thank you, Gavin," Shepherd said. "Theo, why don't you help Gavin get the table set up while I talk to River for a moment?"

My stomach did a somersault at the prospect of being away from River, but he didn't seem bothered. *He'll only be in the next room, Theo. It'll be fine.*

River picked up my hand and kissed the back of it. "I'll be right out," he assured me.

I swallowed, nodded, and stood, going to the door with Gavin.

Thirteen

River

"MOM SAID I'M NOT allowed to harvest your organs," I said as Shepherd placed two highball glasses on his desk. "She and Tatty also send their love."

Shepherd spun the top off the bottle of imported liquor with a snort and splashed a dash of amber in each glass. "Coming from Mom, that's practically a threat. I can't possibly think of anything I've done to warrant such a thing." He sat back, putting his feet up on the desk, crossing one ankle over the other as he swirled the drink around. He peered into it as if he expected to find a fly in his drink.

I shifted in my seat, throwing an anxious glance at the door. I didn't like leaving Theo alone, especially in Shepherd's apartment with someone I didn't know.

"You don't need to worry about your pet," Shepherd said, cradling his glass. "Gavin isn't interested."

"How do you know?"

"Because Gavin is the most sex repulsed asexual ace to walk the face of this Earth," Shepherd said with a twinge of disappointment. "And while his morality is flexible, it is much more grounded than mine, hence why I keep him around."

I eyed the drink in front of me. "You're drinking again. You know you're not supposed to drink with your meds."

"Which one of us has the medical degree again?" Shepherd pretended to consider the ceiling. "That's right. I do. You have a *certificate*. Cheers to you." He lifted the glass and downed it in one go.

I considered him as he refilled his glass. "Are you off your meds?"

Shepherd gave me a bored glance. "I had a naughty little grad student who hasn't had an orgasm all semester waiting for me at my club when you showed up. Given the immense amount of preparation he and I have both put in for our session tonight, I was disinclined to cancel, so I've only postponed our meeting by a few hours. Every minute that I'm up here with you is one he's not licking my boots and begging me to let him come, so let's finish this quickly and go back to pretending to tolerate each other at a distance, shall we? What is it you want from me, River? You do realize I can't take on your boy toy as a patient?"

I put my arm on his desk, leaning forward. "I want you to tell me how to play with him without breaking him, and I want you to help me find the people who hurt him so I can make them pay."

He considered me for a long moment, tapping the end of his pen on his desk. "I'd like to have another session with him. Alone this time."

"You just got finished telling me you couldn't take him on as a patient," I growled.

"I didn't say as a patient. I'd like to study him."

"No," I answered before he'd even gotten the full sentence out. "I'm not leaving you alone in a room with him. He's *mine*."

Shepherd sighed. "I know this possessive display is rooted in your trauma, River, but would you try to think about it rationally? You're asking me to assess and diagnose a patient I've seen for only a few minutes in a less than ideal situation."

You bastard, I thought at him. That was why I couldn't stand Shepherd. He thought he was better than the rest of us. We were all murderers, but not him. He could pass his crimes off on one of his alters, still somehow believing his hands were clean.

"You're not having a session of any kind with Theo." I folded my arms. "Either help me, or I'm leaving."

Shepherd shrugged. "To be clear, I won't object to you leaving at any time."

"And I'm taking Theo with me," I added.

His left eye twitched.

Yeah, Shepherd was definitely off his meds again, which meant I was sitting in an office with a ticking time bomb.

He poured himself another drink and drank it thoughtfully, staring at empty space for a while. "Co-dependency. Complex post-traumatic stress disorder. Possibly even an attachment disorder, depending on how young he was when this began. He clearly lacks a strong sense of self."

"How do I fix him?" I insisted.

Shepherd sighed. "You can't *fix* him. He's not a broken doll. With disorders that complex, I would normally recommend extended therapy under regular supervision, perhaps even an inpatient program. Clearly, that isn't an option here. You'll need to build his autonomy slowly. Give him simple tasks to do, but don't coddle him. Domestic chores would be a good place to start."

I wrinkled my nose. "He isn't one of your house slaves, Shep."

"I'm being serious," Shepherd said, deadpan. "You small-minded cavemen laugh, but BDSM mirrors therapy in a lot of ways. A typical course of therapy begins by breaking down assumptions and barriers that separate the present self from the ideal self. Theo doesn't have those barriers. His self is like...a house with no walls. His trauma is clearly compartmentalized somewhere. It's not in the house. Maybe it's outside the house like a storm. The longer that trauma stays outside, the more damage it's going to do to his whole identity. But if you open all the windows at once, you'll flood the place and wreck it too. Something like this has to be handled carefully. You crack the windows into the trauma, River. You don't throw them all open at once."

I slumped in my chair. "Once more, without the confusing analogy."

Shepherd sighed and shifted, letting his elbow rest on the desk. "It's extremely likely that he's suppressed memories associated with his abuse. Those memories will resurface, but don't force them. Deal with them as they come. He's going to experience all five stages of grief. You know how to deal with those. You've been trained."

He was right. Working in the funeral industry, it was mandatory to get my certificate, even though I rarely interacted with living people. Mom and Dad had drilled the right responses into me, too. I understood grief and knew it well enough that I was confident in how to respond to it when it finally hit Theo.

"What about sex?" I asked.

He massaged his temples. "Without speaking to him, I'm reluctant to give you specifics. However, since I know what a stubborn ass you can be, and since I don't want you to break him before I get a chance to study him... Some victims of sexual trauma disassociate during sex as a coping mechanism. They build a safe place in their minds, separating their consciousness from what's happening to their body."

I frowned. "You think Theo does that?"

I didn't know if I liked that. I wanted him to be present so I could enjoy him. If he wasn't totally conscious of what was happening, he couldn't consent. Not fully.

"I don't know," Shepherd said, shaking his head. "I only said it's common. Given his history, I would expect he views it as transactional, not unlike us, and may attempt to use it to manipulate you into giving him what he wants. He's been taught that orgasms make dangerous men happy, and the fastest way to ensure his continued survival is to provide them to you."

He had tried, but I didn't want him to think of me like another customer to take care of. It was my job to take care of him. "How do I change his mind? Get him to see things differently?"

"Psychotherapy?" Shepherd suggested, lifting an eyebrow.

I gave him a sour look.

"I'm serious, River. As long as he only has you, he can't fully realize his own identity outside of you. Your personality is too big, and Theo will cling to you. He needs to be around other people." His chair creaked as he leaned forward, grabbing a card from the corner of his desk. "I'm giving you the name of someone I trust," he said, scribbling on the back of the card. "She's a former student of mine, and a survivor of a similar situation. She runs a weekly support group in Winchester. Theo should go. It's good for him to realize he's not alone in his trauma, and to have someplace to talk about it where he won't feel judged."

Shepherd held the card out to me. I swiped it from his hand without the promise that Theo would go. That had to be up to Theo. If he wanted to go, I'd take him, even if I thought group therapy was utter bullshit.

"Fuck you," I spat, but pocketed the card anyway. "What about the other thing?"

"You mean hunting down a group of predators who clearly can't be bothered with consent? Predators hunting vulnerable people in *my* backyard?" He sank into his seat, putting his feet back up on the desk with a smirk. "Oh, River. You wouldn't have come to me if you thought I'd say no."

I knew Shepherd would say yes. It was the others I wasn't sure about.

I arched an eyebrow. "You don't want to confer with the others?"

Shepherd's eye twitched again. "Bryce is on board as long as Dex stays out of it."

Not surprising, since Dex was eight and afraid of the dark. It was too bad Dex was the one I saw the least of, because he was my favorite. "And Keres?"

Shepherd's gaze grew more intense, and, for a moment, I saw the monster beneath. He was cold and evil, a being made of pure hate and crafted for the singular purpose of killing whoever was unlucky enough to cross his path.

"Keres is resting in the dark place," Shepherd whispered. "And we don't want to wake him, do we?"

"Are you sure this isn't going to wake him up?" I wasn't trying to be an asshole, but I had to know.

Keres had a thing for hunting people who hurt the vulnerable, which sounded like a good thing, until you realized that, in Keres's twisted version of reality, everyone was guilty. He was the sort of killer who would rip apart a city, killing everyone, until he was the last one standing. And then he'd slit his own throat for the hell of it.

"I'm never sure of anything when it comes to him," Shepherd said, watching me with predatory intent. "But that's the risk of playing this game, isn't it? Put your hand in the cage enough times, even a well-trained dog bites when he's hungry."

"Well, let's hope it doesn't come to that." I stood and polished off my drink.

"River," Shepherd called as I went to the door.

I paused and looked back at him.

All traces of the danger that lurked beneath his skin had gone, leaving in its place the mask of a perfectly normal, functional human being. "Try music to get him to open up. Something other than rap? The CIA uses that to torture people for a reason."

"Fuck you," I said again and stormed out of Shepherd's office.

Fourteen
Theo

RIVER DECIDED WE WEREN'T staying for dinner. It was just as well since I wasn't hungry. My stomach and mind were both churning after my conversation with Shepherd.

All day there'd been this pressure slowly building in my skull. Talking about what happened relieved the pressure some, but not enough. I needed to do something to get it out, but I didn't know what.

I looked over at River as he tightened his fingers around the steering wheel. He hadn't said a word to me since we left, focusing straight ahead on the drive. Irritation, or maybe anger, rippled out of him like heat from a radiator.

I shouldn't have said I wished I could go back. That had to be it. What else did he have to be angry about?

"I don't actually want to go back," I said, breaking the silence of the car ride.

River blinked and looked over at me, his shoulders relaxing slightly. "What?"

"To Master. I don't want to go back. I want to stay with you."

He took a deep breath and let it out slowly. "You're only saying that because you're afraid of me."

"I'm not. I feel safe with you. Safer than I ever have before with anyone."

It was strange, how connected I felt to someone I barely knew. Yet the more time I spent with River, the more I was sure of how I felt. I wasn't afraid of him, only of him getting bored of me. There was this lingering feeling that he'd eventually realize his mistake with me, that he'd look over and finally realize that I wasn't worth all the trouble he was going through. I wasn't worth anything to anybody.

Except maybe River.

My thoughts weren't making any sense. How could I be both worthless and valued? But I felt different things at different times, and talking to Shepherd had only mixed all of those feelings up in the worst way. I needed to figure out who and what I was supposed to be with him. Our relationship felt too loosely defined, and I didn't know how to act, or what was expected of me. Was River my caretaker like Master? Was he supposed to be my friend? My lover?

My chest was suddenly tight. There were too many feelings happening at once and I couldn't breathe.

Then River's hand left the steering wheel and closed over mine, and the fog of confusion began to lift. "I'm not mad at you, Theo. I'm just mad."

I let out a shaky breath, relieved. "At Shepherd?"

"At everything. Everything except for you." He pulled his hand away, putting it back on the steering wheel. "Do you need anything? Hot? Cold? Something to eat?"

I shook my head. "I'm fine. But if you want to eat..."

"What I want isn't food, Theo." The intense look he shot at me across the narrow space between us sent goosebumps breaking out over my skin.

My breath caught for a moment before I whispered, "What do you want?"

"Are you sure you want me to answer that, little finch? It might scare you, the things I want."

"You can't scare me, River." *Please. I need to know.*

He tapped his fingers on the steering wheel until the silence became unbearable.

"You want to fuck me," I said.

River's finger stilled. "I want to do more than that, little finch. I want to mark you, sink my teeth into that pretty, soft flesh and leave bruises behind. Not because I want to hurt you. Because I want everyone to see my mark on you and know that you're *mine*. Especially Shepherd. I didn't like the way he was looking at you tonight. I don't like the way anyone looks at you. Every time they do, all I can think about is biting that pretty neck and sucking on the bruise until it blooms. I want to hold my teeth over your pulse and feel it flutter for me. I want you to ache for me. Only for me."

I sucked in a sharp breath, trying to ignore the way his words made my cock harden. "That's..."

"I told you that you might not want to hear it," he mumbled in a dark tone, staring forward.

"It's not that. I needed to hear it, River. Not knowing what you want is so much worse."

He shook his head. "I don't want you to think that's all I want from you. I don't want to be like the people who hurt you." He glanced over at me, his expression still severe. "I need you to want it. If you don't, it will never happen. I would rather keep you up on your shelf than risk breaking you myself."

I frowned. "I don't understand what that means."

"It means if I can't have you, nobody will," he said, looking forward again. "And I don't know how far I'll go to make sure that remains the case. But I won't allow anyone to hurt you in a way you don't want, not even me. I'll kill anyone who tries."

Just like he killed Rick.

The idea should've made me fear him. Instead, I'd never felt safer than in that moment.

Or more turned on.

Which was even more confusing. I wanted him to leave bruises on me, to bite me until it hurt. Why did I want that? Hadn't I been hurt enough? My neck had felt so naked ever since he'd taken Master's collar off. Was I so ready to wear someone else's symbol of ownership? A collar was a collar, whether it was leather or a bruise.

It's different with him, I thought. *Because I know he won't do it unless I let him.*

But how can I be so sure?

Maybe it was naïve, and I was weak, but I felt sure. I wanted him to hurt me, but not in the way other people had. It had to be different.

"What if I wanted that too?" I asked and watched him carefully. "But...maybe somewhere else? Not my neck?"

River glanced over at me and then quickly away. "It doesn't have to be there, but I'd like it to be somewhere other people can see."

Because he needs people to understand I'm his to protect. The bruise is as much a threat to others as a mark of ownership. That makes it different.

I glanced out the window, recognizing some of the houses and the big sign. A short while later, we passed through the sleepy little town, and then out the other side. We were miles from River's house and I still didn't know what to do. That feeling of dread was getting worse, the pressure in my head pounding.

By the time we pulled down the long gravel driveway and he parked the car, my whole body was vibrating with a need to get that feeling out of me, and thanks to River, I knew exactly how.

"River," I said, as he turned off the car.

He pressed the release button on his seatbelt and looked over at me, waiting.

My mouth was dry and my heart was pounding, but not because I was afraid.

I leaned across the space, reaching out but stopping short of touching his face. He was so beautiful; it felt like a sin to touch him. I wasn't worthy. River's hand closed over mine and he brought it to his cheek. He closed his eyes and leaned into my touch.

"Will you kiss me?" The request came out as a breathy whisper, barely loud enough to hear.

He turned his head and pressed his lips to the inside of my wrist. Could he feel my pulse racing through that kiss?

I licked my lips. "Kiss me more?"

His eyes fluttered open and locked on mine. For a second, he remained utterly still, like a predator locking onto its prey. Then he launched himself across the center console and captured my lips with his. I surrendered against the fury of him, a rabbit in the jaws of a hungry wolf. Strong fingers gripped my hair by the roots, tipping my head back while he caught my bottom lip with his teeth.

Finally, the pressure that'd been building in my head all night released. This was the pain I needed; the only thing that made sense. I didn't have to question it; there was no more wondering where or when or why. That could all come later. Right now, this was what I needed, what I wanted.

He kissed me until we were both breathless and my scalp ached, yet I was so hard it was starting to hurt.

"River," I whispered hoarsely. Had he stolen my voice with that kiss? "I want more."

He considered me for a moment, brushing his fingertips lightly over my cheek. "Are you sure?"

I swallowed and nodded. "Please." *I need something to feel good. I need pain I can understand, pain that reminds me I'm real, that I'm here. I'm still alive.*

"Okay," he said, and got out of the car.

Fifteen

River

I RUSHED AROUND TO open Theo's door for him, my attention catching on his every movement as he got out of the car.

Part of me was still worried he would bolt, despite his claim to want more. After what he'd said at Shepherd's, how could I not worry? Shepherd had warned me he might try to use sex to manipulate me. Was that what he was doing, or was this real? Did it even matter as long as we both got what we wanted?

As long as he doesn't leave me.

My house was in the middle of nowhere, across from a soybean farm. If he ran, he might even get a fair distance before I caught him.

And I *would* catch him. That wasn't the problem. I was more concerned about what I would do when I did. I had promised I wouldn't let anyone hurt him, not even me, but that wasn't true. I'd kill him before I ever let him get away from me. He was mine, every part of him, from the freckles dusting his shoulders to the heart beating in his chest.

My insides ached with the need to claim him so that everyone who looked at him would know he was mine. I wanted him to feel me with every move, even when we weren't touching, and know that I was there with him.

I had never wanted that before with anyone, and the feeling was...confusing. It was as if there were two parts of me at war. One part wanted to bite him, twist him, hurt him, and break him so he couldn't run. The other part desperately needed him to choose me. He wouldn't do that if I hurt him.

Theo walked to the old wooden stairs leading up to my porch, and I relaxed. He wasn't going to run. He was staying with me, choosing to. My heart fluttered behind my ribs, and I shook out my keys, rushing past him to open the door.

The hardwood floors creaked as he stepped inside.

I shut the door, my thoughts racing through all the things I *should* do. I should take care of him, be gentle, take my time, make him feel wanted.

But that wasn't me. No matter how much he deserved that, I couldn't give it to him.

I couldn't take it. I grabbed him and pushed him against the wall next to the old grandfather clock, swallowing his needy groan. His body relaxed against mine and he opened to me, surrendering immediately as he had in the car.

"I need to be inside you," I said when we parted. "Now."

Theo put his arms around my neck. "Can we go to a bed?"

I snarled and bit his ear before lifting him by his ass. Theo squeaked and wrapped his legs around my waist, crossing them over my ass so he didn't fall.

"I'll fuck you in every bed in this house, little finch," I replied, carrying him upstairs.

He blinked as if he were staring into bright lights. "How many beds are there?"

"Three and a hide-a-bed in the sofa," I replied shortly.

I carried him to my bedroom and kicked the door shut behind us even though we were alone in the house. I didn't want the rest of the world intruding on this. They could wait their turn, because I absolutely was going to fuck him in every room of my house.

Theo let out another soft grunt when I put him down on the mattress. I didn't bother with the light. As much as I wanted to see his eyes roll back and his face contort with ecstasy, the dark was a safe blanket that hid the ugliness of the world. Maybe I could hide some of mine in it too.

I started pulling and kicking off my clothes while Theo frantically discarded his shirt. I kissed him again, harder, massaging my tongue over his, greedy to swallow all his softness. Theo moaned beneath me. Was that a conditioned response? Did he mean it? His limbs had gone limp under me, all the will to move gone out of him. What Shepherd had said about Theo disassociating during sex echoed in my mind and I pulled back, gripping his chin to hold him still while I looked down at him. He had that distant, doe-eyed look of someone who was awake, but not present. Seeing it on his face was like a stab straight to my gut.

"Don't do that," I said firmly.

He blinked, and the look was gone. "Do what?"

"Stay with me, Theo." I nuzzled against his throat. "Don't leave me."

His arms closed around my shoulders. "I'm right here."

But he wasn't. I could hear it in his voice. He was teetering on the edge of the safe place he'd made, the place he could go that no one else could reach him. I had to keep him with me, but I was going mad with need. I wanted him enough that I was starting not to care.

With a snarl, I tore at his clothes, yanking his jeans and underwear off. I was being too rough. I was going to hurt him if I didn't slow down. Deep down, I knew I was failing at this on every level. I needed to do something to take the edge off before I destroyed what little trust he had in me.

I forced myself to focus on something else. The ritual of preparation was a good distraction. *I should do that.*

I crawled over him to yank open the bedside drawer. Theo was breathing hard, watching as I laid everything I needed out in a straight line and in order. Lube. Condom. A hand towel for cleanup.

I can't do this the way I normally do, I thought, arranging everything. *I have to do something different with him, something that keeps him grounded in reality.*

"River?"

I looked over my shoulder at him, his brows pinched in concern. Warm, soft fingers trailed over my shoulder. He was touching me, my Theo was touching me like he wanted me, but how could I know that he meant it?

"I don't want you to be afraid of me," I said quietly and then shifted how I was sitting on the bed. "I mean, you *should* be afraid of me, but I don't want you to be."

Theo shook his head. "I told you I'm not afraid of you, and I meant it."

That was a lie. I knew it was. Everyone was afraid of me, and for good reason. People feared what they didn't understand. How could they understand me if I didn't even understand myself?

But Theo's trauma wouldn't let him tell the truth. He'd been taught the truth was dangerous. I had to teach him differently.

I turned around and pulled Theo into my lap, sliding further into the bed so I could lie down with my head on the pillows. When he looked at me in confusion, I said, "I want you on top of me."

"I thought..." He hissed when I picked up his hand and bit the inside of his wrist hard enough to leave a mark behind.

"I'm not going to bend you over and fuck you like everyone else has ever done. I'm not everyone else." I grabbed the bottle of lube and held it out to him. "Get yourself ready for me."

Theo took the bottle with shaky, unsure hands, and I hated that he was uncertain, hated that he kept looking at me, waiting for me to tell him I'd changed my mind, hated that he seemed like he didn't know how to do this. Other people had always done it to him. I didn't know who they were, but I hated them too.

I hated everyone and everything except for Theo. The rest of the world could burn, and I wouldn't give a damn as long as he was safe and with me.

His face was bright red as he carefully spread the lube over his fingers, warming it by rubbing his hands together. Theo pointedly avoided looking at me as his fist closed around my cock and he slicked me up.

"Stop," I barked, and I hated how he flinched. I cupped his cheek, forcing my voice to soften. "Don't worry about me yet." I took his hand, turned it over, and poured more lube over his fingers, pushing his hand back to him. "Finger your ass."

He stared at me as if I'd lost my mind, but he complied. Straddling my hips, Theo leaned forward. My attention flicked to the large standing mirror set up on the far wall so I could watch him do it. There was enough moonlight coming through the window that I could see him clearly circle his entrance with his middle finger before pushing it inside. His eyelashes fluttered, and he bit his lip as he slid his finger in and out.

"Does it feel good?" I asked him, watching his face flush.

He nodded.

I turned my head and scraped my teeth over the inside of his elbow. "Add another finger."

He did as he was told, groaning softly.

I moved my hands to his chest, running my fingers through the sparse curls of coarse, dark red hair. "Fuck yourself on your fingers while I touch you, little finch."

"I thought you wanted to be inside of me." He opened his eyes, but his lids were heavy, pupils blown wide.

"I do," I growled, and I rolled one of his nipples between two fingers, earning a pleasured hiss from him. "But I also need you to enjoy this. I want to be inside you and feel you come while you're riding my cock, chasing the pleasure no one else can give you. I want you to *want* to impale yourself on my cock."

"I already do," he panted and started rocking his hips back against his fingers.

"No, you don't. I need you to need me like an addict needs the needle. I want to be the fire burning in your veins, Theo. When you breathe, I want you drowning in your need to be with me."

"Fuck, River," he panted and tipped his head back, exposing his beautiful, soft throat as he fucked himself. "That has to be the single hottest thing anyone's ever said to me. And probably the most fucked up."

"I know. I don't care. Add a third finger."

He lowered his head, looking down at me, unsure until I sat up enough to capture his nipple between my teeth. Theo cursed again and his hips bucked, his hard cock dragging over my stomach and leaving a smear of pre-cum behind.

"Do it," I demanded and pushed the lube at him. "I need you ready."

"I *am* ready," he whined, but did it anyway, doubling over slightly as he added a third finger. "Ungh. Fuck..."

I reached between us, closing a fist around his leaking cock to give it a single teasing pump. "You know, there's a part of me that wants to watch you come like this. I want to watch you come apart without ever spoiling you. Keep you pristine and know you'll never be touched again except by the hands you want."

"I want *your* hands," he said, panting and trying to thrust into my fist. "I want your cock, River. I want you inside me."

I thumbed the leaking slit of his cock, smearing pre-cum across it. "Only me?"

"Only you!"

"Tell me you need me."

"I do!" He tipped his head back, practically sobbing, desperate, but I wouldn't let him have the friction he wanted, instead grabbing his ass and tipping him forward so that he had to stop fucking himself. He whined, "I need you so bad, River."

I held him there while I slicked myself up. "You need me to claim you?"

"Yes! I need you to make me yours. Fill me up until there's nothing but you left."

"Show me," I demanded.

Theo reached behind him and lifted my cock, positioning it expertly against his entrance. We groaned together as he slid me inside the sweet, tight heat of his body. He bore down, making it a few inches before he had to pull back and add more lube.

"Fuck, River, you're so big," he panted, sinking down even more.

I growled and gripped his hips, fighting the urge to thrust up into him. He was playing a dangerous game by feeding my ego, but damn if I didn't eat that up like candy.

Theo sank onto me until he was flush against my hips. Hands braced against my chest, he started to lift himself up and down, rocking his hips. I gripped his thighs, squeezing tight enough that I left finger indentations. It still didn't feel like enough contact, so I hooked an arm behind his back and pulled him down into a crushing kiss before moving down to scrape my teeth over his collarbone.

"Here?" I asked, licking over the spot. "Can I mark you here?"

"Fuck, yes," Theo panted.

He cried out as I sank my teeth into the skin, but the pained cry quickly morphed into a desperate, choking moan. Theo cursed as I closed my lips over the spot and sucked hard, tasting salt and iron.

"River!" he groaned.

God, hearing my name on his lips like that was so fucking sexy. My control shattered and I gripped his hips and started pumping up into him roughly. He grunted with every impact, the wet smack of our bodies coming together filling the room. My eyes fixed on the bright red spot on his upper chest, watching the bruise deepen and bloom. The stark colors against his pale skin were the most beautiful thing I'd ever seen.

"Oh, fuuuuck…" Theo whined, his voice trembling with each crash of me into him. "Fuck, River. Right there! Right fucking there!"

I slid my hand between our bodies to grip his cock, pumping quickly.

"Don't stop! Please don't stop!" he pleaded, eyes squeezing closed.

I snarled, incapable of words. It hadn't been more than a few minutes and already pleasure was coiling at the base of my spine, a high-powered spring ready to release. I was so keyed up, so fucking horny for Theo. I was surprised I'd lasted that long, but I wanted to make it at least until I was sure he'd finished.

Thankfully, I didn't have to wait long. Theo's hips jerked and his body tightened around me as if he were trying to strangle me through my cock. Cum splashed over my stomach, up my chest, and hit the comforter. Theo stared at it spilling over my fist stupidly, as if he couldn't believe it was real. That wrecked look of disbelief and bliss was so fucking hot, I couldn't hold myself back. I drove my hips up into him, pulling him down in one hard motion and sinking my teeth into the inside of his arm. He shuddered and shook in the last throes of his orgasm as I found mine, spilling inside of him.

Theo collapsed against me, breathing hard and trembling in my arms as if he were freezing.

Still inside of him, I reached to pull the blanket over us and paused with a slight grimace when I remembered something. "Dammit..."

"What? What's wrong?" He blinked up at me, still bleary-eyed and breathing hard.

"I was so worked up I forgot the condom. I'm not supposed to do that if we don't talk about it first."

Mom would kill me if she found out, maybe literally. Consent was not something we were allowed to violate with sexual partners, and she had made it very clear that without an enthusiastic yes to anything, the answer was always no. I had definitely crossed a line with Theo.

"S'alright," he mumbled, dragging his nose across my collarbone. "I like knowing it's there. Plus, it's one more difference between you and them. They always had to wear one. It was in the rules."

Rage flared in my chest like a candle under gasoline. I squeezed Theo harder against me, as if I could somehow shield him from all the awful things that had already happened to him. I couldn't. No one could. He'd never get back the years he lost or fully recover from the trauma. I knew better than anyone that he'd carry that with him for the rest of his life, and nothing I did would change that.

But I could make them pay for it.

Starting with his former master.

Sixteen
Theo

We took a quick shower after, and then River made me sit on the toilet so he could get a closer look at the bruises he'd left. I thought he was just admiring them until he opened the cabinet and got out a jar.

"What's that?" I asked as he unscrewed the lid.

"Arnica cream. It'll help you heal faster." He spread some on his fingers and reached toward the big bruise on my collarbone.

"Leave it," I blurted, and he froze. Our eyes met and I swallowed nervously. Was he mad?

I knew he liked it there, and after how badly he'd wanted to mark me, it seemed like such a waste to make it go away faster. Yes, it hurt, especially when I moved around, but I *liked* that it hurt. Whenever my head started to feel too full, I knew I could reach up and touch the bruise and I'd feel grounded again. Every time I saw my reflection, I'd be reminded of how badly it seemed like he'd wanted me, how good and valuable he'd made me feel.

River hadn't treated me like *a* whore. He'd treated me like *his* whore.

He nodded, shoulders dropping as if he were relieved. "Let me see the inside of your arm."

River spread the cream over the two bruises he'd left on the inside of my arm and a few I hadn't known were on my hips. Then he gave me two little brown pills that he promised would help if there was any pain and took me back to bed to sleep.

Even as exhausted as I was, it was hard to sleep, despite being in River's arms. The house was too new, the sounds of the old wood creaking unfamiliar, and my thoughts were too loud in my head.

Normally, I'd shut my mind off after sex. Just clean up and curl up, numb and empty. I couldn't do that with River. He wouldn't let me. Not that I wanted to, either. While I'd had orgasms before, it had been different with him. So far, he'd gone out of his way to make sure I enjoyed sex, that I was comfortable, and that I wanted what we were doing. He'd been so careful with me, so tender in a way no one had ever been. It was easy to open myself up to him.

What if it's an act? I wondered. *What if this is just how he is in the beginning?* The way River spoke of himself sometimes scared me. He could change at any moment and decide to hurt me instead of taking care of me. What would I do then?

I knew this wasn't healthy, that our relationship was about as toxic as it got, but I couldn't help myself. I wanted this.

Relationship, I scoffed. *Is that what this is? Are you so desperate, Theo? He gets you off twice and you're ready to make your bed with a murderer.*

Well, he couldn't possibly be any worse than all the others that'd come before. At least, that's what I told myself.

The ghosts of faces swirled in my memory, specific features always out of reach. I remembered croaky voices, the smell of stale tobacco and bad breath, calloused hands in places I didn't want them to be.

"Hey," River said, stroking a hand through my damp hair. "You okay?"

I swallowed and wondered again if he had some kind of mind reading power. He seemed to have a sixth sense of when I was sinking into my own head too much. "Yeah, just thinking."

River was quiet, his fingertips brushing over my ribs and sending little shocks of pleasurable sensation through me.

"Do you remember what I told you about my mom?" he said quietly.

"That she died of a heroin overdose." Why was he bringing that up?

River nodded. "I don't know a lot about my father, but I know he was white, and DNA has never come up, so he must not be in the penal system. She was here illegally from South Korea. They think that's why she didn't go to a hospital to have me. There were no records of me. No birth certificates. No social security card. When she died, I was four. I was an only child that no one knew existed, so no one came looking for me. No one came to check on her."

My throat felt tight. I reached behind me to hold his hand, but he didn't squeeze back.

"I didn't know how to use a phone," he continued. "I could reach the fridge, the sink, and two cabinets that contained cereal, chips, and crackers. I was lucky she'd just gotten a big box of food from the food pantry and gone shopping. When it happened, I thought she'd just gone to sleep for a long time. Sometimes, when she took her shots, she did that. Even when she started to bloat and smell, I didn't know what was going on. I was too young to have any concept of death."

"Jesus, River," I whispered.

"They didn't find me until someone from the power company came to shut our electricity off. I told him my mom was sick, and that I was hungry, apparently. They think I was in there with her for over a month. I don't remember. I don't remember a lot of it, actually. Just the waiting. Waiting on her to get better, to wake up, to take care of me."

How could he be so casual about it? He didn't sound the least bit upset, like it didn't matter that he'd been alone with a decaying body for over a month.

I turned over to face him and touched his cheek. "You don't have to tell me, River."

"I'm not telling you because I want your sympathy," he said, staring at me. "I'm telling you because..." He sighed and rolled onto his back. "She left me alone, Theo, and I'll never forgive her for leaving. I can't. I hate her. I hope she's rotting in hell for loving her fucking drug more than she ever loved me."

River closed his eyes and took a deep breath in, letting it out slowly before he turned to face me again. "You can't leave me, Theo."

Like his mother left him, I realized.

Oh, River. My heart felt like it'd cracked in two. This was him at his most vulnerable. He was letting me see who he was under the mask he showed everyone. Somewhere deep down, buried beneath a mile of misdirected anger and unhealthy coping mechanisms, was a scared, hurt little boy who needed to take care of someone, and who needed to be taken care of in return.

I scooted closer, putting my arms around him and tangling our legs together. "I won't," I promised.

"You can't run from me," he said again. "You can't go back there. I won't let them have you."

"I'm not going anywhere, River."

He took a breath and it came out shaky, almost like he was on the verge of tears. "I need to tell you something."

I lifted my head to look up at him. "What is it?"

"It's about my family. My brothers, Mom, Dad, Tatty... We're not *normal*."

I'd guessed as much already. War seemed to have OCD, and Shepherd had four personalities. River was a sociopath and the triplets... Well, one of them was in an institution, probably for life.

River ran his thumb along my cheek. "Have you heard of Big Sister? Some people call her the Angel of Death."

I shook my head.

"They say she killed twenty-three men over thirty years," River said. "All of them were rapists and abusive husbands. Men who deserved it. She worked as a delivery nurse at Mount Carmel Hospital. Some little girl came in pregnant, and within a year, her dad, her uncle, her neighbor—they all went into the ground in a pine box."

"Why are you telling me this, River?"

He studied me in silence for a long moment. "Because Annie is The Angel of Death."

I stared at him in shocked silence. How could that be true? Annie was sweet and kind. Gentle. She'd given me cookies and tea.

And if what River was saying was true, she'd killed twenty-three abusers, freeing twenty-three girls from future abuse.

"Yuri has worked for the Vori since before he came to America in the early nineties," River continued.

"The Vori?" I asked.

"Russian mafia. He's not a member himself, but the connection is strong. His old man had an arrangement with the local boss to dispose of the bodies. Dad's continued that tradition. Sometimes, the bodies he's taken care of... They aren't completely dead, Theo."

I couldn't stop myself from recoiling slightly. "Wait a minute." I sat up. "You're telling me Annie, Tatty, and Yuri are what? Like serial killer mob bosses?"

River shrugged. "Well, technically Tatty is a mafia princess, and there's her husband, Niki, but like that whole thing is complicated. He's *definitely* killed people though."

"What about War, Xander, and Xavier?" I pressed. "You going to tell me they're serial killers, too?"

River's eyes took on a particular darkness that made me shiver. "We're all killers, Theo. You saw me kill Rick. He's not the first. There have been seven others, but I promise you they all deserved it."

Eight people? Fuck, that was enough to qualify him as a serial killer more than twice over, wasn't it?

I was in bed with a serial killer.

A serial killer from a family of serial killers. It was almost too much to believe.

"H-how?" I stammered. "How does no one know?"

"Nikita is a very good lawyer, and we're all very careful. Besides," he said, waving a dismissive hand, "mutually assured destruction is stronger than blood. Like you, I was brought up with strict mental conditioning, except that where your captor abused you, my parents used that programming to try to help me. They recognized what I was early on and decided that my instincts should be used for good instead of evil, just like what Mom did when she was younger. Mom, Dad, Tatty, and Nikita make sure I don't kill people. Only monsters like Rick, and like your Master."

I sighed and crossed my arms, looking away. "What am I supposed to do? Just believe that you're good serial killers?"

"There's no such thing as a good serial killer," he said and squeezed my thighs. "We're not good people, but we can't help who we are. Even if Annie and Yuri hadn't found us, we'd be who we are, but we'd be worse. We'd be uncontrolled."

"You're saying you can control yourself?" I asked, tone harsher than I meant it to be.

River shook his head. "No. Not alone. I know my limits. Shepherd can as long as he stays on his meds, and War and the triplets deal with their issues in their own way, but I need to have other people around me who know. That's why I'm telling you all this. You can help me. Tell me if I'm taking things too far. Teach me to be more...human."

I looked down at him, trying hard not to feel sorry for him. His early life had been a living hell, but that was no excuse to kill people. If the people he was killing did deserve it, though, would that be so bad?

"That's a lot to ask of me," I pointed out. "I can't even take care of myself, and you want me to take care of you?"

"No," he said, shaking his head again. "You don't need to do anything. I just need you to be you. It's hard to explain. There's a lot of noise in my head, Theo, but no direction. Just anger. Other people who aren't like me, they help me know where to direct it."

"Like at Master?"

River's jaw muscles flexed, and anger flashed in his eyes. "He's not your master anymore, Theo."

I sighed and touched my forehead. "I know, but it's not like I know what else to call him. I don't know his real name. I don't know anything useful."

"Are you mad at me?" he asked, finally sitting up.

I considered River, waiting to feel some shadow of anger. It should be there, but it just wasn't. "No," I said at length. "You're right, River. Some people don't deserve to live. If no one else is going to do anything to help, why can't you do it in your own way? You saved me." I sighed. "Tell me how I can help."

River smiled and surged up to catch my lips in a quick kiss. "You don't have to do anything but be with me. But if you do happen to remember something, it would help. Maybe not tonight, though." He glanced at the clock and winced. "I have to be at work in a few hours."

I frowned at the clock. "I don't know if I can sleep. My mind is pretty busy tonight."

He replied with a suggestive smirk. "You want me to suck your dick? That might wear you out."

I pushed his head away, laughing. "You can't solve everything by giving me orgasms."

"I can try." He grinned ear to ear and pounced me, tackling me to the bed, kissing his way over my stomach and hips.

I relaxed and tried not to think about who he was outside of this room. Maybe that would be enough and this would all make sense tomorrow.

Seventeen

River

THE ALARM WENT OFF at seven the next morning.

I shut it off and rolled over to kiss Theo awake. It was tempting to stay in bed with him all day. There was only one body, and it was from a county with no attached services, which meant he was probably a John Doe. It didn't matter if I prepped him today, tomorrow, or next week for cremation, so long as we didn't get overrun with bodies.

But if I tried to call out of work, Dad would lecture me about responsibility and the importance of routine. He'd be at my door in an hour demanding that I come to work because it was good for me, and he'd be right. Theo was good for me, too.

I ground myself against his thigh, savoring the taste of him, the answering hardness of his cock against me.

"What was the alarm for?" he asked groggily between kisses.

"I have to go to work," I replied and kissed him again.

"What time do you have to work?"

"Soon." I reached between us, slotting our cocks together in my fist. "But it's not the end of the world if I'm late this once."

He made a small sound in the back of his throat as I started thrusting against him with more intention. "It doesn't bother you to talk about dead bodies while we're doing this?"

"Should it?" I licked over the bruise I'd left the night before. "Why?"

Theo shifted to look at me. "I don't know. Bodies and funerals aren't exactly regular pillow talk."

"Maybe they should be. Nothing reminds you that you're alive like death. Sex and funerals go together like flies and fruit. It's actually one of the most common places—after bars—for people to hook up."

"I wonder why that is," Theo said dreamily, his voice growing thick.

"Dunno. Shepherd's the shrink, not me."

"I wonder if—"

I closed a hand over Theo's mouth, muffling his next words. "I don't want to talk," I said and sank my teeth into his arm. I wanted to bite his neck, but he'd asked me not to, and I'd respect that, at least until I got him to change his mind.

Theo's muffled moan vibrated through my palm. When he opened his mouth, I pushed my fingers into it and he closed around them willingly, sucking hard, eyes closed, face serene. Fuck, he was beautiful and so damn perfect. It wasn't fair that I hadn't found him sooner.

I let my fist glide over us slowly, working both of us in tandem. It'd take a while to make him come like that, probably even longer because he'd already come three times the night before. I didn't mind, though. I savored every second I was with him, every heated huff of breath, every quiet sigh or moan. Those sounds were mine, and he'd never make them for anyone else again.

The world could wait. Theo was the only thing that mattered.

Slowly, though, his breathing got faster, and he started to tremble. I pulled my fingers from between his teeth to let him have some air.

He immediately gasped and started to come, shaking violently as if he were convulsing, his mouth open in a silent scream as he spilled his release over my fist. I followed him into bliss a second later and then collapsed on top of him, breathing hard.

"I think we need another shower," Theo said absently.

I grunted in agreement. "And then we'll swing by Mom's for breakfast."

After our shower, we hopped in the car and I drove him to Mom's. Theo wasn't happy about my plan to have him spend the morning with her, but I promised to take him to lunch and make up for it in the afternoon. Shepherd had said domestic chores would be good for Theo, and that was Mom's area. She'd have him sweeping floors, baking cookies, and washing dishes until he was too tired to think about what he'd been through. It was what she'd done with all of us in the beginning.

Well, everyone except War, but his OCD made cleaning an impossibly complicated task.

I realized my mistake as soon as we walked into the kitchen and found Xander was already there.

Xander's eyes widened, immediately jumping to the bruise on Theo's chest, which showed brilliantly thanks to Theo's choice to wear a V-neck that day. "Bro. Is that a *hickey?*"

I growled at him. "As if you're not covered in them half the time."

Xander conceded the point with a shrug and forced his pop tart out of the toaster early. He plopped at the table and paused halfway through taking a bite when the front door banged open and a very sweaty War came into the hall, his phone pressed against his ear. His eyes were all puffy like he hadn't slept, which was weird for him. War *loved* his beauty sleep.

"It's not about the money," he was saying. "Ken, we agreed you were going to wait. It was your fucking idea! Well, don't raise your voice at *me*!" He sighed and pinched the bridge of his nose. "Look, if you sign that contract, you won't have time to..." He lowered his hand, sobering. When he continued, his voice was completely flat. "No, I understand. Of course. Yeah. We'll talk later." He hung up and stared down at his phone resting in his palm.

I crossed my arms. "Can I kill your ascot wearing tool boyfriend *now*?"

He sighed and clipped the phone to his hip without looking at me. "He's not my boyfriend. Not anymore." War shoved his ear pods back in and jogged up the stairs.

I frowned. That wasn't like him at all, at least not the complete lack of emotional reaction. The breaking up with Ken bit was pretty standard. They'd broken up and gotten back together half a dozen times over the last three years. I glanced back at Xander.

"Don't look at me," Xander offered, his mouth full of pop tart.

I walked over to kiss Theo's cheek. "Get some breakfast. I won't be long," I told him and then rushed up the stairs after War.

Outside of War's room, I paused. The door was cracked open and he had his music cranked up so loud through his earbuds that I could identify the song. I pushed open the door and hung in the doorway, apparently interrupting a vigorous set of sit-ups.

He paused long enough to scowl at me, yanking out one of his earbuds. "What do you want?"

I crossed my arms. "Taylor Swift? War, if you want to torture yourself, there are better ways."

"Fuck you." He put his back flat to the floor again. "Close the door on your way out."

I sighed and came in, shutting the door behind me. "Come on, War. You and me both know Ken's going to take you back like always. Don't be all dramatic over it."

"He's cheating on me," War said, remaining flat on the floor. "With his manager this time, I think."

"And he's still breathing?"

War sat up and shot me a warning look. "You're not allowed to kill Ken, River."

"Don't tell me you actually liked him?" I lifted an eyebrow. We all knew War and Ken were only together because War wanted kids and he thought Ken was an ideal dad for some reason. They had this five-year plan to get married and adopt a couple of orphans from some war-torn country or something. I didn't care about all that. What I cared about was that Ken was a jackass jerking my brother around.

War stared past me at nothing. "I bought a ring, River. I thought..."

I sank to the floor, sitting across from him, arms crossed. "You'll find someone else, War."

He shook his head slowly. "That's easy for you to say. Do you have any idea how few people want to put up with all my stupid tics and compulsions? Ken was perfect. He didn't care as long as I didn't embarrass him in public. I mean, the sex was crap, but we had the same goals, came from the same socio-economic bracket...I didn't even care the first three times he cheated. I don't know why this time is bothering me so much."

"He was the wrong person for you and you know it," I said flatly.

War's eyes met mine briefly before darting away.

I sighed and stood again. "You know what you need? Something to distract you. Now that you're not flying back to Miami, you have plenty of time to help me and Theo."

"Maybe," he muttered.

My watch beeped. "Shit. I'm going to be late for work. Just think about it, okay? It's better than exercising until you throw up, War. Don't punish yourself for that jackass's stupidity. He's the one who deserves to be miserable, not you."

I came out of War's room and almost ran straight into Xavier, who was frowning down at his phone.

"Fuck," he said, paling when he saw me, and he jerked his phone to his chest like he was trying to hide the screen. "When'd you get here?"

"I was just leaving." I looked him up and down. "Don't let Xander be an ass to Theo today."

Xavier rolled his eyes. "As if I can control *anything* Xander does."

"Just do it," I told him and hurried down the stairs.

I collected my coffee thermos from Mom, made sure Theo had everything he needed, kissed him goodbye, and walked across the yard to the funeral home. I was early for once, judging by Dad's car being absent, but I'd wanted to be. Once the organ started playing upstairs, it'd be hard to get my work done, especially if they played "Amazing Grace," which they almost always did. It was like nobody could be original with the arrangement of their funeral music. When I finally kicked it, I hoped they played something more interesting, like bagpipe dubstep. Something *unexpected*.

My keys jingled loose in my hand, ready to unlock the transport bay doors, but I paused halfway up the ramp when I saw the door was already cracked open. I glanced back at the parking lot, verifying that

Dad's truck wasn't there. He lived too far away to walk, especially with his bad knee. Could he have left it open when he closed up yesterday? No. Dad had never been that careless.

I shifted my grip on the keys, going on high alert, and grabbed the door, yanking it open. Nothing in the immediate area seemed out of place, and when I went through the office, nothing was missing from there. The computers were still locked with no signs of tampering, and the filing cabinets were all in order. I even went upstairs to make sure no one had messed with the displays or the flowers we had all set up for the service happening in a few hours.

Nothing was missing or out of place. Everything was exactly where and how it was supposed to be.

I was still on edge as I suited up and prepped for my first and only job of the day. Why would someone break into a funeral home and not take anything?

And then I froze.

The bodies.

Still half garbed, I shoved through the double doors and into the work room, where I stopped dead in my tracks. There was a body on the table. One that wasn't supposed to be there.

He was a young man, late teens or early twenties. Attractive, even if he was a bit on the waifish side, with messy blond hair and pale skin, even for a corpse. He was lying fully clothed on my worktable, wearing a worn white t-shirt—the kind that came in multi-packs at department stores. There was a vomit stain on the shirt.

That never should have happened. Clothed bodies meant contamination had been brought into the workspace. Now everything was polluted, and I'd have to clean the whole room from top to bottom.

"River?" Theo's voice echoed down the hall.

Shit, what was he doing here? I'd told him to stay with Mom.

"River, you forgot your breakfast. Annie sent me to..." He trailed off as he pushed through the doors and into the lab.

I turned around with a sigh. Now everything was doubly contaminated. Thankfully, I'd only have to clean and sanitize once.

My worries about cleaning and contamination disappeared when I saw Theo staring at the body, his face paler than normal.

The paper bag containing my breakfast trembled in his fist. "Oh my god."

"First time I've ever had a body show up here without having to go get it myself," I said.

"No," Theo said, shaking his head, a terrified look on his face. "River, I know him!"

Eighteen
Theo

I COULDN'T BREATHE. MY chest was too tight, my throat closed up. Cold sweat coated the back of my neck and my chest. I tried to pull in air, but it was like my lungs refused to expand.

Memories punched their way to the front of my brain.

David. His name was David. He'd been my roommate as long as I could remember. Sometimes, we even went places together, worked together. He liked Diet Coke and dancing. We passed stickers and stolen bubblegum late at night and sat together at movie night.

I knew his name. I knew *him*. And now he was dead.

Not theoretically dead, as in I didn't know what happened to him and he never came back one night dead, either.

He was right there, still and pale and dead.

I blinked and River was right in front of me, his hands on my face. He was talking to me, but the blood was pounding so loud in my ears I couldn't hear what he was saying, so I focused on the movement of his lips.

Breathe. Was that what he was saying?

"Breathe, Theo."

I gulped in a short breath, and it stuttered its way out of me in jerky puffs.

River nodded. "One more. In and hold it, little finch. There you go."

"I think I'm gonna throw up," I said, my voice squeaky.

River spun me, curled an arm around me, and hurried me through the double doors. There was a big trash can for discarded gloves and aprons in the next room. I doubled over it, emptying the contents of my stomach. My arms trembled as I heaved, and tears ran down my face.

It took me a long time to recover, but River stayed right there with me, rubbing my back. When I could finally think, I forced myself to let go of the trash can. My knuckles were white and ached from the death grip I'd had on it.

"David," I said, my voice trembling. "His name is David. He was my roommate."

"Fuck," River spat and got out his phone. He pressed a single button and held it to his ear. When whoever was on the other end answered, he replied, "We have a problem. A big one. I need a family meeting now at the funeral home." River hung up without waiting for a reply and put his hands on my shoulders. "When was the last time you saw him?"

I put my palm to my head, pushing back my hair, trying to think. Had I seen him the day Rick and Vince took me to that dive bar? The days were all starting to run together, and that felt like another life, even though it hadn't been more than ten days. It couldn't have been. "Um. I don't know. The day I met you? Maybe the day before? He was still there when I left. We both had assignments that night."

"Do you know who he went with?"

I shook my head. "No, they don't give us that kind of information until we show up."

"Didn't," River corrected and cupped my cheek. "That's all in the past now, Theo."

I nodded numbly. How could he be dead? It felt surreal, like I'd walked into an alternate universe without realizing it. And what was he doing here? We were nowhere near Master's home. At least, I didn't think so. It seemed like it took a long time for River to drive me from the dive bar to this small town we were in.

"I've called everyone over," River said calmly. "We're going to talk about this and decide what to do. In the meantime, there's some toothpaste and a toothbrush in a travel kit upstairs. Let's get you cleaned up."

I nodded again.

I was only half-aware as River guided me into the main part of the funeral parlor. He brought me to a small bathroom with fake flowers and a jar of potpourri. There was a picture on the wall with cute little animals and a bunch of words I couldn't read. I stared at it while I brushed my teeth, waiting for the numbness to fade.

River hung onto me the whole time, his arms wrapped tightly around me or a hand on my back. Normally, I would have hated to have someone touch me that much, but with River, it was grounding. He was the only thing that felt real.

I started to feel nervous again when we left the bathroom, but River didn't bring me back into the room with the body, instead hustling me into what looked like a break room.

Annie, Tatty, Xavier, and Xander were all already there, chatting amongst themselves. All their talk stopped as soon as we came in. Eyes crawled over my skin and I shifted uncomfortably under their stares.

"Theo, love," Tatty said, rising. She opened her arms and embraced me. "Are you all right? Come sit by me, *rybka*." She guided me to the table to sit.

War came in shortly after us, his hair still wet. Unsurprising since he'd been in the shower when I left the house. He sat at the table with the others, a glass of something green in his hand. "What's so important that it couldn't wait until this afternoon?" War mumbled, sipping his green smoothie.

"I'm certain River will tell us," said a grim-faced man as he entered the room and went straight for the coffee. He must've been in his fifties with his short, salt and pepper hair and his neatly trimmed goatee. Laugh lines crinkled at the corners of his eyes and near his mouth. "Hello, Theo," he said without glancing up at me. "You can call me Yuri. I'm afraid we haven't had a chance to meet yet."

I frowned. He didn't look like someone who burned people alive in an incinerator for the Russian mob. He looked...friendly and refined. The sort of grandfather who might've been eccentric, but in a fun way.

"That's Nikita Volkov," Yuri continued, gesturing to another man who'd come into the room.

Volkov? I glanced over at Tatty.

She smiled warmly. "Yes, love. My husband."

"Her much better looking half," Nikita said with a wink. He extended his hand to me. "Very pleased to meet you, Theo." He had a very slight accent that I couldn't quite place. The tattoos on Nikita's fingers, though, I had seen before. Despite his crisp, clean suit and clean-shaven face, Nikita looked like someone who had done time.

"Likewise," I said and resisted the urge to shake out my hand to get circulation going to it again.

"I presume this has something to do with the unauthorized body in the prep room?" Yuri sank into the seat across from me, stirring his coffee. Nikita took the seat next to Yuri while River sat on the other side of me.

"It does," River said. "Theo's former roommate."

I stiffened in my seat as I realized I was going to have to explain my story again, except this time in front of all of them. Sweat broke out on the back of my neck and nausea started to churn in my stomach.

"Tatty and Annie have filled us in on the relevant details," Nikita said, much to my relief. He pulled a yellow legal pad out of the briefcase he'd brought with him and clicked a pen, setting both on the table. "Do you mind answering some questions, Theo? That would help us get a better idea of who these people are so we can help."

River gave me an encouraging nod.

"What do you want to know?" I asked.

Nikita put his pen to the paper. "How many were being held at the same location as you?"

I chewed on my lip. "There were seven of us, including Master."

He scribbled something on the page. "All boys?"

I nodded and then added, "Yes. All around my age. We were raised together like brothers."

He looked up. "So would you say you knew this young man well?"

I shrugged. "We shared a room. I knew David better than anyone."

A horrifying thought occurred to me, and I suddenly felt sick again, putting my hand over my mouth. "Oh, god. What if they killed him because of me?"

"We won't know anything until we've done a more thorough examination of him," Yuri said calmly.

"Do you know who his last clients were?" Tatty asked, massaging my shoulders.

I shook my head. "It was a first names only kind of business, and a lot of people didn't even use their real names. I could probably point out places better than faces, and even then only if I saw them again. I..." I blushed. "I don't know how to read well enough to know what the signs said."

"Maybe the body has some clues," War said, crossing his arms.

Xavier frowned. "Am I the only one concerned that these people know where we live? Like, they broke into the family business and left a body on the table. That's a warning, right?"

"Fuck," River spat. "Bet they pumped the bartender for information. I had to show my ID to buy a drink there. Fucking prick."

"If they did that, then the bartender knows something." Annie looked at Yuri, who nodded.

"I wouldn't be surprised," Yuri added, glancing at Nikita.

Nikita nodded. "They didn't choose that place of business by accident to drink in. That bar sits on the edge of Russian and Greek territory, not a place anyone would care too much about. Between the cracks, you might say. Not a good place."

"Rick took me there a bunch of times," I said. "Nobody ever asked any questions. Nobody asked me for ID either."

Xander took a loud slurp of his coffee. "Best case scenario, he was taking money under the table to look the other way."

"Worst case," added Xavier, "he was actively participating. Maybe even scouting out future victims."

"Future victims?" My chest felt tight again.

Annie took one of my hands and squeezed it. "Sweetie, these types of operations aren't profitable with so few workers. It's likely your Master was either one of many, or he had multiple safehouses holding boys like you."

"Unless they found another way to turn a profit with them," Yuri said with a frown.

I swallowed, sure I didn't want to hear, but I had to ask anyway. "Like what?"

"Did anyone else come or go from the house?" Nikita cut in, ignoring my question. "I know you said your Master. But was there anyone else?"

"There was this doctor," I said slowly. "Doctor Harris." I watched Nikita scribble something down. "You're not going to hurt him, are you?"

"We'll do whatever's necessary to get the information we need to free those other boys," Yuri said firmly.

"Harris is probably a common enough name that he'll be difficult to find," War said. "Think you can pick him out from a picture, Theo?"

I nodded.

War grunted and gripped his weird green smoothie. "I'll put together a lineup and then go pay him a visit. See if he wants to spill his guts or *spill his guts*."

"Not yet." Nikita cast his son a firm glance. "Your medical expertise will be needed here first."

"I want your help looking over the body, War," Yuri said. "They dumped him here as a warning. They know we have Theo, and they want him back. They made sure we knew they could come and go as they pleased, too, by leaving the door open."

Tatty snorted and leaned back in her chair, crossing one leg over the other. "They clearly don't know who they're messing with."

"Probably not," Yuri agreed, "and we want to keep that advantage as long as we possibly can. War, Annie, and I will go over the body to search for clues. We'll need your help with that too, Theo."

"Me?" My voice went high, and I glanced up at River for confirmation. "But I don't know anything."

"You knew David, sweetie," Annie said. "The places he went, the people he spent time with. There might be something you can tell us that will help."

"What do you want us to do?" Xavier asked.

"Please tell me it involves stalking someone," Xander said, rising to go refill his coffee.

Xavier snorted. "Yeah, you could use the legwork. Your ass is getting fat."

Xander pitched his empty cup at Xavier's head.

"You two are going to sober up," Yuri said, reaching to collect the fallen cup and calmly depositing it in the trash.

"And Tatty and I will run down a few leads of our own," Nikita offered, glancing at his wife.

"I'll go down to the salon and see what the word on the street is," Tatty mused. "If they dumped a body here, then maybe word is circulating."

"I want the bartender," River insisted.

Yuri shook his head. "He's inconsequential. A middleman at best. The chances he knows names, faces, or locations are slim."

"I don't care," River said, crossing his arms. "If War gets the doctor, I want the bartender."

"This isn't a contest," War scoffed.

"If you can behave yourself and follow the rules, you can accompany War," Yuri said.

"But—"

Yuri cut War off with a glare. "When you are sitting in this seat, young man, you can hand out assignments. Until that day, you'll do as you're told."

War let out an irritated huff and scowled at River before turning away.

"In the meantime," Yuri continued, "Nikita confirmed that this operation is not one of theirs, nor are they getting a cut."

I gave the handsome older man another glance, trying once again to figure out exactly how he fit into things.

Nikita folded his hands. "I spoke to my father briefly. Because the locations we've identified so far are all skirting the border between Russian and Greek territory, he doesn't want us to handle the situation directly, but he's given his blessing for me to give you some indirect assistance."

"Oh my god!" Xander said excitedly. "Are we getting Uncle Sacha? Please tell me he's sending Uncle Sacha."

"Ugh," Xavier groaned and rolled his eyes.

"Your Uncle Sacha is coming in from Paris tomorrow," Yuri confirmed, beaming.

"Yes!" Xander pumped his fists in the air.

"And you two will be retrieving him from the airport as part of your errands," Yuri continued. "River, he'll be staying with you."

"Does he have to?" River said with a sigh.

"Yes, because you have space."

"He could have my room at your house," River pointed out.

"River." Yuri's tone held a warning. "Show some respect."

"Fine, but no pickled herring. My house, my rules."

I almost chuckled at how pouty River sounded. At least some of the initial shock had worn off.

"Feeling better?" Annie asked, patting my hand.

I swallowed and pulled my hand away from her. "I think so."

"He's free in his own way now," Tatty said gently.

I nodded numbly. She meant that to be comforting, but I wasn't sure if it was. There were many times during the darkest times of my life that I'd wished for death, and I knew I wasn't alone. It had felt like that was the only escape. River had shown me there was another way, and now I wanted that for everyone. Knowing it was too late already for some made my heart twist and clench.

"We are shutting them down," Nikita said, standing and adjusting his jacket. "One way or another, this operation's days are numbered."

Nineteen

River

THE CAMERA FLASHED AND whirred and images appeared on the mobile computer monitor, all pieces to a puzzle I was desperate to solve.

"Early rigor," War said, flexing the elbow joint. "He hasn't been dead too long."

"Rectal temperature confirms that," Dad said. "Two, three o'clock this morning, probably."

I moved to snap another picture at a new angle.

"The vomit stains on his clothing aren't old." Mom leaned in with a pair of scissors and carefully cut the shirt from the body in strips.

Normally, if a body came in with belongings, we tried to preserve them and give them to the family, but David didn't have family. Theo was probably the closest thing he'd ever had.

I turned to Theo. "What should we do with his clothes?"

Theo stood in the corner, a dark look in his eyes, arms crossed and jaw set. "Master bought them for him. Burn everything."

I nodded and we carefully stripped off the body's clothes. Mom brought a white towel to lay over his genitals out of respect and we kept working, starting with the head.

Dad used a fine brush on the hair, gathering fibers into a small plastic scoop. "Might be carpet. Hard to say."

"He had pretty blue eyes," Mom commented. "Good teeth. I wonder if we can get Harry to run a dental match for us? See if he has pediatric records."

"Maybe," Dad agreed.

"Signs of obvious trauma to the torso." War pointed to David's chest before lifting one of David's arms to examine it. "Bruising is pre-mortem, but consistent with the bilateral bruising on the posterior biceps. Bicep contusions are oval-shaped, four in number, consistent with human fingers."

"What does that mean?" Theo asked quietly from the corner.

War lifted his head, looking at me. "It means he was held down with significant force shortly before his death."

"What's that on his arm?" I took his right arm and rotated it so that the inside faced out. A wave of *something* rushed over me at the sight of the bruises there. For a moment, I was back in a dark room, covered in filth, sitting on the carpet and looking up at my mother, watching the flies swarm. I knew what it was even before War spoke.

He leaned over the arm briefly. "Subdermal hematoma from an intravenous injection. See this thin band of bruising up here? Probably from the tourniquet."

He walked over to a cabinet on the wall, pulling out a huge syringe. He came back, pressing his fingers firmly into the body's abdomen as if he were looking for a specific spot. Theo flinched as War jammed the syringe into David's side.

"Should be able to get enough to do a preliminary screen for the usual suspects," War muttered, drawing back the plunger on the syringe. "If he was an addict, we'll definitely know."

"He wasn't," Theo cut in, drawing everyone's attention. His face flushed and he looked at his shoes. "We weren't allowed to do anything too heavy. Poppers and pot were fine, but nothing else, even if the clients wanted us to. He wasn't shooting up."

"The mark inside his elbow suggests otherwise," War said, finishing up.

Mom frowned and leaned over the arm I was looking at. "Theo, dear, was David right or left-handed?"

Theo's face went blank the way it did when he was actively remembering something he didn't want to. He came out of it with a shudder and looked at the floor. "Right, I think. He always held his Diet Coke in his right hand, anyway. Why?"

"Because nobody shoots themselves up in their dominant arm unless they've already blown the ones in their other arm, and there's no evidence he was injecting anything on the left arm." Mom looked up and gestured for me to take a picture. "And nobody would tie a tourniquet this tight with their off hand."

War finished labeling the vial of blood he'd taken from David and deposited it in the cooler before coming around to the end of the table. He picked up David's foot, rotating the ankle with a frown, first one and then the other. "Ankle fractures are pre-mortem as well. Check the airway?"

I carefully massaged the jaw open further and Mom connected a small tube to the digital camera, running it down the throat. There were obvious signs of trauma.

"Ten to one there's fluid in his lungs," Mom said.

"What are you saying?" Theo asked.

My fingers twitched inside their gloves, the ache for violence returning. "Someone broke his ankles so he couldn't escape, then held him down and forcefully injected him with a fatal dose of drugs, probably opiates. He choked to death on his own vomit."

"Opiates this so-called Doctor Harris could've supplied," War said.

"But he didn't feel any pain other than the initial stab of the needle," Mom added quickly.

"Oh my god," Theo muttered and hid his face in his hands.

"What's that?" Dad pointed to the body's left hand.

I moved around to the other side and carefully turned his hand over with a frown. "There's some kind of mark here, but I can't make out what it is. Definitely not a tattoo. A stamp maybe?"

"Do you have a blacklight?" Theo said, uncrossing his arms and stepping forward.

"Top drawer there." Dad nodded to the cabinet.

"I'll get the lights," Mom volunteered.

Theo went digging around in the cabinet and found the blacklight, bringing it over to us. Dad thanked him and nodded to Mom, who dimmed the lights. I held the body's hand while Dad's blacklight danced over it, illuminating the image of someone sitting on a stool wearing a dunce cap.

I squinted and frowned. "What is that?"

"It's a club," Theo supplied. "They take us there sometimes. I... I'm sorry. I don't know the name, but I've been there a few times." His throat worked and he looked away.

Arson wasn't one of my preferred vices, but I immediately considered burning the club down once we figured out which one it was. I looked to Dad. "Shepherd would know his competition, wouldn't he?"

War nodded with a grunt.

Mom turned the lights back up, and I snapped a picture with my cell phone before I stepped away. On my way to the computer alcove, I peeled off my gloves and other PPE, discarding all of it. Given the time, Shepherd might be teaching a class, so I didn't expect an immediate answer when I texted him the picture and asked if he knew what it was. Yet my phone buzzed with an answer almost right away.

Shepherd

Where did you find that?

River

On a body that got dropped on our doorstep.

You'd know that if you came to family meetings.

Shepherd

I can't help it that I have a real job and people who depend on me.

I almost crushed my phone. Shepherd really was an infuriating dick.

River

Just tell me what club it belongs to.

Three dots danced on the screen for a minute before they disappeared. My phone vibrated a moment later, Shepherd's name dancing over the screen.

"That'd be the Time Out Room," he said as soon as I answered. "It's a fetish club for people who can't afford membership at the Playground. They cater more to curious first timers and broke idiots than people actually in the lifestyle. You said you found it on a body? Please tell me said body can definitively be linked to the club."

"Why?" I demanded.

"Because getting to go after Jeff Dimori would get me harder than spanking a senior after they missed class all semester and then showed up asking for extra credit two days before grades are due."

"Gross." I wrinkled my nose. "And oddly specific. And yeah, the stamp's on the dead kid's hand. It's pretty obvious they forced him to OD and then dumped the body here for us to find."

"Tacky," said Shepherd with a snort. "Any idea how they're wrapped up in the trafficking ring you're trying to bust?"

"Not yet, but I think I'd like to find out."

"Me too," Shepherd said too enthusiastically. "Give me a few hours and I'll secure you memberships so you can go check out the Time Out Room."

I frowned and pulled the phone away from my ear to make sure I was still talking to Shepherd. "Why are you being so accommodating?"

"We all have our kinks, little brother. One of mine happens to be watching dirtbags like Jeff squirm. I'll meet you at my place at seven. Bring the boy." Shepherd hung up before I could object.

I sighed and lowered the phone.

"I want to go," Theo said behind me.

"Theo..." I turned around and put my hands on his shoulders before thinking better of it and raking my nails through his hair instead. "If you go, it might trigger some memories you might not want to remember."

"Yeah, but if I'm not there, you won't know who to look for." He uncrossed his arms and pushed my hands away. "I know the faces of the men who took me there, and I might even see someone I know. If I don't go, there's no way for you to know who's worth questioning and who isn't."

Theo was right and I hated it. I hated having to put him out in front of me, back in danger. Back where other people could put their hands on him.

I ghosted a kiss over his soft lips. "You understand we're not just going to question people. Tonight is going to get messy, especially since Shepherd wants to help."

He took a deep breath and let out, nodding slowly. "I know. I can handle it. Please, River. I can't sit back and do nothing. I need to help."

"Okay," I agreed at length. "But you'll stick close to me, and whatever you do, don't let anyone else touch you, even Shepherd. If you do, I don't know what I'll do."

"I won't," he promised and put his arms around me. "Thank you, River."

I had a feeling he wouldn't be thanking me by the end of the night, not once he truly saw what I was capable of, but I put my arms around him just the same and kissed his ear.

Dad suddenly filled up the doorway, tugging off his PPE. "Before you go check out this club, you need to run down the doctor lead."

"If this Doctor Harris gives us a location, we might not need to go to the Time Out Room at all," War pointed out.

Dad shook his head. "I want every lead run down, either way. We can't rush this or we'll be walking in blind. The more information we have, the better. In the meantime, I have a service to conduct upstairs."

War sighed and peeled off his gloves. "I'll go put together a lineup of Doctor Harrises in the Columbus Metro area. I'll swing by your place later this afternoon with it, River, and we'll go pay him a visit once Theo picks him out."

I nodded and finished washing my hands before threading my fingers through Theo's. "Let's go home," I said, planting a kiss on his cheek.

Twenty
Theo

River looked up from the fridge, frowning at me. "Did I do something wrong?"

I looked up from the tabletop, snapping out of my thoughts. I hadn't even been thinking about anything, just staring blankly at the table, waiting for something to happen. I did that a lot. It was the worst part about living with Master, all the waiting.

"What? No." I said, shifting in the seat.

"You haven't said a word to me since we left the funeral home." River closed the fridge and came over to squat in front of me. "What's wrong, Theo?"

I sighed and rubbed my forehead briefly before letting my arms fall limply to my sides. "What are we, River?"

He blinked rapidly as if the question was a shock. "What do you mean?"

"We don't even know each other well enough to call this friends with benefits. We're not friends. You definitely can't be my boyfriend."

"Why not?" he asked, cocking his head the other way.

"Because I've only known you what? Ten days? Two weeks?" I threw my hands up vaguely. "I don't know anything about you, River."

"You know that I've killed people."

"Besides that! I don't know your favorite color, or what food you like… I don't even know what *my* answers to those things are! How can we be a thing when I don't even know who I am?" My chest was tight again, and my mind was racing through a thousand different worries. I was saying all the wrong things, making him not like me. Making him *angry*.

Stupid, Theo. Stupid! That's dangerous, making someone you know to be a killer angry with you.

I couldn't help myself. I felt like I was going to explode if I didn't get what I was feeling out into the open.

He held my face in his hands. "We'll find all of that out together."

"That answer's not good enough!"

I didn't know why I was near tears over something as stupid as not knowing what River's favorite color was, but it felt like my whole world was suddenly falling apart. There was a balloon swelling in my chest and it was about to burst. My cheeks were wet, and my breaths came out as panicked gasps.

And then River's lips were on mine, and it was like he was breathing for me. I gripped his sleeve in a fist as he bit down on my bottom lip. The bitter tang of copper and salt flooded my tongue, the pain pulling me back from the edge of a spiral into the abyss. I groaned as his tongue slid over the bite, licking up the blood.

"It's red," he said when we parted. "My favorite color is red."

I couldn't stop myself from laughing, despite my tears. "Of course it is."

"And my favorite food is a cheese pizza with extra cheese." He kissed my cheek before tracing his tongue over the wet trail my tears had left. "I don't like TV or movies. I prefer nonfiction books."

I shuddered as he repeated the action on my other cheek.

"I consider myself pansexual, and I've had fourteen sexual partners of varying genders. I don't believe in virginity, but if I did, I'd have lost mine when I was eighteen to a girl who asked to sleep with me. I agreed because I was curious and not because I actually liked her, and to be honest, it was awful. You're so much better at sex, and I like that about you, even if you lack the confidence. My favorite organ is the liver."

"Okay," I chuckled. "Now you're *over*-sharing."

"I'll tell you anything you want to know," River said and pressed his lips gently to mine. "And I'll give you anything you want. All you have to do is ask."

"Anything?" I gave the fridge a long look, considering.

"Anything," River promised. "Tell me what you want, Theo, and it's yours."

I sighed again, trying to release more of the pressure. "What I want right now is a sandwich, another orgasm, a shower, and a nap, but I'm not sure what order I want it all in."

"Food first," he said and stood.

River made us grilled cheese sandwiches and served them each with a pickle and a glass of chocolate milk. It reminded me of a lunch a four-year-old would ask for, but it was better than what I usually ate at Master's. He kept us on a strict diet of mostly vegetables and lean meats so we'd be *useable*.

After lunch, we went upstairs and I curled up in bed with River, my head resting on his shoulder while he scrolled through pictures of mushrooms on his phone and told me about them. A bone deep exhaustion had settled in my limbs, and I was desperate to sleep, but I couldn't bring myself to close my eyes. I was too afraid I'd see David's dead eyes staring back at me if I did.

"How do you do it?" I asked River quietly.

His thumb paused on the screen and he looked down at me. "Do what?"

"Your job? Touching and cleaning and caring for dead people all day. Kill people. All of that. I've only seen a few bodies, and I'm terrified they're all I'll dream about."

River lowered his phone. "Those two activities aren't even remotely related."

"They aren't?" I tipped my head back to look up at him.

"Of course not. I can kill people because they deserve it, or at least they don't deserve to live. Murder is..." He tapped his chin as if he were trying to find the right word. "It's like absolution. These people will never confess or repent any other way. They won't ever be useful to society. They're a cancer feeding on the healthy parts of society. When I kill them, it's no different to me than when you step on a cockroach."

"You don't get a thrill out of it?" I asked.

River put his phone down on the bedside table before sliding onto his back and pulling me on top of him. "Will you be disgusted if I said I did? Not a sexual thrill. That's not my thing. But I want them on their knees. I want them to beg and plead. I enjoy seeing the terror in their eyes the moment they realize the only choice left is to scream or stay silent. I like knowing they felt the fear they instilled in others, and that I made them feel it."

"It makes you feel powerful," I clarified.

He nodded.

"And you like to be powerful." I chewed my lip, considering.

He said he liked being powerful, but the last time we had sex, he'd given me all the control, letting me be on top. I'd never done that before, never wanted to. Now that I had, though, I could almost understand the rush he was talking about. I'd felt it looking down at him. There was something thrilling about knowing that a terrifying killer was willing to submit to me.

I gripped his wrists and raised them over his head, pinning them to the headboard behind him. "What about this? How does this make you feel?"

His eyes darkened. "Is this how you want me?"

I snorted and rolled my eyes, letting go of him. "We both know you're the one who gets what he wants in the end."

River surged up, pausing with his lips next to mine. "And if I said I wanted you to dominate me?"

A rush of something fell from my chest straight to my groin. It felt like suddenly dropping two stories in an elevator. I licked my lips. "I wouldn't know how to do that."

"I could teach you." His hands closed around my ass, squeezing. "But I think deep down you know exactly what to do, don't you?"

I bit my lip as he rocked my hips against his. He was already hard, his erection digging into me in the most distracting way. I wasn't far behind him, but nerves were slowing me down. There was still too much noise in my head, and I wasn't sure.

"Go on," he said, lying flat again and putting his hands back where I'd held them. "I'm yours to do with as you wish."

The words sent a pang of lust straight through me, and I started imagining doing all kinds of things to him. Things that I shouldn't want to do to anyone.

"What if I hurt you?" I said quietly.

"Pain means I'm alive. As long as everything's still attached and functional when you're done, I'm good." He rolled his hips into me again. "Do your worst. See if you can make me scream."

I looked down at him, stretched out beneath me, his t-shirt riding up on his belly just enough to show off that perfect line of dark hair trailing beneath his jeans. River didn't have a lot of body hair like some men, but he didn't bother with shaving or waxing like others either. He had the perfect amount sprinkled over his body, and it was screaming for me to run my fingers through it all.

I pushed his shirt up, exposing him from the chest down. He'd said my nipples were the color of bubblegum. His were a pinkish brown, the color of dried rose petals. The rest of him was pale, though he was by no means as pale as I was. He'd said his favorite color was red. Maybe he needed some red to match me.

"Last chance," I warned, meeting his eyes. I planted my fingernails firmly against his chest below his collarbones.

River's pink tongue flicked out over his full lips and his nostrils flared, but he didn't utter any objections.

I dug my fingernails in more and raked them downward over his skin. Little pink lines blossomed in three neat rows. River tipped his head back against the pillows with a low moan, but that was nowhere near a scream, so I did it again.

"Ngh. Shit!" River's hips bowed off the bed, taking me with him.

I panicked and lifted my hands. "Oh my god. Was that too much? It was too much, right?"

"Why'd you stop?" He lifted his head. "Did I say stop?"

"I thought I hurt you."

"You did," he panted. "Do it again."

I swallowed and brought my hands shakily back to the top of his chest. This time, when I raked my fingernails over his skin, the marks were red and angry. I shouldn't have liked it, but I did. Seeing those marks on him, knowing he was letting me, that at any moment, he could pounce on me, hurt me, kill me... It was a thrill unlike anything else I'd ever experienced. My dick was so hard and throbbing that it ached, but it wasn't just a sexual thrill. There was something visceral about knowing I had marked him as mine.

I bent down and gently tongued the worst of the marks, drawing a small hiss out of River. Whether it was pain or pleasure, I didn't know. Maybe both.

"You might have to tie me up to do this right." His arms twitched, fingers clenching in and out of fists, but he didn't move.

The very idea of binding him in place so he couldn't squirm away was enough to have me peeling off my shirt and throwing it aside. I fell forward, pinning his arms in place with all my weight. River was strong, though. He could've gotten free. He could've tossed me off that bed, tackled me to the floor and snapped my neck with his bare hands. Instead, he let me hold him down. Even when I moved my weight off him, he stayed as I put him except to breathe and twitch.

I realized I could get to more of him if he wasn't wearing his clothes. "Get naked," I demanded.

His lip curled up in a smirk before sitting up to pull off his shirt and shimmy out of his jeans and underwear.

God, he was so perfect, so out of my league. I almost couldn't believe he was real. Maybe I was asleep in my old room, and this was all the most wonderful dream. If it was, I didn't want to wake up.

When he laid back down, I raked my nails over the soft flesh on the insides of his arms, over his shoulders. His cock was leaking by the time I made it to his thighs. It twitched as I clawed through the coarse hair on his legs, leaving a glistening puddle of pre-cum on his abs. I leaned down and pushed his dick out of the way so I could lick it up.

"Fuck, that's hot," he turned his head and moaned into his bicep.

"Is it? What about this?" I closed a fist around the base of his cock, holding it steady so I could drag my fingernails over the flushed head.

He groaned and shuddered. "Fuck, Theo. You hurt me so good, little finch. Look at those beautiful marks you're leaving all over me."

His praise made me brave enough to try it harder and I felt him throbbing in my fist.

"Fuuuuck..." He started panting loudly.

There was something about how his voice came out all whiney and desperate, so vulnerable. I needed more of that like I'd never needed anything before.

I lifted my hand and spat in it before I started twisting a fist over the red scratch marks I'd left behind. His thighs started to shake until he couldn't take it anymore. He suddenly grabbed me and hauled me up his body.

Hot lips slotted against mine briefly before he demanded, "Need you. *Now*, Theo."

I rose onto my knees, fumbling to get my fly open. He jerked my jeans past my hips. I had to climb off him briefly to get them all the way off, but the minute I was back, he was circling my entrance with a slick finger. I grabbed the lube and squeezed some more into his hand so he could push two fingers inside.

I kissed him again, moaning and rubbing my drooling cock over his abs while he worked his fingers inside of me, getting me ready for him.

When River sank inside of me, it was like feeding a fever. I couldn't ride him fast enough or hard enough. His breaths came out in angry snorts and growls, and he started to fuck up into me quick and hard. He surged up, and the next thing I knew, we'd changed positions. He flung my ankles up over his shoulders and I cried out at the new position. With every brutal thrust, he dragged his cock over that sensitive bundle of nerves inside of me, building pleasure to a fever pitch.

"I'm close!" I shouted.

"Good. Me too." River's hand closed around my cock and he gave it two rough pulls before his hips stuttered and he groaned, flooding me with his release.

The dam burst and my orgasm ripped through my entire body, different and more powerful than all the ones I'd had so far. It felt like it ripped a part of my soul out with it.

When I started to come back down, River was kissing and biting my chest, breaths coming hot and heavy against my skin.

"Holy fuck," he murmured against me, lowering my legs. "That was so fucking hot, Theo. I think I might be into this whole letting you dominate me thing."

I chuckled and wiped sweat from my forehead. "Well, I wouldn't exactly say that's what happened. Although I think you're right about one thing. If you want me to keep you from pouncing on me, I am going to have to tie you up."

"Mmm." He nosed against my neck. "I've never let anyone tie me up before, but I'm so into it."

"Seriously?" I propped myself up on my elbows so I could look at him. "You'd let me do that?"

River cupped my cheek. "There isn't a lot I wouldn't let you do to me. Let's just say I was imagining something a lot sharper than fingernails slicing into me."

I frowned. "I don't know if I trust myself to go that far."

"Yet." He kissed me deeply, tangling our tongues together briefly before answering. "One thing at a time. You don't have to do anything you don't want to. Not with me."

I nodded and pulled his head to my chest, warmth blooming deep inside me. I didn't know what love felt like, and it was probably too soon to be feeling it with River, especially knowing he might not be able to love me back, but there was something there. Something I wanted a lot more of.

Twenty-One

River

I WOKE UP TO someone pounding on my bedroom door.

"Get up, love birds," War shouted through the door. "I didn't spend all afternoon doing this research to stand out here and listen to you snore!"

Theo frowned and looked at me. "I don't snore, do I?"

He did, and it was adorable, but I wasn't going to tell him that. I kissed his cheek, throwing back the covers. "Two minutes," I told War, searching the floor for my jeans.

It was probably closer to five minutes before Theo and I made it downstairs. In that time, War found my kettle and started some hot water. I scowled when I saw he had his tea bag in my favorite mug. It had a death cap mushroom on it and read in comic sans font: I'm a Fun-Gi.

I shouldered past him to use the hot water to make some coffee, snorting at the box of tea he'd brought over. "Weight loss tea? War, there's not an ounce of fat on you."

"First thing I grabbed," he lied.

I gave him a stern look. "Did you eat today?"

He snorted. "What are you, my mom now? I've already got two of those, thanks."

I sighed. "War, he's not worth it."

"I have no fucking idea what you're talking about, River." He walked away from the counter, stirring his tea and gesturing to the laptop that sat open on the table. "Have a look, Theo. Recognize any of them?"

Theo glanced between us before turning to the laptop screen and bending over it. While he wasn't looking, I grabbed War's box of diet tea and buried it in the trash. It wouldn't make much of a difference long-term; it might take Tatty or someone else to talk some sense into him before his obsession with losing weight got bad again. He didn't need to lose another ounce, but it was one of his go-to behaviors whenever he and Ken were on ice.

"This one," Theo said, pointing at the screen.

I came around behind him to get a glimpse of one of the men responsible for Theo's years of mistreatment. Maybe the old middle-aged obese doctor with bushy eyebrows hadn't been the one to kidnap or hurt Theo, but he'd allowed it to happen, and that made him just as guilty as the people who had in my book.

"Doctor Peter Harris," War said, turning the laptop toward him. "Pediatrics."

I made a face. "You're telling me this asshole treats *kids*?"

"Makes sense if Theo and the other boys had been with this Master guy since they were young." War's fingers raced across the keyboard before he hit the return key. "And we're in luck. He's got a Ewing's Crossing address. Our deadbeat doctor is a local."

"Well then, what are we standing around here for?" I put the coffee cup down and started toward the door, pausing only when I realized War wasn't following. "What?"

"He has a wife, River. Kids." War glanced over at Theo.

I didn't give a shit about this doctor's wife and kids. If he was guilty, they were better off without him. *But Theo might*, I realized. And not just that. This doctor would recognize Theo. He couldn't come with us, but leaving him alone in the house… *He should be with somebody.*

I crossed the room and put my hands on Theo's shoulders. "We're going to drop you off at Mom's house for the evening, Theo."

His eyes flared wide. "What? Why?" He gripped my shirt in his fists. "I want to come with you."

Theo's voice was so desperate and small that I had to kiss him. War rolled his eyes, but I ignored him.

"Not this time, little finch. This is a delicate operation, and we have to be careful. War and I are trained for this. You'll be safer with Mom and Tatty tonight."

He glanced at War as if he expected to get his support, but War was firmly on my side. He was too rational a thinker to be moved by Theo's puppy dog eyes.

"Get your phone, Theo," I said and gave his ass a pat. "Mom and Tatty will take good care of you."

"Annie and Mom were making gnocchi," War added. "You'll like it. It's potato pasta. Carb city."

"We'll be back before you know it," I promised Theo, and he finally moved to the doorway.

War watched him leave, frowning. "Is he going to be okay while we're gone?"

"I'll tell Xavier to put on one of his musical movies," I said with a shrug. Theo seemed to like movies with singing and dancing.

Theo was still tense when we dropped him off, and I was nervous about leaving him, but Mom promised to feed him and they were trying to pick something from the streaming program when we left.

He seemed happy enough on the couch with Xavier, and he barely noticed us go out the door.

We took War's rental car, mostly because I didn't want to drive. Plus, he'd rented a BMW with a premium sound system. It was a shame that all he fed the speakers was female pop singers of the early 2000s.

I frowned down at the stereo knob as Brittney's special brand of bubblegum pop filled the car. "So. Ken."

"Give it a rest, River." War rolled his eyes.

"Look, we wouldn't have to talk if you had decent taste in music."

He scowled over at me. "Don't trash on Brittney, River. She's the princess of pop for a reason."

"Yeah, and that reason is called autotune."

"Fine." He reached down and hit the button skipping to the next thing in line on his iPod, which wasn't any better.

"Ugh, really?"

"You just hate pop music," War complained.

"I do not. I like some."

He picked up his iPod and shoved it at me. "Prove it. Find me one song on there you know the lyrics to."

"I will then." I scrolled through the iPod quickly. There were probably half a dozen songs in War's collection I knew, even if I didn't like them. Sometimes, songs were hard to avoid. When they got popular, they played *everywhere*. I paused when I hit one song in particular, a wicked smirk appearing. "Found your new theme song."

War actually growled when the opening riff for Queen B's "Single Ladies" started to play. "I'm going to kill you, River."

"If you keep driving with your lead foot, probably."

He sighed and backed the speed down from the ninety he'd been going. "Look, you were right, okay? Ken was an asshole and I never should've let it go on as long as it did. Is that what you want to hear?"

"Not quite. What I'd like to hear you say is fuck Ken. You're way too blasé about this breakup. I'd expect this level of non-reaction from one of the triplets or Shepherd, but you?"

War shrugged. "It's been a long time coming. If anything, it's a relief. I'll never have to wake up and find his stupid beard hairs in my toothbrush again."

"That's the spirit," I said with a nod.

"No more five am wakeups just so he can go practice his swing at the country club," he continued. "No more of his five hundred pairs of stupid white shoes. No more hanging out with his boring golf buddies. No more..." He paused before shaking his head. "No more talks with social workers and adoption agencies."

"War, I know kids are important to you, but—"

He acted like he hadn't even heard me. "I'm getting too old."

"You're thirty-six!"

"They look at everything, River," he insisted. "Do you have any idea how hard it's going to be with that OCD diagnosis hanging over my head? Ken was fucking perfect because there was nothing wrong with him. He was boring, average, and mentally stable. I've got no chance by myself, and without a stable relationship of at least three years?" He shook his head and hit the steering wheel. "Fuck, River. I'm not just losing my shitty boyfriend. I'm losing my chance at a *family*."

"I'm your family," I snarled. "Me, Xavier, Xander, Shepherd... What about us?"

War sighed and shook his head, his shoulders slumping in defeat. "Never mind. You don't get it."

He was right. I *didn't* get it. Why did he keep going on about having a family when he already had *us*? War was supposed to take over for Dad so he could retire, run all our operations, and be the one we all came to. As the oldest, that was his job. He couldn't do that if he was saddled to small, helpless humans for the rest of his life. We were all the family he needed. Why couldn't he see that?

"We're here," he announced, turning the steering wheel.

I frowned and turned away to look out the window. That was War's way of shutting down the conversation, and getting him to keep talking about it would be all but impossible once he decided he was done. He was even more stubborn than me.

We'd pulled down a narrow rocky driveway that led through the thick woods. Deep evening shadows clung to everything. "I don't see a house. You sure this is the right driveway?"

"This is a service road for the electric and gas workers," War said. "Harris's house is a quarter mile down the road. It'd be stupid to pull into the driveway, River."

I huffed out a sigh. "I was hoping not to hoof it through the woods for this one."

"You should know better." He pulled the car in behind a pine tree with a thick skirt and opened the center console, pulling out two black ski masks and tossing one to me.

I tugged mine on, adding black gloves before we got out to get some gear out of the trunk.

War brought his briefcase full of knives and syringes around to the back seat, prepping two syringes. "How much do you think he weighs based on that photo we saw?"

I shrugged, tugging up the carpet in search of the tire iron. "Three hundred? Depends on if that's an old photo or not."

"You're right. Better assume three-twenty, just in case." He prepped his syringes in silence.

"What's the plan if we run into the family?" I asked and then added, "Where the fuck's the jack in this caviar car?"

His eyes flicked up to meet mine. "There probably isn't one."

I stood up. "How do you change a flat tire if you get one then?"

His turn to shrug. "Call AAA?"

"God forbid War should break a nail." I snorted and shut the trunk. If there was no tire iron, I'd have to use my fists if it was called for. This was supposed to be War's interrogation anyway. I was there for backup. "Anyway, about the family..."

"Don't run into the family."

"Yeah, but if we do."

"Don't."

Great plan, I thought, but I wasn't going to argue. I didn't want to have to hurt a woman and kids, especially since they weren't on our approved list of targets, but I'd do whatever needed to be done to keep the operation on track.

War checked his watch. "Okay. Everything on silent?"

I checked my phone, half expecting to see a text from Theo. I was disappointed when there wasn't one. "Silent," I verified, switching off the sound.

We tossed our phones into the back seat and started through the woods, keeping to the shadows as much as possible. Dry leaves crunched under our feet, but it didn't matter because no one was around to hear it. The only building was a two-story farmhouse style home in the distance. When we got closer, it was a relief to find there weren't any cars in the driveway.

That doesn't mean the wife's not home, I thought, crouching next to a tree. *Other car could be in the shop. Plus, there's the kid to worry about. Let's hope the little snotgoblin has practice after school.*

War signaled for me to go around back while he took the front. I nodded and crept out of my hiding place. Rather than go straight for the back door, I checked the windows, peering in to find all the lights off, no sign of anyone. I checked the back door and found it locked before moving around to try all the windows, which were also locked.

"Anything?" War whispered as he came to join me in the back.

I shook my head. "Locked up tight."

"Same on the other side. Doesn't look like anyone's home, but be careful." He pulled his lockpick kit out of his pocket and got to work.

I sighed and stepped back to play lookout. War's style of killing was *boring*. He preferred stealth and care. I would've stayed in the woods until the doc came home. The best place to pounce on someone was when they felt safe and were distracted. That'd be when he was fumbling with his keys to unlock the front door. One good whack on the back of the head with the tire iron to disorient him, and then drag him off into the woods, put him in the trunk, and drive him somewhere else.

The door clicked. "We're in," War announced and pushed open the door.

I went in first. The back door opened into a neat and orderly laundry room. The kitchen was just as clean, but I spotted some pictures on the fridge of their kid. He was probably eleven or twelve, and he was posing in a basketball jersey.

"We're in luck," I said, holding the photo up so War could see. "Junior made the basketball team. Probably has practice after school."

"That gives us two, maybe three hours, depending on how much of an asshole the coach is." He checked his watch and adjusted his timer.

"Any idea what the wife does?" I pulled open the fridge.

War pushed it closed before I could grab anything. "She's a math professor. I checked while you were kissing your boyfriend goodbye. She won't be back until after eight. He should be here any minute."

As if on cue, we heard a car pull into the driveway. War gestured for me to go to the back door in case he came in that way while he readied a syringe and stood by the front door.

Don't know what you expect me to do if he does come in the back, I thought, stepping into the laundry room. *There's not much around except...* My eyes fell on a sledgehammer. I smirked and picked it up, holding it on my shoulder.

Keys jingled, and a moment later the front door opened. Heavy feet took two steps into the living room before a masculine voice cried out. The front door swung closed and there was the sound of a heavy body collapsing as War grunted.

I poked my head out of the laundry room. "Everything okay?" I asked as I watched War struggle to hold up the doctor's limp body.

"Get over here and help me!" War growled.

"Calm your tits, Barbie. I'm coming." I sighed and put the sledgehammer down. *Until next time, beautiful.*

I helped War carry the man out the back door and to a tiny tool shed we'd spotted on our way in. The smell of motor oil and cut grass permeated the air in there while I searched for something to secure him to. We found an old camping chair and an orange electrical cord to bind him with. War put an IV in each arm once he was secure and clipped an oxygen sensor onto his finger. War yanked off his smart watch, hitting a few settings and sliding it onto the man's wrist where it immediately began displaying his heart rate. War started laying out several pieces of equipment.

I frowned. "Does he need all that?"

"Do you want him to die before we get any answers?" War retorted. He readied a syringe at the IV port. "Ready?"

"I was ready ten minutes ago," I replied.

War pushed the plunger down. There was a brief moment where nothing happened, and then the man's eyes snapped open. He took a desperate breath, and the watch started beating as his heart rate soared.

Doctor Harris's eyes darted back and forth between us. "Who are you? Please, take what you want but don't hurt me!"

"Unfortunately, what we want is you," War said, moving around in front of him. "Or at least information that you have."

I grabbed the doctor by his shirt. "What do you know about a man they call Master? A group of boys that live with him?"

Recognition sparked in his eyes. There was no missing it, even if he was about to insist otherwise. "I don't know what you're talking about!"

"You've been treating them for years," I snarled and let him go.

"Please, you've got the wrong guy! Oh my god, my chest!" He started crying and I rolled my eyes.

"That's the adrenaline I gave you," War said casually, lifting another syringe and passing it to me.

The doctor's eyes widened, tracking the movement of the syringe. "What's that?"

"That is Pavulon," War replied. "Not one you know? Not surprising since you're a pediatrician and not a surgeon. You see, Pavulon is a paralytic agent. Once it goes in, you'll be able to see, hear, and feel everything, but you won't be able to move." War nodded to me.

I jammed the needle into the port and pushed down the plunger. He didn't deserve to have it go in slow.

War snapped his fingers. "Damn. I forgot. Problem with Pavulon is it's notorious for depressing your breathing, and I've given you a rather large dose. So in six, seven minutes, you're going to have a lot of trouble breathing. Lucky for you, I brought everything I need to intubate you so you don't die." He held up a few pieces of equipment.

The doctor let out a helpless sound as his heart rate skyrocketed higher. "Please. I have a wife, a son!"

War went back to his briefcase, retrieving a scalpel in its sterile packaging. The doctor's chair creaked as War sat on his lap, carefully removing the scalpel. "You have until you run out of air to tell us everything you know about this Master's operation, the boys, and where to find them. But talk fast because between now and then, I get to practice my incisions."

Twenty-Two

Theo

I STUFFED MYSELF FULL of gnocchi and Italian sausage while River was gone. Xavier put on a musical about a man-eating plant. The movie was confusing and strange, but the songs were catchy.

"So when are you going to become a dentist?" Xander teased, throwing popcorn at his brother.

"When you open a floral shop," Xavier replied and pitched a candy at him from across the room.

"Fuck you. I am way too hot for retail," Xander replied, sitting forward on the sofa. "What time is it?"

Xavier tapped a button on his cell. "Just after midnight. Hey! I was watching that!"

Xander smirked at me. "Want to see a real scary movie?" He wiggled his eyebrows.

I sat up from where I was curled on the other end of the sofa, clutching the pillow tighter. "What kind of scary movie?"

"Xander, don't," Xavier warned. "River said stick with kid-safe stuff. He'll be pissed if you show him anything actually scary."

I flushed hot, anger and hurt flaring in my chest. River thought I couldn't handle anything scary? After everything I'd seen and been through? Just because I couldn't function on my own didn't mean I should be treated like a child.

I squared my jaw and looked straight at Xander. "Show me the scariest movie you know of."

"Are you sure?" His voice dipped an octave, and it was enough to send a small shiver down my spine.

I nodded stiffly. "I can handle it."

"Xander, don't," Xavier warned again.

"Too late," Xander said, selecting a shadowy image of a man standing outside a house.

"When River finds out, it's your funeral," Xavier mumbled.

I clutched the pillow tighter as the opening credits started to play. At first, I didn't think much of the movie. It had a lot of characters at the start that were difficult to keep track of, and there wasn't any singing. I started to drift off to sleep until Xander moved over to elbow me awake just as the little girl, who was the main character, started screaming and being thrown around on the bed by an unseen force.

As the movie went on, I started to feel more and more on edge, gripping the couch pillow so tight that my knuckles ached, yet I couldn't force myself to let go of it. I knew the movie was fake and that demons weren't real, but I still couldn't shake that feeling of dread hanging over my head. Such terrible things were happening to that little girl, and there was nothing anyone could do to help her. It wasn't the violence, or the horrible things the demon said that terrified me, but the poor girl's helplessness. It felt too familiar. Even worse, the ending did nothing to soothe those feelings. In the end, the demon won, claiming the lives of two good men.

Xander stood as the credits started to play and I flinched. "Well?" he said, stretching. "What'd you think?"

Xavier frowned and leaned forward to look at me. "Bro, are you okay? You look like you're about to have a coronary."

"I'm fine," I snapped and glared at Xavier. "Why wouldn't I be? It's just a movie."

Xavier got up and snatched the remote from where Xander had left it. "Why don't we watch something else?"

"You do what you want," Xander said with a yawn. "It's almost two-thirty in the morning. I'm going to go jerk off and go to bed."

Xavier wrinkled his nose. "Gross. Did not need to know that."

"Now you know not to bother me. Night, Theo. And remember, kids, don't play with Ouija boards." Xander waved to us and took the stairs up two at a time.

Xavier sighed and hit a button on the remote. "How about some Scooby-Doo?"

I frowned at him. "You don't have to treat me like a kid, you know."

"Bro, what? Seriously?" He rolled up his sleeve, revealing a tattoo of the cartoon dog. "Not everything is about you. Maybe I just like Scooby-Doo."

I sat back against the sofa, loosening my grip on the pillow as the theme song started to play. "Do you think River's okay?"

Xavier shrugged. "Probably. Him and War are good at what they do. They are taking a long time, though." He looked over at me, his voice softening. "Hey, I'm sure they just got caught up chasing a lead. They'll be back soon."

I hoped he was right, but it didn't stop me from worrying. What if they'd gotten caught? What if they were hurt? Or in a car accident? Anything could have happened. I got out my phone and glanced down at it, considering sending River a text, but then I remembered the instructions he'd given Xavier and Xander. I didn't want him to think I was even more helpless than I was, so I tucked the phone away with a sigh and stretched out on the sofa, my head resting on the pillow. Eventually, even Scooby-Doo couldn't keep me awake, and I drifted off to sleep.

My dreams were full of deep shadows and strange angles. Disembodied voices called to me from rooms I couldn't reach. I wandered around a run-down house where the walls shifted and moved on their own, trapping me in a labyrinth of dusty rooms full of spiderwebs and rotten furniture. There was a child crying somewhere, but no matter how hard I tried or how many rooms I moved through, I could never find him.

"You *what*?"

My eyes snapped open, heart racing, fighting the urge to jump behind the couch and hide at the sound of River's fury. He stood toe to toe with Xavier in the living room doorway, fists clenched at his sides.

"Re-*lax*," Xavier said, calmly crossing his arms. "First of all, it wasn't me. Second of all, he's fine. It was just a movie."

"I told you not to watch anything scary with him for a reason!" River's fists trembled at his sides.

Xavier shrugged. "I don't see what the big deal is."

"The deal is I told you not to do it, and you did it anyway."

"River?" I sat up, rubbing sleep from my eyes.

River shot one more threatening look at Xavier before pushing past him and coming to sit with me on the couch. "I'm here, little finch."

I blinked at him and then frowned. "I told Xander to play a scary movie."

"Xander?" River glared at Xavier.

Xavier shrugged and uncrossed his arms. "Guilty."

River turned back to me. "Theo..." He reached to touch my face.

I pushed his hand away. "I'm not a kid, River! I...I should be able to watch what I want. I should be able to go places, and do things. I want to be treated like a *normal* person."

"But you're not a normal person, Theo," River said quietly. "None of us are."

I sat there on the verge of tears, knowing he was right. It didn't matter what I wanted. I was never going to be normal. I was always going to be just another helpless victim of the shit that had happened to me. No matter what I did, I couldn't go back to change it, but that trauma had changed me. I'd never get to know who I was without it.

That realization broke something in me. I threw myself forward, clutching River's shirt and sobbing into his chest.

He sighed and put his arms around me, gently kissing the top of my head.

"You want me to get Mom or Tatty?" Xavier volunteered.

River shook his head. "No, I've got this." He scooped me up in his arms. "Let's go home, little finch."

I was still crying as he carried me to the door, but I didn't want to be. For all my insistence that I wasn't a child and shouldn't be treated like one, I was doing a fine job of proving it.

I forced myself to stop the same way I did when men started yelling at me not to cry. I held my breath until I was lightheaded. When I let myself breathe again, we'd moved outside and Xavier was opening the passenger door of River's car for me.

River deposited me in the seat and strapped me in before turning to Xavier. "Make sure Xander knows I'm pissed."

"River, come on. You know how he is. It wasn't malicious. He was just..." Xavier shrugged. "Acting out?" He rubbed the back of his head. "You know he's been off lately."

"Well tell him to get his shit together, because—"

I flinched as River shut my door, the rest of their conversation too muffled to hear through the car.

A minute later, River stomped over and got into the driver's seat, starting up the car.

I watched the house shrink as he backed out of the driveway, feeling numb again. "Did you get the information you needed?"

"What?" River hit the brakes and frowned over at me.

"From the doctor," I said quietly. "Did you and War get the information you needed? You were gone so long."

"I'm sorry about that, Theo." He reached to cup my cheek. "Are you sure you want to hear that right now?"

I closed my eyes and swallowed, trying to ignore the pang of guilt in my chest. It was stupid for me to break down crying now, when everything was finally going well. "I need this to be over. I'll be better when it's over."

River considered me in silence a moment before backing out of the driveway and pulling onto the road. "He gave us an address," he said eventually. "We drove up to check it out, but the house was empty. There were signs people had been there recently, so we think he's already moved the others to another location."

"Fuck." My heart sank into the pit of my stomach. River wasn't saying it, but I could hear it in his voice. There was a chance we'd never find him.

"We'll find him," River promised. "Even if he leaves Ohio, we'll find him. There's nowhere he can go that we can't reach."

"How, River?" I asked, throwing up my hands. "There's only what? Eight of you? It would take years to scour the country for him."

"There's a whole fucking army behind me and my brothers, Theo. You just haven't met them yet."

River's house looked sad and empty as we pulled up to it. I dragged myself up the stairs behind River, too exhausted to think about anything other than crawling into bed with him. I wanted to forget this whole terrible day had ever happened.

We went straight upstairs, and I stripped out of my clothes, climbing into bed in nothing but my underwear. When River spooned up against me naked, I half expected him to make a move, but he didn't. He ran his fingers over my side, drawing tiny circles on my skin.

"Is there anything I can do to make you feel better?" he whispered against the back of my head.

I shook my head. "Not unless you can bring back the dead." I still couldn't believe David was gone. "Did the doctor say anything about David?"

"Yes," River said after a slight hesitation. "He confirmed he wrote a prescription for opiates recently. We tried to get him to give us the name he wrote it for, but he stopped breathing before we could."

I swallowed, trying to imagine Doctor Harris gasping for his last breath. "Did he die quickly?"

"No," River promised. "He suffocated on his own bloody vomit. It took almost six minutes. Last thing he did was piss himself in terror."

"Good," I said coldly and rolled over onto my back. "Does it make me a bad person that I'm glad he suffered?"

"No." River shook his head and cupped my cheek. "He knew people were hurting you and chose to let it continue so he could make extra money every month. Money he was using to feed his gambling addiction."

I closed my eyes, but they snapped open again when River tilted my face toward his.

He closed his mouth over mine in a quick kiss. "Some people don't deserve to live," he said when we parted. "And I don't think you're a child, Theo. I just want to protect you. I know you want your life to be normal, but—"

"I know," I said, my voice rough from the kiss. "I know I can't ever be normal."

River's hands closed over mine. "We make our own normal."

He kissed me again, this time slower, almost sweetly, teeth nipping at my bottom lip. Warm fingers slid under the elastic band of my briefs, brushing against the head of my cock. My breath caught as River's lips left mine and he started kissing his way down my body. River's warm lips closed around me, my eyes fluttered closed, and I forgot all about everything outside of that room. I forgot about how helpless I was, how hurt and confused I was about everything else. None of that mattered. All that mattered was that he was here with me, that he desired me.

I never felt more precious than when River's mouth was on me. No one had ever done that for me or even offered before him, and that made those moments more special, especially since he genuinely seemed to enjoy doing it. He moaned around me, the sound vibrating up my spine, making the pressure build faster.

My fingers clutched the back of his head, not to ask for more, but because I needed to touch him everywhere I could. I let out a strangled sound as he sank further, letting me slide to the back of his throat. His hand closed around my balls, massaging them with firm strokes almost as if he were begging for me to come.

My lips parted in a silent shout as I slid over the edge. He didn't stop squeezing my balls or sliding his tongue up and down my shaft as I started to come, trying to coax more out of me until it was too much. I pushed his head away with a hiss. River immediately crawled up my body and forced his tongue into my mouth, feeding me my own release. I groaned and shuddered as he did it, taking everything he gave me.

We parted only long enough for him to grab the lube from the bedside table, and a second later, I yelped as slick fingers probed at my ass. "You know, nothing we do in here is normal either," he said with a smirk as he worked his fingers, getting me ready for him. "We could try that if you wanted. Just normal, boring, vanilla—"

"Don't you dare." I gasped, grabbing his shoulders. I slid my fingers up to gather a handful of his hair by the roots, drawing a pleasured growl from him as I pulled hard. "Forget normal. Fuck me like I'm your whore."

Something dark flashed in River's eyes. "Is that what you want to be, Theo?" he asked, speeding the pace of his fingers until I was panting and squirming. "My whore? Just for me?"

I licked my lips. "Yes. Only for you."

I shouldn't have liked to be called that. I should've hated it, and I knew it, but I didn't. I *was* his whore. He'd paid for me with cash and blood. There was no denying that River owned me now, body and soul. I'd never wanted anyone else but him.

"Fuck, Theo," he growled and pulled his fingers free to give my ass a small swat. "Hands and knees for me, little finch."

I trembled as I turned over, rising to my hands and knees as I had for hundreds of other men. But River wasn't those other men, and this was different. I needed him to do it this way, maybe because of the bad memories, or maybe because I was as sick and twisted as the rest of his family. Maybe I needed to prove to myself that I could do this, that I wasn't weak and helpless, that I could make my own choices. Untangling all that could wait for later. All I knew was that I wanted this, and I wanted it from him.

River positioned himself against my entrance and sank in slowly, groaning loudly while I panted and winced against the pillows. His hands slid down my back, thumbs tracing the bumps of my spine. I flinched when his lips pressed against my shoulder like a brand.

"You okay?" he whispered against my skin.

I nodded, but that wasn't good enough for him. His hand closed around my throat and he forced me up off the pillows.

"Don't go somewhere I can't follow, little finch," he murmured, teeth tugging at my ear. "Stay with me. Let me show you how much better this can be."

I swallowed against the weight of his fingers. "Okay. Yeah. I trust you."

He nuzzled against my ear, kissing along the nape of my neck before he started to move. My jaw trembled and I squeezed my eyes closed, biting the inside of my cheek to keep from sinking into that safe space in my mind.

Hot breaths panted against the little hairs on my neck, and River's fingers flexed against my throat. "Say my name, Theo."

I licked my lips. "River."

"And who do you belong to?"

"You."

His hold on me tightened. "Fuck, you're so goddamn perfect. Do you have any idea how long I've needed this? Needed you?" Teeth scraped against a tendon in the back of my neck. "You're my favorite thing, Theo. My most prized possession."

I shuddered at that, my cock giving a needy twitch as he started to speed his pace.

One of his hands traveled to my hip, fingertips digging in hard. "The things I would do in your name... There isn't any line I wouldn't cross for you. You understand that, don't you? I'd burn this whole world to ash just to have you. I own you, but you own me too, Theo."

Something in my chest swelled at the confession, some emotion I couldn't name and had never felt before. A heady mix of pride and need and fear. That was so much to process, too much to make sense of in this moment.

"Fuck, River..." I didn't think I could come again so soon, but to my surprise, my cock had decided to rally.

River closed his fist around it. "Come for me. Be completely mine. All of you, Theo. Even the parts you try to hide from me. Be mine, and I'll be yours."

Panic squeezed around my heart as I realized I was going to come again. The rising wave of pleasure was too big, too much. I clawed at the pillows and squeezed my eyes shut tight, letting tears fall as River drove his body into mine, pushing me over the edge. I came with a scream like a sob, drowning in pleasure. My muscles jerked violently, almost as if I were possessed. Maybe I was. Maybe River was the demon I had let inside of me.

His hips jerked and he buried himself deep inside me with a grunt, spilling in me with aborted little thrusts, each one sending a new wave of bliss through me.

When it was over, we laid there in a pile, panting, sweating, and shaking. I wasn't sure I could move, even if River's considerable weight hadn't been pinning me to the bed. I wasn't sure I *wanted* to move.

"Fuck, Theo," River muttered. "That was...Are you okay?"

I nodded sleepily. "Tired."

He chuckled and kissed my cheek. "I bet. It's... Fuck, it's almost five in the morning. That took a while. Worth it, though."

He slid free of my body and walked away to grab a towel to clean us up before gently tucking me back into bed. I'd still barely moved.

"Get some sleep, little finch," he whispered, fingers feathering through my hair. "I'll watch over you."

Twenty-Three
River

I WOKE UP TO the sound of Xander and Xavier arguing downstairs instead of my alarm clock. Their voices echoed through the hall, and I sighed, unsticking myself from Theo to roll onto my back. He was still asleep, so I kissed him awake.

He rubbed the back of his hand across his freckled face. "Mmngh. What time is it?"

"About six-thirty," I told him, peppering kisses along his jaw.

We got up and took a quick shower, dressed, and headed downstairs. Xander and Xavier were still arguing, and I could hear them all the way up the stairs.

"...No way he knows anything useful," Xander was saying. "I told you not to answer!"

"What was I supposed to do? Ignore him forever?" Xavier replied.

I came off the last stair and let out a frustrated growl. "Why are you two freaks arguing in my house at this hour?"

Xander and Xavier, who were dressed in opposite colors for once—Xander in white and Xavier in black—exchanged a glance.

"Xion called again yesterday," Xavier said.

I glared at them, irritated because they'd woken me up still. "So?"

Xander smacked Xavier in the back of the head. "So this idiot answered."

"That still doesn't explain why you're here *before sunrise*."

Xander blinked. "Is it that early?"

Xavier sighed. "We didn't sleep. I wasn't even going to bring it up because it's Xion, but then War came back from his run early this morning and told me what happened last night. Xion's lead might be worth chasing. You've got nothing else to go on, River."

I narrowed my eyes at the two of them. "He's been in a locked ward for years. How the fuck would he know anything?"

"A better question might be how he even knows we're looking for anyone at all," Xander said, giving Xavier a hard look.

I grabbed Xavier by the front of his black hoodie and yanked him forward. "You *told* him?"

Xavier shoved me away. "Look, I know Xion is fucked up, and I wasn't going to talk to him, but dammit…" He spun on Xander. "You've been showing *symptoms*. I had to, Xander. Don't you get it? I already lost one brother to our broken brains. I don't want to lose you, too. I thought if I knew how it happened, I'd be able to help you before it was too late."

Xander let out a snort and turned away, arms crossed, while Xavier hung his head.

"Symptoms?" Theo asked, glancing between them. "Symptoms of what?"

Xavier fidgeted with his fingers and looked at me.

I shrugged. "Don't look at me. You brought this into *my* house."

His shoulders slumped. "We have schizophrenia. Well, sort of. Xion has it, and since we're identical triplets and there's a definite genetic component…" He shrugged. "It's only a matter of time before it eventually triggers, and we're the prime age for the first symptoms to start appearing."

"I am *not* having symptoms," Xander insisted, turning around, throwing his hands up.

"Yeah?" Xavier shot back. "Well then why did you scribble out all the eyes on your posters with black marker yesterday?"

Xander was quiet for a moment before he folded his arms. "There is no way in hell I'm going up there with you, so you might as well call Serena and cancel our visitation."

"It's already done, Xander," Xavier protested. "I'm going whether you want to or not."

I honestly didn't give a fuck about their sibling drama. I'd figured eventually one of them would cave in and accept Xion's desperate daily calls, and it was no surprise that it was Xavier. He'd always been softer than Xander.

What I cared about was this lead Xion claimed to have. We were painfully short on information, and if he did have something, I wanted to hear it, even if the chances that it'd be something useful were incredibly small.

I pushed past them and went to the closet to grab my coat.

"Where do you think you're going?" Xander demanded.

"With Xavier to see Xion." I pulled one of my extra jackets out of the hall closet and helped Theo into it.

"The fuck you are," Xander said, folding his arms.

I zipped up Theo's jacket and shot him a look to let him know I was considering making him regret his words, but Xavier stepped between us.

"You can't stop me from going," he said, staring his brother down. "You don't get to dictate everything I do, Xander."

"You don't want to go? Fine. Go pick up Uncle Sacha." I retrieved my car keys from where they hung on the wall.

"You can leave those," Xavier said with a smile, jingling his keys. "I just had Shrek detailed."

Theo frowned. "What's a Shrek?"

"It's his dumb Kia, and we're not taking it. We'll take my car." There was no way I was riding all the way to Columbus with his dumb video game soundtrack remixes blasting in my ears.

Xavier stuck his bottom lip out. "Fine. Guess I'll meet you there," he said and palmed his keys.

"Xavier," Xander called. When Xavier turned back, Xander had his hands in his pockets and wore a worried expression. "Don't let him get to you."

"I won't," Xavier promised, and we left him standing in the foyer.

THE TWIN VALLEY FORENSIC Behavioral Health Hospital didn't look much like a hospital, or a prison. It was a sprawling single story brick compound without any walls, razor wire, or guards. There were trees and shrubs everywhere with well-maintained sidewalks weaving in between them.

Inside was a different story. Walking through the doors, we were immediately asked to surrender anything and everything that might be used as a weapon, from our cell phones to our shoelaces. The grim faced orderly handed me a key and pointed me to a lockbox where I could leave my keys and belongings. While Xavier, Theo, and I shoved our things into the box, she called down to the unit to let Xion's social worker know we were here.

Almost as soon as she hung up, another door buzzed open, and a middle-aged soccer mom looking woman propped it open, tucking a stack of papers against her chest. "Party for Mr. Loomis?" She pronounced Xion's last name almost as if she were calling us to be seated for lunch.

The woman smiled as we came up to her, but it was one of those fake smiles, the kind that made me want to break all her teeth. "Good to see you, Xavier. Is Xander not with you?"

"No, but this is my brother River and his partner, Theo." Xavier gestured to us.

Theo's hand tightened around mine as the woman looked us over with a sharp gaze, her smile never wavering.

"I'm afraid only family and visitors on Xion's designated guest list are allowed back," she said. "Theo will have to wait here."

That was unexpected. Not that Theo wouldn't be able to go back with me. I thought that might be the case. I'd also not expected to be on Xion's list of preferred visitors. My plan was to have Xander go in and have him change the list so we could go back, but maybe that wouldn't be necessary.

"It's all right," Theo said, releasing his death grip on my fingers. "I'll wait here." He almost sounded relieved.

I didn't blame him. Given his history, entering a locked ward was probably terrifying. That didn't mean I liked the idea of leaving him behind.

He planted a quick kiss on my cheek. "I'll flip through some magazines and look at the pictures. It'll be fine."

"Don't leave the lobby," I told him and followed Xavier through the door the social worker was propping open for us.

The door closed with a thud that echoed down the pristine white hallway, and she scuttled out in front of us. "I'm glad you finally decided to come up for a visit," said the woman, leading us down the bland hall. "I think you'll be pleased with the progress Xion's made, and seeing you will be good for him. Well, seeing both of you would be better, but it's good the two of you are here. He'll be thrilled to see his brothers."

"Xion's no brother of mine," I muttered, earning an elbow from Xavier.

The social worker slid her name badge through a magnetic reader and a pair of double doors opened, letting us into the belly of the hospital. We followed her down the hall and past a woman with ratty hair curled up on the floor muttering to herself. Further down, an older man shuffled by wearing a pair of those infamous blue grippy socks instead of shoes. He moved as if every step was more effort than the last, his sagging eyes fixed on some point far away while a worker in scrubs walked alongside him.

The windowless room we were let into next looked more like an elementary school cafeteria than anything else. Half a dozen round tables were scattered around, three plastic chairs waiting at each. In the center of each table was a laminated number, taped down, the edges all worn. There were no drawings or paintings on the walls, no vending machines, no nothing except for a beefy worker in white scrubs blocking the opposite door.

Xion sat at a table near the center of the room. While he, Xander, and Xavier all shared the same DNA, time hadn't been quite as kind to Xion. He looked thinner, his cheeks gaunt, his eyes shadowed from poor sleep. His curly, dark hair hung long and limp past his ears, and a dark beard covered the bottom half of his face. The worn sweats and white t-shirt he wore were both too big on him. Xion was what Xander or Xavier might look like after a two-week bender; he was a shallow, haunted version of himself.

Next to me, Xavier sucked in a deep breath and froze in place as his brother's eyes fell on him.

Xion's thin lips spread into a Cheshire smile. "Hello, Xavi. River. Won't you join me?"

Xavier glanced at me before moving slowly toward the table. He jerked out a chair and sat. "Okay, we're here. Tell us what you know about the guy we're looking for."

Xion stared at Xavier, utterly still for a long moment before he slowly folded his hands on top of the table, mimicking his brother's posture exactly. "Hello, Xion," he prompted. "It's good to see you. You look good. Sorry we haven't been up to see you. The last five years have been a real bitch." His chair creaked as he leaned forward. "Now, you try."

Xavier looked over at me as if he were expecting me to provide some guidance.

I shrugged. Xion was *his* brother.

"Go on, brother," Xion said, his left eyelid twitching. "Don't be rude. They're watching."

Xavier's eyes suddenly darted around the room in a momentary panic, almost as if he expected to find the room full of people. It wasn't. We were the only ones there, the guard and social worker aside.

"I'm sure they're tired, Xion," the social worker offered. "It's a long drive up here."

"A five-year drive apparently." Xion leaned back and crossed his arms across his chest. "And no Xander, huh? Let me guess. He's still pissed about the puppy."

Xavier's lip curled. "The puppy? Fuck the puppy. You tried to kill *him*."

Xion shrugged. "Honestly, I thought he was you. But then, I also thought you were clones sent by Donald Trump to spy on me. I had a psychotic break. It happens. I'm doing much better now, thanks."

"As heartwarming as this little reunion is," I interjected, "it's not why we're here. You said you had information, so spill or we're leaving."

Xion's chestnut eyes fell on me with weight. "Just like you, River. It's always what other people can do for you. Not a single thought about how you can help other people."

"It's a gift." I jerked my chin toward him. "Talk. Now."

"Talk. Now," he parroted in a mocking tone. "You should be more careful about how you speak to me. Apparently, I'm a dangerous psychopath." He said the last line in a stage whisper, exaggeratedly lifting his hand.

"That's it." I stood while he was still cackling like an idiot. The chair legs scraped over the polished floor. "I knew you were wasting our time. Come on, Xavier."

Xion moved so fast even I didn't have time to react. He slapped his palms down on the table and shot up out of his chair, the mirth falling from his face like a mask. "Don't you fucking move, Xavi." He blinked and the malice was gone, replaced by a pleasant, smiling face. "I missed you. And I do have something that you might find useful." He looked at me, through me. "Your little boy toy isn't the only broken doll that's turned up lately. There was another here recently who talked about this *Master* the same way yours apparently does."

I gave Xavier a wary look before sinking back into my chair. "Where is he?"

"Six feet under," Xion spat with malice. "She overdosed. Apparently, she was hoarding her meds and trading some with other patients to get her fatal cocktail just right."

"Xion," the social worker said in a warning tone.

He rolled his eyes. "Anyway, it was a she, not a he. Some tweaker bitch. She kept going on about how angels took her baby. Freaked out every time the mention of religious services came over the loudspeaker on Sundays." The stool creaked as he leaned forward. "I traded her two trazadone and a lorazepam for a blowjob and she spilled right after. Bitch was into pillow talk or some shit. She told me she sold her baby to the Master for two hundred bucks and a couple of speedballs at some church. I thought she was talking about some guy she made up until Xavier mentioned this Master you were looking for."

"Which church?" I pressed.

He shrugged. "How the fuck should I know? Wasn't like I paid a lot of attention. People in here are kinda crazy. Besides, this was months ago. With as many drugs as they have me on, you're lucky I remember anything at all."

I sighed. If his information was good, it still wasn't helpful. All he had were the ravings of an addict coming down from her high, and we couldn't even talk to her. His information was months old. Nothing he'd told us would get us closer to finding where Master was hiding out or shutting down his operation, which meant we'd wasted the trip.

"Is that it?" I asked.

He pulled back his lips, scowling at me. "What do you mean, 'Is that it?' Like I gave you nothing? You fuckers don't write or visit. You don't even answer my calls for years, and when you finally do, it's only because I'm *useful* to you."

"Xion," warned the social worker, "let's save our feelings for group."

"No!" shouted Xion, rising. "I have a right! They abandoned me, treated me like I was nothing! Well, I've got news for... Let me go! I'm not finished!"

The big orderly that'd been standing near the other door had put his hand on Xion's shoulder. Xion flung it off. The next thing I knew, Xion's chair was tipped sideways and the table jumped. Xion was face down against the table, his arms twisted behind his back while the orderly held him.

"We need some assistance in here," the social worker shouted through the cracked door.

A second later, three workers in a rainbow of scrubs rushed in to help restrain Xion while we backed away, herded toward the door by the social worker. Somehow, Xion wrestled his way out from under two of the orderlies only to be taken to the floor immediately after.

"Take a long look, Xavi!" Xion shouted as the orderlies worked to restrain him. "This is what you have to look forward to!"

Xavier's face blanched as Xion went from screaming to laughing.

"I'll save you a spot!" Xion shouted from the floor.

Xavier spun on his heels and stormed through the door.

When I finally caught up with him, he was by the exit, hyperventilating and pulling at his hair. "Xander was right. We shouldn't have come!" He hugged himself tightly and tried to blink back tears.

I sighed, unsure of what to do. If he made a scene, it'd be inconvenient, but if I walked him out like that, Theo would want to know what happened, and I didn't want to stress him further.

Xavier suddenly grabbed my arm in a vice grip, his eyes full of panic. "I'd rather die than ever be in a place like this," he said in a small voice, eyes darting around. "You can't ever let them put me in the hospital, River."

I pulled away, wrinkling my nose. "First of all, that will never happen."

"How can you be so sure?"

"Because you're my brother," I said with certainty. "If you ever lose it that bad, I'll kill you myself before I ever let you rot in a place like this."

Xavier wasn't Xion. He didn't want to lose himself to his demons the way Xion had. Xion had chosen to crawl into bed with his demons, and he liked it there. He'd never be family to me.

That seemed to calm him down. Xavier pushed the tears away. "Thanks, River."

I TOOK THEO TO lunch and a movie. Apparently, he'd never been to a movie theater. I didn't care what we saw, but I read him the selections and let him pick. Thankfully, he picked some PG romcom instead of another horror movie. I bought him the biggest popcorn they had, some candy, and a drink, and we made our way into the theater.

Since it was the middle of the day, we had the theater to ourselves. I thought it was the perfect opportunity to give Theo a blowjob, but he seemed really into the movie, so I wound up scrolling on my phone instead. While the boring vanilla heterosexual couple on the screen declared their undying love to each other in the rain, I was reading about experimental mushroom shrouds that were being used in Europe.

When the movie let out, it was late enough that I figured it was time to head over to Shepherd's. Our plan was to hit the Time Out Room and hopefully get something useful out of the day.

Gavin once again answered the door, this time decked out in tight leather pants and a leather vest. "Oh, hey, River. Theo. Come on in."

"Please tell me Shepherd isn't dressed like you," I said as he closed the door behind us.

"Fortunately for you, my leather bondage gear is reserved for private use," Shepherd said, stepping out of the back of the apartment. Thankfully, he was wearing his everyday suit, though he didn't have a tie for once. "Not that it matters since I won't be going in with you tonight."

I frowned and narrowed my eyes at Shepherd. "Wait a minute. Are you expecting us to babysit your grad student in there? Shepherd, there's no way."

Shepherd smoothed his hands over his sleeves. "Not at all. Gavin can look after himself. I'm persona non grata at The Time Out Room, so I'll be your man in the van tonight, watching the back door and walking you through who is who and where to go."

My lip curled. "I don't need you to tell me what to do, Shepherd."

Theo wrapped his arm around mine and huddled in closer as Shepherd's gaze pierced us.

"Think of me as your voice of reason," Shepherd said. "I'm there to keep you from going off half-cocked and killing everyone in there the moment someone bumps into your pet, and to keep Theo from disassociating or sinking into panic. Gavin will be my eyes and ears, and my voice will be in your head the entire time."

Shepherd reached behind his leather sofa and brought out a pristine metal briefcase. He popped open the clasps and held a tiny earbud out to each of us.

Theo took one and slipped it in his ear. The thing practically disappeared.

"Our goal tonight," Shepherd said, slipping one into his ear while Gavin did the same, "is to locate at least one player in this operation, isolate him, extract him from the Time Out Room, and relocate to a pre-prepared secondary location for phase two."

I glanced over at Gavin. "And you're totally on board with kidnapping somebody tonight? That part of your grad thesis, too?"

Gavin licked his lips and glanced at Shepherd before replying. "If I understand this correctly, these people are involved in human trafficking. They're kidnapping people and forcing them to work against their will. We're talking about modern slavery. I have no problem making someone like that disappear."

"And he gets thesis hours for his trouble," Shepherd said, snapping the case shut. "Now, shall we go? I'm dying to see how all this plays out tonight."

Twenty-Four
Theo

Shepherd drove a souped-up SUV, one of those expensive models with all leather interior, state of the art sound, and a high-tech display in the center console. Well, he didn't exactly drive it. He made Gavin drive, as if his grad student was his chauffeur.

The car stood out like a sore thumb in the part of town we drove to, where there were bars on the windows and graffiti on the walls. Trash littered the streets and people crowded the corners in coordinating colors, staring us down. We passed pawn shops, payday loan places, and alcohol drive-throughs.

I recognized some of the buildings and had even been in a few of them. While I didn't know the street names, I could easily point out which alleyways were safe to pull down and which ones weren't.

"I know this neighborhood," I muttered as we drove by one of the alleyways I was in often enough to remember the smell. "I've been here before. Lots of times."

"We're almost there," Gavin said.

I turned to look at River next to me. "What did you learn from Xion?"

"You went to see Xion?" Shepherd twisted in his seat to look back at us.

River sighed. "Yeah. Apparently, someone was in his ward a couple of months ago talking about someone they called Master and a church where she sold her baby, but the information's not reliable. It's months old, and so far nothing we have indicates Theo was being held anywhere near a church."

Shepherd turned around in his seat. "The church could be the front of the operation. Perhaps that's how they're finding their victims."

"They're taking babies?" I stared at him in horror. It was one thing for them to abuse older kids, but babies?

How old had I been when it all began? I couldn't remember much from my early life. What if this had been going on almost since I was born? My stomach turned.

River shrugged. "Makes sense, given that you said Master raised you since as far back as you can remember. If they're not putting you in school, you might not exist on paper, which means they have to have some way of acquiring victims illegally. Why not from addicts desperate for a fix?"

"Oh my god." I turned away, covering my mouth.

"We don't know when you were taken," Shepherd said firmly. "Perhaps you were older and don't remember. Acquiring infants would be incredibly labor intensive, but they'd need to bring victims in young for the type of psychological programming they're using, children under six. That's not to say children that young are being rented out, but I wouldn't put it out of the question. The younger the victim, the higher the price."

River slipped an arm around my shoulders, massaging gently. "What do we need to know about this place before going in?"

"It's members only, but I've taken the liberty of having one of my other assistants secure you memberships," Shepherd said. "They're under the names Lewis and Stephenson using your own first names." He brought up his phone, tapping lightly on the screen. "A six thousand square foot space for you to enjoy, complete with four private themed rooms." He snorted. "That right there is a red flag. People left to their own devices with torture equipment in a closed room? He's asking for a liability suit."

"If they've got private rooms, that's where we're more likely to find the kind of people we're looking for," River said next to me. "How can we see what's going on inside there?"

Shepherd tapped his phone again, pulling up another picture and zooming in. "Well, we all know privacy is an illusion. There are undoubtedly cameras set up in there, and he'll have in-house security watching the feeds. That's one way. Alternatively, you could knock, though no guarantee they'll answer. That's odd."

"What is?" I leaned forward, looking over his shoulder.

"The website says there's six thousand square feet of usable space, but the floor plan only accounts for fifty-two hundred square feet. It could be they're rounding up..."

"Or there are rooms in there that aren't on the plans," River said.

I grasped River's arm tightly. "We have to find out for sure. If there are people being held in there..."

"If there are, I strongly suggest we take care of it quickly and quietly," Shepherd said. "It's places like The Time Out Room that give the lifestyle a bad public image. Taking them down publicly will only further that negative perception."

River sighed. "We don't know if that's the case yet, and I don't know if the three of us will be enough to canvas this place in a single night."

"I'm sure you'll do your best."

We stopped in front of a run-down building with neon lights out front. I'd always thought the place looked more like a dirty strip joint than a club. My insides immediately clenched at the sight of the familiar building.

Flashes of memory shot through me like a bad drug, and I turned to bury my face in River's chest. "I don't know if I can do this."

"I'll be with you every second," River promised. "You'll be safe with me. I won't let anyone hurt you."

"You'll be fine," Shepherd said dismissively. "Chances are, everyone in there will be too interested in someone else to even notice you. And if the staff gives you any trouble, I'll swoop in to make sure they're more focused on me than you."

River kissed my temple and got out of the car, coming around to open my door for me. I was trembling as I wrapped my arm around his, and it felt like he held me up all the way to the door. The heartbeat of bass music thrummed in the walls as if they were alive, the sound only getting louder when Gavin opened the doors and held them for us.

The woman at the front counter had pink and purple pigtails, blue lipstick, and wore a blood red corset. She looked up from her phone as if she were irritated that we'd interrupted her. "Membership?"

"Under River Lewis," River said and gripped me roughly to his side. "And this is my plus one." He jerked his head toward Gavin. "He's Gavin Stephenson"

She tapped the keyboard a few times before looking up and scanning over us briefly. "You got anything to check?"

"No," River said.

She shrugged and started stamping the backs of our hands. "Then you're good to go in. Lounge through the curtains to the right.

If you want to rent a private room, we charge by the hour, max two-hour blocks. With your premium membership, you're entitled to one discounted drink at the bar per person, per visit." She spoke in a bored monotone, as if she said it a hundred times a day. "Enjoy your time out." And with that, her attention was back on her phone.

River's grip on me remained tight as he led me through the curtains. At first, I avoided looking around, not wanting to see any familiar faces, but then I remembered that was why we were there. I glanced up, scanning unfamiliar faces of people in the lounge area, which was more like a bar than a proper lounge. The place was busy, nearly every seat taken. How many of them were there to hurt people like me? How many of them knew?

"You recognize anyone?" River whispered in my ear.

I shook my head.

But we were just getting started.

The lounge was connected to the main area, where a variety of equipment was out on display, none of which I'd ever used.

"Most of the time, they brought us to the bar," I said numbly. "We didn't go into the big room, except..."

My breath caught and a memory hit me full force. The feeling of being trapped, bent over, humiliated. Masked people laughing. I was high up, above them on a stage, but my feet were barely touching the floor. My shoulders ached from the way my arms were bound behind my back.

I shook my head. "I think they do special events here sometimes. Themed parties? There was a stage and masked people were watching while someone I couldn't see was hurting me."

"I'm going to burn this fucking place to the ground," River snarled.

"Arson isn't off the table," said Shepherd in my ear, "but let's try not to immolate the evidence we're looking for."

"I don't think what we want is here," Gavin said, looking out over the main floor. Most people were at the bar, acting as if they were afraid to wander beyond it. "Let's try the private rooms."

No one stopped us as we left the main area, walking down a hallway that ended in a T. There were two rooms to the right and two to the left, plus a mystery door with a no entry symbol straight ahead.

River squeezed my hand. "Anything coming back to you?"

I swallowed and tried to keep my breathing even, turning my head right and left. "This way," I said and took a right. The first door was open and the room unoccupied. It was done up like a nursery with a giant crib, a changing table, and a wide array of stuffed toys. I didn't recognize it, so we moved on to the next one. Soft grunts were coming from beyond the closed door. I turned to go, but River held onto me.

He raised a fist and pounded on the door.

A second later it popped open to reveal a balding man who was half-dressed. "What?" snapped the man.

River glanced over at me. I shook my head.

"Sorry, wrong room," River said.

"Learn to fuckin' read," the man growled and slammed the door shut.

We tried the two rooms on the other side of the hallway—one room made up to look like a castle dungeon and the other a classroom—but I didn't recognize them either.

I frowned after the last door slammed in our faces. "Maybe I'm wrong. Maybe I've never been here."

"Let's try the last door before we come to that conclusion." Gavin gestured to the one with the no entry sign.

My heart jumped up into my throat and I braced myself to be hit with a barrage of memories as he threw it open. Relief washed over me when all we found on the other side was a storage closet.

And then the smell hit me. It wasn't a bad smell, but it was strong. It stung the insides of my nostrils like paint thinner, yet it was softer somehow, a fake chemical smell that I recognized immediately.

"It's through there," I said and pushed past Gavin, dragging River along with me.

"In the storage closet?" Gavin asked.

River let me go long enough to walk to the back where he started pressing along the walls. After a minute, he found a nearly invisible seam in the wall and pulled it open, revealing a numerical keypad. He glanced back at Gavin. "A lot of security for a closet."

"What do you have?" came Shepherd's voice in my ear.

"A keypad," River replied. "Numerical. We need to code to get any further."

There was a beat of silence before Shepherd asked, "How many digits?"

"Looks like five."

"Try six-nine-four-twenty," Shepherd suggested.

"That can't possibly be it," River mumbled as he typed it in anyway.

The keypad beeped and the little red light above it turned green. A rectangular section of the wall popped open revealing a door.

River blinked in surprise. "Fuck, it worked."

"We're clearly not dealing with geniuses," Gavin agreed.

Shepherd's chuckle made the hairs on the back of my neck stand on end. He sounded like a very pleased hyena. "These primates fuck like drunk middle schoolers all their lives and think cannabis is a god. Proceed accordingly."

River carefully pulled open the door. The space beyond was chillingly familiar. It looked like a break room in a busy factory, if that factory had been out of operation for decades and taken over by porn addicts. There were posters on the walls of naked people being restrained or beaten. Magazines full of extreme pornography littered the table. A chalkboard on one side of the wall held words in a grid with numbers in the column beside them. The next column over had numbers with a dollar sign attached.

"What the fuck?" River muttered as we filed into the room. "Is that what I think it is?"

"What are you looking at, River?" Shepherd asked.

River pulled out his phone and snapped a picture of the wall, sending it to Shepherd.

"It looks like a dead pool," Gavin said, walking up to the wall.

I frowned. "Like the superhero?"

"Sort of. Well, he's named after one." Gavin tilted his head back to take in the many, many names scribbled there. Whoever kept track of it would've needed a chair to reach the top.

"Somebody is certainly betting on something," Shepherd agreed. "Fourth column from the bottom. I can't quite make it out. Read it to me under the pick column?"

"D.C. R-seven," Gavin read. "The other name associated with him is Travis K."

"Travis?" I shuddered and turned away from the wall.

"You know someone by that name?" River asked.

I nodded slowly and hugged myself tightly, trying to will the bile down my throat. "Most clients just wanted sex, but people like Travis... He wanted to hurt people. I only went with him one time, but when he was done with me, I had two fractured ribs and a concussion. I don't remember what he did. I think I was drugged. I woke up in the worst pain of my life. I thought I was going to die."

A door on the other side of the room opened and a greasy looking man in a trucker cap stepped in, still zipping up his pants. He froze, taking us in and sneered. "You're not supposed to be in here!"

River tackled the man to the floor. Before the man could even scream, River had his hands around the man's throat, squeezing tightly. The man let out wet gasping sounds, his face slowly turning red, then purple. He clawed desperately at River's hands, movements getting more uncoordinated with each passing second until he eventually fell limp.

"That doesn't sound good," Shepherd mused in my ear. "What's happened?"

"We got interrupted," River said, letting go of the man and sitting back on his heels. "Don't worry. He's not dead. Yet. But there might be a change of plans." He looked at me. "Do you recognize him?"

I swallowed and nodded slowly, numbness spreading through my limbs. What were the chances? "That's Travis."

"Jesus Christ," Gavin muttered.

"Then we have great timing." River stood. "Gavin, help me find something to tie this asshole up with, and then we need to get out of here STAT."

Don't look at him. I tore my eyes away from Travis's pockmarked face and they settled on the door he'd come through. My heart throbbed in my ears, and I was moving past him before I could stop myself.

"Theo! Theo, wait!" River's voice sounded like it was under water, but I couldn't stop myself. I *had* to see.

There was a tiny room on the other side, no bigger than the cell where I'd spent my entire life. In fact, it looked a lot like my cell. A naked mattress lay on the floor, a threadbare blanket tossed haphazardly over it. The floor slanted in the center toward an industrial drain, the area around it marred by dark stains.

But it was the woman huddled in the corner I was concerned about. She was older than me by several decades, and sporting several new looking bruises and a crooked nose. One eye was already starting to swell shut. She looked up at me with blank terror, the kind of haunted fear that no one should have in their eyes. A familiar fear. Tears tracked their way through her filthy face, but she didn't make a sound, just staring at me, her knees pulled up to block the lower half of her face.

"There's a woman," I said, my voice distant and devoid of all emotion.

"Jesus Christ," River muttered. "What are we supposed to do with her?"

The woman glanced between us and surged up with a feral snarl. I jumped out of her way, and she pushed River, knocking him into Gavin, before running through the door we'd left open on the other side.

River struggled to his feet. "Shepherd! Bogie headed your way."

Shepherd sighed. "Always cleaning up your messes."

I swallowed and looked at River. "He won't hurt her, will he?"

"Probably not," River said, raking his fingers through his hair. He looked at Gavin, who was still standing there, dumbfounded. "Well? Are you going to help me with this asshole or what?"

Twenty-Five

River

THEO WAS NOT OKAY, but I couldn't focus on that. I had to focus on the job at hand, which was torturing information out of Travis.

The sick fuck was currently hanging from a meat hook by the chains we'd affixed to his wrists and ankles. At first, the only thing we'd been able to find was duct tape, but that wouldn't hold, so Shepherd got out the kit he kept in the back of his SUV, once again proving that he was prepared for anything.

Shepherd had driven us to the old meat packing plant and dropped me off with Travis and Theo before speeding off to deal with the woman we'd found and to drop off his grad student. I was pretty sure he was going to drop the woman off near a hospital and hope she found her way. She didn't speak a lick of English, and my Portuguese was shit. Shepherd had managed to say a few things to her, enough to get her to stop attacking us, at least.

Travis was pretending not to be awake, but he was. I'd noticed the change in his breathing a while ago. His long, greasy hair hung limp to his shoulders. He'd been wearing a trucker cap, a red flannel overshirt, blue jeans, and a white t-shirt, but he'd lost the hat while we were chaining him up.

I shifted my grip on the sledgehammer I'd stolen from the doctor's house in my hands, pacing back and forth in front of him. Without my normal tools, this was going to be messy. Good. Theo had said Travis had hurt him badly. I was going to hurt Travis worse.

"How do you know he won't lie to you to get you to stop?" Theo said nervously behind me. "Isn't torture a notoriously unreliable way to get information?"

I glanced back at him, wishing again that I'd convinced him to wait in the old lobby instead of coming into the belly of the factory with me. He'd said it creeped him out, that he'd rather be close to me. I wasn't so sure that was a good idea. In theory, he knew what I was, but once he saw me in action, he might try to run.

"I'm not doing it just for the information," I said, turning back to Travis. "I'm doing this because I want to. How long I draw this out for, that depends on how entertained I am. If I get bored with his answers, I'll have to make things more interesting, won't I?"

I tapped the hammer against my palm twice before slapping him in the face with my palm. "Wake up, asshole."

His head jerked up and he stared at me with wild eyes. He started to look past me at Theo, but I grabbed his jaw and jerked his face back to me.

"Don't look at him or I'll take out your fucking eyes," I said. "You don't need your eyes to answer questions."

"I don't know shit," he spat.

"Honestly, I don't care what you know and what you don't. I'm here for the entertainment value." I took a step back and swung the sledgehammer low. It cracked against his shin with the deafening crunch of bone.

Travis screamed, cursed, and spat, wiggling back and forth on the hook, but he wasn't going anywhere.

Behind me, Theo doubled over and threw up.

"What the fuck!" Travis screamed and sobbed. "What the fuck, man!"

"Here's how this game works." I gripped the chain to stop him from swinging. "I ask you questions; you answer. If I like your answer, I ask you another and the cycle repeats until I get an answer I don't like. Then I hurt you. And trust me when I say I can get real creative. Way more than you were when torturing all those people."

"I didn't torture anybody!" He kicked his one good leg. "You've got the wrong guy!"

"Liar!" I spat through clenched teeth and brought the sledgehammer down, smashing the bones of his foot.

He choked on his scream before gagging.

While he was still recovering, I grabbed a handful of his greasy hair. "You tortured Theo."

"Who the fuck is Theo?" he managed weakly.

I jerked his head up and pointed him toward Theo, who'd curled up in the corner, drawing his knees up to his chest.

Travis let out a weak grunt. "Oh, I get it. You're the one who bought the runt off Rick, eh? What's the matter? Pissed you got damaged goods?"

With a growl, I jammed the handle of the sledgehammer into his armpit, relishing how his mouth opened in a silent scream and his body convulsed in pain. "I want to know where the Master is. What's his real name? Where does he live? How do I find him?"

I yanked the sledgehammer away and let him hang there limply, catching his breath.

He lifted his head, showing bloody teeth. The fucker must've bitten his tongue. "You have no fucking idea who you're messing with, boy."

"Oh yeah?" I pushed the hammer into his chest hard enough to make him swing back. "Why don't you enlighten me?"

He lifted his chin more. "You're dead," he shouted in Theo's direction. "You know that, don't you? When they catch up to you, they're gonna—Ungh! Fuck!"

The sound of the sledgehammer striking his stomach echoed through the concrete room, and I'd only hit him with a quarter of the force I normally used.

"Tell me what you know about the Master!" I demanded.

He panted for a minute before finding the air to snarl, "Fuck you!"

"What's he doing with the babies he takes?" I pulled the sledgehammer back to strike again.

Travis' eyes widened. "Wait, wait, wait!"

"Sounds like I'm just in time for the entrée course," Shepherd said, strolling in. He'd changed into white scrubs and white tennis shoes and carried a rolled-up cloth under one arm. He huffed at me as he walked by, grabbing a surgical cart from where it rested against the wall. "He looks nice and tenderized, River, but you won't get anything out of him like that."

"He's mine," I growled at my brother.

"Honestly, River," he mused, pulling on a pair of blue nitrile gloves, "you're like a dog with a bone, shouting 'he's mine' over and over. So dramatic."

"Who're you supposed to be? Hannibal Lecter?" Travis spat, blood dripping down his chin.

"Hannibal is a fictional boogeyman," said Shepherd as he unrolled his tools. "An austere and refined gentleman monster. He had a sense of justice, a moral code that limited his choice of victim to those who he felt had personally wronged him. Thankfully, I have no such compunction."

Metal *shicked* as he pulled a fileting knife free, the polished silver gleaming in the harsh factory light. Travis's eyes widened and he started kicking as Shepherd approached. I stepped back and went to retrieve one of the empty paint buckets stacked in the corner.

Travis screamed, the sound echoing. I held out the bucket, and a moment later, Shepherd deposited an ear.

"Restraint," he said, turning to me. "That's the thing about torture you never learned, River. You keep brutalizing him with that sledgehammer, and you'll break something important. Not only that, but broken bones will release endorphins much faster, dulling the pain. You'll have him in shock or dead before he talks, if you don't render him completely useless beforehand." He turned back to Travis. "Now, where was I?"

Travis sobbed quietly, all the fight gone out of him.

I grabbed him by his hair again. "How do I find the Master?"

"I don't know," he bawled. "Please don't kill me! I won't tell anyone; just let me go!"

"I'm afraid that's off the table," Shepherd said, feigning sympathy. Sick bastard was enjoying playing with him far too much.

"I have a wife. A daughter," Travis pleaded.

"Do they know you're a violent rapist in your spare time?" I spat.

His only answer was more sobbing. Fuck, I hated when they did that. It was so annoying to listen to.

I gave him a shove. "Answer my questions and maybe they'll get a body to bury."

They wouldn't. He was going in the incinerator when I was done with him, but I needed him to talk. Without the hope of survival, I had to give him something.

Shepherd smoothed a hand over his bloody chin. "Shhh. Don't cry now. Not at the end. You don't want that to be how you go out, do you? Alone? Kicking and screaming and sobbing? Poor thing. It's not your fault you're this way, is it? Nature is cruel."

"I-I never wanted to hurt anybody," Travis stammered, lying through his teeth. "They don't listen. And they fight. I can't help it if they fight me."

"Whoever brings them in should train them better," Shepherd agreed.

He didn't mean it. Shepherd didn't give two shits about any of this. No, he was getting off on manipulating this guy to give me the information I was after. As long as I got to kill him once we had it, I didn't give a fuck how it happened.

Shepherd gripped Travis's pimpled chin almost tenderly, holding him up. "Tell me, what were you doing at The Time Out Room? Why is your name up on a board with all those other losers?"

Travis was shivering, hyperventilating, his pupils dilated, but he was fully invested in whatever was happening between him and Shepherd. "I...I... I got some prize money. There's a pool. It's random. I don't know how they pick. But you pick a name, put down a bet, and once a month it pays out and that name goes away. I won, so I came back to spend my winnings, but the bitch... She bit me. Tried to fucking bite my cock off! It's not my fault. I don't know anything about any babies, I swear!" His eyes darted to me.

Shepherd jerked his chin back so Travis had to look at him. "And who paid you your winnings?" Shepherd asked, massaging Travis's jaw. "Who runs the pool?"

"Some guy named Dmitri. He runs it. He lives over on Garfield and Livingston, man. That's all I know!"

"Dmitri?" I caught Shepherd's eye. "Could be Russian. I thought Niki said his people weren't involved."

"Either someone is lying, or it's coincidence. As a psychiatrist, I can tell you the former is always more likely." He turned back to Travis. "Thank you for your help," he said and promptly slit Travis's throat.

"What the fuck!" I growled. "He was *my* kill!"

"My territory, my kill," Shepherd said, calmly walking back over to his tools while Travis bled out. "You got all the information he had. Someone this low on the menu barely knows anything. We were supposed to be after bigger fish." He started cleaning his knife with a cloth from the kit and glanced over his shoulder at me. "Besides, don't you have a caged bird to look after?"

I looked over at Theo, who was curled up even tighter than before, rocking in place with his chin resting on his knees. Something twisted in my chest. I dropped the sledgehammer and went to him, taking his face in my hands. "Theo?"

He didn't answer, didn't look at me, still staring off in the distance at something that didn't exist.

"Theo, talk to me." I leaned in and brushed my lips over his.

He blinked rapidly, pupils coming back into focus. Tears welled in his eyes, but he didn't acknowledge them. "Can we go home now?"

"Of course, little finch. Why don't you go around the corner and wait for me? I'll just be another minute."

He nodded slowly and rose only to freeze when he found his feet. Theo teetered, breathing quickening as he stared at Travis's lifeless body hanging on the chain.

"Theo."

He flinched at the sound of my voice.

"Go to the next room," I said, injecting as much gentleness in it as I could.

Theo turned, almost as if he were moving on automatic, and walked away without a word.

"What do I do with him now?" I asked Shepherd, who was watching Theo carefully.

"Spoil him," Shepherd said unexpectedly. "Give him time and space to process what he's feeling. Encourage him to feel it and to express what he's feeling however he thinks is appropriate. And in the meantime, you spoil the hell out of that young man, River. It isn't every day you find someone willing to put up with you."

I pushed up to stand, casting one long glance back at Travis. "You're not going to eat him, are you? 'Cause you kinda inferred that you would."

"Cannibalism is taboo for a reason," he said calmly. "Contrary to popular belief, it actually has very little to do with the uncleanliness of corpses and more to do with the intimacy of the act. There is nothing in this world more intimate than taking someone else into your body, whether that is for nourishment or pleasure." He wrinkled his nose as he looked at Travis. "I wouldn't feed him to pigs, let alone dine on him myself. That honor is reserved for worthy prey."

"You could've said no," I pointed out.

He smirked. "And you could have not asked."

Twenty-Six
Theo

I WAS BARELY AWARE of the long drive home and spent it curled up in the back seat of River's car. We must have been nearly there when I snapped out of it enough to realize he was on the phone with someone while driving. I stared at the back of his head, trying to understand the words he spoke in the unfamiliar, frantic tone. It sounded like he was speaking in another language, but I knew he wasn't. I was too out of it to make sense of the words at first.

"No, he's not hurt." A long pause. "Obviously. I don't know." He glanced at me in the rearview. "He's just lying there. It's like he's catatonic. I did ask Shepherd, but his answer didn't make any sense." Another pause, this one longer than the rest. "No. No, Mom. No, I don't want to talk to him." River sighed. "I *know*, but what was I supposed to do? Xavier was adamant that he go. He's an adult. Technically. I know that. He's fine." River sighed. "Well, Xander will have to get over it or go find Xavier himself. I have to take care of Theo. All right. Okay. Yeah. Uh-huh. Thanks. See you tomorrow."

His phone beeped as he hung up. River flung it into the passenger seat, clearly irritated.

I closed my eyes and heard the crunch of bone. My bones. Travis's bones. David's bones. The bones of people I'd never even met.

"Theo?" River's voice.

Cool air washed over my bare arms and I shivered. The direction it was coming from didn't make any sense.

My eyes fluttered open, and I realized we'd stopped. He was holding the door open above my head, waiting for me to get out.

Instead, I rolled my head back to look at him upside down. "I don't want to move."

"Then can I come in to sit with you?" he asked.

I nodded and scooted, sitting up enough to make room for him.

River slid into the back seat with me and closed the door. I lowered my head, letting it rest on his thigh and closing my eyes again.

I should've been terrified of him. It hadn't been that long since I'd watched him brutally beat a man with a sledgehammer after nearly choking the life out of him. Travis had deserved it though, had done worse to other people. He'd probably participated in killing people, or at the very least looked the other way when it happened. Travis was a bad man, and River had helped destroy him, making the world safer. He was like a superhero without the leotard and the cape. A vigilante superhero that killed people and liked it.

But he was my killer. As twisted as that was, I felt safer with him than I'd ever felt in my entire life.

"Can I touch you?" River asked quietly.

I nodded.

Strong fingers combed through my hair, and I smiled. He was petting me.

"When I was ten, I found a stray cat," he said into the darkened, stuffy air of the back seat. "He wasn't very friendly. Wouldn't even take food from my hand. But he'd sit in his tree and watch me, tail waving back and forth. I liked having him there, watching over me. I never felt alone, and he never hurt me or asked for anything from me."

River's hand paused, fingers twitching against my scalp. "Then, one day, he was hit by a car. I tried to take care of him, but he died anyway. And then I couldn't sit under that tree anymore. It didn't feel like a safe place. It felt...haunted."

I looked up at him. "Why are you telling me this?"

"To demonstrate that I can relate to your pain," he said, deadpan. "To empathize."

The ache in my chest deepened. There was a vast canyon between losing a cat he hadn't even named and what I'd just been through, but he was trying so desperately to connect with me. It was like he was standing on one side of that canyon, screaming at the top of his lungs, but when the sound reached me, it was barely a whisper.

I reached up to cup his cheek.

He turned his face and kissed my palm. "It's not the same, is it?"

I shook my head and buried my face against his stomach. "I don't want to talk about it."

"Do you want me to talk about something else? I don't know if I can talk about anything that doesn't involve death, though, so maybe I shouldn't. It's kind of my whole life."

I sighed against him. "It's not that Travis is dead, or even that you tortured him. He deserved to die. I'm glad he's gone, and I'm glad we could help that woman, but seeing him brought back some memories I wish had stayed forgotten."

River moved his hand down from my head to caress my shoulder. "Is there anything you'd like me to do to help? You want some food or a blanket? I can go inside and get a book and read it to you. It'd probably be another science book. I have a new one about mushroom growing I can read to you?"

I smiled into him and sat up, putting my arms around his neck and letting my head rest against his shoulder. "You really like mushrooms, huh?"

"I like understanding life cycles," he explained, rubbing my back. "Mushrooms feed on dead matter and can grow in the most amazing places. Things most life would deem untouchable or inedible are the perfect home for fungi. They thrive on death, but more than that, they're mostly harmless. While they feed on dead organisms, they don't give anything in return. They don't pollute. They're like...the purest form of life."

I chuckled against him, nuzzling in closer. "I like how you explain them."

"Mushrooms were integral to the development of humans," he said, as if he hadn't even heard me. "We've been using them since the dawn of time for food, for altered states... Hell, there have been whole religions that sprang up around them, and there have been so many pieces of great art or scientific breakthroughs thanks to mushrooms. Yet to us, they're ordinary. Just humble little fungi that grow on trees or you put in a salad. They're like... an ordinary miracle. Why are you laughing? They are."

"It's bizarre to hear a serial killer so in awe of life."

River frowned. "Killing is a part of life. Everyone does it on some level. Maybe not to other humans, but anyone who eats meat is contributing to a whole industry that slaughters animals. Vegetarians eat dead plants. Most things are alive at the expense of some other organism, whether that's a bacterium or a cow. Life needs death to thrive. I'm just..." He waved a hand. "Another cog in the machine. A corrective action the universe sometimes makes to right wrongs."

"That's a nice way to think about psychopaths and sociopaths," I mumbled sleepily. "Do you really believe that?"

River shrugged. "Seems about as likely as mushrooms inspiring a world religion. If that can happen, anything can."

I closed my eyes, listening to the sound of his voice as he talked more about the unlikely pairing of atoms and the cycles of life and death. Sometimes, he spoke of it on a cosmic scale, talking about whole galaxies being born, living, and dying in a single breath. The next moment, he'd jump to explaining the life cycles of a particular fungi.

I could've listened to him talk about that nonsense for hours. Whenever River spoke of life and death, he came alive in a way he didn't at any other time. His eyes sparkled and his hand gestures became more animated. Excitement built in his voice, clearly depicting how much he enjoyed the topic.

And then the light suddenly went out of his eyes, and he dropped his hand to his side. His expression flattened and he looked down at me. "I've been talking about myself too much and not letting you get a word in. Mom told me not to do that so much."

I shook my head. "I like listening to you talk. It's comforting."

He smiled and kissed my cheek. "I'm glad. Would you like to go inside? As much as I'd love to stay out here all night talking about mushrooms, it's getting chilly."

"Yeah, I think I need a shower and to brush my teeth again. Then maybe another shower."

"How about a hot bath? It'll feel better."

I agreed to the bath, and we went inside. The house was dark, and there was no sign of Xander, Xavier, or their Uncle Sacha who was supposed to be there. Upstairs, River ran me a hot bath while I brushed my teeth. Then we undressed together and got in the tub where he held me some more.

"This is nice," I said with a contented sigh as I leaned back against him.

"Mmm," he agreed and pulled me closer, running his fingers through my chest hair. "You smell nice when you're wet. The only time you smell better is right after you come."

I chuckled. "That's because I smell like sex and you."

"Well, yeah. I don't see a problem there."

I relaxed against him, letting him slowly explore my chest and stomach with light touches while my cock hardened. An hour ago, I hadn't thought I'd ever want to have sex again. There were too many bad memories associated with those moments. When I was with River, everything felt different. He was the exception to every rule.

I turned my head until my cheek was resting against his chest. "Is Xavier going to be okay?"

River shrugged. "He was shaken, but that was to be expected. Xion's not well, and Xavier is terrified he's going to wind up like him."

"Is it inevitable?" I looked up at him.

"I don't know," he answered earnestly. "But I do know that Xavier has more support than Xion did. Xavier doesn't want to fall apart. Xion did."

I was quiet for a while longer, enjoying his touch. "Did you mean what you said earlier? About letting me tie you up?" I asked after a few minutes had passed.

"Absolutely," came his immediate reply. He dipped his hand below the surface of the bath water, curling his fingers around my cock.

I laughed and spun around, straddling his hips, hands resting on his chest. "You realize you won't be in control? You'll be the one who's totally helpless for a change. I'll get to do whatever I want to you, and there'll be nothing you can do about it."

"Are you hearing any complaints from me?" He grinned and thrust his hips forward, his erection grinding against mine. "You can tie me down and ride me like the prize I am anytime."

I chewed on my lip. "What if I wanted to, say, top you?"

River smirked and gripped my hips, grinding against me. "You want to fuck me, Theo?"

I flushed, fighting the sick feeling starting to rise, pushing it back down. "I've always bottomed. Always, River. I don't know. I thought maybe..." I turned my head and slid away from him. "Never mind. It was a stupid idea."

"No, it isn't." River pulled me back to him. "You want to know what it feels like to be the one with all the power. To be in a role completely opposite the one you associate with what happened to you. Like unearthing that part of you."

I swallowed and nodded. River had put it into words better than I ever could have.

"Okay," he said with a shrug.

My eyebrows shot up. "Seriously?"

"Why not?" He stood, water cascading off his body as he extended a hand to me.

My heart jumped. "Right now?"

River pulled me to my feet and kissed my lips gently. "I thought I made myself clear on day one, Theo. Whatever you need, if I can give it to you, it's yours."

We barely dried off before we tumbled into bed together, kissing, licking, biting at whatever skin we could reach. It wasn't frantic or hurried, just a slow, playful testing of comfort zones. I ended up on top of him and started kissing my way down his body while he massaged my scalp and shoulders. River giggled like a madman when I dragged my tongue over his ribs, so I grinned and did it again.

"I like the sound of your laugh," I told him.

"You might not like what happens if you do that a third time," he warned, a genuine smile on his lips.

"I'm not afraid of you, River Laskin," I teased and licked his ribs again.

He surged up from the bed. I squealed as he tackled me to the mattress, pinning my hands above my head, and then gasped and kicked when he dragged his tongue over my underarm. "Oh my god, River! You're insane!"

"Certifiable," he agreed and kissed me hard.

When we parted, we were both panting. Despite the playful nature of all our wrestling in bed, my cock was painfully hard and throbbing.

River dragged his cock over my hip, leaving a wet smear behind. "You going to fuck me or what, big boy?"

"A little hard to top you when you're holding me down," I pointed out.

He hummed in answer. "True, but I like the view from up here. You're adorable when you're horny and your face is all flushed. Maybe I could ride you instead?"

My cock bucked at the suggestion. I squirmed free of him enough to retrieve the lube from the bedside table and tossed it to him the same way he'd done to me before. "Get yourself ready for me then."

"I've got a better idea," River said, lifting my hand. "Since this is your first time, I want to teach you how to do it."

Before I could object, he slid my fingers into his mouth. My other hand went to my dick, stroking absently as he gave my fingers a sloppy coating with his tongue. "Fuck, River."

"Now, get me ready," he teased, moving my hand behind him and lifting up on his knees.

I shouldn't have been nervous, but I was. I was shaking like I'd never even been with a man before, terrified that I was going to do everything wrong. But River guided my fingers to his entrance and gave me a reassuring kiss, telling me to take my time, so I did. I swirled my finger around his opening, enjoying the way his eyelashes fluttered with pleasure when I did. He groaned when I pushed a single digit in, testing.

"Push deeper, baby," he urged. "You're not going to hurt me."

At least I could be sure of that. I'd already seen River take a lot of pain and knew he could handle it. Still, I didn't want to treat him the way I'd been treated. I wanted him to enjoy this. *I* wanted to enjoy it.

I eased my finger in past the tight ring of muscle at the entrance, marveling at how hot he was inside. It almost seemed like he'd turned into an inferno, burning for me.

River rocked his hips back, pushing my finger even deeper, thighs flexing. He retrieved the bottle of lube and I slicked up my fingers more, adding a second. He moaned loudly and started moving his hips, fucking himself on my fingers. "That's it, little finch. Do you know where my prostate is? A little further forward. A little..."

I knew I'd hit it when his eyes rolled back and he let out a long, low sound.

"Fuuuuck...Theo..."

My cock pulsed, hearing my name like that on his lips. He looked so serene above me, his bottom lip between his teeth, muscles flexing. With each roll of his hips, his cock dragged over my stomach, leaving a trail of glistening wetness behind.

"River," I breathed, stricken suddenly by the sight of him. "God, you're beautiful."

"Fuck, don't say that."

"Why not? It's true."

He leaned forward, his dark hair falling in front of his eyes so that all I saw was his gleaming grin. "Because when you're massaging my prostate, I have no filter. I might say what I'm thinking."

"And what are you thinking, River?"

He shuddered when I said his name, and I gained more confidence, moving my fingers in and out of him more roughly.

I gripped his hip with my free hand, helping him rock back to meet my thrusting fingers. "What does my beautiful, strong, River think about when I tell him he's so goddamn perfect that he looks like a god when the moon hits him just right?"

His fingers curled, nails digging into my chest. "So I'm a god now, am I? If that's true, I might expect you to worship me."

I wanted to, maybe more than anything. I wanted to get down on my knees for River and bask in the glow of him, to lick the sweat from his body and feel his fingers curl in my hair while he fed me his cock like it was my last supper. I wanted to kiss his feet, to cling to him and know that I was his forever. By the dark glint in his eye, I could tell he wanted the same thing.

He leaned forward, seizing me in a claiming kiss that ended with him nipping my bottom lip. "I want you inside me, Theo."

I swallowed my nerves and carefully extracted my fingers. "What should I do?" I asked as he slotted my cock against his opening.

"Just breathe and don't move," he replied as he started to lower himself onto me.

It sounded easy. Just lie there, and sink into the warm, tight bliss that was River. Like most things, though, it was far from it. The minute I felt his body squeeze around mine, my hips tried to jump. I had to clench my muscles tight to keep myself from thrusting up into him.

I was barely in an inch before he pulled back up and I whined at the loss. "Fuck, you're bigger than you look." He grabbed the lube and applied more, both to himself and to me, before trying again.

"River," I whined when he lifted himself once more after having only gone a tiny bit further.

"'Sokay," he mumbled between desperate pants. "I can take it. Just...gimme a sec."

I didn't know if I had a second. His body was so hot and tight around me; I already felt like I was going to explode any second.

Something inside him released and he sank down further with a small grunt. "Fuck."

"Are you okay?" I asked him.

He lifted his chin from his chest and smiled up at me, his forehead glistening with sweat. "This is probably the worst possible time for me to say this, but I've never done this before either."

"River!" I struck him in the shoulder. "Why didn't you tell me?"

"Because I thought if I did, you'd change your mind, and that's the last thing I wanted. I want this." He rolled his hips once, and every ounce of irritation I had with him disappeared into thin air. "I wanted your big cock inside me. I wanted to see that look on your face while I rode you, and I wanted to know that I'm the only one who gets this from you."

He punctuated every sentence with a graceful roll of his body against mine, each one more like heaven than the last. My fingers dug into his thighs, my body already beginning to tremble.

"You can move now," he said, "unless you want me to do it?"

"Yes," I panted. "Make me come."

He smirked. "I can do that."

I shuddered as he started to ride me in earnest, moving on top of me as if he'd done this a thousand times. My hips started to drive up into him. I couldn't stop them. It was as if he'd awakened something in me I hadn't known was there, and all I could think about was chasing my own pleasure. Somewhere distant in my brain, it registered that I should be touching him, pleasuring him, but I couldn't force my body to move the way I wanted it to.

It didn't seem to matter to River, because he gripped his cock with a slick fist and started pumping it in time with my thrusts. "That's it, little finch. I need to feel you come inside me. Make a fucking mess of me and fill me up. All I want is you in there."

"F-f-fuck, River!" I gasped and yanked him down hard as I came almost without warning.

He grunted as my cock spilled inside of him, his hand twisting over the head of his cock. With a loud curse, his body tightened around me, spasming in time with mine. River doubled over, stomach muscles clenching as he coated my stomach with his cum. I tried to keep moving, to find a rhythm that worked between us, but it was like we'd both short-circuited and nothing worked. For a minute, we were lost in the chaos of each other, and it was pure bliss.

"Fuck," River panted when he could finally draw a full breath. "Just...fuck."

"Are you okay?" I reached up to touch his cheek.

He leaned into the touch, kissing my palm. "Yeah. Better than okay, actually. If I'd known it'd be like that, I'd have been riding a lot more dick. That was fucking amazing."

"Hey!" I gave his ass a slap. "This is the part where you say it was amazing because it was me and not some random hookup."

He chuckled and leaned down to kiss my nose. "Of course. That's exactly what I meant."

We separated with a small groan, and I cleaned myself off with a discarded t-shirt before doing the same for River as he stretched out in bed beside me.

"It's all right," I relented once I'd fully caught my breath. "I'm kind of bad at topping, though, aren't I? I mean, I still wound up on the bottom. Or does it still count since I was the one doing the penetrating?"

River shrugged and slid an arm under my shoulders, drawing me to him. "Top, bottom...whatever. End of the day, what matters is you enjoyed yourself and so did I. Whatever it was you'd call that, we gotta do it more often. I don't think I've ever come so hard in my life."

I laughed, but it was cut short when River lifted my chin and I found myself staring into one of his intense gazes.

"You did enjoy that, right?" he asked. "It wasn't...triggering or anything?"

"Not triggering at all," I said, and it was true. If anything, that experience had given me a ridiculous boost of confidence, even if it hadn't gone the way I planned it in my head. I kissed his chin. "Thank you, River."

He cocked his head to one side. "What for?"

"For being you."

He laughed like my statement was ridiculous and feathered his fingers through my sweaty hair. "Who else would I be?"

Twenty-Seven

River

THEO WOKE UP WITH a sudden gasp and sat straight up, panting, unfocused terror in his eyes. Bright sunlight washed over his pale skin, making it look more milky white than usual.

I was barely awake myself, but I already wanted to raise Travis from the dead and take him apart limb by limb. "It's okay," I murmured, sitting up and lazily throwing my arms around his shoulders. "You're safe now."

He relaxed against me. "I'm sorry."

"Don't be. It's just a nightmare." I pressed a kiss to his shoulder and inhaled deeply. He smelled like fear, sweat, and sex with a hint of the strawberry shampoo I'd bought for him. The combination had me harder than steel.

I was tempted to pull him back to bed and fuck him until he forgot all about his nightmare, but Mom had told me I should be careful not to let him avoid dealing with his emotions. Sex was an avoidance technique, and I wanted him to get better so I could have all of his attention. Still, I couldn't stop myself from peppering kisses down his back.

Theo twisted in my arms. "What time is it? Aren't you going to be late for work?"

"Screw work," I said and sank my teeth into his shoulder. "Let's stay in bed all day and fuck."

"Won't your dad be mad though?"

I growled as he untangled himself from me. Dad was the last person I wanted to talk about when Theo was naked in my bed. "Let him be mad," I said and pounced on him.

Theo gasped as I pinned him to the bed and whined loudly when I bit his collarbone, but he rolled his hips into me just the same, already hard. "Jesus, River."

Someone was suddenly pounding on my bedroom door.

"Go away," I snarled over my shoulder.

"Good morning to you, too," came Uncle Sacha's voice through the door. "When you're done fucking, you need to come downstairs for a family meeting."

"Ugh." I groaned and rolled off of Theo. Uncle Sacha really knew how to kill the mood. "Does nobody in this family respect a locked front door? C'mon. Let's go shower real quick," I muttered, pulling on my robe.

After a quick shower, Theo and I made our way down to the formal dining room, where most of the family was already gathered. Everyone except for Shepherd, of course, who never came to family meetings and yet somehow always knew everyone's business.

Uncle Sacha stood at the head of the table, leaning over some printouts of the photos we'd taken the night before. Mom and Tatty sat to one side and Dad was on the other, examining the print outs. His eyes flicked up to me, a vague hint of irritation on his face. He didn't like it when I wasn't on time, but it wasn't like this meeting had been scheduled.

"There he is!" boomed a deep voice with a heavy Russian accent.

Uncle Sacha was a big man, both in height and width. Every time I'd ever seen him, he'd been in a brightly colored track suit and enough gold chains to rival Fort Knox.

His bald head shone in the low light as he stood and extended his meaty hands to grasp mine. "Hello, nephew," he said in Russian. "How are you, eh?"

"I'm fine," I replied in English. "Good to see you too, Uncle Sacha. This is Theo."

"His boyfriend," Xander said in a stage whisper.

"Good thing I brought my ear plugs!" Sacha boomed with laughter and patted Theo's back.

Not that he'd need them. Uncle Sacha snored so loud we'd probably be the ones sleeping with earplugs in.

Theo coughed and shied away from Uncle Sacha. "Um. Hi."

Niki appeared practically out of nowhere, stepping out from the shadows to my right.

"Jesus, man," I hissed. "Fucking make some sound when you walk."

He grinned. "How will I sneak up on you then? Hello again, Theo."

"Morning...sir," Theo offered politely.

Dad cleared his throat, his glare silently demanding that we come to order.

"Now that we're all finally here," said Dad, throwing a look at me as Theo and I sank into the last two empty seats in the dining room, "we can go over what we have from all our different sources. But before we begin, Theo... How are you? Are you feeling up to revisiting the events of last night?"

Theo's fingers closed around mine and he nodded.

"Are you sure?" War asked. "Because we are going to talk about some uncomfortable topics."

I squeezed Theo's hand and gave him a reassuring nod.

He blew out a slow breath. "Yeah. I'm good."

"Okay, then." Dad stood and handed the business part of it over to Niki with a glance.

Niki crossed one leg over the other, his trusty legal pad in his lap. "Let's start with what we know about this operation. We know that The Time Out Room provided space and access through a man known as Dmitri. Last night's interrogation provided a vague address. We know that Theo was being held with others in a house that has since been vacated, which means any other boys in Theo's age group were likely moved to a new house."

"If they weren't killed outright," Xander said.

Everyone glared at him.

He shrugged. "What? It's a possibility."

"I have men watching the corner of Garfield and Livingston," Sacha said. "Traditionally, that's the edge of Greek territory, and we have a strong relationship with them, so Niki and I reached out to them. They'd heard of someone named Dmitri who ran a betting operation and gave me what they had. He's some kind of small-time gang banger with lots of little fingers in lots of little pies."

"Another middleman," Xavier said with a sigh. "When do we get to the good stuff?"

"Dmitri Federoff," Niki said, passing papers around the table. "Assault and battery, possession with intent, vandalism and petty theft. Most recently, he did four years of a six-year sentence for armed robbery and found God in prison. Officially, he's employed as a custodian at Saint Niklaus Orthodox Church, which also runs a soup kitchen and a homeless shelter."

That piqued my interest. Xion had mentioned a church. Maybe his information was good after all, even if it was frustratingly vague.

"Sounds like someone that should have been on our radar already," War said.

Tatty took one of the sheets of paper, frowning at it. "Why don't I know this name?"

"Because he's never dealt in big money," Niki clarified. "On the inside, he ran with the NLR and not the AB."

"NLR? AB?" Theo asked. "What does all that mean?"

"AB stands for the Aryan Brotherhood," War supplied. "White supremacists."

"Our organization occasionally has to do business with the AB," Niki said, "but nobody likes it."

Xander sat back, folding his arms. "And the NLR are the Nazi Lowriders. Yeah. Those kind of Nazis. Bad dudes."

"We do not do business with Nazis," Niki clarified firmly.

Tatty clicked her tongue. "We're killing this one, *da*? My grandmother didn't survive the Holocaust so scum like this could breathe in our city."

"As quickly as we can," Dad agreed.

"He has easy access to vulnerable populations and connections," Sacha said. "Perfect hunting grounds for trafficking."

I took the page and scowled at it, the words blurring together. "What's this piece of shit doing working with women and kids?"

Theo shook his head. "I've never seen him before."

"You wouldn't," Sacha explained. "I believe he's a scout and a money man. His job would be to single out potential targets. Someone else does the grab."

"And he has plenty of targets to choose from," Mom said. "Poverty in this area is very high. Teen pregnancy is through the roof, and access to proper medical care is daunting. Saint Niklaus has an outreach ministry that specifically caters to pregnant women with nowhere else to turn. It's one of the oldest operations in the city, stretching back to the fifties. Paperwork on what happens to the babies is...sketchy. They seem to get sent to a private children's home in Westerville, but as far as I can tell, the Westerville home only exists on paper."

"Fuck," I muttered and exchanged another knowing look with Xavier.

"Xion *was* telling the truth," Xavier said and deflated in his chair.

"It's a baby farm," I said, fingers curling against the table. "Or a version of one. They target impoverished women, addicts, and teenage mothers who can't afford to raise a kid and don't have access to abortion care either due to their circumstances or religious background. Tell them they'll take care of all the paperwork, get them to sign their babies over to them, maybe even deliver them in-house to keep the hospitals out of it, marketing it as a discreet delivery. Then the babies are given to wet nurses who've already been secured. Usually immigrants here illegally. They're essentially raised from birth to be free labor."

"That seems likely," Sacha agreed grimly.

"Shit," Xander said, lip curling. "You're talking about *slavery*."

"If you're right, this operation has got to be, like, massive," Xavier added. "We're talking a multi-level scheme."

"That's not even the worst of it." Sacha held up one of the printouts of the chalkboards we'd taken pictures of the night before. "I believe each one of these rows is someone in that system, and the secondary operation that Dmitri Federoff is running is a dead pool. They're letting frequent customers bet on who the organization is going to kill first, and he takes a cut."

"You mean like David?" Theo asked, his tone flat. His leg was shaking under the table.

I put my hand over his knee and he instantly relaxed.

"I doubt David is the first or only victim," War said carefully.

Niki tapped his pencil on the table. "Keeping helpless people alive is expensive. The people behind this operation had to provide food, clothing, medical care, transportation, and time for each of you. They looked at each of you as an investment. If the return on that investment were to dwindle enough, they'd have no qualms about cutting ties and moving on, making space for a new one."

"Younger victims bring in more money," Sacha said with a nod. "Young boys are the most profitable investment, but that investment would lose value as the boy ages, especially if he begins to talk back."

Theo shuddered and leaned into me.

I massaged his thigh. "So Dmitri's double dipping, and The Time Out Room is what? Just renting space?"

"That's how it looks on paper," Xavier said. "Their books register a monthly rental fee from a DMF every month on the first."

"You hacked their books?" Theo said, dumbfounded.

Xavier snorted. "Not like it was hard. They're using QuickBooks."

Shepherd wasn't going to be happy that we hadn't found a definitive way to link his archenemy Jeff to this, but he could deal.

"So, when do we get this Dmitri guy?" I demanded.

Niki huffed. "*You* don't. We don't operate inside Greek territory, and he's across the line, but I've arranged something with the Greeks to make sure he's delivered to us alive so we can question him."

"I'm sure Nigel will be happy to let us take out the trash for him," Dad said, pushing up to stand at his full height for the first time.

Mom crossed her arms. "I'm more concerned about the women that are still being lured in."

Tatty nodded. "We should shut the church down if we can."

Theo glanced around the table, blinking rapidly. "You can do that?"

"Temporarily," I said with a shrug. "All we have to do is cut through the right pipe or bribe someone at the gas company to say there's a gas leak. Nobody questions an attractive blue-collar guy in a uniform and a name badge."

"It will buy us some time," Mom agreed.

Theo's head moved as he looked around the table, his breathing still fast. "Why are you doing all this? This is… It's a lot. You're going through a lot of trouble, putting yourselves at risk, and you barely even know me."

Mom smiled and reached across the table to put her hand over his. "Theo, sweetie, you're *family*."

"Even if that were not the case," Niki said, standing, "this has been operating under our noses all this time, and neither the Volkovs nor the Costas have been cut in. That makes them competition. Disrespectful competition. The Costas don't appreciate that, and we Volkovs certainly don't either."

Theo shuddered.

"This is what we do, Theo. When we see something wrong and we can fix it, we do." I lifted Theo's other hand and kissed his knuckles.

Xavier made a gagging sound. "Gross."

I snarled at him like a feral dog, showing my teeth.

Xander shrugged. "You gotta admit, bruh, PDA is kinda cringe."

"But what if you get caught?" Theo insisted, ignoring Xander and Xavier. "You could go to prison for life, River. You could get the death penalty if they ever find out what you've been doing!"

"That is my job," Niki said with a bob of his head. "You let me worry about all the legal issues. I didn't spend all those years in law school and perfecting this gorgeous American accent for nothing, you know."

Dad flushed slightly when Niki grinned at him.

I rolled my eyes and thought, *Get a fucking room, preferably far, far from me.*

Sacha nodded. "And if all else fails, there is a place in Paris if you ever need it."

I grinned and winked at Theo. "I'll help you with your French anytime."

Xavier gagged again. Xander punched him in the shoulder.

"So, what are our assignments?" I asked, more to keep Theo from hyper focusing on his worry than anything else. I knew this was going to be a hurry up and wait operation, and I always hated those. But if the Greeks and the Russians had a deal, even I wasn't stupid enough to get in the middle of that.

"War and Annie will pay a visit to Saint Niklaus'," Dad said. "Xander and Xavier will run down this little black book that Dmitri was so kind to tell us about. Let's get the paper trail set up to lead straight where we want it."

"Follow the money it is," Xander quipped.

"I'm going for a spa day," Tatty offered. "One of the ladies there has an ex she's still friendly with whose brother is a guard up at Youngstown. If anyone knows about Dmitri's NLB days, it'd be in the system. Maybe I can get some juicy deets."

"And I have legal paperwork to do," Niki said.

Dad nodded. "As for us, River, we have two bodies to cremate this week. I suggest we focus on the work at hand and let Sacha and Niki's people do their job."

Sacha came around and patted my shoulder. "Clean your basement and sharpen your tools. Let me bring this one to you, nephew."

Twenty-Eight

Theo

River and I went back to the funeral home where Yuri decided we'd work a half day. Routine, he said, was good for everyone. While River prepared the bodies, Yuri handed me some spray and a soft rag with instructions to dust the place from top to bottom. When I was done dusting, he showed me how to use the vacuum to take care of the carpets and how to wipe down surfaces with special wipes.

Around four o'clock, Yuri interrupted my work with a somber apology.

"David's body has been prepared for cremation," he said, folding his hands. "We were wondering if you'd like to say a few words?"

I chewed my bottom lip, glancing past him to the stairs and nodding. No one else was going to say anything. Might as well be me.

My stomach was tied up in knots as Yuri escorted me to the back of the building, but we didn't go into the embalming room, instead going down the hall into a large, open space. There was a large furnace encased in metal, the sound of it running loud enough to drown out the sound of my own heartbeat in my ears.

There was a short mechanical belt, and on that belt was a coffin made of thin wood. The lid was off, leaning against the belt next to where River stood. Even though I had already seen him, I steeled myself before stepping up to the thin coffin.

He looked like he was asleep. Peaceful. They'd done as I had asked, discarding the ratty clothes he'd been wearing when he was dumped, and instead he was fitted with a nice jacket, a clean white t-shirt, and plain black slacks. His hair was swept to one side, trimmed, and styled. He looked like a Bible salesman who'd fallen asleep in the wrong place, not a sex slave who'd been murdered.

It looked like David if David had lived a better life, a nicer life, but it wasn't David. David was gone. These were just his atoms. Hydrogen, oxygen, and all the other things River had named off the night before. A common miracle in a box who'd had sentience for a little while. Now that part of him was gone, and all that remained was to return him to an inert state.

Ashes to ashes.

I realized everyone was waiting for me to say something, but I didn't have any stories to tell. What little I had to say about him to other people had already been said, so I spoke to the shell that remained.

"I'm sorry you didn't get to know freedom in life," I said, looking at his serene face. "You deserved better. We all did. I wish I could promise you that we're going to get these bastards for what they did to us, but the truth is, I don't believe in a big, cosmic scale. Vengeance doesn't balance trauma. It'll never bring you back so that you can know what I know, that there are good people in the world. Vengeance isn't for the dead. It's for the living, so I can't promise it to you. But I can promise you that you won't be forgotten."

With that, I lowered my head and stepped back. Yuri nodded to River, who carefully lifted the lid and secured it on the coffin, covering him one last time.

Yuri's hand closed on my shoulder. "Would you like to do the honors?" he asked, gesturing to a big, red button on the wall.

I walked over and pushed it. A large black door on the cremator opened and the belt whirred to life. Heat breathed on my face, making the air go wavy as the box rolled into the cremator. The black door slid shut, and that was that.

"We are going to get them," River promised me.

I blinked and tears fell, but I didn't feel sad. I was furious. David had died afraid and alone in dirty clothes, never knowing what it was like to have someone hold him and tell him he was made of the same atoms as far away galaxies. He'd never known what it was like to have a family, to be taken care of, to fall asleep safe in someone else's arms. It wasn't *fair*.

I pushed the tears away with a fist and looked straight into River's eyes. "When you go for Master, I want to be the one to finish him. I need to look him in the eyes and watch them go dull. I need to do it, River."

River glanced over at Yuri, who nodded once. "It's your right," River said.

Yuri patted my shoulder. "The rest will take some time. Why don't you two go home for the day? I'll bring the urn by in the morning before tomorrow's service."

I WAS QUIET FOR the short drive home, my mind empty. While I wasn't as numb as I'd been the night before, everything I'd been through was beginning to weigh on me. I was tired. Just...tired.

River put the car in park and looked over at me. "Tell me what you need, Theo."

My hands clenched where they rested on my knees, but I didn't know how to answer him. I didn't know what I needed, and even if I had, I couldn't put it into words. There was a balloon in my chest swelling and swelling and swelling, getting ready to pop.

Hot tears raced down my cheeks. I didn't even try to stop them. "Why didn't I run away?" I asked no one in particular. "There were so many opportunities to escape, so many people I could have asked to help me. I could have fought back, could have screamed. Why didn't I fight harder?"

"Because you'd been conditioned since birth not to," River said plainly. "They used psychology to make you docile."

I shook my head and sniffled. "No. I knew I should run. I thought about it a lot. I'd look at the doors and think, 'If I'm quick, I can make it.' But I never even tried. I'm such a fucking coward, River. I couldn't even save myself."

River took my face in his hands, making me look at him. "If you'd run, they would have caught you, and then you'd be the one dead now."

"I should have tried." I was breathing hard, the balloon in my chest stretched to its limit.

"Even if you had gotten to the authorities, it would have been too late to do anything," River insisted. "People like this, they have multiple safehouses, multiple people in charge at several sites. If they thought they were about to be exposed, they'd have executed everyone and burned wherever they were holding you in to the fucking ground only to pop up somewhere else three months later."

My jaw trembled. "How do you know?"

"I know because it's what I would do." His gaze softened and he brushed a hand through my hair. "Why do you think I'm so good at hunting and killing these parasites? Because I can think like them. For normal people like you, it'd be unthinkable. But for monsters like me?" He shook his head. "I'd be like them if not for Mom and Dad."

"You're nothing like them, River," I exclaimed and threw my arms around his neck. "You're not a monster! Stop saying that!"

"Theo..." He said it with a sigh, as if he were frustrated with me.

Why wouldn't he be? I was weak. Pathetic. I had let people do all those awful things to me, just laid there and let them put their hands on me. I never even said no. I didn't fight. Didn't scream. Most of the time, I didn't even cry. I did what I was told. Why didn't I fight harder? I didn't deserve the freedom I had. I didn't deserve to escape Master.

I held onto River and sobbed into him, wallowing deep in my self-loathing. Disgusted. Angry. Drowning in guilt over something I couldn't control.

"I should be dead," I managed through shaky gulps of air. "I wish I was."

"I don't." River pulled my head back, darkness flashing in his chestnut eyes. "If anything ever happened to you... Fuck the Russians.

Fuck the Greeks. Fuck them all, Theo. Everyone who isn't us. I would rather burn it all down than lose you."

I shook my head. "I don't want to die. I just don't want living to hurt anymore. I'm so tired, River. I'm tired of the flashbacks and the nightmares and flinching every time someone touches me. Living like this is worse than being dead. I'm trapped in this state of half-existence, surviving but not living, and I don't know how to make it stop. I want to remember what it feels like to be *alive,* dammit!" My fists flew to my forehead as if I could somehow fight my own mind.

River's hands closed gently over my tight fists and eased them down into my lap. "I think I can help with that part," he offered quietly. "At least tonight."

He got out of the car and came around to open the door for me. Instead of letting me get out, he leaned in and hit the release for my seatbelt before scooping me up in his arms in a bridal carry. I was half afraid he was going to drop me as he carried me up the stairs, but he didn't. River was strong. River was brave. He was good. Not a monster, even if he could think like them. He was the darkness monsters feared.

River put me down to unlock the front door and then guided me through it, pulling my lips to his once we were on the other side. My breath caught, and I braced for teeth in my skin, but they never came. He kissed me slowly, gently, as if I were made of glass.

The thought made something in me snap. I surged into him with enough force to knock him against the wall. He hit it with a grunt that barely made it out of his mouth before I had him pinned in place, one hand wrapped around his throat, my teeth in his bottom lip. I pulled my teeth away and moved my hand up to grip his jaw, a thrill going through me at the sight of blood on his lip.

Jesus, maybe I was disturbed too.

"I shouldn't like seeing you bleed," I said.

River smirked, red smearing across his front teeth. "But you do, don't you? Admit it."

"Yes," I growled and kissed him again.

He parted the seam of my lips with his tongue, filling my mouth with the taste of copper and salt. I couldn't stop the groan that bubbled up from my throat. The balloon swelling in my chest seemed to shrink, the pressure releasing.

He leaned into me, grinding against me through our clothes.

I pushed him back against the wall, holding him there by his shoulder. "Why do I like hurting you?"

"Who cares about the why? I'm into it. I like this side of you. Go on. Take charge. Tell me what to do. Manhandle me, Theo."

I wasn't sure I liked that side of me, but fuck it. We were already there. If River was into it, why not?

He made a disappointed sound as I reached to undo his belt. "Giving up already?"

"Not even close." I undid his belt and yanked it through the loops. "Hands," I demanded, and River presented his hands, wrists together.

The belt wasn't the most effective restraint, especially if he struggled, but I'd had one tied around my wrists enough times to know exactly how to use it to my advantage. I tried not to think about how fucked up the thrill I got was. Here I was, taking something that had been done to me against my will, and using that knowledge with River. I hadn't wanted what happened to me, but he did. I couldn't explain why, but it felt like a reclamation of sorts. I needed to do it, fucked up as it was.

River gave his bound hands a testing tug. "Not bad."

I didn't answer him, sinking to my knees to unzip his pants. I yanked them and his boxers down in one swift move, freeing his already hard cock. He hissed as I ran my tongue down his length, looping his bound hands behind my head for leverage.

"I want you to know I can make you come in less than three minutes if I wanted to," I said. "I'm a fucking expert at blowjobs."

One of his eyebrows shot up. "And why do I need to know that?"

"Because I don't want you to come until I say you can."

He pursed his lips. "Ooh. I like this game."

"You might change your mind in three minutes," I told him and wrapped my lips around him.

"Fuck," he murmured and leaned his head back to hit the wall.

River moved his hips, chasing the slick heat of my mouth as it retreated, and I let him. He was only torturing himself, and he knew it. I'd laid the rules out, and he'd agreed. Maybe he thought I'd cave, but I was determined not to.

Even with his wrists bound, he found a way to grip me by the hair, but he didn't push or try to direct the pace other than thrusting his hips. That, he left up to me, and I swallowed him until I gagged. The wet sucking sounds filled the empty hallways, echoing. I hoped Sacha wasn't there. Actually, I didn't care. Let him walk in on us. Let him see how fucking perfect we were together, how much River needed me and I needed him.

"Fucking hell, Theo," River panted. "I'm close already."

I pulled my lips off of him with a loud, wet sound and he groaned in frustration. River's cock was hard as steel, jutting straight forward and flushed. His soft, velvety skin shimmered in the afternoon light. I kissed his thighs, dragged my teeth over his hips while he instinctively tried to chase my mouth, seeking the relief I wouldn't allow him to have.

I gave him about thirty seconds to cool down and then I was back at it. The bitter, salty taste of his pre-cum coated my tongue and I moaned, the sound vibrating down his shaft. That was what I needed, a taste of life to wash the sour flavor of death from my tongue.

"Theo..." His voice came out in a whine, and he started to squirm so I pulled away. River made a sound halfway between a laugh and a sob. "Oh, you..." He inhaled sharply through his teeth. "You're awful."

I smirked and gave his twitching cock a flick, making him double over and shiver. "You like it."

Before he could make one of his smart comebacks, my lips were on him again, teasing him back to the edge once, twice, three times more. Each time I denied him, he got more desperate, even trying to get free of the crude restraint I'd fashioned. I stilled him by kissing and sucking on his balls, running my teeth over his hip, massaging his thighs and stomach in soothing circles.

"Theo," he barked after the fifth time I pulled away, denying him the release he sought. "You need to let me come."

"I don't *need* to do shit," I shot back at him, earning a growl that sent a shiver through me. There was the feral River I was after.

"Are you trying to make me tackle you?"

"Good luck with your hands bound," I told him and licked a heavy drop of pre-cum from where it was dripping freely. "Unless you think you can get free?"

He growled and wrenched his right hand down with a slight twist. Fear flickered through me as the belt came free, and I scrambled to my feet to run for the bedroom.

River caught me in the sitting room. Strong fingers twisted in my hair, and he spun me around to slam his mouth into mine. I'd never thought a kiss could be so full of anger and heat, but that one was. River's rage was boiling over, and knowing I had brought him to that point sent a shuddering thrill to me. He might have been the one calling the shots, but he wasn't in control. I was. I'd turned him into this needy, snarling beast that only I could satisfy, and I was proud of my work.

He yanked my head back by the hair mid-moan. "I'm going to fuck you so hard you can't move."

"Promises, promises," I chided with a smirk.

He spun me and shoved me against the arm of the sofa. Weight settled between my shoulders, bending me in half. Old habits kicked in and I submitted without so much as a whimper of complaint. My head started to go to that place, separated from my body.

River brought me back with a bite to my shoulder. "Don't do that," he whispered into my skin. "Don't check out on me. Fight me."

I stiffened, aware of that swelling balloon in my chest again. Fight him? Why would I fight him? I wanted this, had practically begged for it.

Because I couldn't fight before, I realized. Was this his way of drawing a line between then and now? Was it manipulation? Or maybe he got off on overpowering a victim.

This was a dangerous game to play with a killer, maybe the most dangerous game.

"Fight me," River insisted and spun me around to face him, "or I'm gonna lose interest."

"Fuck you." I shoved him back.

"That's the idea." He reached for my hands.

I pulled away, keeping my arms out of reach. River leaned into me with all his weight, pinning me in place to the point that it made my legs ache, but there was something exciting about this new game. I wanted him to catch me, to make me, but I wanted him to work for it. The harder he was willing to do that and the more he was willing to endure to get me, the more excited I got. Maybe it was the adrenaline, but I drew back a hand and slapped him across the face. Hard. His head jerked to one side, and I panicked, immediately dropping the act.

"Oh my god. Are you okay, River?" I pushed his hair back to have a look. At first, the bright red mark on his cheek sent a shock of horror through me. I had done that. I'd *hit* him. He'd rescued me and I'd hurt him.

Then I saw his smirk. He looked back at me, the earlier cut in his lip opened again. His pink tongue dragged over the fresh smear of dark blood. "You'll have to do better than that if you want to hurt me, little finch," he said and crashed our mouths together.

The fresh taste of blood and his demanding touch drove me wild. I started pulling off my clothes so fast that I heard fabric rip. River yanked his shirt over his head and threw it behind him. When we were both naked, we fell onto the sofa, him on top of me. The wooden frame groaned under the force of our impact, but we were too lost in each other to care. His hot lips roved over my chest and arms. Hungry teeth nipped at my skin, pinching it into little lines of fiery pain that he soothed with his tongue.

I gave as good as I got, biting and sucking on any skin that I could find. My fingers coiled strands of dark hair around them and yanked until I worried I'd pull his hair clean out. I squirmed under his weight, kicking half-heartedly until he pushed my legs apart and settled between them.

River paused long enough to fish out his wallet and retrieve a tiny disposable packet of lube. "Get your legs up on my shoulders," he ordered and ripped the packet open with his teeth.

"Make me," came my breathless reply.

He did, grabbing them one at a time and forcing my calves onto his shoulders. I lifted my hips off the sofa in one last challenge, but it wasn't enough to keep him from spearing me with two slick digits. I gasped and tipped my head back with a loud curse.

"Who do you belong to?" River demanded, working his fingers in and out of me.

I bit my lip, refusing to let him win that easily.

"Fine with me if you want to keep playing the brat." He pulled his fingers free of me and shifted my hips, lining up to seat himself in a single rough thrust.

I gasped as he filled me, the dizzying mix of pain and pleasure impossible to process at first.

River didn't give me time to recover either, rolling his hips and making my toes curl. "Whose ass is this?" He thrust into me hard enough that I couldn't keep my mouth shut.

I cried out, the answer coming out of me on automatic. "Yours!"

"That's right," he snarled and closed his fist around my leaking cock, jerking violently. "And this big cock, who's that belong to?"

I propped myself up on my elbows, watching him drive himself in and out of me, watching him work his slick fist over my cock with enough force I could barely think. "You! It's yours!"

Teeth grazed the inside of my thigh. "Say my name, little finch."

"River," I panted, pleasure and pressure coiling low against my spine.

He shifted his angle, driving into me harder, dragging over my prostate with every thrust. "Louder."

"River!"

"I didn't hear you," he taunted. "Give it to me *louder*, Theo."

I came screaming his name over and over again, so loud that the neighbors might have actually heard me. I was too far gone to care, too wrapped up in the orgasm quaking through me.

River's mouth found mine as his hips stuttered, moaning against my tongue as he came.

"Fuck," he panted and went boneless on top of me, letting my legs fall. "Fuck, Theo. That was..."

"Worth waiting for?" I grinned at how wrecked he sounded.

River nodded. "Very worth it." He lifted his head, letting his chin rest on my sternum. "Are you okay?"

"Yeah," I replied, voice hoarse. "My throat's sore from screaming, and I'm sure I'll be feeling some of that tomorrow, but I'm fine."

"I meant up here." He tapped my forehead. "Hell of a mindfuck, what you just did."

I let my head fall back and stared up at the textured ceiling. "Jesus Christ. I hit *you*. I should be the one asking if you're okay."

"That made me hard as fuck, just so we're clear. I asked you to fight me, remember?"

"Yeah..." I ran my fingers through my messy, sweaty hair. "It was kind of fucked up, though, right?"

"Who cares if it is? We're both breathing and you enjoyed yourself. There's cum all the way up in your hair, Theo. You clearly needed that."

I blushed so hard, I thought my face might catch fire.

River rose on his arms and planted a kiss on the end of my nose. "Second, I like having to work for it. You're worth it. You could fight me a lot harder, and it'd just turn me on more."

"I don't want to be like Travis," I said quietly.

"You're not, little finch. He hurt people who couldn't fight back. I can. Everything you give to me, I can give you back twice over. You aren't going to hurt me."

I ran my thumb over his split lip. "This says otherwise."

"I'll heal," he promised, kissing my hand. "Our power exchange is consensual. That's what makes it hot, knowing you're fighting me because you trust me not to lose it with you. No one's ever trusted me like that before."

My throat was suddenly tight, emotion threatening to overwhelm me.

"Besides," River cut in with a grin before it could, "I look hot as hell with a bloody lip."

That made me smile. "Yeah, you do."

"Anytime you want to get feral and fight it out, little finch, you let me know." He kissed me playfully before sitting up. "Now, how about some chicken nuggets? I'm starving."

River hopped up and went into the kitchen, not even bothering to retrieve his pants.

Twenty-Nine
River

THE NEXT FEW DAYS were routine, or at least as routine as they could be. Theo and I woke up, fucked, went to work, ate food, fucked some more. Bodies came in, went out, went in the dirt, went in the cremator.

All the while, my hands itched to feel the crack of bone. I dreamt of faces I'd never seen and smashing them in with crowbars and hammers after they confessed to the horrible things they'd done to Theo. My dreams became a landscape of wrecked bodies and bloody concrete, broken only by my name on Theo's lips.

On the fourth day, Theo and I curled up on the old sofa in front of some animated movie he'd wanted to see while I skimmed the latest digital edition of *Morgue Science*.

Keys jingled and Uncle Sacha appeared like a shadow on a brick wall next to the sofa. Theo stiffened and started to sit up.

"Is it happening?" I asked, pausing the movie.

He nodded. "I'm off to pick up your present. I'm told he's in a very talkative mood. It'll be a few hours. I'm taking the hearse up."

"Thank you, Uncle Sacha," I said with a nod.

"Bah, it's nothing. But if you want to thank me, you can give your cousins some relationship advice. Aleksi in particular. That boy needs someone to keep him in line." He shook his head.

I snorted. The day Aleksi Laskin took advice from anyone would be the day the world ended. He was as hard-headed and stubborn as they came. It was a moot point anyway, since I was pretty sure Aleksi was also a total closet case in denial. Anybody who spent as much time as he did bragging about being straight was most definitely not.

"I'll see you in a few hours, yes?" Uncle Sascha said, spinning his key ring on a finger.

I nodded and Uncle Sacha left. As soon as he was gone, I unpaused the movie, kissed Theo, and slid out from under him.

"Where are you going? Don't you want to finish watching *Encanto* with me?" Theo asked.

I shook my head. "I have to get ready."

"Then let me come with you." He picked up the remote and paused the movie in the middle of yet another song.

I studied Theo. Watching me and Shepherd torture Travis hadn't gone well, and I was starting to worry that he might not have the stomach for that side of my life, despite his objections. If I denied him, though, he'd be upset with me, and I didn't want that.

"You can come," I said, nodding.

The ritual always began the same way; I took a shower. Even though Theo was with me, it wasn't like our normal showers, which usually ended with one of us giving the other a blowjob or a hand job. I scrubbed myself head to toe, working the lather in and visualizing washing my skin away so that I only existed in the barest sense of the word.

I shaved, even though I didn't need to, and applied aftershave, standing naked in front of the mirror. For a moment, I allowed myself to think of my mother.

It was the only time I allowed such melancholy. Sometimes, I wondered what she would think of me, if she'd ever thought of me at all. I didn't remember a lot from those early days, but I had never thought of my mother with any fondness. She'd always loved heroin more than she'd ever loved me. Maybe the addiction had robbed her of her ability to love. Maybe she was like me and never had it in the first place. They did say certain disorders had a genetic component. Or maybe it was because my father was like the men who'd hurt and tortured Theo. Maybe that was why she'd never wanted anything to do with me, because I was the living, breathing manifestation of her trauma.

That trauma ate her from the inside out, flowed through her veins from little black dabs heated in burnt metal spoons. I had watched her rot, watched the flies crawl in and out of her nostrils and lay eggs in the places no life had been for a long time. Her death gave birth to a thousand swarming flies, and to me, or at least what I became.

Life was a cycle, and I was simply the next evolutionary step in a closed circle.

So was Dmitri Federoff, but I couldn't look into his eyes and see myself. We were not the same. He operated out of filthy back rooms, dirt and blood under his fingernails and the stink of cigarette smoke in his hair.

I stood in front of the mirror, running a fine-toothed comb through my hair until it was perfect, and then I trimmed my fingernails with meticulous attention, scrubbing under them for good measure. Then I donned my white scrubs, opened my closet, and retrieved one of eight pairs of white tennis shoes I owned.

I was hungry when we made it downstairs, but I didn't eat, nor did I offer anything to Theo. It would be better if he only had liquid in his stomach. When I offered him water, he took it and sipped it.

"Are you ready?" I asked him. "This won't be like last time. Shepherd isn't here and his methods are...different from mine. More psychological."

Theo nodded slowly, considering his sweating glass of water.

"I'm going to kill this man," I said, to make sure he understood. "He's going to beg and bargain. Probably cry and piss himself. You don't have to watch, Theo, but that doesn't change what I'm going to do."

"I know." His voice was strained.

"He might say things that will hurt or trigger you to get a rise out of you."

"I know that too." He lifted the glass to his lips for a sip. "I wasn't ready last time, but I am today."

I believed him. If Theo said he was ready, then he was ready.

We went downstairs into the basement. It was his first time seeing my setup, so I walked him through it, pointing out various pieces of equipment and explaining what it was all for.

"Jesus," he said, sucking in a breath. "It's like the embalming room."

"Not quite. I'm still on a residential drain system, so I can't go pumping bodily fluids into the sewer here." I walked over and stomped on the drain. A small recess popped open and I clicked on a flashlight, illuminating a collection of blue waste barrels. White drainpipes fed into a large, rectangular septic system beneath. "I have a lye powder that goes down in there to help break down any solids, but it's not usually an issue. We put them in the hearse when we're done and take them over to the funeral home to go in the cremator."

"Sounds very well thought out," Theo said, his voice flat.

"We're not going to get caught," I assured him. "No one is looking for this guy."

He met my eyes, brows pinched together. "Whoever dumped David's body in the embalming room knows what you're doing."

I dismissed his concerns with a wave. "I'm sure Rick just blabbed about seeing me and somebody put the dots together. We're going to put an end to this before that can happen again."

Theo nodded, and we didn't speak again for a while.

I moved around the basement, laying out the tools I'd need, polishing and arranging them neatly on the surgical tray. Wet wipes. Pliers. A claw hammer. An assortment of different lengths of nails. A staple gun. An old needle injector that I'd already replaced in my embalming kit. And, of course, the coup de gras, my trusty trocar.

Theo jumped when someone pounded on the basement door. I frowned at him.

"I'm okay. Just wasn't expecting that," he said.

I adjusted the angle of the trocar and went to open the basement door. Sacha was there with a body bag slung over one shoulder, which presumably contained Dmitri Federoff, who was grunting and wriggling.

Sacha smiled. "Presents!" he announced and stepped into my office. He paused by the door to kick off his muddy boots before bringing Dmitri to the table.

He flailed like a madman inside the body bag, making it annoyingly difficult to unzip it. When I unzipped his face, he blinked and squinted at the bright light.

Dmitri had looked like a punk ass gang banger in his mugshot, but in real life, he looked like shit. The Greeks had clearly already warmed him up for me, handing him over with one swollen eye, a broken nose, and plenty of bruises. Blood had caked under his nose and dried on the white cloth they'd shoved in his mouth. His white t-shirt had several stains ranging from what looked like grease to vomit and blood.

His eyes widened as I leaned over him.

"*Zdravstvuyte*, motherfucker," I spat and yanked the bag free.

He jerked, fighting against the zip ties around his wrists. He'd been fighting enough that they'd started to dig into his skin, leaving deep red bruises to blossom.

Sacha helped me peel away the bag and secure him to the table using the straps, which I'd copied from an ECT table diagram. If they could survive electroshock and still hold somebody in place, they'd work just fine for shit stains like Dmitri. I cut through the zip ties binding his ankles. He tried to kick at me with his bare feet, but Sacha caught him and held him so I could strap his feet in. Then we repeated the action with his arms before I pulled the filthy gag from his mouth.

"I told those Greek fuckers everything," Dmitri spat as soon as he could.

"Well, now you're going to tell me." I stomped down on the hydraulic lift, which tipped the table up so that he was vertical.

"C'mon, man," he half-sobbed.

I ignored him, making a show of examining my tools, deciding where to start.

He struggled noisily as I ran my fingers over each piece, one by one, eventually giving up with a defeated, "Fuck!"

I closed my hand around one of the smaller nails and my claw hammer, walking back to him. He squirmed as I carefully wedged the nail under his big toenail.

I looked up at him, hammer at the ready, listening to him pant. His nostrils were too clogged with blood to breathe through them.

"Tell me about the church," I demanded. "Which church is it?"

We already suspected it was Saint Niklaus', but we needed to be sure before we made a move.

"What fuckin' church, man?"

He screamed as I struck the head of the nail with half force, just enough to drive it in an inch.

"What's the Master's real name?"

He shook his head, sobbing. "I'm just the bookie, man. I'm just the fucking bookie!"

I gave the nail another tap. He kicked so hard, I worried he'd break his own ankle, so I grabbed another nail and moved to the other foot. "Where do they keep the people you were putting in that room in the club?"

"I don't know, man!" His voice cracked.

I put in a second nail, deaf to his wailing, and stepped back to wait. That was the key to torture. A lot of people wanted to keep swinging, but overload the body with too much pain at once, and the adrenaline dulled it. In males, adrenaline spiked early, at about the fifteen-minute mark, before it gradually declined over the next hour. So, I left him there and started a timer for twenty minutes before pacing to the other side of the basement to get a pop out of the fridge.

Dmitri lifted his chin from his chest. "Help me!" he screamed in Theo's direction. "For God's sake, fucking help me, man!"

I watched Theo closely, but he didn't crack. If anything, his face hardened.

He stepped up to Dmitri, looking up at him. "Help you? I'm the fucking reason you're up there, asshole."

Dmitri's eyes widened as Theo grabbed the pliers. "Wait, wait, wait!" He broke off in a scream as Theo wrenched the nail on his tiny left toe free.

I casually reached to reset the timer.

"Shall we give him some soothing music, nephew?" Sacha asked, passing a cold pop to Theo, who'd come to join us.

"Good idea." I got out my phone and queued up a playlist of songs specially curated by Xander and Xavier for that purpose. It was mostly hyperactive europop with lots of heavy distortion and repetitive lyrics. They called them meme songs. I had no idea what that meant, but auditory and visual torture was kind of their thing.

I slipped the linked Bluetooth earbuds into Dmitri's ears and stepped back, wrinkling my nose. "A little early to be shitting yourself, dude. We haven't even gotten to the good part."

"What now?" Theo asked.

"Now, we let him stew until the adrenaline wears off and the earworms break down his cognitive function, which will take about..." I checked the timer. "Eighteen minutes. In the meantime, we can do whatever."

Sacha shrugged. "I'm going to go make myself a bologna sandwich. You boys have fun."

Theo waited for Sacha to make his way upstairs and for the door to shut behind him before looking at me and repeating his question. "What do you want to do?"

I licked my lips and gave him a slow once over. "You still haven't proven your three-minute blowjob claim."

He wrinkled his nose. "I'm not giving you a blowjob inches from a Nazi on a torture table."

"Your loss." I shrugged and went to polish my tools.

"Do you really think he has all that information?"

I shrugged. "Probably. If not, he knows who does. This doesn't end until I have names and addresses. Once he realizes that, life will get significantly less painful for him."

"And then what?" Theo's voice wavered slightly.

I turned around to look at him. "Then we go and get the bastards."

"Yeah, but how do you make sure someone else doesn't take over? How do you stop the cycle?"

I pressed my lips together, considering. "I don't know. Maybe we can't. There's always going to be evil in the world. Stopping things like human trafficking, kidnapping, and murder is going to take a lot more than I can accomplish. But I can take this guy out. We can shut down *this* operation." I walked over to cup his cheek, planting a kiss on his freckled forehead. "Focus on what we can do, not everything all at once, okay?"

Theo nodded slowly. For the first time, it felt like I'd gotten through to him. In the last few days, he'd changed. Hardened, but in a good way. When it was just me and him, he was still soft in all the right places, still my sweet little finch up on the shelf, even if he'd lost some of his innocent façade. That had been a mask. An act. The real Theo wasn't a helpless, meek little slave. He was defiant and taunting with a lust for life. He glowed bright like fire against my shadowy nature. Theo was everything I wanted, and I was everything he needed.

The timer ran down and beeped, filling the room with a sharp shriek. I shut it off and popped the earbuds out of Dmitri's ears, sliding them into my pocket.

"Please," Dmitri pleaded weakly. "Please stop..."

I picked up the bloody pliers and pulled over a chair, turning it around to sit on it backwards. "That's up to you, Dmitri. All this stops the minute you tell me what I want to know, and I want to know where to find the Master. I want to know where he is, and I want to know everything you know about this operation."

He lifted wet brown eyes to mine. "If I tell you, you'll let me go?"

I almost laughed at the ridiculous notion. "I think we both know you're not coming back from this."

Dmitri let out a soft sob and lowered his head.

"But," I said, rising from the chair, gripping him by his greasy hair to pull his head up, "the faster you answer my questions, the more of you stays attached."

He whimpered.

"So how about it, Dmitri?" I asked, waving the pliers in front of his face. "You ready to talk?"

Thirty
Theo

It didn't take Dmitri long to break.

I was numb listening to him spill everything through snot and tears to River, listing names and places I had never heard of, but must have been to. It was like he was talking about another world.

It should have been shocking to hear River was right about the baby farm angle. It wasn't. It should have been upsetting to know that I—and the other boys—had been raised nearly from birth to be treated as cash cows. He said they started renting us out to the highest bidder when we were five.

Five.

I didn't remember.

There were flashes here and there of hotel rooms, toy cars, fast food kids' meals, ice cream, and cartoons. I remembered feeling sad and dirty, even when I took a bath. Was that why?

Apparently, it was like Sacha said. The older we got, the less they could charge for us because there was less demand. The people in charge started to look for other ways to make money, no longer caring if we survived their schemes. There were rumors of red rooms and torture chambers where people could pay exorbitant sums to enact their disgusting fantasies on us, but if they existed, Dmitri wasn't getting a cut of them.

He did have his hands all over the dead pool, which was a sick betting game about which one of us would die next. The same people who raped us were betting on when and how we'd die. It probably even incentivized them to participate in killing us so they could collect their winnings, though Dmitri didn't admit that much.

"How many boys are left?" River demanded, fist clenching around the pliers. He no longer needed them. Dmitri was telling him everything.

Dmitri shook his head. "Six, I think. They moved them to the basement of this old abandoned elementary school in Franklinton that's connected to this church."

"Saint Niklaus?"

Dmitri nodded slowly. "That's the one."

River looked over his shoulder at me, probably to see my reaction, but I had none. I didn't know any of those places.

River turned back to Dmitri. "What is the Master's real name?"

Dmitri swallowed. "His name's Earl. Earl Maynard."

Earl. Master's real name was Earl. It was a stupid name and I hated it. I couldn't believe I had ever let someone named Earl run my entire life.

"There's a book," Dmitri offered. "A black book with all the names of all the regulars. I kept it in case I ever needed to blackmail the guys for more money so I could get out quick. It's stashed in the safe at The Time Out Room. Jeff let me keep it there. He got a cut of everything in percentages. It's all there, in the book. Everything you want."

"Thanks. That's real helpful." River stood up from the chair he'd been sitting in. "Just one more question, Dmitri, and then we'll be done."

Dmitri glanced down at the pliers and back to River's expressionless face and dull eyes. "I told you everything!"

"You didn't tell me if you watched." River walked over to his tray of instruments and picked up a long instrument that looked like the spout to a garden hose. It was hooked up to a long tube that ran to the wall. "Or if you participated, or if you looked the other way and took money from pedophiles to line your own pockets."

"What?" Dmitri's face was white as a sheet.

River stomped over and gripped him by the back of his head. "Did you ever put your hands on any of those kids, you sick fuck?"

"N-n-no!" he stammered. "I'd never! Fuck, man!"

"He's lying," I said in a small voice and felt my body swaying in place. I was oddly lightheaded, disconnected. My head was a balloon, threatening to float away from my torso. "I remember you now. I wasn't a kid, though. You made sure. You asked twice if I was eighteen."

Dmitri's eyes widened and darted to River. "He... He's lying!"

"You gave me poppers," I continued. "Said it'd make it feel better. You were nervous. Barely stayed hard. I had to suck you off and wound up throwing up all over your shoes."

"What the fuck!" Dmitri shouted.

"Wrong answer," River spat.

I flinched as he drove the sharp end of the trocar into Dmitri's abdomen. The sound that came out of Dmitri's mouth was caught somewhere between a gasp and a groan. I couldn't see what River was doing, but he seemed to be moving the long, sharp wand around inside of Dmitri. The tube connected to the trocar lit up with a bright green liquid and a strong chemical smell filled the air.

I turned away, unwilling to watch. The sick feeling that'd been there when Shepherd killed Travis was absent, but so was my anger. River had enough rage for both of us, and he was injecting it into Dmitri, cleaning him from the inside out with it.

My feet carried me to the stairs, which were just out of sight of the table. Upstairs, I could hear Sacha moving around, the dull hum of the TV. So normal, the same sounds one would find in any suburban house at night. The sounds coming from Dmitri and River were anything but.

I don't remember going up the stairs and through the kitchen, and I don't remember sitting down on the sofa, but I must've. I came out of my trance staring at the television screen, watching the attractive middle-aged news anchors relate the story of a gang-related shooting on a street I'd never heard of. She seemed as detached as River, uncaring as she read facts from her teleprompter.

Even though I was staring at her, and I heard her words, I was back at The Time Out Room two days after my eighteenth birthday, throwing up on Dmitri's shoes. They'd been Nikes, red, the laces only half-tied. I remembered thinking he was lazy for not tying his shoes. Why hadn't I remembered that when I looked at his mugshot? Why did it take watching him sob and piss himself for me to remember?

Because there were hundreds of Dmitris in my past, nameless faces. People hiding in suburban neighborhoods. Parked in soccer mom SUVs with stick family bumper stickers. School principals, city officials, motorcycle mechanics. People from every socioeconomic level and walk of life. The same people probably filling pews on Sundays and cheering on their kids at ballgames.

Everyday monsters hiding in plain sight.

A shot glass plunked down on the coffee table in front of me, clear liquid spilling over the edge. I blinked up at Sacha.

"Drink, little fish," he commanded.

I picked up the glass and poured it in my mouth, eyes stinging and throat burning. I coughed as I lowered the glass. "What the hell is that? Rubbing alcohol?"

"Close," he admitted and produced a bottle full of letters that weren't in English. "Water from the motherland. Good for what troubles you."

"Good for burning off all my nose hairs, you mean." I sat forward and put the glass down.

Sacha laughed and patted my back. "Moves it from your nose to your chest, yes?" The sofa creaked as he sat down next to me with another glass, refilling both. "The privilege of an easy life is not for men like us, is it?"

"I wish it was," I said as he handed me the vodka. "Does it ever get easier? This life?"

"Only when we die," he said and threw back his drink. "But we aren't the type to feel sorry for ourselves, are we? Nor are we like River, whose rage is his righteous outlet. You are like me, caught up in the wild current of bigger personalities. Let me give you some life advice, little fish." He gripped the bottle and turned it over in his hands. "Let the current carry you. Do not swim against it. You'll wind up where you're supposed to be."

"I don't know how to deal with all these intrusive memories." I swallowed the vodka and winced, though it wasn't nearly as bad the second time.

"Take them as they come, and stop blaming yourself," he suggested, refilling my glass. "Pace yourself through it as best you can. Develop a vice or two. It's good to be bad sometimes."

I lifted an eyebrow. "Like vodka?"

"Exactly." He grinned and handed me the refilled glass, tapping his own against it and declaring, "*Nah zdarovhyeh*!"

"What does that mean?"

"To your health," he explained and emptied his glass.

I could drink to that, I decided, and drank mine too.

Thirty-One
River

"ARE YOU DRUNK?" I gave my Uncle Sacha a chastising look. "Did you get Theo *drunk*?"

"He got himself drunk, nephew," Uncle Sacha slurred in Russian.

"I like being drunk," Theo protested, swaying on the sofa.

I snorted. "Well, you won't like it in the morning. Come on." I helped him to his feet, half carrying him to the stairs.

It took a while for Dmitri to die, longer than I expected, actually. The trocar was dull, and I'd intentionally missed piercing his heart, but I was pretty sure shock got him before he suffocated. Embalming fluid wasn't meant to go in living bodies.

After cleaning up, I'd used the secondary lift to put him in a box, and I'd covered that box with waterproof plastic. Getting it into the back of the hearse by myself had been a bitch, but I was glad I hadn't bothered to ask Uncle Sacha for help. Apparently, he'd been upstairs getting smashed while watching the news. At least Dad and Niki had agreed to meet me at the loading bay. Dmitri Federoff was on his way to being charred bones, and the world was a much better place without him.

"What's the deal with your mom and dad and their..." He waved vaguely. "You know. Tatty and Niki." Theo stumbled on the next step, but I caught him, throwing one of his arms around my neck to keep him upright. "Aren't they all like, married?"

"Ever hear of polyamory?" I said with a smirk.

"Poly...Pol...what?"

"Mom and Tatty are a couple," I explained. "And Dad and Nikita are a couple. Also, Nikita and Tatty are a couple. Dad and Mom are married, but they aren't a couple. It's for appearances only."

Theo scrunched up his face and stopped, thinking hard. "So when they fuck, it's like a giant orgy or..."

I laughed. "I try not to think about it too hard."

We reached the top of the stairs, and he threw his arms around my neck, practically throwing himself at me. "Carry me?"

I scooped him up without question and carried him into our room, kicking the door closed behind me.

"Are we going to fuck?" he asked, nuzzling into me.

"Not until you're sober. Mom would kill me. Literally." I put him down on the bed and went about stripping off his shoes and socks.

"You're not like that, are you?" he asked quietly. "Polyalimony or whatever."

I snickered. "No, little finch. I'm all yours."

"Well good, 'cause I don't want to share you." When I lifted his shirt over his head, he caught my lips in a sloppy kiss. "I love you, River."

For a second, it felt like I'd jabbed the trocar into my chest by mistake and twisted it around. I cupped his cheek. "Why do you love me?"

"Just 'cause," he said, shrugging. "You get me, and even I don't get me. Plus, you've got a big dick and you know how to use it. You're like some sort of...sexy psycho killer wizard with a big dick."

I snorted, holding back a laugh. "Technically, I'm a sociopath, not a psychopath."

"Whatever you say, dick wizard."

I grinned and pulled the blanket up over him. "I think I like drunk Theo. What I don't like is not being able to fuck you to sleep, so hurry and sober up so you can get some of my big dick." I kissed his cheek and stepped away from the bed.

"What're you gonna do? Not sleep?" Theo asked.

"I have to make a phone call, and then I'll be right with you."

That seemed to placate him. He curled up, tucking my pillow under his chin, and was snoring before I even had my phone out.

I called Shepherd, because he'd be pissed if I didn't update him immediately. He didn't pick up the first time, so I immediately tried again.

"What?" he snarled into the phone after the third ring. "There had better be a body I care about, River."

I smirked when I realized he was breathless. "Doing a late-night grading session with your grad student, eh? Hi, Gavin."

"Who's Gavin?" came a muffled voice.

A muffled *feminine* voice.

My eyebrows shot up when I realized it was a woman. "Expanding your horizons, I see. Good for you, Shepherd."

There was the muffled sound of a door closing. "What do you want, River? Make it quick."

"I assume you've been filled in on most of the details of our little mission so far?"

"I know about the Russians and the Greeks, yes." There was the sound of a tap running. "What's any of that got to do with me?"

"I just had a chat with Mr. Federoff. I have all the information we need to make a move," I told him, sinking into the armchair near the bed to watch Theo sleep.

"And?" he huffed, impatient.

"And I thought you'd want to know that Jeff, the owner of The Time Out Room, was definitely taking a cut. We'll need a scapegoat to dump all this on when we're done, so I figured..."

"You figured Jeff was perfect. Makes sense. Adjusting the paper trail to lead straight to him will be easy." He paused briefly. "Remind me again why you're not my favorite brother?"

"Because I like my steaks medium well and think wine tastes like someone pissed on perfectly good grapes," I replied.

Shepherd snorted. "You're an uncultured swine, River, but I owe you for this."

"Damn right you do, and that's the other reason I'm calling." I glanced over at Theo, making sure he was fast asleep before shifting to sit sideways in the chair, my legs draped over the arm. "Theo said he loved me."

"Congratulations," Shepherd said dryly.

"I'm serious, Shepherd. What am I supposed to do about that? I don't know how to...I mean, I know what I should've said, but..."

Shepherd sighed. "There are whole libraries of books dedicated to this subject, River. Even if that's beyond you, you could try the self-help section of the paper."

"Why? You're a sex therapist. Aren't you, like, an expert in this stuff?"

He sighed again. He was turning into a broken record. "I'm a licensed clinical psychiatrist, not a sex therapist. It just so happens that my area of interest is the study of kinks, sexual fetishes, and human desire and their comorbidities with psychiatric disorders. Second, sex and desire exist on a spectrum that don't always include love and attraction. Human sexuality and relationships are far too complex a subject for me to break down over the phone at..." He paused. "Fucking hell, River. It's two in the morning! I should have my face buried in the dean of the psych department, not on the phone with the likes of you."

"Oh, is somebody finally getting *tenure*?" I teased. At least that explained what he was doing with a woman in his bed. I didn't think Shepherd swung that way, but then I'd never paid much attention to his love life except to bust his balls about banging his grad students.

"Why am I telling you any of this?" he growled. "I don't even know why we're still talking."

"Because you secretly like me." I shifted again in the chair, sitting upside down. Theo was even cuter from that angle, especially when he was drooling on himself. "Tell me what to say to him, Shep. Please?"

"Just tell him you love him back."

I frowned. "How do I know if that's true?"

"Look, River, it doesn't matter if it's true or not. It's what he wants to hear. Neurotypicals tell people that expecting it to be parroted back at them. It makes them feel secure."

"Even if he knows it's not true?"

"Goodbye, River." Shepherd hung up on me.

I sighed and let the phone fall to the floor, remaining upside down. Why'd he have to say that? Of all the drunken confessions to make, why was it "I love you, River"? Hadn't I made it clear that I probably couldn't return the sentiment?

I mean, what was love? Just a chemical response in the brain, one that didn't happen to me. I liked Theo, found him adorable and intriguing, and wanted to always have him with me, but I wasn't ever going to be capable of putting his needs before mine. The only reason

I took care of him was because it benefitted me. There wasn't an altruistic bone in my body. I just wasn't capable.

Obsessive, yes. Possessive? Absolutely. But in love?

I tried to think back to the few movies I'd had to sit through, the ones with romantic subplots. There were always these deep, moving confessions of feelings. The characters looked at each other and got all swoony and teary-eyed, confessing they couldn't live without each other. I could live without Theo. I didn't want to, but I wouldn't die of a broken heart if something happened to him. That was a ridiculous notion that never really happened anyway.

Truth be told, if Theo ever did try to leave me, I'd probably completely lose my shit and have to kill anyone who ever tried to be with him. I saw him as a possession, one that I wanted to snuggle, and kiss, and hold, but he was still a possession to me. I knew it would hurt him to hear that, especially given his history, but that was the truth.

That wasn't love.

Was it?

All this angst over a stupid four-letter word, I thought, dragging a hand over my face.

An aching tiredness settled in my bones all of a sudden, so I shucked my clothes and crawled into bed behind Theo, spooning against him.

He gave a tired hum as I kissed the back of his neck, shifting against me. "Hey."

"Hey," I replied, nuzzling against his shoulder. Maybe I'd get lucky and he'd forget all about his drunken confession tomorrow. Then we could move on and go back to the way things were before.

Thirty-Two
Theo

HANGOVERS SUCKED, BUT AT least I didn't have to work.

I spent most of the day in bed with River watching over me. He sat in the chair next to the bed, alternating between scrolling through articles and having hushed conversations on his phone. I knew he was making plans for what was to come, but my head hurt too much to engage.

The shadows grew longer and the day dragged on with me alternating between periods of deep sleep and semi-wakefulness. In the late afternoon, I woke up and found River's chair empty. Frowning, I sat up and looked around, but there was no sign of him.

For a minute, I didn't know what to do. We'd been apart a few times, but I'd always known where he was or how to get in touch. Waking up alone was strange and scary. What if something had happened to him?

"River?" I called, rubbing sleep from my eyes.

There was no answer.

I frowned and sat up. Maybe he was in the bathroom. I went down the hall to check, but the bathroom was empty. I checked downstairs, but the whole house was empty, and I didn't see his car in the driveway.

With nothing else to do but worry, I dragged myself back upstairs to shower. I smelled awful anyway. All through the shower, thoughts raced through my mind. Had he gone to get Earl by himself? After I told him I wanted to be the one to kill him? No. River wouldn't do that to me. Maybe he got called to a family meeting, or over to the funeral home for something, or he could've gone to the store. There were a hundred places he might've gone, but my brain decided to fixate on the worst possible one.

I didn't bother dressing after my shower, dragging myself back to bed, feeling sorry for myself.

I'm so stupid, I thought, hugging the pillow tight. *If River ever does get tired of me, what am I going to do?* I wasn't set up to function in the world. I'd need to get a job, find someplace to live... I didn't know how to do any of that. Didn't have any skills that might translate into actual work. Sure, I could dust and sweep floors, but that wasn't an actual job, was it?

I was tired of people's pity, tired of the way they looked at me and only saw me as a victim, tired of the way that other people were so careful about what they said around me. Everyone was always asking me if I was ready, if I was sure I could handle things.

What they really wanted to know was if I was going to have a fucking breakdown. Maybe I was. Maybe I already had, but dammit... I wanted to be treated like a person, not a broken toy. I wanted to be more than the trauma, and that was all anybody seemed to see when they looked at me.

I fell back into a dreamless sleep, feeling angry at my own helplessness.

It was dark when I heard the bedroom door open and close and the familiar shuffle of River's feet approaching. Instead of immediately waking up to ask him where he'd been, I laid there in sullen silence, pretending I was still asleep. That'd piss him off more than confrontation and better to convey my irritated mood. River liked attention, even if it was the negative kind. Refusing to acknowledge him would be torture.

So, I stayed face down on the bed, eyes closed. The mattress shifted under his weight as he climbed onto it, and still I didn't move.

"Theo?"

I bit the inside of my cheek when his hands slid up the backs of my legs slowly. My cock started to stir where it was pinned against the mattress, but I didn't show any other outward signs of acknowledging him.

"I know you're awake," River said firmly. "Don't ignore me."

I turned my head the other way, snuggling harder into the mattress to hide my erection.

River gave an irritated huff. Strong hands closed around the backs of my knees, pushing my legs apart so he could settle between them.

"I'm sleeping." I started to get up so I could move to the other side of the bed.

River pushed me back down with a hand firmly between my shoulders. "I was enjoying the view."

His weight settled on top of me. I bit my lip when I felt his hard cock rub against my ass through his jeans. Teeth grazed my shoulder.

"I've been thinking about being inside you all day," River murmured into my skin. "It's been impossible to concentrate on my work."

"Is that where you've been all day?" I sounded pouty because I was.

River's hand closed around my chin, and the other gripped my hip while he slowly ground against me. "You're mad at me."

"I woke up and you weren't here," I grumbled sullenly and bucked up with my hips. "Stop that."

River capitalized on my sudden movement, slipping a hand between my hip and the sheets to grip my leaking cock. "Poor little finch. Nobody to take care of this for you? Is that your problem?"

I rolled, trying to throw him off of me, but he compensated by sitting up on his knees and coming down hard to pin my arms at my sides. I gave him my best threatening scowl, which probably still looked more like a pout, even as I enjoyed the rough friction of his jeans against my dick. "I don't like waking up alone."

"Well don't get drunk and pass out and then you can come with me to pick up the body at the nursing home next time," River said, thrusting against me.

I frowned. "Is that where you went?"

"Yeah. Normally Dad would do it, but this close to the holiday, he wanted to rush planning with the family, so he did that while I played chauffeur for Grandma Mabel's corpse."

"You're terrible at pillow talk." I gave his shoulder a half-hearted shove.

"I've got no concept of romance, Theo."

"Yeah, but you've got to know that talking about dead grandmas is a definite mood killer."

"For some people."

I made a face. "I'm some people."

"This says otherwise." River closed his hand around my cock again, giving it slow, lazy pulls.

"That has nothing to do with dead grandmas." I squirmed away, kicking enough to at least seem like I was trying to swim out from under him. "You still should've woken me up."

"I thought about it." He pushed up, the look in his eyes pure lust as he raked them over me. "But then I saw you all naked and splayed out in my bed, completely helpless. So out of it. I thought about punishing you with my cock for being such a bad boy last night and getting drunk before I could fuck you into the mattress."

I shuddered.

"I knew if I climbed in this bed with you, I was going to have to hold you down and bury myself in the tight heat of your body, and I wasn't going to care if you were awake for it or not."

My cock twitched, weeping a heavy teardrop of pre-cum. I licked my lips. "You could've."

"I could have," he agreed.

"No, I mean... You can next time. If you want. If the urge ever strikes you again. I don't mind. I think it'd be kind of hot to wake up with you already inside me."

"It's dangerous to give me that kind of access, Theo," he said and bit my lip.

I couldn't stop the groan that came out of me. My hips rolled against him. "It's not. I trust you. More than anybody."

Something changed in his face. The cocky grin faded, replaced by an uncertain expression.

I stopped moving. "What is it? What's wrong?"

He shook his head. "Nothing."

"River, if something happened..."

"Nothing happened," he insisted and sat up on his knees again.

I yelped when he roughly turned me over, but it was an exaggerated sound. He hadn't actually hurt me, and the mild fear churning in my belly at what he might do to me was more an aphrodisiac than anything else. I started to crawl away when he yanked the bedside table drawer open, but not too fast and not too far. Just enough to give the illusion of attempting an escape.

"Where the fuck do you think you're going, little finch?" he growled and yanked me back in place by the ankles.

I gasped when I kept sliding backward and realized he was dragging me to the end of the bed. He dropped my feet and they hit the hardwood floor, though my upper body above the waist was still pressed to the mattress. I tried to lift myself with my arms, but he pushed me back down hard enough that I bounced.

"You can get up when I'm done with you," he declared. "And by then, you're going to have cum leaking out of a very sore hole."

I tensed as a slick finger pushed its way inside me.

"C'mon, relax for me. That's it, Theo."

For some reason, hearing my name on his lips instead of little finch again instantly calmed me. River didn't call me little finch except when he was playing at being the big bad predator he thought he was. I knew the truth. Underneath that murderous exterior, he was just a giant nerd who ate his chicken nuggets with ketchup and showed me pictures of cool mushrooms he found online. I couldn't bring myself to be afraid of him. Not even when he was torturing information out of a Nazi.

Maybe it was because I totally lacked any self-preservation instinct. That had been beaten and programmed out of me at an early age, to the point that the only scenario in which I could bring myself to fight back was when I felt safe enough to do so. Safe with him. It was fifty shades of fucked up, but then so were we.

I rocked back against his finger, saying yes with my body while resisting with my words. "Stop, River."

"You don't mean that. I know you don't. This greedy little hole is practically sucking my finger in." His free hand closed around my throat before he added a second digit. "Fuck yourself on my fingers, little finch."

"No," I said even as I did it. "I don't want to."

"Liar," he scoffed, amused. "Look at how bad you want it. I see the little smears of pre-cum you're leaving on my sheets. You can't help but want it, can you? And you want more than my fingers. You want this big, hard cock in you, don't you?"

"No," I lied, fingers and toes curling as he found my prostate. "Fuck..."

"Give me one good goddamn reason not to impale you on my cock right now and fill you so full of my cum that it's leaking down your leg."

I tried to think of a reason—I really did—but what he was doing to me felt so good, I could barely think of anything at all. It wasn't just the physical sensation either, although River knew far too well how to manipulate my body to respond. I needed him, craved reconnecting with him like a drug. Though he'd only been gone a few hours, it'd felt like he'd abandoned me forever, and I needed to know that wasn't the case. I needed River to reclaim me as his.

Fuck, he was right. I was a needy little bird.

"Please don't," I whimpered in a small voice.

"That's it, little finch. Beg me not to." He was panting behind me as if he were the one desperate to be claimed.

"Please, River," I said, curling my fingers into fists. "Please don't hold me down and fuck me hard. Please don't claim me. Don't make me yours. I can't take it."

"Fuck," he growled, and his fingers retreated long enough for him to undo his belt. There was the telltale sound of his zipper coming undone.

We groaned together as he seated himself inside me in a single rough thrust. It hurt, taking him all at once like that, but I loved the pain, loved knowing it was him. Who was I kidding? I loved *him*.

Once he was inside me, River didn't move except to brush a soft kiss against my temple. In the wake of his brutal treatment, that kiss was like ice on a burn. "You okay in there, Theo?"

No hint of pity or probably even any real concern beyond whatever related back to getting more of what he wanted. River wasn't capable of that.

I swallowed against the pressure of his fingers around my throat. "Fuck, yes, I am. This is the hottest thing... I mean..." I cleared my throat and continued in an exaggeratedly dry tone, "Oh, no. I hope you don't make me come against my will. That would be *terrible*."

He snorted and bit my earlobe. "You're a fucking brat, you know that?"

"Less talking, more destroying my ass," I mumbled, wiggling my hips.

River shifted his weight, rising so that he could grip my shoulders. He withdrew nearly to the tip before plunging back into me hard enough that the shockwave went all the way up my spine. My mouth opened in a silent scream when he did it again. And again. River set a brutal fast pace that wouldn't have been the least bit enjoyable if it'd been anyone but him.

He paused with a grunt and moved his hands from my shoulders to grip me under my arms, long fingers brushing against my nipples on either side. I shuddered, eyes rolling back, and the fight in me died. All I could do was squirm as he rolled my nipples between his fingers while he fucked me, everything beyond that fading into the background. Even though neither of us was touching my cock, I could feel the pressure starting to build. I opened my mouth to tell him, but he chose exactly that moment to start thrusting harder, chasing his own orgasm. I was already on the edge when his hips slammed into me and he cursed in my ear, movements going jerky.

"River," I half-moaned, half-whined in warning. When I slid over the edge, part of me was in a full-on panic. I was shaking so hard, I thought I might be having a seizure, the orgasm so different, so intense that I thought I was going to pass out. My cock pulsed, spilling cum everywhere, more than there'd ever been before. Some distant part of me had the gall to be angry about it, like my body had betrayed me by not ever letting me have an orgasm that intense before.

"Fuck," River panted before smiling against my shoulder. "Did you just...?" He moved his hand lower, closing it around my sticky cock.

I shrieked at the overstimulation and immediately tried to squirm away, choking on my next breath.

He chuckled. "I didn't know I could make you do that."

I groaned and slid an arm under my head. I felt hot enough that I worried I'd developed a fever. River did not need that to pump up his ego, even if he deserved it.

He pulled free of me with a small grunt, and I crawled up the bed, turning over in time to catch him licking my cum from his fingers.

I shuddered. "You're a menace."

River grinned and fell into bed beside me. "A menace who made you come without even touching your dick. Careful, I might start to actually believe I'm a god. I sure worked miracles on you, huh?"

I turned onto my side, throwing my leg lazily over his and my arm over his stomach to trace over the coarse line of hair there. "Did you really go to do a pickup?"

He looked down at me, confused. "Where else would I go?"

"I thought you'd go kill Earl without me."

River frowned and pulled me up to straddle his hips. My legs still felt like jelly, so he had to adjust my knees and hold my ass to keep me upright where he wanted me.

"I thought you said you trusted me," he said, sounding...disappointed.

"I do, it's just..." I looked down at my hands splayed over his bare skin.

Even though he spent more time indoors than was probably healthy, River's skin was several shades darker than mine and smooth beneath the fine dusting of dark hair. There was nothing gentle or delicate about the way he was built, but there was a subtle, rough beauty to him, the kind that made him seem almost otherworldly sometimes.

I sighed. "I know people think I'm weak. That I don't have the stomach for this or that I'm not ready."

"Nobody thinks that, Theo."

"Yes, they do!" I snapped roughly. "Sacha does. Xander and Xavier do. Yuri does. War definitely does."

"First of all, War's a dick, and I forbid you say his name in my bed. Second..." He cupped my cheeks with both hands, giving me a stern look. "Since when were you able to read other people's thoughts, huh?"

"I don't have to. I see the way they look at me."

"Maybe you're reading in them what you think of yourself then," River said.

His words were so stark, so honest, it shocked me, and I knew he was right.

"You're doubting yourself," he continued. "Any sane person would, especially after what you've been through."

"You don't," I pointed out.

River arched an eyebrow. "I said *sane* people, Theo. I'm pretty sure me and my brothers don't qualify. Hell, maybe no one in my family does. But you do." He drove a finger into my chest and then flicked my nose lightly. "And you know what? It's okay to do that."

I blinked and swatted his hand away from my face. "It is?"

He nodded. "It's good that you can do that, because I can't. If I didn't have you constantly pulling me back, anchoring me, quelling the rage in me, I'd have already killed again. And I don't even know if it'd be someone who deserves it."

"I don't understand," I said quietly. "I'm not doing anything."

"You are, even if you don't see it," he said and sat up to kiss my forehead. "When I get angry, people die. And the night I saw you, I was so pissed off. I think I went to that bar looking for someone to kill to take the edge off. I was directionless, lost at sea without a beacon. You've become that for me. You're my lighthouse, Theo. No matter how far I go, as long as I can still see you, I know I can come back from the dark."

I laid down against him, letting my head rest on his chest. "I've never been anybody's anything before. What if I'm not good at it?"

"You can't possibly be bad at being yourself," River said as if it were obvious. "And that's all I want from you, Theo. I want you to be with me, and to be happy. I like seeing you happy."

I frowned, feeling something twist in my chest. "What about love?" I didn't know if someone like River was capable of love.

River's fingers started tracing little circles over my ribcage. He was quiet for a minute, deep in thought about his answer. "I always thought of love as a chemical process in the brain, the release of dopamine and oxytocin to promote bonding. That doesn't happen in my brain the way it does for normal people. But maybe I'm wrong. Maybe love can look different sometimes. It can be this. It can be us."

"Can it?" I shifted to look up at him.

He smiled and stretched. "Who says it can't be? It's like everything else. Fuck labels. Fuck the assholes in lab coats and their stupid psych degrees and the whole DSM series. You make me happy. Why can't that count as love?"

I didn't think happiness and love were the same things, at least not to me, but that was part of it. What River and I had was a mutual obsession with each other. We were drawn to each other like magnets from the first moment our eyes met across the bar, and nothing was ever going to keep us apart. Maybe that didn't look like love to anyone else, but I felt like it was as close as we were ever going to get.

So, I tested it out.

I looked up at him and said the words I'd been dreading saying because I was so afraid he wouldn't return them. But maybe he didn't have to return them. Maybe love wasn't about give and take on both sides. It could be just me giving, and him taking what he needed, when he needed it, if that's what worked for us.

"I love you, River."

"Thanks," he said with a big grin and a wink. "I love me, too."

"You're such a fucking jerk," I muttered and twisted his nipple.

He hissed and surged up to kiss me. "But you love me anyway," he teased, still smiling.

And he was right. I absolutely did.

Thirty-Three

River

No one questioned it when two dozen men in suits rolled up to a funeral home in expensive cars. Such a gathering of notorious figures wouldn't have gone unnoticed by police surveillance if they'd met anywhere else. The Greeks and the Russians didn't meet in numbers very often for obvious reasons.

We cleared out the main viewing room, putting a long table in the center where mourners usually sat. Theo was tasked with laying out the bowls of bread and salt while I stood at the door with Dad, shaking hands and kissing cheeks with mobsters.

The Russians were the first to arrive with a handful of grim-faced *vory* I didn't know coming through. Dad seemed to know them all by name, greeting them each with the utmost respect, standing next to Niki.

The first one I recognized was my cousin, Aleksi, Uncle Sacha's oldest. He looked good for someone pushing forty, tall with a thick head of dark hair that he wore combed back. Piercing blue eyes scanned the parlor entry as he paused in the doorway, filling the air with the smell of his expensive cologne. He peeled off his leather driving gloves, revealing a pair of cross tattoos on his right hand, one for each occasion he'd done time. Like the rest of the *vory*, he had a ton of other tattoos under his clothes, each of which told a story.

"*Kak dyela*, River," he said to me only after he'd taken Dad's hand.

"*Nyeplokho. A u tyebya*?" I replied, answering his bone-breaking squeeze with one of my own.

Aleksi grinned. "Your Russian's getting better, cousin. You've been practicing."

"Not as much as I'd like," I said with a shrug. "Been busy."

"So I hear." He tapped out a cigarette, haunting the doorway instead of going in.

I stiffened as his eyes slid past me and settled on Theo.

"This is him?" Aleksi asked in Russian, gesturing to Theo. "He's paler than you. You should take him to one of those nude beaches down south. Let him get some sun."

I coughed and waved away his smoke. "As if you're not three shades whiter than snow."

"Yes, but I'm meant to be white. Ohio's no good for you. We should go together. I have a guy in the Keys. A Cuban with a very nice boat. You bring your boy toy and I'll bring his sister. I hear she likes to watch boys fuck."

"You mean *you* like to watch," I pointed out, punching him lightly in the shoulder. "Just come out of the closet already."

He laughed it off, puffing on his cigarette. "You're just pissed I got all the girls when we used to hang out and you could only pull their little brothers. But now I have to find a new wingman. Maybe I'll ask Shepherd. Are all of his personalities queer or only the one?"

My fingers started to itch at the mention of Shepherd's name. "He's out of your league."

"Nobody is out of my league, cousin. I could have the boys *and* girls if I wanted. Lucky for you, I only like pussy. Leaves some for the rest of you."

"You keep telling yourself that," I muttered.

"Aleksi! Hello, good morning!" Niki called, coming to put an arm around Aleksi's shoulder. "How are you?"

The two weren't related but had somehow wound up looking a lot alike. Because Niki and his Tatty had let Mom and Dad raise War, everyone understood Aleksi was Niki's heir. Of course, Simeon the Immortal would have to die first. He'd been in and out of the hospital for half my life, dodging death. The old geezer was pushing a hundred and two. But if the reaper wanted his soul, he'd be in for a hell of a fight. Simeon was the meanest, stubbornest old Russian I'd ever met.

The air changed when a spotless blue Lincoln Continental pulled up. Aleksi immediately put out his cigarette and ran his fingers through his hair before tugging on his suit jacket. The driver got out first, a middle-aged man with a star-shaped scar on his cheek. He opened the rear passenger door for his employer first.

Nigel Costas was an elderly man with liver spots and a thin white beard. He was always dressed impeccably and walked with a cane that he probably didn't actually need. Every time I'd seen him, he looked like the sort of man who would walk into his own funeral and only lay in the coffin because he chose it.

His only son, Leon, had met a tragic end not long ago thanks to a long bout with bone cancer rather than a bullet or any of his many criminal activities. That left his twenty-two-year-old grandson, Izzy, to inherit the Greek throne. Problem was, Izzy was gay as fuck. That might not have been such a big deal to the Greeks if he was more of a pitcher than a catcher, but that wasn't the case, at least not according to the three-minute clip that had circulated a couple years ago. It was one of those open secrets in the underworld that everybody knew but never acknowledged out loud.

Izzy Costas got out of the rear driver's side door, dark, broody eyes sweeping over the scene.

"Holy crap," Theo whispered, suddenly appearing next to me. "Who's the underwear model?"

I scowled at him.

"What?" he said with a shrug. "I do have eyes, River, and he's so hot, he might set this place on fire."

"He's all right," I muttered. "That's Isador Costas, Nigel's grandson. The stone-cold shrew next to him is his wife, Hillary."

"Only in the barest sense," Aleksi chimed in, watching the newcomers carefully. "If they've ever shared more than a chaste kiss on their wedding day, I'll sprout wings and fly."

There was a dull thump as Sacha slapped Aleksi in the back of the head and demanded, "Show some respect."

Nigel and his family approached, stopping first to trade grips with Niki. "Nikita, it's good to see you. How is your father's health?"

"Better than yesterday," Niki replied, as always. "Strong as an ox still. He asked me to thank you for the vegetable basket you sent last fall."

"I'll send him another. I have pumpkins as big as your head," Nigel promised and stopped in front of us. "Yuri Laskin," Nigel remarked, planting his cane. "It has been some time."

"It has," Dad agreed. "You look well."

"I look amazing for an octogenarian, you mean," Nigel replied sharply. "I don't think I'm ready for one of your caskets yet, so you can stop measuring me with your eyes, young man." He turned and smacked Izzy in the chest with the back of his hand. "Give the man the vegetables, eh?"

Izzy stepped forward, holding out a basket overflowing with tomatoes, cucumbers, and several kinds of peppers. "Thank you for your hospitality," he said politely.

Dad accepted the basket with thanks, but we weren't done. No exchange with the old Greek was ever complete without him bragging about the size of his stupid vegetables.

"Look at the size of those cucumbers, eh, Yuri? You know how you get cucumbers that size? Fertilizer. Good fertilizer, not that pig shit Americans sell at the Home Depot." He lifted his cane and shook it. "I heard human ashes are good for the soil."

"Coffee grounds are better," Izzy offered, drawing a scowl from his grandfather. He was soft spoken enough that many would mistake his demeanor for shy, but there was a ruthless edge to the way he spoke. If Nigel was a baseball bat wrapped in barbed wire, his grandson was a knife whispering in the dark. "You need magnesium and sulfur for tomatoes. Not enough of that in human remains."

"They're mostly carbon," I agreed.

Hillary looked me up and down. "And how do you know anything about growing tomatoes? Aren't you an embalmer?"

"River reads a lot of books," Theo volunteered, drawing everyone's eyes to him.

I stiffened, my fingers twitching at my sides. I didn't like all that attention on him. He was *mine*.

Hillary wrinkled her nose. "Oh, you're him, aren't you? The whore."

Dad's hand clamped on my shoulder, keeping me from surging forward to strangle the life out of the heiress. He gave me a subtle shake of his head.

"Hillary," Izzy said, his tone quiet but full of warning. "Don't."

There was a loud gasp and Tatty stepped out, extending her hands. "Hillary, love! Don't you look amazing? Is that last season's Louis Vuitton? Darling, you must go shopping with me! Nudes are out and pastels are coming in."

Hillary put on a fake smile, taking Tatty's hands. "Tatty, how are you? You look like you haven't aged a day. Are you doing Botox or did you get a lift?"

"Neither, darling. It's all natural," Tatty replied. They exchanged cheek kisses before Tatty continued, ushering Hillary into the building, "Come with me, darling. I'm dying to show you the diamond broach Niki bought me last week. You can help me put it on."

Izzy encased my hand in both of his. "I apologize for my wife's rudeness."

I was still simmering when he let go of me and turned to Theo. How dare she call him that. I was the only one allowed to call Theo that, and it'd taken so much work to get him that comfortable with me.

"Theo. Is that short for Theodore?" Izzy asked.

Theo swallowed and looked at me briefly before answering. "I don't know. I think it's just Theo."

"It's a name with Greek origins," Izzy said. "Do you know what it means? It means gift of God."

"I don't believe in God," Theo said, fidgeting.

"We all have our gods, and we are all sinners first," Izzy said. "Even if we don't ascribe to the gospels." He inclined his head and moved on.

"Don't take it personal, eh?" Aleksi said to Theo. "They're Greek. They can't help being assholes." To me, he said in Russian, "Relax, cousin. Go take your boy in the back and work it out, huh? You look like you're going to pop." He made a lewd gesture with his hand before patting my back and wandering off.

Dad sighed and swooped around to stand in front of me. "Control yourself, River."

"If that bitch calls Theo that one more fucking time—"

"You'll do nothing," he said, cutting me off. "You'll bite your tongue and walk away. It's been a long time since we've all been in the same room, and the way they see it, they're doing you a favor by involving us. Niki put in a lot of legwork to make this happen, and I won't have you starting a war in my house."

Theo came to my side, wrapping his arms around me. "Your dad's right, River. I've been called a lot worse. Their opinions of me don't matter."

"I'm not going to stand here and let them insult you," I said, squeezing him back.

"If she gets out of line again," Niki said calmly, "I will correct her."

"You will sit and be gracious, or you'll leave," Dad said firmly.

I didn't bother arguing with him, even though I felt like it. When Dad used that tone, it meant he couldn't be swayed. He was right anyway. While we didn't need the Russians or the Greeks to find and execute Earl, it was too late to back out now. If we did anything without their blessing at this stage, they'd take offense, and offending mobsters would only end in more bodies. One of them might even be Theo's if I didn't tread carefully.

I let out a long sigh, adjusted my suit jacket, put a hand around Theo's waist, and we walked into the main parlor.

Most people were still standing, shaking hands, and having light conversation, but things shifted as soon as everyone was there. People instinctively took their seats with all the Russians filling out one end of the table and Greeks the other. We sat at the center, Theo at my side. He slipped his hand into mine under the table and I gave him a reassuring squeeze back.

A small bowl of coarse salt and several loaves of freshly baked bread made their rounds on the table, symbols of welcome and friendship, as business opened up.

"Thank you all for coming," said Niki. "I'm sure you're all very busy, so let's get straight to it. We need access to Saint Niklaus Cathedral, or rather, the operations going on there."

"Unsanctioned operations," Nigel clarified.

"How could they operate inside your territory for almost two decades without being noticed?" Aleksi scoffed, resting an elbow on the back of his chair.

"Human trafficking is your area," Nigel said. "You tell me."

Aleksi glared at Nigel. "Not children. Not *babies*."

"Good to know there's a line somewhere you Cossacks won't cross." Nigel lifted his water and took a sip.

"And it's good to know you Greeks care so much about what happens in your territory," Niki volunteered. "Perhaps some restructuring is in order if this could go undetected on your side for so long."

The two mobsters glared at each other from across the table.

"It doesn't matter," Sacha said, giving his son a cutting glare. "We know about it now, and we are shutting it down. While we can get into the church, access to the sub-basement and the operation itself is incredibly limited. If we go in guns blazing, these people will put a bullet in every head in the basement before we ever get downstairs."

Theo squeezed my hand tight.

I moved my hand to his thigh and felt him relax slightly. "We don't want that to happen."

"The only way to avoid that outcome will be to get someone inside the operation," Sacha said. "Infiltration could take time. Months, maybe years."

"We don't have that kind of time," Theo said.

"Not if they're dropping bodies on our doorstep," Dad agreed, meeting Nigel's displeased glare.

"Who currently has access?" Izzy asked, and all eyes turned to Theo.

Theo's throat bobbed. "Um. I don't know anything about the church. I don't remember ever going there."

"What about the doctor?" Dad asked, looking to War, who sat next to him.

"Dead," War confirmed.

"My intelligence says he has someone else at his practice who fills in when he can't make it, a man named..." Aleksi tapped his fingers on the table, thinking. "O'Neil. O'Neil took out a second mortgage on his house, and with two ex-wives and five kids between them, he's paying alimony and child support out the ass. A lot to exploit there."

"All you need is for him to leave a door unlocked," War pointed out.

"And not tip anyone off," I said firmly.

"All I have to do is twist his arm," War said. "He's a doctor, not a soldier. He'll break like fine china under pressure."

Aleksi sat forward to look at War. "Can you do it?"

War snorted. "In my sleep."

"And once you've gotten in, then what?" Nigel asked.

"Fire purifies all sins," Izzy offered, folding his hands on the table. "I'm sure the church has a nice insurance policy, and if not, we can help them out with that. As for the prisoners, they will likely need medical attention. Rehabilitation."

"Fold them in with our whores and let them work for it," Nigel proposed.

I almost jumped to my feet, but Theo beat me to the objection.

"No," he demanded, face hardening. "They've been through enough."

"Well," Nigel scoffed, "we should get something for our trouble."

Izzy frowned. "The insurance money will more than cover our expenses, baba."

"We'll take them," Dad offered.

My attention swung to him, eyes widening. He and Mom weren't exactly young anymore, and raising a handful of people like Theo to be functional wasn't going to be easy or cheap, but I knew better than to argue with the old man.

"Annie and I will see that they get the care they need," Dad said.

"We want Earl," I said instead. "The one they call Master."

"I did some looking into him, too." Aleksi shook his head. "He actually has ties, albeit distant, to us. He has a cousin who owns the butcher shop under one of our safehouses. He's brushed elbows with us enough times that he wasn't even hard to find. I can give you his addresses, but he has about two dozen low-rent multi-family units. Fucker's a slum lord. It seems he's gone to where he feels safe, in his proverbial castle. If he goes to ground again, it will take time to run him down."

"Then let's make sure he doesn't." Nigel planted his cane and stood, prompting the rest of his people to do the same. "How soon can we execute this?"

"My *boyeviks* are ready to go," Aleksi said. "Doctor O'Neil and I will have a chat tonight and we can move this Tuesday."

"Two days before Thanksgiving?" Dad shook his head. "We're booked up with back-to-back services."

"I'll work overtime to make sure everything is ready here," I offered. "And Xavier and Xander can fill in wherever you need."

I was anxious to get it done, and I knew Theo was too. The longer we waited, the more likely someone was to get spooked or the more things could go wrong. The sooner Earl was dead, the sooner I could have Theo all to myself, body and mind.

"Then it's settled." Niki stretched to his full height. "We will keep eyes and ears on Earl Maynard and the church."

"And we will speak to our insurance broker," Neil promised.

Neil and Niki clasped hands over the table. It was a historic event, the kind someone was sure to write about in history books. The Russians and the Greeks coming together for anything was rare. I barely cared. All I wanted was the opportunity to watch Theo cut into Earl. As long as that happened, I didn't care who was involved.

Thirty-Four

Theo

River worked hard the next few days, getting up early and staying at work late. Sometimes, when there were services, I went with him to work, but I didn't see him all day. Mostly, I swept, dusted, and pointed the bereaved to the sign-in books or to the restrooms.

At the end of the day, River was often tired enough that he fell asleep on the couch while I was still watching TV with Sacha or Xander and Xavier. We didn't talk much, but we touched often, every chance we got. It still never felt like enough.

It felt like the world had inhaled and was holding its breath, waiting for Tuesday.

I started to wonder what would happen once I woke up Wednesday morning. It would be a new world then, one without Earl in it. For the first time in my life, I would be truly free.

Sunday night, I laid on River's chest, listening to him breathe, and wondered what I should do with myself. I supposed I could leave him. Go try to establish myself somewhere, see the world. But I didn't want to go anywhere without him. Before, I'd stayed because I had nowhere else to go. Master would have hunted me, and I'd never be safe without River.

Things would be different come Wednesday. I wouldn't need River to protect me. I knew how to cook and clean, and I could probably find a shelter somewhere that would take me in, agencies that would help me get jobs and all the documents I needed. I had needed River to save me, but I didn't need him anymore. At least, not like that.

The more I thought about it, though, the more I realized I *wanted* him, which was different than needing him. Even though I could leave, I didn't want to. I wanted to choose him and this wild and crazy life he'd brought me into. It was comfortable now.

What if he doesn't want me anymore after this? I lightly traced a finger down the center line of his chest. *What if he only wanted to save me and his interest disappears once that's done? What do we have but a shared enemy?*

Love? Maybe. Could I love someone I'd known for such a short time? Less than a month and I was ready to spend the rest of my life with him.

I looked up at him, watching him sleep. *Is that what I want?* We were both still young. The rest of our lives was a long time. It seemed like a lot to ask from him. From anyone. If he asked me, though, I would do it. I was in love with River, and I didn't know how to love anyone else, nor did I want to.

When the alarm went off early the next morning, River rolled over and pulled back the curtains, squinting at the outside world with a displeased look. "Dammit."

"What is it?" I pushed up from the mattress, rubbing sleep from my eyes, my heart in my throat. "What's wrong?"

He let the curtain fall back into place and sat up. "It snowed."

That got me up and moving out of bed, my heart thumping with excitement. I went to the window and pushed the curtain aside with a big smile. The whole world had been blanketed in a layer of white, and more was falling. It looked like a painting outside.

"What's the matter, River?" I asked, landing on top of him. "You don't like the snow?"

River groaned and turned over, pulling the pillow on top of his head. "Not when I have to drive on it. Roads will be a mess. That's the cherry on top of having to get everything finished up for the whole week today. I'm not looking forward to work today."

"I thought you loved your job?" I snuggled up to him, kissing his cheek.

"I like being able to take my time to do it," River explained. "When I have to rush, it's hard to make everything look as good."

"You take pride in your work, and it shows." I kissed him again, this time on the mouth, slipping my tongue inside to taste him.

He gripped my leg and started tracing lazy circles on my thigh. "You keep kissing me like that and we'll definitely be late for work," he said and nipped my ear.

River's phone rang and he reached for it while I tried to seduce him back to bed. "What's up, Dad? Yeah, I saw. Really? Are you sure? They're okay with it? Okay, yeah. Makes sense. No, it's fine. Thanks. Bye." The phone beeped as he hung up. River tossed the phone back onto the nightstand and pulled me on top of him with a big grin. "Looks like we both get a snow day."

"Really?" I asked, bracing myself on his chest. "What about the viewings you had scheduled for today?"

"Rescheduled. Nobody wants to drive in this." He pulled me down into a lazy kiss, his soft tongue dancing against mine.

We rolled and his weight settled overtop of me. I wanted to be in the moment, to be totally into the slow seduction of his lips on my skin, but my mind had hooked on something else. Something I couldn't fuck away or forget. I laid there, drifting between the urge to disassociate completely and to ask him the most dangerous question of all.

Eventually, the question won out.

"What happens after tomorrow, River?" I asked as he kissed his way down my neck.

He hesitated, looking up at me. "What do you mean?"

"I mean us."

He frowned. "Why would anything change?"

"Are you sure you'll still want me when I don't need you to save me?" I combed my fingers through his hair.

He wrinkled his nose as if the whole notion was ridiculous. "I'll never stop wanting you. How could I?"

"So I'm supposed to sweep floors and pass out pamphlets at the funeral home forever?"

He sighed and shifted to hold his head up, planting his elbows on the bed. "What do you want to do?"

My mouth fell open and then quickly snapped shut. No one had ever asked me that before. Even if they had, I wouldn't have known how to answer them. I still wasn't entirely sure, but I was beginning to get a few ideas.

"I want to travel," I said. "See the world."

After spending my entire life in a tiny cell and only being allowed out to service strangers, it seemed like the natural thing.

"Did you know the world's largest living organism is a mushroom?" River said, drawing me out of my thoughts.

I blinked, surprised by the rapid change in topics. "I did not."

"Yeah, there's this giant colony of honey mushrooms in Oregon. There's like ten kilometers of them growing out there, all clones of each other. I've always wanted to go see them myself."

My lips turned up in a smile when I realized why we were talking about mushrooms. He wanted to travel too, but of course it had to involve one of his interests. I didn't mind. I'd never been to Oregon, and that was as fine a place as any to start exploring the world.

I kissed his forehead. "I'd love to go see a giant colony of mushrooms with you, but then what?"

"What do you mean?" he asked, sitting up.

I sucked in a breath and forced myself to say it, even though I was dreading the answer. "I mean us, River. Where do we go? How does this end when there's nowhere left to travel, and no more mushroom colonies left to visit? What happens to us?"

He stared at me for a minute, as if he couldn't quite process the question. Maybe it had never occurred to him that there would be life after this, or what it would mean once this job was done. Sometimes River had trouble planning ahead, especially when emotions were involved. I could understand. Despite his insistence otherwise, he was a man with big feelings, and those often got in the way of being able to see a path ahead. Up until recently, planning for the future had been impossible for me, too, but once Earl was gone, the future would be all that remained.

"You want to get married?" he asked me deadpan.

I stopped breathing, my lungs seizing.

Get married? To River?

I'd never even considered it. Never thought of marrying anyone, but I didn't want this to end. I wanted to be with him forever, so marriage seemed like the natural thing to do. Wasn't it? This was insane, but so was everything else that'd happened to me.

"Do you?" I asked quietly.

He shrugged. "I couldn't care less about all the formal stuff. You've been mine since the day I bought you, and that's never going to change, but if you want a ring and a big ceremony, I can do that."

My throat was suddenly tight. "Really? You want to marry me?"

River leaned down, wrapping an arm around the back of my head to lift my lips to his. "What I want is to see you every day for the rest of my life. I want to see you when I wake up every morning, and every night before I fall asleep. When I wake up in the middle of the night, I want to feel you next to me. I want to be the one to hold you when you cry and when you laugh. I want to sit with you on the couch downstairs and read my science articles while you watch your silly animated musicals that I hate. I want to wash your back, and taste your skin, and still be the only one to make you come." He punctuated each sentence with a kiss along my jaw. "And that applies now, as well as when you're eighty and your teeth are falling out."

I giggled and gave him a lighthearted shove. "How romantic."

He caught my hand. "And when we die, I want to be with you then, too, Theo. I want us together forever, until we're nothing but ash and memory." River nuzzled against my chin and kissed my neck.

I touched his cheek, bringing his lips back to mine, and kissed him until he pulled back.

River's brows knitted in concern, his eyes softening, like he was concentrating hard the way he did when he was trying to figure out my emotions. It shouldn't have been sexy, but it was, partly because I knew he'd never look at anyone else that way. Just me.

"I want that too." I gave his shoulder a firmer push, and he went onto his back without any resistance.

River's hands went to my hips as I straddled him. "You're fucking perfect, Theo, and all this perfection is mine."

I smirked and ran my hands over his arms, feeling the goosebumps there. "And all *this* perfection is *mine*."

River's eyes darkened and he twisted, sliding open the bedside table. I thought he was reaching for the lube, but when I saw him grab a box cutter, my cock gave an excited twitch. He held it out to me. "Show me."

"How?" I already knew what he wanted me to do, but I needed to hear it from him.

"Carve it into my skin," River said, sounding breathless. "Mark me, Theo."

I stared at the box cutter, my mouth dry, then reached to take it with shaky hands. "Are you sure? This will probably scar."

River rolled his hips up against me, grinding his cock against mine. "I've never been more sure of anything in my life. I want you with me forever, and I want the whole world to know I'm yours."

"Fuck," I murmured. "Okay. Where?"

"Right here." He patted his bare chest just above his heart.

I clicked the box cutter up two notches. My heart was pounding as I pressed the blade to his skin. River groaned as I made the first downward slash, his eyes rolling back and fingers kneading my ass. The blade was sharp enough that it parted the skin like a scalpel. Blood welled to the surface and spilled from one cut into the next. I tried to keep my hand steady, but it wouldn't stop shaking. By the time I'd finished the second letter, a strangely powerful euphoria settled over me. I wasn't just carving my name into River's chest, claiming him; he'd put his life in my hands.

When I was finished, I clicked the box cutter closed and tossed it aside, shivering like I was freezing, but I wasn't. I was warm everywhere, vibrating with an emotion I barely understood. River's blood flowed freely down the planes of his stomach like a little river. I watched it move with his body as he breathed hard, staring at me with wide eyes, pupils blown so huge, I'd have thought he was on something if I didn't know better. I felt like I was high too, and I'd never been harder in my life. My cock was leaking, pre-cum dripping into the rivulets of blood running down River's stomach.

River's hand snaked into my hair, gripping it by the roots. "I need to be inside you. Now," he snarled roughly.

I hurriedly retrieved the lube, but he barely let me prep myself before he was thrusting into me. I cried out at the rough burning pain of being suddenly stretched to my limit, but that pain was everything I wanted, everything I needed. The only thing that felt real.

"Fuck, Theo," he moaned and started fucking up into me hard. "You feel so fucking good."

"I'm already so close," I panted.

"Good." River snarled and swiped through the bloody mess on his stomach before closing around my cock. I moaned loudly and tipped my head back as he started to stroke me.

River groaned and let go of my head, thrusting into me with more intention. Every movement sent sparks of nearly unbearable pleasure racing up my spine until his hips stuttered and I felt him spill himself inside of me. That sent me careening over the edge, spilling thick ropes of cum over his bloodstained stomach and chest. Seeing the essence of us mixed together like that sent another shuddering wave of euphoria through me, the feeling so intense, my vision whited out.

When it was over, I collapsed against the right side of River's chest, shaking and panting.

River turned my lips up to his. "Say it again?" he asked as soon as he could speak.

I smiled, knowing what he was asking for. "I love you, River Laskin."

"God, I'll never get tired of that." He nosed against me and added, "Theo Laskin."

The words sent a shudder up my spine.

I could be that, be his in every way. I didn't know what my real last name was, and the one I was using didn't fit. His fit much better.

We cleaned up as best we could, but the sheets were ruined. We'd probably have to replace the mattress, too, but that could wait for another day. I got the bleeding stopped, even though it took a while, and helped River bandage himself before we curled up at the end of the bed to avoid the wet spots on the mattress.

I snuggled against River, my head on his chest. My finger moved over the bandage, gently tracing out the letters I'd carved into him. "What will your brothers think?"

"Of what?" he asked, scrunching his face up.

I looked up at him. "Of us getting married."

He shrugged. "I don't care what they think."

I pinched his side. "Be nice."

"Ow, what? Seriously. Shepherd's too busy teaching and fucking his grad students. War's so obsessed with finding a *new* family he probably won't even notice, and Xander and Xavier will be too busy partying. They have their own lives, and I have you."

I hummed lightly and closed my eyes. "I think they'll approve."

"They'd better, or I'll feed them to my mushrooms."

"No you won't," I said, tickling his hips, making him laugh and kick. "I won't let you."

He pushed me away only to pull me back instantly and kiss the top of my head. "Are you ready for tomorrow?"

Something in my chest tightened, threatening to squeeze until it broke. "I don't know. I think so, but going back there, seeing it all again..."

"You don't have to go in," River offered gently. "You can always come in after."

After someone else took care of Earl. He was offering to kill him for me. The thought was touching, but if I wasn't there when it happened, I didn't know if it'd feel real. I wanted to pull the trigger myself after what he'd done.

"I want to go," I said quietly. "I think I need to."

"Okay," was all that River said, and he kissed me again.

We spent most of the rest of the day in bed, only being drawn downstairs by the scent of warm food. Sacha had made borscht and served it with buttered rye bread. I'd never had anything made of beets before, but it was easily the most hearty and delicious thing I'd ever had.

After the sun set, we sat down to watch the news together, which seemed to be Sacha's favorite thing. River mostly ignored the television, scrolling through his phone. I tuned most of it out, too, paying more attention to the warmth of River against me.

Theo Laskin. I kept running the name through my head, feeling giddy every time I thought it. River had promised me a ring and a proper proposal once all this was done, but I didn't need all that for it to be real. I knew he meant it. Once River said he was going to do something, he did it, and that was that.

I was mostly zoned out until the news anchor cut in with a breaking story.

"Breaking news tonight out of the German Village," she began in a tense tone. "A local nightclub owner is missing, and police say they suspect foul play. More from Andrea, who's on the scene. Andrea?"

The camera cut to a two-story house in an upscale neighborhood. Yellow police tape marred the front and a whole crew of people in uniforms moved around behind her.

A serious looking woman with a dark brown bob stood in front of the camera. "Tiffany, I'm here at the home of Jeffrey Dimori, owner of The Time Out Room in Easton, which investigators are now calling a crime scene. It began with a call to emergency services around two o'clock last night placed by Dimori, who believed he was the victim of a home invasion. By the time police arrived, Dimori was gone, the only sign that he'd been here at all was a drying pool of blood on the kitchen floor, and this black book full of names investigators are saying may link him to a pedophile ring they've been investigating for months."

I sat up and elbowed River as they cut to an interview with a policeman. "River, look."

"I hear it." He frowned at the screen and immediately got up, punching some buttons on his phone.

"What are you doing?"

"Calling Shepherd." River put his hand on his hip and paced back and forth quickly for several minutes before he cursed, lowered the phone, and tried again. "He's not answering."

"Do you think it's him?" I asked.

Sacha shrugged. "Hard to say. Men like Jeff have made many enemies. Shepherd Laskin is only one of many people who would be all too happy to make him disappear."

"It worries me that he's not answering," River said, lowering the phone. "Maybe we should go check on him."

"But the operation at Saint Niklaus is tomorrow," Sacha said, sitting forward. He folded his hands in his lap. "You are not your brother's keeper, River. If Shepherd is involved in Jeff's disappearance, then there is nothing you can do."

"I'm less worried about Shepherd and more worried about Keres," River said, sinking onto the couch. "I think he's off his meds."

"And what will you do if he is?" Sacha asked. "Nothing. Sometimes, River, it is best to keep your head down and let things play out. *Chimu byt, tavoh ni mihnovat.*"

I looked over at River. "What does that mean?"

"It means you cannot avoid what is bound to happen," Sacha explained. "Keres is a caged beast. If Jeff fell into the cage, then it is more suicide than murder." He lifted his glass of vodka and downed it in a single swallow. Then Sacha stood and patted River's shoulder. "Let us focus on our task, and leave Shepherd to his."

Thirty-Five
River

Saint Niklaus' Church of the Holy Rosary was a sprawling brick compound that took up a quarter of a city block. At its height, the building had housed a private preschool and a small shelter for the homeless in addition to the church itself. A decline in attendance and income led to the church's closure in the mid-nineties. It changed hands three times in eighteen months, though the church never officially reopened in its full capacity.

A cardboard sign jammed into the overgrown grass shuddered against the wind, announcing that the free clinic was around back. Worn letters on the yellowing sign spelled out directions to a soup kitchen dinner being held on Thanksgiving.

On the surface, it looked like a community center designed to connect the poor with badly needed resources. No one would ever look at the historic stained glass or the worn brick and think this was the face of a human trafficking operation that'd been running for two decades.

"How are you doing, little fish?" Uncle Sacha's eyes were glued to the rearview mirror, watching Theo in the back.

I twisted to look at him and frowned at how pale and sweaty he was. "You don't have to go in there."

Theo's fingers twitched against his knees, but he didn't look away from the front door. He swallowed. "I don't know if I can do this."

"You don't have to," I reiterated. "Between us, the Russians, and the Greeks, we have more than enough manpower."

It wasn't like Theo would be useful in there. He didn't know how to operate a gun, and we wouldn't need a guide. War's conversation with O'Neil had gone better than expected. He'd agreed to wear a small camera on his clothes, which had mapped out the maze of subterranean hallways. We were just waiting for a signal from Aleksi's team.

Theo finally tore his eyes from the front door to look at me. "If I don't go in there, what am I supposed to do? Just sit here while all of you risk your lives?"

"We've done this a hundred times," Sacha said dismissively before glancing at me. "Well, most of us. What my nephew is too kind to say to you is that it would be best if you remained here. Since you're not part of the operation, you're just one more body to protect. In those narrow hallways, that makes you a liability."

I scowled at Uncle Sacha.

"What?" Sacha said with a shrug. "You both know I am right. We already know we will have a handful of civilian targets to secure and protect. That will be difficult enough."

Theo sighed. "He's right," he said, squirming. "I guess I'll wait here."

I gave Sacha a pleading look.

Uncle Sacha smiled and patted my shoulder. "I'll stay with him. He's safe with me."

The speaker in my ear chirped and Izzy's voice broke the silence. "Gamma in position."

"That's my cue." I popped open the glove box and retrieved the .357 Magnum in there, doing a quick check to make sure all the chambers were loaded. When it came to murder, I usually preferred to do the job with something more hands-on, but that wasn't practical in this case. The .357 was more for protection than anything since I was going in with the second team.

I got out of the car and opened Theo's door, stealing a quick kiss, savoring the taste of him before gripping the back of his head briefly and letting my forehead rest against his.

He gripped my black turtleneck in his fists. "I love you."

"Same." I said back with a coy grin before standing and pointing at Sacha. "Take care of my fiancé." A little thrill fluttered through me when I said the word out loud for the first time.

Sacha's eyes widened at the announcement, too keen to miss it. He was the first one outside of us to know.

I didn't linger long enough for him to ask questions, instead pulling down the black ski mask to cover my face and quickly jogging across the street to where Xander, Xavier, and War were already in position.

We'd tried to call Shepherd to see if he wanted a piece of the action, but he wasn't picking up his phone. That still worried me, but it wasn't the first time. It was like Uncle Sacha said. He had to see to himself for now.

I nodded to War as I approached and heard his voice in my ear. "Beta team in position."

"Alpha is good to go," Aleksi answered from his entry point. "Let's party."

Everything seemed to happen all at once.

War threw open the door and we filed into the church foyer, fanning out, guns up. I took my place in the center of the formation next to War, covering the thirty-to-sixty-degree section of the arc. The foyer was a wood paneled room, mostly empty. It smelled like all old churches and courthouses, like dust and sweat and paper. It was empty so we closed on the sanctuary doors. I took the right side while War held the left, watching the hallways while Xander and Xavier came forward to grip the sanctuary doors.

"On a three count," Xander announced. "One, two..."

Xander and Xavier yanked open the sanctuary doors and we made our way slowly down the center aisle between the pews. It was a pain in the ass, but we had to check every single row to make sure nobody came around behind us. We leapfrogged down the rows two at a time. Three rows in, we found a pair of old ladies cowering between the pews. They looked harmless, but then so did Mom, and she had the highest body count of all of us.

"Reach for the sky, grannie!" Xander howled, approaching.

The old ladies' hands shot up and they started wailing.

Xander snickered. "Always wanted to say that."

Xavier rolled his eyes. "Herd them into the confessional."

Shots rang out deeper in the church, sounding like popcorn. Aleksi's voice quickly followed over comms. "Two down! Watch your six, Gamma. These fuckers are armed and move like fucking pros."

Flashes lit up the room just off stage at the front of the dusty sanctuary and gunfire barked. War and I sped our pace, rushing to the front only to be met with a rather calm looking Izzy as he stepped out of the shadows, slapping a fresh magazine into his tiny Italian-made handgun.

"Jesus, fuck," Xander whispered next to me. "Am I the only one with a raging boner right now?"

"Ugh," War groaned.

"You're such a simp," Xavier muttered.

"What? *Look* at him," Xander insisted with a dreamy sigh.

Izzy paused at the sight of us before giving us an acknowledging nod. "Boys."

"Bodies?" War asked, ignoring Xander's drooling over Izzy.

Izzy tipped his head casually back toward the room he'd come from. "Two in the hall. You?"

"None yet," Xander replied.

"Still early. I'm sure you'll get one, Tiger," Izzy smirked and winked, obviously aware of Xander's interest.

"We have two witnesses in the confessional," War offered. "Couple of old ladies."

He turned, regarding the image of the Madonna in stained glass behind him, expression going cold. Long, thin fingers closed over the hat he wore and he removed it, placing it against his chest. "I'll take care of them. You boys go on."

Without another word, War and I came up the short steps, taking a right to go through the stage doors. I didn't think Izzy would kill the old ladies, but who knew what he would do? He wasn't exactly known for being merciful, and collateral damage was better than a live witness.

I let the thoughts slip out of my brain, focusing on the task at hand as we came up on a heavy iron door that'd already been pried open. There were two bodies slumped over near it, one on either side. Aleksi's work. Only one of the guards was dead, but the other would be in a few seconds. I nudged him out of the way with my foot and we stepped through the door.

The stairs that led down from the security door were so narrow, even I felt claustrophobic. They turned ninety degrees twice, descending into an underworld of a sterile white hallway with flickering fluorescent lights above. White doors were staggered on either side of the hall. A whiteboard hung on each, some of them bearing initials while others had a big X. The rooms closest to us were open.

I swung into the one on the right and immediately stopped. It was a six by nine windowless room, the walls painted white like the hallway. There was no bed, just a thin mattress on the floor. A bucket with a lid sat in the corner furthest from the bed. There was a boy in the room, a teenager with dirty brown hair. His big, brown eyes had the same furious yet defeated look in them that Theo's had the first time I saw him. Seeing that again, and the conditions Theo must've lived in, turned my vision red with rage.

Before it'd even registered what I was doing, I was stalking down the hall to where Aleksi had cornered a man in scrubs near an opening with a tile floor. The man had his hands up and was trying to back away, but there was nowhere to go. Behind him were a series of showers and drains. No effort had been made to provide privacy for anyone using those showers.

I shoved Aleksi out of the way and grabbed the man by his green scrubs, slamming him against the shower wall, demanding, "Where is he?"

"Holy fuck, man! What the fuck!" the man exclaimed, his voice breaking. His hands flew up in surrender, the coward. "Just tell me what you want! I'll tell you anything!"

I shoved the barrel of the .357 against his stomach. "The Master. Where the fuck is he?"

"He's not here!"

"Where is he?" I demanded again.

"He went out the back." The man pointed. "Once there were shots, he ran. Told us to liquidate the assets."

Assets.

Was that what they'd called Theo? An asset? Like he was a fucking product on the shelf?

I didn't need to shoot the man, but I did. I squeezed the trigger once, twice, three times, pumping his stomach full of lead. I would've done it again except that Aleksi yanked me away from him. I brought the gun up, pointing it at him on instinct, but he pushed it toward the ceiling just before it went off again.

"Stupid boy," he snarled in Russian, twisting a pinky in his ear. "You killed him before I could pump him for more info."

"We have another," announced one of his men in the hall.

"Doctor!" someone shouted from one of the rooms. "Need some help in here!"

War pushed his way through the pair of Russians hovering in the doorway. "Who's got Narcan? Check the others!"

I spun away from the scene. There was nothing I could do for the kids they'd purposefully overdosed in their hurry to clean up their mess. I was there to find Earl. I started down the hallway that stretched ninety degrees from the one with the boarding rooms.

"Where are you going?" Aleksi called after me. "River! Earl's in the wind! He's gone by now!"

I knew he was right, but I didn't care. I didn't want to believe it without verifying it with my own eyes. Stomping down the hall, I stopped to shove open every single door, finding an office, a medical exam room, a tiny little kitchen, and a storage room. At the end of the hallway, another stairway wound up to a dirty concrete room with an elevator. I slammed a fist into the button, clicking it repeatedly.

How had this all gone so wrong? We'd done exactly what we set out to do. They'd seemed surprised by our arrival, and yet somehow Earl still got away. I couldn't imagine telling Theo that we'd gone through all this for nothing, that the monster who'd tortured him for years was still out there. If he really was in the wind, there would be no finding him. He'd move to a new city, set up another operation, prey on more vulnerable people.

The thought made my stomach turn. Not because I gave a damn about people, but because I knew that the news would break Theo. He'd never feel safe, not until Earl was dead and in pieces.

The elevator doors finally opened with a ding that the hallway seemed to swallow. I stepped into a dirty metal car with graffiti scrawled on the back. The doors were about to slide closed when a black gloved hand slid between them. I glared at Izzy Costas as he forced the door open. His dark eyes raked over me, but he said nothing as he stepped into the elevator, standing off to the side. He ignored me as if I wasn't even there, checking the slide on his gun.

I glared at him as the doors slid closed. "What the fuck are you doing?"

"Making sure I have one in the chamber," he replied casually. "You?"

I crossed my arms and looked away. "I have to find him."

"And when you do, what then?" He opened his suit jacket, tucking the gun out of sight after turning on the safety. "You're about to walk into a public parking garage to find a ghost who may already be long gone."

"What's that got to do with you?"

"We are inside my grandfather's territory," he said casually, folding his hands in front of him. "If Sweet Sacha Laskin's favorite nephew gets killed on our soil, you can bet our peace will fall apart." Izzy considered me, his gaze cold and distant, as if he were staring at the inner workings of the elevator instead of me. "I'm here to make sure your young love doesn't get you killed and start a war that my family will bleed for."

The elevator slid to a stop and the doors opened. I stepped out, checking either side of the car with my gun at the ready. There was no sign of Earl, nor any cars on that floor. No sign anyone had been there at all except for a few old stains in the concrete.

The sound of gunshots echoed out from below, sending a chill up my spine. I ran to the edge of the parking garage, peering down at the street from behind the concrete barrier. The sun had set, but there were ample streetlights, and I recognized immediately that I was looking down at the street where Uncle Sacha was parked.

Uncle Sacha's beat up junker was on the corner, the driver's side door opened. My blood ran cold when I saw the silver-haired man yank Sacha's limp body out of the driver's seat. Earl.

Sacha fell in the snow, leaving a streak of red pooling beneath him while Earl jammed himself into the driver's seat. Tires squealed.

"Fuck!" I snarled and ran for the elevator, slamming my fist twice on the button. It was too slow so I ran for the ramp, knowing that no matter how fast I moved, I was too late. Earl had shot Uncle Sacha, jacked his car...

And now he had Theo hostage in the back seat.

Thirty-Six
Theo

I STARED AT THE back of Master's head.

At the back of Earl Maynard's head. He was no one. He was just a man with graying hair, glasses, and a lying smile. A man who had held me captive for most of my life, had gotten rich from selling me to worse men who would have killed me.

A man who had killed David.

At first, he didn't acknowledge me in the back seat, taking off to drive over the speed limit. We sped by parked cars with Earl constantly looking in the rearview mirror. I was in shock. It'd all happened so fast. He'd just opened the door, shot Sacha, yanked him out of the car, and then we were moving.

What can I do? My mind was racing. I knew I should do something to stop him, but what? I was unarmed. Helpless and at his mercy again. The thought made me sink further into the seat, wishing I could disappear.

We took a hard right turn onto a ramp, merging onto a busy freeway.

"Bet you think you're pretty clever right now, huh, kid?" Earl said as we accelerated into traffic. His dull blue eyes peered at me in the mirror, illuminated by passing headlights. "You always were dumber than a can of pebbles. Almost as fucking stupid as your whore mother. At least she put up a fucking fight. But you won't. No, we made sure you didn't have an ounce of fight in you."

I lowered my head, knowing he was right. What could I do? Even if I was armed, I couldn't shoot him, not while we were going eighty miles an hour down a busy highway. I didn't know how to drive or where we were. If I somehow managed to survive flinging myself from the car—which was unlikely—where would I go? I didn't know how to get back in touch with River.

I was alone. Helpless yet again.

My fingers curled into fists. "Why?"

"Why what?" he snorted.

"Why do all this?"

Earl shrugged. "Why the fuck not? I saw an opportunity and took it. Most of the people who were coming into the fucking clinic were hookers asking for opiates anyway. All I ever did was give them what they wanted. When they started squeezing out brats nobody wanted, I saw dollar signs. You should be fucking grateful. Without me, half of you kids would've been shoved in dumpsters and drowned in public toilets. I saved your fucking life."

"Did you save David's life?" I snapped, glaring at the back of his head as if I could shoot bullets out of my eyes.

His face twisted into a sneer. "Who?"

"David," I said. "The body you left at the funeral home for us to find."

Earl gave a cold laugh. "Oh, him? He was asking too many questions. Wanted to know where you were, why you hadn't come back. Started a rumor that you'd *escaped*. Where there's one that gets away, everyone thinks they can. We needed to send a message, make sure the others shut the hell up and kept working without questions. As for your friends…" His hands flexed on the steering wheel. "They needed to know there was a price for interfering in my business."

"Seems to me you made a mistake." I leaned forward. "Do you have any idea who it is that's going to come looking for me, *Earl?*"

"You mean the Russians and the Greeks?" he huffed. "Yeah, I ain't worried about a couple of mobsters. Once the heat dies down, I'll grease what palms I need to get the hell out of dodge."

"I mean the other people," I said, letting my voice drop an octave. "The ones even the Russians are scared of."

His eyes darted to me in surprise, but he quickly recovered, focusing back on the road.

I couldn't help but laugh. "You don't fucking know who you're messing with, do you? Or did you think the Greeks and Russians considered you enough of a threat to team up to take you down? You're small time. They didn't give a shit about you until my people put a target on your back."

"What people?" Earl spat. "You don't have *people*. Your mother was a crackhead whore and your daddy was some trucker with a spare fifty and twenty spare minutes outside a truck stop."

"You'll find out," I said, sitting back and praying that I was right. "Eventually."

My phone buzzed in my pocket and I nearly jumped out of my skin. Sweat broke out on the back of my neck as my eyes swung to Earl's reflection, hoping he hadn't heard it. He hadn't, he was too focused on the heavy traffic.

I leaned forward, hunching over, and fished the phone out of my pocket, turning the brightness down all the way and turning off the vibration before typing in the passcode. In the dim backlight, I could barely make out that I had a text from River. I opened it but couldn't read the words. I still couldn't read well enough to type a message back either, so I hit the dial button and slid the phone to the floor. It was the best I could do, the only way I knew how to help.

When I heard him pick up on the other end, I talked over his frantic hellos. "Where are you taking me, Earl?" I demanded loudly.

"Airport," he said distractedly.

"I'm not getting on a plane with you."

Earl made a disgusted sound. "As if I'd invest another fucking penny in you, let alone buy you a fucking plane ticket. No, this is where the buck stops. This is the day you die."

"They'll find you, you know," I said, mostly to distract myself from the terror threatening to make me break down. "Even if you kill me, you're not getting away with this."

"I already have, idiot," he scoffed. "You're my last loose end, and you're too much of a fucking pussy to do anything. You always have been. Honestly, I'm fucking relieved I don't have to look after you needy pricks anymore. You make me sick, how pathetic you are. Killing you is a favor too, isn't it? Just the natural end that's been a long time coming."

I clenched my jaw and looked down at the phone. The call timer was still running. Was River listening? If I stopped talking, he might think something happened to me. I had to keep Earl talking, had to get more information from him, anything that would help River find me. Even if he came too late, River deserved a body to mourn.

"So this was always your plan, huh?" I ventured as Earl took an exit. "I was always meant to die when I got to be too much trouble?"

"Don't take it personally, kid. Every product has a life cycle. You can only sell damaged goods second hand so many times." He shrugged. "Usually, I try not to just off you, though. Most of you have good kidneys, good eyes, good livers. One last gold mine." He laughed and shook his head. "Cash from the cradle to the grave. That was the whole fuckin' idea." He snorted. "Of course, that was before I realized how fucking expensive you all were. Then the clinic we used as a front needed to be legit, which costs even more. I'm always greasing palms, always paying people off. Fuck, in this economy? You're not worth it once you're over fifteen. I should've started gutting you bastards for parts younger. Something I'll keep in mind next time. Do you know how much rich old farts will pay for a good, gently used kidney?"

I felt sick. He wasn't going to stop. I'd known that, but still, hearing it come out of his mouth left me with a sour taste on my tongue. Earl intended to set up in another city, prey on more families, destroy more lives. And he could do it, too. He had the money, had people willing to take bribes. The cops weren't going to stop him. Nobody cared about addicts and prostitutes and the unwanted babies they made. Nobody cared about people like me who didn't exist on paper. The invisible people.

But I wasn't invisible to River and his family. They'd taken me in, looked after me, giving me a home, a life. Treated me as human for the first time in my life. They were my family now, and I needed to get back to them if I could.

Traffic thinned out as we drove closer to the airport, weaving through a complex maze of roadways, following signs I couldn't read. Some of them were color coded, and I clung to that, hoping that would help. When we pulled into one with a big blue sign overhead, I sighed. "Blue lot, huh? At least I get to die under my favorite color."

"Don't get your hopes up about them finding you in time neither," Earl spat. "I promise you'll be cold by the time they find you."

"It won't stop them from hunting you down," I told him.

Earl didn't seem to care.

The huge parking lot was mostly abandoned, with only a few snow-covered cars scattered around. He drove us to an isolated section of it and parked. As soon as he got out of the car, I grabbed my phone and shoved it in my pocket, still on, so he wouldn't see.

The second he opened my door, I launched myself at him, tackling him to the icy pavement. I must've surprised him because he hit the ground, and I took off running. The bark of a gunshot made me freeze. I thought at first that I'd been hit, but, checking myself over, I realized he'd missed, so I started running again. Another shot came closer, hitting a snow bank off to my right. The gun roared again, and fire traced a line across my arm. I fell to my knees, the impact reverberating through my body strongly enough to take my breath away. I covered my hand over the wound. My sleeve was soaked in blood.

Get up. Run. Survive. The thoughts pounded through my head, but I was in so much pain. I tried to push myself up, but my arm hurt too bad. The second I put pressure on it, I folded.

Brown loafers slammed into my ribs with a gut-wrenching kick. I doubled over, choking on stomach acid and pain.

"You son of a bitch!" Earl snarled and flipped me onto my back. He stood over me. Breath erupted from his nostrils like smoke. "I'm gonna fuckin' enjoy this," he said and pointed the gun at my head.

He jerked before he could pull the trigger, a dark stain spreading across his chest. He looked down at it like he was confused and then jerked two more times before crumpling and lying still in an expanding pool of blood.

I managed to push myself up on my elbows, still trying to process what'd happened. River stood there, a gun pointed at where Earl had been standing. A sleek black SUV idled behind him, spewing exhaust into the night. Both front doors were open, but Izzy was still only halfway out of the car.

Half a dozen other cars were on the road, speeding through the entrance to the blue lot, but I didn't care about them. I only cared about the man in front of me.

"River," I breathed in disbelief.

He dropped the gun and ran to me, falling on the pavement and taking me in his arms, kissing me fiercely. "Fuck, I was so worried I wouldn't make it in time."

"You came for me," I said, throwing my arms around him only to wince.

"You're hurt," he observed and twisted. "I need a doctor!"

"It's nothing," I assured him, snuggling into him. One pull of River's scent into my lungs was enough to bring me down from the terrifying ledge I'd been on for the last hour.

I was okay. I was going to make it.

Aleksi appeared out of nowhere, closing on us with his gun drawn. He kicked away Earl's gun. "Everybody okay?"

I was startled when Earl groaned and then coughed.

"Fuck," Aleksi spat, pointing the gun at Earl. "He's alive?"

"Where's War?" River demanded.

"Back at the compound," Aleksi said. "They'd already OD'd half the kids before we got there. He's keeping as many alive as he can."

I pushed away from River and limped over to retrieve Earl's gun from where Aleksi had kicked it in the snow. A ball of ice settled in my gut as I came back to where Earl was bleeding on the pavement.

Earl tried to get up, but he couldn't. He looked up at me, nothing but pure hate in his eyes. He was sub-human. Less than that. How had I ever been afraid of him?

My hand shook as I pointed the barrel of the gun at him, even when I steadied it with another hand.

River reached to adjust how I was holding the gun slightly. "You can do this."

I took a deep breath and let it out in a wispy cloud. "I can do this."

He nodded and took a step back.

"You think this makes you better than me?" Earl spat, defiant to the end. "You're still trash. You were born a nobody, and that's how you'll die. Nothing but—"

I pulled the trigger.

The sound echoed through the mostly empty lot in the middle of the night. That gunshot was a scream, a whisper, a prayer answered with a bullet to the brain. It was the end of Earl Maynard and his reign of terror.

He fell over like he wasn't real, hitting the pavement with a muffled thud. My pulse pounded in my ears as I looked down at him. He looked like nothing, like he'd never been anything. How could I have ever been afraid of him? Just blood and bones and a paper-thin skin to hold it all in.

Just an evil, evil man. One of many.

River's hand closed over the top of the gun and he tipped the barrel toward the sky, gently twisting it out of my hands. "You did well, Theo."

I realized my lungs hurt and let out a breath. A blink and tears fell. I turned away from the body, putting my arms around River's neck and burying my face against his shoulder, sobbing freely.

"It's over," he promised, handing the gun off to Aleksi, who caught it with a tissue. River put his arms around me and pulled me close, his heart thumping against my ear. "You're free."

Thirty-Seven
River

The aftermath was chaos.

Theo had only been grazed by a bullet, so once we got the bleeding stopped, he was all right. Aleksi and his *boyeviks* loaded up the body, wrapping it in a tarp, and then came back with shovels to collect all the bloody snow. It went into an ice chest that'd probably find its way into the Ohio River or the bottom of a coal mine soon enough.

Earl's body was on its way to the Laskin Funeral Home by the time Izzy came over. He spoke quietly with Aleksi, who immediately turned away, nodding. Izzy put a hand on Aleksi's shoulder before turning his icy gaze on us.

I moved in front of Theo protectively when he approached. "I never got to thank you," I said, extending a hand. "If not for your driving, I never would've made it in time."

He took my hand and shook it firmly. "I'm glad to have helped. I only wish I had better news to bring you."

I stiffened, but it was Theo who appeared at my side and asked, "What is it? What's happened?"

Izzy took a deep breath, letting it out slowly. "It's your Uncle Sacha. He was taken to the University Hospital in critical condition. I had a nurse inside the OR that I trust with my life. They did everything they could, but..."

"He's dead, isn't he?" I said.

Izzy nodded. "I'm sorry, River. Deeply sorry. Your Uncle Sacha, he was a good man."

It was telling that I didn't feel any grief over the loss. Uncle Sacha had lived a full life. He'd known the risks. I would miss him dearly, but all I could feel at the moment was relief and worry.

My eyes slid to Aleksi, who was bent over the hood of his car, hands folded as if he were in prayer. "Is Aleksi going to be okay?"

"For better or worse," Izzy said quietly. "Aleksi is strong, and he has a good heart. He's well suited for his lot in life."

He extended his hand to me again, and I took it.

"You have my condolences," Izzy offered, "but I'm afraid my duties as my father's heir call me away. Apparently, a rather devastating fire has broken out in one of our investment properties. A church. A pity. It was a historical building, as I understand it. It will be very expensive to renovate."

"I'm sure you'll manage," I replied, shaking his hand.

Izzy's mouth turned up in the slightest hint of a smirk. He glanced over at Theo, and it took everything in me not to scoot Theo behind me. "Farewell, Theo Christianson," he said and turned.

"Actually, it's Laskin," Theo offered. He dipped his head and mumbled. "Or it will be soon."

Izzy hesitated, his smirk blossoming into a playful smile that looked surprisingly natural on his face. He dipped his head. "Congratulations," he said and walked away.

It was after midnight before the scene was clean enough that I was comfortable leaving. Theo was shivering and exhausted, but he didn't want to leave my side. He tensed when I walked him back to the car, but calmed down when I told him I'd be there with him.

"That was a smart thing you did with the phone," I said as we pulled out of the parking lot. "I'd never have found you if you weren't feeding me all that info."

"I didn't want to be helpless again," he said sleepily.

I watched the headlights and streetlights wash over him in waves, taking in the familiar blank stare. My hand closed over his and squeezed. "You did the right thing."

"I know," he whispered, voice hoarse. "I know that Earl had to die. He wasn't going to stop. Killing him was the only way to end this. And yet..." He turned his head, the weight of his gaze falling on me. "How do you do what you do?"

"I don't know." I pulled my hand away. "Some people say it's because I don't have a soul, but I don't believe in souls. You shouldn't feel bad about killing Earl today."

He closed his eyes and tipped his head back against the headrest. "I don't feel bad. I feel...dirty. Like by killing him, he's infected me in a way. He's a part of me now, whether I like it or not."

"You fought him," I said firmly. "You survived him. He's like a scar. Old news, a memory that you'll live with. Maybe it'll hurt once in a while, and maybe it'll change you, but it's over, and you're stronger now."

Theo didn't say anything all the way home.

I thought about stopping at Mom's. She'd probably be awake, waiting on Xander and Xavier, and sitting with Dad while he grieved Sacha's loss. Theo needed to be taken care of, and I wasn't sure I was the right person to do it, but taking him into a house full of grieving people didn't seem wise. Besides, he was exhausted, and I was getting irritable. I needed him to myself.

He moved sluggishly from the car into the house and barely seemed aware as I ushered him up to the bath. Other than wincing slightly when I cleaned the blood from his arm, he barely acknowledged anything. He was in his own head, somewhere else. Somewhere away from me.

Once I got him out of the bath and dried off, I helped him put on his favorite pajamas and took him to bed where he lay next to me and stared at the ceiling for a long time.

"River?" he whispered eventually.

"Yeah?"

The mattress creaked as he turned his head toward me. "What was in that text you sent me? I…I can't read well enough to know what it says."

I traced my fingers over his stomach lightly. "Don't worry about that. We'll teach you. Annie's a good reading teacher. It said, 'I love you. Stay calm. I'm coming.'"

"Did you mean it?" he asked without missing a beat.

"Of course. I mean, I didn't know how to find you before you called. Xavier was talking about how he'd turned on the GPS on your phone, and he was going to try to track it, but—"

"No, I meant the other part." He sat up, looking down at me. "The part where you said you loved me. You've never said that before."

That fact hadn't escaped me either. I had thought maybe it would be calming to hear when I sent it. I'd been so worried about him panicking or being hurt that I'd forgotten he couldn't read.

The reason I sent it, however, didn't make it any less true. I'd had all evening to think about those three little words I hadn't been able to say before and what they stood for.

People said those words all the time to each other. I love yous were cheap. They were easy. Anybody could say they loved someone else. The words had meant nothing to me until I said them to Theo. Telling Theo I loved him had been like describing the proliferation of mushroom spores in a closed space. It was an indisputable fact, and one that sent little flutters of something light and happy through me.

I had thought it wouldn't count if it was a text message, but it did. Loving Theo was like putting down roots in good soil. It just made sense.

I sat up, cupping his cheek, and brushed the ghost of a kiss against his soft lips. "I love you, Theo."

Finally, he smiled. "I love you too, River," he said and kissed me back.

Epilogue
Theo

"SMILE!"

I was blinded by an unnecessary flash as Xander squished his face against mine for his stupid selfie. When I took a playful swing at him, he danced away, thumbs already racing over the keyboard on his screen.

"Oh, that's definitely going to need a filter," Xander mumbled. "Hashtag: just because you work in a basement doesn't mean you have to look like a corpse."

"It's November in Ohio," I muttered, bouncing a frozen pea off his head. "There's no such thing as sun."

"You could try a tan," Xavier said as he stirred the gravy on the stove. "Amy's cousin's roommate works at this upscale salon. I can get you a discount."

"Do not," War said without a hint of mirth, pointing the blade to the carving knife at me before slotting it into the electric carver. "With your fair complexion? You want skin cancer? Premature aging? Fastest way to damage your skin is UV rays. I will literally kill you myself if you ever set foot in one of those, Theo."

I cringed, half convinced that War was serious. I didn't think the man knew how to joke.

"I'd think you'd be happy to push that, considering how much Botox you sell," Xander mumbled, still typing. He shrieked when Tatty snatched his phone away.

"No phones at the table," Tatty chided and went to help Mom.

War snorted. "Botox is only a small percentage of my income. I don't put people under the knife for fun. I *help* people look their *best.* It just so happens that sometimes their best look is six feet under."

Xavier rolled his eyes and snatched his brother's phone back, passing it to Xander behind his back. "You do tummy tucks and lipo for rich assholes who want to look good in bikinis on the beach."

"Actually, I was thinking about a change of scenery." He eyed me with a small smile. "Maybe it's time for me to come home. Florida was too humid anyway."

"You're moving back to Ohio?" I asked excitedly.

River would be ecstatic. He'd never admit it, but he liked War. Having him close would be good for both of them.

"Probably. Got nothing to keep me in Miami now that Ken's gone." He shrugged. "Besides. I saw there was an opening at Best Face Forward."

"Bro..." Xander frowned. "Isn't that a non-profit? You can't just go from plastic surgeon to the rich and famous in Miami to fixing burn victims for free. That's weird."

"I think it's honorable," Tatty said, swooping in to kiss War's cheek. "We should all do our part to give back where we can."

"I agree," I said and grabbed two beers from the fridge.

War frowned, eying me. "Are you even old enough to drink?"

"Are they?" I gestured with my chin toward Xander and Xavier.

"Let the boy have his fun." Tatty winked and waved me off. "It's his first Thanksgiving. Let him indulge."

I went from the busy kitchen into the living room where Yuri, Niki, and River were glued to the television, watching the football game. Well, Yuri was. River's eyes were glazed over, betraying his obvious boredom as he sat next to his dad. Ever since the news about Sacha had broken, Yuri had been distant.

As far as I could tell, the only thing Niki cared about was Yuri. He had Yuri practically in his lap, watching him more than the game.

"Hey," I announced and leaned down to kiss River from behind, passing a beer to him and one to Niki.

"Hey," River replied and grinned up at me.

I settled in against the back of the sofa, arms folded, giving the screen a bored glance. "Who's winning?"

"Umm..." River wrinkled his nose and looked over at Yuri. "The blue guys I think?"

"Michigan," Yuri said with obvious distaste. "We're down by three. Plenty of time for a comeback."

I found it endearing how he seemed to have some sense of ownership of a college football team, saying we and ours whenever he talked about the Buckeyes. At least he was doing something other than hiding with Niki. I hadn't seen much of either of them since it happened.

The warm smell of roasting meat drifted into the living room as Annie peeled the foil back from a giant turkey. I'd never had turkey before, but it smelled delicious. She'd been in the kitchen all day baking pies and roasting that big bird. Apparently, there was this tradition to stuff yourself to bursting with food on Thanksgiving. That was news to me since Earl had never let us celebrate holidays or birthdays. I didn't understand it, but I was happy to indulge the tradition, especially since it meant I got to spend more time with the Laskins.

In the last two days, things had been crazy. River had taken time off work, and Yuri had closed the funeral home with no plans to re-open until after Sacha's funeral, which they were handling personally.

Aleksi had called, and I'd talked to him briefly on the phone to thank him for his help, but he'd seemed distant. Understandable since he'd lost his dad. He'd promised that he and his men would hunt down anyone connected to the operations at Saint Niklaus and that something like that would never, ever happen again in their city.

I watched the news every night while River scrolled through his phone. Neither of us mentioned how empty the room felt without Sacha in the big armchair, but neither of us sat in it either, even though I knew it was River's favorite chair. He was mourning in his own way.

The news mentioned the fire at Saint Niklaus', and how it had gutted the historical building, but nothing else related made the news. Not the shooting at the airport, not the six surviving boys from the basement. Sacha's carjacking made the papers, but it'd been buried deep. A detective called the day before to talk to me, and I told him the story I'd been coached to tell. A stranger shot Sacha, forced his way into the car, drove to the green lot at the airport and then abandoned the car on foot. They, of course, found no traces of the event, and since there were two murders a day in Columbus, the case would go cold in short order, especially once Niki bribed the right people.

I glanced over at Yuri and caught River's eye, trying to communicate non-verbally that he should tell him already. We hadn't yet announced our engagement and I was getting antsy, especially since River had gone right out and bought me a ring that I wasn't allowed to wear. I had it in my pocket, and if he didn't break the news before dinner, I was so putting it on and sitting next to Xander. Xander would *absolutely* notice and ask me about it.

River rolled his eyes and shook his head, taking a long pull from the beer as if to say, "Fine." He didn't think it was that big a deal, acting like everybody probably already knew. "Hey Dad. I—"

"Yes!" Yuri shot to his feet, clapping as the crowd in the stadium on the screen started screaming. The announcers were talking a million words a minute while people ran around in excited circles on the field. I didn't understand what was happening, but whatever it was, it must've been good for the red team. I think that was our team, at least.

I was about to ask when the doorbell rang.

Everyone in the house stiffened, eyes shooting to the door. Everyone was present and accounted for except for Shepherd, whom no one had heard from in days. War had even gone up to Shepherd's apartment to check on him and found the place ransacked, but no sign of Shepherd.

Before anyone could move, I pushed away from the sofa. "I'll get it."

I bounded for the door and pulled it open, stunned to find Shepherd standing on the other side. He was wearing a nice black jacket and a white button down, looking as impeccable as the last time I saw him, not one hair out of place. He was also holding a foil-covered casserole dish.

"Theo!" he declared, smiling. "Good to see you're well."

"Shepherd," I said, surprised. "Are you...I thought..."

"I see you're as eloquent as always," he said lightly and stepped past me. "Cold out there."

"Shepherd!" Annie shuffled down the hall to take the dish from her son. "Welcome home!"

"It's so good to see you, love," Tatty said, exchanging cheek kisses with Shepherd.

"Likewise, Tatty, and I've brought something special for you." He held out a bottle of very expensive looking wine.

"Oh-ho. So you do love me!" She pinched his cheek.

Annie peeled back the foil on the casserole dish Shepherd had brought. "Mushrooms?"

"Stuffed with sausage, breadcrumbs, and some pecorino Romano. Italian style." Shepherd clarified. "It's my own recipe."

"I'll add that to the table. Come in, sweetie. Dinner's almost ready." Annie turned and shuffled back to the kitchen.

"I'll go get this on some ice," Tatty said of the wine and followed Annie to the kitchen.

River appeared next to me, frowning while Shepherd shed his coat and scarf. He crossed his arms. "Where the fuck have you been? I've been trying for days to get ahold of you."

"Busy," he said dismissively.

I exchanged a glance with River, who charged forward and spoke to his brother in a low tone. "War checked your apartment. He said it looked like it'd been tossed. Are you okay? Is something going on?"

"Ah, that." There was irritation in Shepherd's tone as he dragged his fingers through his hair. "I had...a vermin problem."

"A vermin problem?" River asked dryly.

"Yes, a church mouse got loose in my apartment, and he proved rather difficult to capture." He hung his scarf on the coat rack and tucked his hands into his pockets. "I had to let the cat out, you see. Cats are very good at hunting sly little church mice, and this particular cat..." He gave a Cheshire grin. "Well, let's just say no one has escaped him yet."

I had the distinct feeling that we weren't talking about a cat and a mouse at all.

Shepherd pushed between us, patting River's shoulder. "There's no need to concern yourself. Both the cat and the mouse are where they belong."

"Everybody?" Annie called from the dining room, placing the huge turkey at the head of the table. "Dinner's ready!"

"I'm right on time," Shepherd said, flashing another wide grin. "Come, River. I'm desperate to know what you think of my mushrooms. I made them just for you. Personally, I think they're to die for." He walked into the dining room.

River caught my arm. "Whatever you do," he whispered, "do not eat the mushrooms."

"Only if you promise to announce our engagement over dinner." I pulled away and folded my arms. The truth was, I had no intention of going anywhere near those mushrooms, but River didn't know that.

River scowled at me. "You manipulative little shit."

"Learned it from the best. You can punish me later." I flashed him a wink and a smile, and we went hand in hand into the dining room as War took the carving knife from Annie.

"I'll carve," War volunteered with a warm smile.

River sighed and we sat down. Xander and Xavier immediately started elbowing each other and throwing insults while War shot them menacing glares. Shepherd busied himself adjusting how the forks and spoons were laid out while Tatty poured glasses of wine. Annie smiled at everyone. Yuri and Niki came to the table with hands clasped and sat down, talking quietly about the game.

Everyone at that table had killed someone, including me. I hadn't thought of killing Earl as a rite of passage, but in many ways, it was. His death had closed a chapter of my life forever, and there was nothing left in my future but blank pages waiting to be written. That didn't erase what I had been through. I knew I'd still wake up in a cold sweat and gasping for many years to come, but knowing I would get to do it next to River made it bearable. I could do anything if I knew I had him, and he had me.

As for everyone else...

Well, I almost felt sorry for the next fool who crossed the Laskins.

Almost.

THE END

Want to keep reading about River and Theo?

Get a bonus epilogue when you sign up for my newsletter at:

https://subscribepage.io/DarkMMLEveland

Want more of the Laskin brothers?

Read War's story in book two...

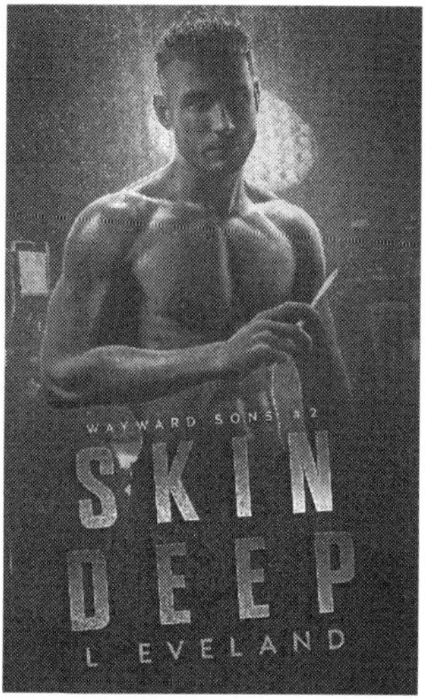

Turn to the end of the book for a preview of *Skin Deep*...

One
War

"HAS THAT UGLY TRUCK been tailing us?" I squinted at the truck in the driver's side mirror.

It was parked two rows over and three spaces to the right. While I couldn't see the driver in the dim lighting, I could vaguely make out the shadow of the man sitting behind the wheel. He'd been parked there for the last twenty minutes and still hadn't gotten out. Neon from the signs in the bar window danced over the rust-speckled frame. It had Ohio plates, Franklin County. No front plates.

"Where?" Xavier hung out the window of the passenger side, straining his neck to see.

I grabbed him by the collar and yanked him back in. "For fuck's sake, don't look at it!"

"How am I supposed to answer you if I don't look at it?" He shoved my hand away.

I went back to staring at the truck in the mirror. "You're not. You're supposed to be watching the front door of the bar for our mark."

I was sure I saw that same truck at the last bar we'd trailed our target to, but maybe not. After spending all night sitting in the dirty parking lots of dive bars on the south side of Columbus, every vehicle was starting to look the same.

We had been following our target—a pedophile named Alvin Telaris who dealt in kiddie porn—from watering hole to watering hole, waiting for the right time to grab him. After he spent an hour in the last stop with no signs of slowing down, I made the executive decision to speed the process along by sending Xander in as bait. He was a little old for Alvin, but with a little makeup and the right clothes, he could look a lot younger than twenty. It was Xander's specialty, playing the lure, and assholes like Alvin ate his act up hook, line, and sinker.

I hated to do it though. It put Xander in the line of fire and out of my sight. If I was sitting in the van, I couldn't be in there making sure nothing went wrong. No matter how many times we did this and things turned out fine, it only took one wrong move to fuck us all over forever.

I tried not to think about that as I tapped my fingers on the steering wheel, still staring at the oddly familiar truck. Of course, trying not to think about it only made me think about it more.

I grimaced as horrific images of my younger brother flashed through my mind. Xander beaten and bloody, lying on a dirty bathroom floor. Xander pinned to a wall, crying for help. Xander dead in the alley behind the bar.

I tried to shake the unwanted images away, but it was no use. It happened a lot, a symptom of my oh-so-fun diagnosis that got filed under obsessions. An obsession with macabre worst-case scenarios, maybe. Worst-case scenarios that I could never let come to pass.

"Come on, Xander," I growled. "How long does it take to convince a pedophile you're down to fuck?"

"You talking about that ugly green rust bucket two rows over?" Xavier squinted at the rearview mirror.

I nodded once. "That's the one. Was it at the last bar?"

Xavier was quiet for a minute, pressing his lips together. He dragged his fingers through his hair, which used to be dark all over. He'd bleached it a few weeks ago and colored the ends orange and blue. It made him look like his head was on fire, but at least no one would confuse him with Xander anymore at a glance. "I don't know. Maybe."

"Helpful," I grunted and rubbed a hand over my stomach, turning my attention back to the dented front door of the bar.

I should count the cars. My eyes darted nervously to the row of cars across from me. Why had I thought that? I didn't want to count the cars. It didn't matter how many cars were in the parking lot, but I'd already started counting without meaning to, and I couldn't stop. *One, two, three, four...*

Sweat gathered on the back of my neck as I stared at the fifth car in the row. There's an empty space between the last two. Why didn't I park there? *Stupid War. Stupid, stupid. Now there are only five cars in that row, and you know that's bad. Five is a bad omen. A death omen. What if Xander's in there right now, bleeding out? He could be dead. He might be dead. It's a sign. You know it is. Maybe I miscounted. I should count again to make sure.*

"Maybe one of us should go in there to check on Xander," I said, forcing my eyes away from the row of cars.

Logically, I knew there was no connection between any particular number and whether my brother was alive or dead, but OCD didn't work on logic. I didn't even know where that association had come from. It felt random. In my life, though, there was nothing more terrifying than *random*.

"He's fine," Xavier said with a shrug. "I'm sure he's just doing his Pinocchio act."

I wrinkled my nose. "Pinocchio act?"

Xavier exaggeratedly fluttered his dark lashes at me. "Make me a real boy, Daddy," he chirped in a high voice.

"Never fucking do that again," I said and gave him a shove.

"Hey, you're the one that asked." He snorted and picked up his energy drink, loudly slurping it down.

The bar's front door swung open, and I stiffened at the sight of my younger brother walking out of the place, practically falling all over our mark. Every protective instinct in me flared to life and it took all the effort I had not to immediately throw open my door and go waste that motherfucker then and there.

Alvin, our mark, was a short, middle-aged man with glasses a size too big for his face and a mustache he apparently thought made up for the fact that he was balding. He looked disturbingly like every middle schooler's creepy gym teacher, the one that lingered a little too long in the locker room to watch you change. Fuck, he even looked like a slimeball.

Xander played his part well, wearing a big smile, his lip gloss shimmering in the neon, the glitter sparkling on his bare midriff. There was a part of me that envied how confidently he wore crop tops and short shorts, just not in this situation. Watching him walk out with Alvin, all I wanted to do was go scoop up my brother, wrap him in ten layers of bubble wrap, and pry Alvin's eyes out of his fucking skull.

"Easy, killer," Xander said. "Let him come to us."

"I know the fucking plan," I growled. *Doesn't mean I have to like it.*

Xander stumbled like he was drunk, but he wasn't. At least, I hoped he wasn't. He usually wasn't stupid enough to drink anything on the job, even if he was good at making it look like he had.

They made it about five yards before there was movement from that truck behind us. My eyes swung to the mirror as I watched a man climb out of the driver's side. He was *huge*, easily six and a half feet tall and a wall of pure muscle with flawless dark skin. The man fished around in the bed of his truck before coming up with a baseball bat.

"Shit, we might have trouble," I mumbled, pointing him out to Xavier.

"Fuck," he replied and threw open his door.

We scrambled to get our equipment ready. Xavier yanked open the center console, drawing out the portable blowtorch he'd made and I flung open my work briefcase, grabbing one of the ready-made syringes of remimazolam, a super-fast acting muscle relaxant. Normally, it was used to relax nervous patients before outpatient procedures, but in larger doses, it could knock a man flat in under a minute if administered correctly.

This would blow our cover for sure, but we didn't have a choice, not if we wanted to maintain control over the situation. Alvin was exactly the type to have made plenty of enemies to compete with us, and we had to get to him first.

As soon as Xander saw us coming his smile morphed into an irritated scowl. He flung himself at Alvin, making it look like another drunken stumble, but it was enough to throw Alvin off. He tripped and went down to the pavement, laughing like an idiot. We were seconds from reaching him to extract our target.

But that was a few seconds too many. The guy from the truck got there first. He grabbed Xander by the collar and flung him away from Alvin.

I cursed and broke into a run, reaching him just in time to grab the bat before he could bring it down on Alvin's head.

Xander brought his designer boot down on Alvin's head. "Prick!" He spat on him before kicking him once again for good measure.

The man spun around, yanking the bat out of my hand, but before he could swing at me, I jammed the syringe into his shoulder and pushed down the plunger. His eyes went wide, and his hand swung up to slap the hole in his arm when I pulled the syringe out. The look in his eyes morphed back and forth between rage and terror as he stood there.

For a second, I was worried I'd miscalculated the dosage. The guy was big, over six and a half feet tall and muscular, built like a fucking tank. I didn't have a second dose, so if he didn't go down, we were fucked.

I took a half a step back, reaching for the knife hidden in my sleeve.

Then the guy's eyes rolled back and he fell.

"Shit!" I jumped forward to catch his slumped body, or tried to. He was big enough that I could barely hold him up. I grunted, shifting my hold on his obnoxiously thick arms. "A little help here?"

Xander snorted and folded his arms, eying Xavier. "Don't look at me. I played bait."

"Dick," Xavier grumbled and came to help me drag the big guy out of the line of sight. Xander leaned forward, clutching his knees while he tried to catch his breath. "Who the fuck is he?"

"I don't know," I panted.

"Shit." Xander looked at me. "Are we supposed to kill him?"

I winced. I'd never had a job go this wrong before. People had walked in on me while I was working, and I'd taken care of them, but they were always people that deserved it. Bodyguards, henchmen, enabling spouses. I knew nothing about the man passed out at our feet, which meant it was technically against the rules to kill him. We didn't kill people without thoroughly vetting them through Annie, Yuri, Tatty, and Nikita first.

What the fuck was the procedure for this? Why didn't I know it?

I closed my eyes, trying to calm the rising panic in my chest. My brothers were relying on me to keep control over this situation. If it even started to look like I was losing it, they might spiral. I had to keep it together, for them.

I blew out a slow breath. "Xander, get Alvin in the van. We stick to the plan."

"What about him?" Xavier asked, gesturing to the big Black man with his blowtorch. "We can't leave him here. He's seen our faces."

I held out my hand. "Give me your zip ties."

Xavier did as I told him. "You're going to tie him up?"

I took the zip ties and knelt, carefully binding our unexpected guest by the wrists and ankles. "We've got less than an hour before he starts to come around, and I expect he's not going to be too pleased when he does. We need to get him out to the factory and into a room before then."

Xavier stared at me in disbelief. "You're taking him with us?"

"What choice do I have?" I snapped rougher than I meant. I stood, tugging a travel-sized package of baby wipes from my pocket to clean my hands. "You two are going to work on Alvin. Stick to the plan and finish the job we came to do. I'm going to get to the bottom of who he is and why he's been following us. Now help me drag him to the van."

Read the rest of the story in Skin Deep, available February 28th!

From the *Author*

Thank you for reading Body Count!

This was my first foray into dark romance and contemporary romance. War's book, Skin Deep, is coming up next.

Long before I was a romance author, I wrote extreme horror, so when I found out I could combine both my love for steamy MM romance with some elements of horror, I was all-in. Granted, they're very, very light in this series, but that's by design. Can't put everything in one book, right?

This book was also somewhat inspired by my own interest in criminal psychology, and some family history with the Italian mafia. One of my uncles used to drive for them part-time and he had some crazy stories to tell!

But most of all, I blame this project on Hannagram. If you're not familiar, that'd be the popular fan ship between Hannibal Lecter and Will Graham from the TV show *Hannibal*. I've been obsessed with that show for a while and couldn't find near enough books to feed that obsession, so I decided to write one myself. Of course, Shepherd's character is based somewhat on Hannibal himself, but I decided to tell the stories of a few of his brothers first. But his book is coming...eventually.

If you absolutely cannot wait for the next book in the series, you can become a superfan to read ahead. I'm usually 1-2 books ahead of whatever's available on Amazon, so it's perfect if you want to binge read. If you're looking for something a little darker, you'll also enjoy Twisted, a much darker and psychological story that's currently exclusive to Ream. It's all about a psych patient stalking and falling for his therapist. The first 3 chapters are free. In fact, I publish a lot of free content there every month.

Thank you again for reading!

Join my email newsletter to stay in touch.

ABOUT *the* AUTHOR

L EVELAND LIVES IN West Virginia with their three cats, two children, a dog, and their poor husband, who has to put up with it all. Eveland enjoys Italian food, fancy coffee, and fantasy video games.

When they're not writing, they probably should be! But they're likely watching a cooking video or true crime on YouTube instead. When they are writing, it's probably about men who are kinky, queer, and morally gray. L Eveland is a genderqueer and trans author who uses they/them pronouns.

Visit L Eveland online at:

www.levelandbooks.com/

https://reamstories.com/leveland

Printed in Great Britain
by Amazon

54422864R00211

Le mouvement beat, le minimalisme, le New Wave et Robert Smithson

Les adeptes du *New Wave* ont actuellement tendance à nier tout objectif commun avec les minimalistes. Ceci reflète profondément la rivalité entre générations et le climat de méfiance qui caractérisent l'art moderne depuis le XIXe siècle, situation à laquelle New York n'a bien sûr pas échappé. A un niveau plus conscient, on peut constater que ce sont à la fois les artistes du *New Wave* et ceux qui en font la promotion qui s'engagent franchement dans la voie de la négation de l'Histoire. Les artistes sont mus par une colère incontrôlable ; les promoteurs doivent nier toute relation réelle entre le *New Wave* et le passé s'ils veulent maintenir l'illusion de la nouveauté, illusion indispensable quand l'art vise un marché axé sur une classe grandissante d'entrepreneurs spéculant de plus en plus en fonction du concept d'obsolescence planifiée.

Mais pour comprendre la signification du mouvement *New Wave* actuel, il est nécessaire d'identifier correctement ses antécédents. En fait, le *New Wave*, le minimalisme et l'écriture *beat* traitent tous du même problème. Tous les trois expriment la fascination / répulsion de l'Amérique pour ses racines culturelles si superficielles et sa vulnérabilité face à l'impact du changement technologique.

Au départ, toute correspondance entre le *New Wave* et l'art minimal semble impossible dans la mesure où l'une des manifestations les plus évidentes du *New Wave* est justement son opposition à ce que Jeffrey Deitch appelle «l'académie post-minimaliste [1]». Cependant, c'est précisément cette académie post-minimaliste qui a présenté une «normalisation» [2] des objectifs que s'était fixé le groupe minimaliste d'origine à l'époque difficile de l'administration Nixon. L'intention politique du minimalisme fut alors transformée par les diverses échappatoires du post-minimalisme, échappatoires formelles, anthropologiques ou tournées vers l'idée de nature et d'artisanat.

On peut néanmoins trouver la preuve qu'il existe bien un lien entre les sensibilités *New Wave* et minimaliste dans la série d'essais que Robert Smithson a écrite à la fin des années soixante et au début des années soixante-dix. Dans ses derniers écrits, Smithson a lui aussi élaboré une stratégie pour traiter des problèmes posés par la normalisation et l'autodestruction, qui avaient miné les mouvements *beat* et minimaliste et menacent maintenant les artistes du *New Wave* au moment même où ils apparaissent.

En 1966, Smithson publiait son premier essai, «L'Entropie et les nouveaux monuments», où il décrivait la fascination que la culture post-industrielle exerçait sur les premiers artistes post-minimalistes, leur passion pour les films et les salles de cinéma, la «matière imprimée», la science-fiction, la théorie de l'information et la géologie. Il prétendait que la nature embryonnaire et brutale du travail de ces artistes était le résultat de leur propre torpeur «entropique», elle-même écho de la condition léthargique de notre civilisation [3].

Arrêtons-nous à cette description des «sorties au cinéma»

chez les artistes minimalistes, dans «L'Entropie et les nouveaux monuments» : «Certains artistes voient un nombre invraisemblable de films. [Peter] Hutchinson, par exemple, au lieu d'aller à la campagne étudier la nature, ira plus volontiers voir deux ou trois fois le même film sur la 42e Rue, par exemple *Horror of Party Beach,* et y repensera pendant des semaines. Les films confèrent un aspect rituel à la vie de nombreux artistes, et introduisent alors une sorte de mysticisme à bas prix qui les maintient en état de transe perpétuelle. Le «sang et les tripes» des films d'horreur répondent à leurs «besoins organiques», alors que la «froideur de l'acier» des films de science-fiction comblent leurs besoins «inorganiques». Les films sérieux s'appuient trop sur les «valeurs», c'est pour cette raison qu'ils sont rejetés par les artistes les plus lucides. Ces artistes ont des rayons X à la place des yeux, et sont capables d'y voir clair dans le magma qui passe pour de la «profondeur de nos jours [4].»

Écrite il y a une quinzaine d'années, cette description peut être considérée comme une véritable décalcomanie de l'approche d'un artiste *New Wave.* Peter Hutchinson, comme le groupe musical des *B-52s,* s'intéresse à la culture plagiste post-industrielle. Il préfère même voir ses films à Times Square, s'appropriant ainsi un autre symbole de la génération actuelle. Comme les artistes minimalistes, ceux du *New Wave* rejettent aujourd'hui le «magma» dépassé des «valeurs» humanistes traditionnelles en leur préférant la perception et les émotions déclenchées par la pornographie (Jimmy DeSana, Jane Dickson), la science fiction (Steve Keister, Ronnie Fischer) et les nouvelles images (Ilona Granet, Becky Howland).

Comme les minimalistes, les artistes *New Wave* se tournent vers les images produites par les médias plutôt que vers une conception nostalgique de la nature pour appréhender la substance du réel. Mais les minimalistes et les artistes *New Wave* n'ont pas eu la même réaction devant les mêmes images d'horreur. Là où les minimalistes étaient figés dans leur attente catatonique (ce que Smithson appelle leur «transe perpétuelle» et leur «état entropique»), les artistes *New Wave* plongent délibérément dans la convulsion hystérique (ce que Ronny Cohen appelle leur «énergisme») [5]. C'est là la différence essentielle entre la froide répétition métallique d'une sculpture de Judd et le fusain sur carton, maladroit et tortueux, de Becky Howland, *Transmission Towers,* qu'on a pu voir à l'occasion du *«December Colab Show»* chez Brooke Alexander. (Il faut noter que les minimalistes, entropiques et catatoniques, s'efforçaient de traduire physiquement leur propos par la forme abstraite, alors que les artistes *New Wave,* hystériques et «énergétiques», ont tendance à représenter des phénomènes spécifiques.)

Toujours dans «L'Entropie et les nouveaux monuments», Smithson explique quel matériel visuel intéresse l'artiste minimaliste : «Comme les films et les salles de cinéma, la «matière imprimée» joue un rôle entropique : les cartes, les graphiques, les publicités, les livres d'art, les livres scientifiques, l'argent, les plans d'architecture, les manuels de mathématiques, les diagrammes, les journaux, les bandes dessinées, les dépliants et les brochures des compagnies industrielles. Judd a une collection labyrinthique de matière imprimée, qu'il «regarde» la plupart du temps plus qu'il ne la "lit"» [6].

Depuis cette explication de 1966, la «matière imprimée» (sous forme de «livres d'artistes») est devenue le domaine exclusif de la fixation post-minimaliste sur la philosophie phénoménologique et la réalité privée. A la fin des années soixante, comme aujourd'hui, elle donnait aux artistes le moyen d'enregistrer radicalement leur appréhension de la société. Smithson explique que Donald Judd «pourrait prendre une équation mathématique et, à vue, la traduire en une progression d'intervalles métalliques», ce qui est un moyen d'échapper à la convention suranée de la composition «relationnelle». «L'écriture de Judd, poursuit Smithson, se rapproche beaucoup des descriptions précises et purement matérielles, que l'on peut trouver dans sa collection de manuels de géologie [7]». L'intérêt que des artistes comme Judd ont éprouvé pour la science-fiction les a aidé à rompre avec les valeurs culturelles et les modes artistiques traditionnels admis.

La matière imprimée, telle que Smithson l'a décrite, joue aujourd'hui un rôle similaire dans la culture *New Wave.* Dans la chanson, *«Don't worry about the Government»,* le groupe musical, les *Talking Heads* met l'accent sur sa fascination pour la conscience cartographique et les slogans publicitaires. L'artiste Peter Fend a récemment présenté *Future States,* un dessin où apparaissaient, sur une planisphère, des frontières politiques potentielles. La thématique de l'argent, vient, elle aussi, de réapparaître. Au *«Times Square Show»,* Christof Kohlhofer a présenté *Billion Dollar Bills.* Dans une exposition récente au *Colab*, Andréa Callard a proposé une pièce intitulée *I made this money, what can I buy* ?

A partir de là, nous pouvons même remonter de 1966 à 1956. Cette préoccupation, cette conscience douloureuse de l'impact du changement technologique sur la culture, trouve sa source dans l'œuvre des écrivains de la *Beat Generation.*

Contrairement aux artistes *New Wave*, les minimalistes semblent bien avoir eu conscience de leur dette envers l'écriture *beat*. Smithson, par exemple, reconnaît volontiers l'influence que les *beats*, et plus particulièrement Allen Ginsberg et William Burroughs, ont pu exercer sur l'évolution de son propre travail. Conscient de cet héritage, ce n'est pas sans fierté que Smithson fait référence à ses liens avec diverses figures *beats* à l'occasion d'un entretien autobiographique pour les *Archives of American Art* en 1972. Il précise à cette occasion qu'il est né à Passaic, New Jersey, tout près de Paterson, où Allen Ginsberg avait vu le jour. Il se souvient qu'il allait voir le vieux William Carlos Williams et comment celui-ci «parlait souvent de Ginsberg sortant à n'importe quelle heure de la nuit». Influencé par l'idée *beat* du voyage libre, Smithson a fait le tour des Etats-Unis et du Mexique en stop, de 1956 à 1958. «Quand je suis revenu, *Sur la route* avait été publié, et tous ces gens-là venaient de se faire connaître, Jack Kerouac et Allen Ginsberg. D'ailleurs, je les ai rencontrés tous les deux» [8].

Considérons, par exemple, l'imagerie de *Howl*, cette protestation de Ginsberg contre la structure tortueuse de la société post-industrielle. L'enfer qu'il y décrit est vécu dans des «appartements de robots» et des «faubourgs invisibles», des «terrains et des arrières-cours vides» des «rangées branlantes des salles de cinéma», des «toits d'appartements» et face aux «néons clignotants des feux de circulation» [9].

L'obsession de Ginsberg pour la vie urbaine, les produits terrifiants de la science et de l'industrie, la structure du commerce, sont autant de thèmes du minimalisme et du *New Wave*, présents dans cette strophe de *Howl* :

«(J'ai vu les meilleurs de ma génération détruits par la folie) ... qui furent brûlés vivants dans leurs innocents complets-vestons en flanelle sur la Madison Avenue parmi des éclatements de vers en plomb et le fracas emmagasiné des régiments de fer de la haute-couture et les cris de nitro-glycérine des pédés de la publicité et la suffocante moutarde des rédacteurs en chef intelligents, ou qui furent écrasés par les taxis ivres de la Réalité Absolue[10].»

William Burroughs est un autre précurseur, encore plus sombre, de cette sensibilité. Smithson avait lu *Le Festin nu* à Rome en 1961. Il disait alors que «l'imagerie... correspondait... à une espèce d'accumulation massive et grotesque de toutes sortes de rituels de rejet... Le fait d'ériger ces situations rituelles me fascinait» [11]. L'intérêt de Burroughs pour la violence, la fantaisie sexuelle, les secousses de la technologie et le Tiers Monde, le désigne aussi comme un précurseur important du *New Wave,* comme on peut le constater dans ce passage typique de *La Machine molle* (1961) :

«Dans le matin bleu venteux masturbant un corps idiot souillé de chairs scarifiées froides – mains calcaires catatoniques croisées sur son yen – un ami de n'importe quelle structure-garçon coupé par un genre de mollusque – enfants des rues du vert ensemble – sourires lents de bronze d'une terre herbeuse sans mémoire – petits fantômes frais insouciants d'un spasme adolescent – excrément en métal et ténèbres de cristal de la cité-poisson – sous un crépuscule violet nos vêtements lacérés linge de momie sur parquets d'obsidienne – Panama se gluait à nos corps».

«Tu viens avec moi, Mister ?»

Aurores boréales clignotent de son «Oui» – La corde est ajustée – Se tortillant dans le vent des poils noirs crèvent sa chair – Grandes canines déchirent ses gencives avec le plaisir exquis d'un mal de dent – Les garçons taxis verts vont jusqu'au bout avec n'importe quel baratin [12].»

Sur le plan émotionnel, le mouvements *beat* et le *New*

Wave sont tous les deux *hot.* Leur art est basé sur un investissement affectif intensif dans l'expérience. Pour de nombreux adeptes, ce type de participation s'est avéré mortel. L'autodestruction apparaît alors : Neal Cassady, Jack Kerouac et Sid Vicious sont tous morts tragiquement. Dylan frôle la mort dans un accident de moto en 1966. Burroughs était un junkie.

Au contraire, le minimalisme a été un mouvement *cool.* Ses pratiquants étaient «détachés». Ils se protégaient par la distance intellectuelle. Pour eux, le danger consistait à devenir académiques, d'être neutralisés. Et c'est justement ce qui est arrivé à la plupart des leaders du mouvement : Carl André, Donald Judd, Dan Flavin, Walter De Maria, Sol LeWitt. L'incapacité de ces artistes à pousser leur travail au-delà de leurs concepts initiaux constitue l'échec de la génération minimaliste.

Les écrits de Smithson sont un lien entre la *Beat Generation* et les minimalistes, puis entre le minimalisme et le *New Wave.* Bien sûr, Smithson est mort prématurément et tragiquement. Mais sa mort était accidentelle, sans rien d'autodestructeur.

Cependant, les deux dernières années de sa vie, Smithson avait élaboré une méthodologie pour négocier la voie étroite entre la normalisation et l'autodestruction. Dans l'entretien de 1972, il n'est pas loin de codifier cette stratégie, largement basée sur des idées «marxistes», quand il confronte les illusions et les problèmes du capitalisme moderne. Les trois principes interdépendants de cette méthode sont la Conscience, la Réalité et le Dialogue [13]. Smithson insistait sur le fait que les artistes doivent être conscients des motivations de leur travail, de leur rôle dans la société, et du rôle de leur travail. («Vous savez bien que beaucoup de gens ne veulent pas entendre parler de ce genre de choses. Ils préfèrent que l'artiste soit un peu niais, inconscient et même complètement cinglé».)

Il insistait sur le fait que l'artiste doit essayer de traduire ce qu'il croit être la nature de la réalité, et non se laisser séduire par la création d'échappatoires, de «mondes rêvés» (qu'ils soient d'ailleurs agréables ou cauchemardesques). Il soutenait que les artistes «suffisamment idiots pour penser qu'ils sont sur un nuage» aidaient en fait à renforcer les valeurs politiques réactionnaires en perpétuant l'illusion sociale et politique dans les mondes rêvés qu'ils créaient. (Il a dit que l'art était l'opium de la bourgeoisie.)

Pour finir, il soutenait que le dialogue était le seul moyen pour un artiste d'atteindre la conscience et la perception du vrai. Son travail contient des dialogues entre l'art et l'environnement, l'artiste et le monde de l'art, le monde de l'art et la société. Il s'est attaqué au «mythe kantien» définissant l'objet d'art comme une «chose en elle-même». Il luttait au contraire pour imposer l'idée que le travail des artistes est dialectique : les choses n'existent pas en elles-mêmes. Elles sont liées à d'autres choses. Il parlait d'une méthode dialectique «qui cherche un monde en dehors de l'enfermement culturel».

«Ce sont de relations dont je veux parler. On a tendance à voir l'art en termes d'isolation, de neutralisation, de séparation, et c'est ce qui est d'ailleurs encouragé. L'art serait alors sur orbite, complètement indépendant des expériences de ce monde, et je m'intéresse davantage à ces expériences, non pour réfuter l'art, mais pour l'intégrer à ces expériences ; en d'autres termes, tous ces facteurs en font partie».

La génération *New Wave* a déjà eu ses laissés-pour-compte. Au moment même de leur apparition publique, certains de ses artistes se sont détruits, d'autres ont rapidement accepté que leur travail soit neutralisé. Pour combattre la montée croissante de ces dangers, l'artiste doit acquérir une méthodologie cohérente. Adopter des principes comme ceux de Smithson est peut-être le seul moyen pour la génération actuelle de survivre assez longtemps pour mener son travail à maturité.

Publié pour la première fois dans *Arts Magazine*, (New York), vol. 55, nº 9, mai 1981.

Notes sur les peintures (1982)

1. Ces tableaux représentent des prisons, des cellules et des murs.

2. Ici, le carré idéal devient une prison. La géométrie est révélée comme enfermement.

3. La cellule rappelle l'appartement, le lit d'hôpital, le bureau d'école – les points de chutes isolés de la structure industrielle.

4. Les tableaux constituent une critique du modernisme idéaliste. On trouve une prison dans le *Color-Field.* L'espace vaporeux de Rothko est emmuré.

5. Des conduits souterrains relient les éléments entre eux. Les «fluides vitaux» y entrent et en sortent.

6. Le stucage est une réminiscence des plafonds de motels.

7. La peinture *Day-Glo* * désigne le «mysticisme bon marché». C'est la lueur résiduelle de la radiation.

* Marque de peinture fluo vendue dans les années soixante.

Publié pour la première fois dans *Peter Halley, Collected Essays, 1981-1987*, Bischofberger Gallery et Sonnabend Gallery, Zürich, New York, 1988.

Déclaration (1983)

Même si mon travail est apparemment géométrique, sa signification se veut l'antithèse de l'art géométrique antérieur. L'art géométrique est généralement lié aux divers idéalismes de Platon, de Descartes et de Mies. Mon travail, en fait, est une critique de ces idéalismes.

J'ai tenté d'utiliser les codes du minimalisme, de la *Color-Field Painting* et du constructivisme pour révéler la base sociologique de leurs origines. Après Foucault, je vois dans le carré une prison ; derrière les mythologies de la société contemporaine, un réseau camouflé de cellules et de conduits.

Pour définir plus avant mon travail, j'aimerais aussi évoquer le travail de Robert Smithson. Alors que Smithson désignait la désolation du paysage industriel avec les symboles de la géométrie pure, je cherche, quant à moi, à injecter dans le monde idéal de l'art géométrique une trace de ce même paysage social.

Publié pour la première fois dans *Peter Halley, Collected Essays, 1981-1987, op. cit.*

Contre le post-modernisme : une relecture d'Ortega

De nombreux critiques ont montré depuis quelques années un intérêt grandissant pour l'idée de post-modernisme. Ils définissent le concept de différentes façons, mais tous sont convaincus que l'art moderniste touche à sa fin et qu'un nouvel ensemble de théories est nécessaire pour décrire l'art, aujourd'hui.

Aucun critique, cependant, ne semble avoir envisagé le fait que l'art, dit moderniste, ne soit pas simplement passé de mode, mais encore plus simplement, et avant tout, victime d'une mauvaise interprétation. Les critiques d'aujourd'hui semblent étayer l'idée de modernisme sur les analyses formalistes développées par Clement Greenberg dans les années cinquante. Mais cette définition du modernisme par Greenberg n'a jamais pu fonctionner quand il s'agissait de définir l'ensemble de la production artistique moderniste du XXe siècle. Ce modernisme formaliste n'a pas plus défini le passé qu'il ne définira le présent. Une autre définition du modernisme, esquissée par l'écrivain espagnol José Ortega y Gasset dans son essai de 1925, *La Déshumanisation de l'art*, sera à la fois plus adéquate et plus utile.

Toute définition du champ et de la typologie de l'art moderniste est à la fois un exercice descriptif et prescriptif, dans la mesure où aucune définition des caractéristiques de la production artistique, dans une société donnée, ne peut être détachée des aspirations de l'auteur pour cette société. Le modernisme de Greenberg tentait de trouver un équivalent artistique au rôle de leader international que l'Amérique recherchait après la guerre. Aujourd'hui, alors que ces aspirations se sont effondrées, il n'est pas étonnant que les idées, sous-tendant le mouvement esthétique qui en dépendait, paraissent hors de propos et éculées.

Greenberg cherchait aussi à donner une théorie du modernisme aux Etats-Unis, alors que le pays, contrairement aux nations européennes, n'était pas encore dans une phase post-industrielle, mais toujours dans sa première phase de croissance. L'art de l'Amérique après guerre, l'expressionnisme abstrait, était transcendantal, expressionniste et sûr de lui, comme l'art européen du XIXe siècle, quand l'Europe s'industrialisait. Le modernisme de Greenberg offrait à la promotion de l'art américain une théorie positiviste et déterministe, liée, ironiquement, à la fois aux valeurs du capitalisme du XIXe siècle (l'accent mis sur le «goût», la «qualité») et au marxisme du XIXe siècle.

Pour forger sa théorie, Greenberg a soigneusement ignoré une grande partie de l'art européen du XXe siècle. Dada, le surréalisme et Duchamp ne trouvaient pas leur place dans son système. Il fut obligé de taxer le cubisme analytique de «contre-révolution» envers le modernisme, et de faire commencer l'ère moderniste au milieu du XIXe siècle pour y inclure les impressionnistes (tout spécialement Monet), qui étaient paradigmatiques à sa théorie [1].

Cette stratégie a occulté des distinctions importantes entre ce siècle et le précédent. Dans le modernisme formaliste de Greenberg, le XIXe et le XXe siècles sont abordés comme une période historique unifiée. Les différences fondamentales entre le XIXe siècle industriel et le XXe siècle post-industriel sont ignorées. Mais en fait, le XIXe siècle représente la phase de l'industrialisation du monde occidental, du mécanisme, de l'empirisme et de l'art populaire (le romantisme et le réalisme). C'est le siècle de la confiance et de la passion.

Le XXe siècle, au contraire, est celui de la relativité et du doute : la physique d'Einstein remplace le mécanisme de Newton, comme la subjectivité freudienne succède à l'absolutisme victorien. Sur le plan philosophique, le positivisme marxiste est remplacé par le doute existentialiste et phénoménologique. L'automatisation, l'électronique et l'Etat-providence mettent fin à l'influence du travailleur dans les industries lourdes.

Créer une théorie du modernisme, qui rassemble des époques si différentes comme Greenberg a cherché à le faire, ne peut que créer des difficultés. Chez Ortega, nous trouvons au contraire une théorie du modernisme qui se limite à l'art du XXe siècle.

Comme Greenberg, Ortega remplit un rôle normatif par rapport à l'art moderniste. Il voit en lui l'art du XXe siècle et de la société libérale, dont il chante les louanges. Pour Ortega, la première force intellectuelle du XXe siècle, c'est le relativisme. Ce relativisme naît chez des individus pour qui le doute est fondamental, il nécessite l'invention d'un système politique tolérant apte à intégrer ce doute. Pour Ortega, ce système politique c'est le libéralisme : «Le cri le plus noble qui ait jamais été poussé sur cette planète [2].» En 1930, à l'époque où le fascisme montait partout en Europe, et alors que la révolution russe était tombée dans les horreurs du stalinisme, il écrivait :«Le libéralisme est un système basé sur les droits politiques, selon lequel le pouvoir public, malgré sa toute puissance, limite volontairement son influence et tente, même à ses dépens, de laisser une place au sein de l'Etat qu'il dirige à ceux qui ne pensent et ne réagissent pas comme lui...»

A la base du libéralisme selon Ortega se trouve la croyance suivante : les progrès technologiques et politiques de la société sont dus à des individus exceptionnels, séparés de la «masse» de l'humanité par leur «nécessité intérieure... de s'élever vers quelque chose de plus haut qu'eux-mêmes, de se dépasser, et d'accepter librement ce que cela implique». De tels individus, grâce à leurs efforts exceptionnels, sont ceux qui «créent» les institutions caractérisant notre civilisation, bien que leur travail soit le plus souvent laissé dans l'ombre. Des progrès comme l'eau courante, la protection de la loi ou l'automobile sont considérés par la «masse» comme des droits naturels, alors qu'ils sont le résultat des luttes de ces individus engagés.

A l'opposé de cet individu exceptionnel, Ortega définit «l'homme-masse». L'homme-masse se distingue de l'homme du commun. Il n'appartient à aucune classe socio- économique particulière, c'est plutôt un individu qui «se considère comme parfait». L'homme-masse «ne ressent aucun manque en dehors de lui-même». Rien ne l'incite à respecter les principes de légalité quand ceux-ci ne servent pas son intérêt personnel. Il considère les bienfaits de la civilisation comme des droits naturels, et non comme la résultante d'une chaîne complexe d'interactions sociales. L'homme-masse croit en «l'action directe». Quand il est au pouvoir (comme sous l'Allemagne nazie ou la Russie staliniste), «la masse homogène pèse de tout son poids sur le pouvoir public et écrase, annihile tout groupe opposant», car la masse «éprouve une haine implacable pour tout ce qui ne lui ressemble pas».

Le libéralisme d'Ortega rejette les aspirations populistes qui ont assombri la pensée artistique dans ce pays pendant tout le XXe siècle. L'aspiration au populisme est due en partie à la croyance en l'opinion de la majorité, qui est la base même de l'approche démocratique américaine. C'est aussi l'aboutissement des aspirations humanistes des intellectuels américains, après-guerre. Des tentations marxisantes de Clement Greenberg et de Meyer Shapiro au populisme socialiste de Gregory Battcock et de Kim Levin, jusqu'à des enfants terribles de l'extrême droite comme Jedd Garet récemment, il y a toujours eu un malaise par rapport au libéralisme chez ceux qui écrivent sur l'art, d'où le désir d'adapter d'une façon ou d'une autre l'art moderniste au moule populiste. Ortega, à l'encontre, soutient non seulement que l'art moderniste n'est pas seulement impopulaire par nature, mais anti-populaire, dans la mesure où l'idéal qu'il exprime est l'antithèse de celui de l'homme-masse.

Selon Ortega, le modernisme artistique est un art essentiellement basé sur le doute. Dans *La Déshumanisation de l'art*, il en définit les caractéristiques. Le «style nouveau» tend à :

1) déshumaniser l'art,

2) éviter les formes vivantes,

3) ne voir en l'œuvre d'art rien d'autre qu'une œuvre d'art,

4) considérer l'art comme un jeu et rien d'autre,

5) être essentiellement ironique,

6) se méfier du factice et donc rechercher une réalisation scrupuleuse,

7) considérer l'art comme non transcendant.

A travers chacun de ces points, il cherche à différencier

l'art du XXe siècle, celui du doute, et l'art passionné, positiviste et confiant qui a caractérisé le XIXe. Cinquante ans plus tard, l'héritage de l'art du XIXe est sans doute toujours présent, et il sera d'autant plus utile d'étudier le raisonnement d'Ortega.

Ortega déclare tout d'abord que l'art moderniste est «déshumanisé». Il tente ici de distinguer l'effet produit par l'art, le «plaisir de la vue», de la sensiblerie autobiographique qui a dominé le XIXe siècle. Par déshumanisation Ortega entend l'«a-émotionnel». L'art moderniste, celui du doute, doit se tenir à l'écart de la «contagion» des «sentiments personnels». Ortega illustre ce phénomène dans le domaine musical : «De Beethoven à Wagner, la musique visait essentiellement à exprimer des sentiments personnels. Le compositeur érigeait de grandes structures sonores conformes à son autobiographie... Wagner a utilisé son adultère avec Mathilde Wesendonck dans *Tristan et Isolde*, et si on veut apprécier cette œuvre, il faut devenir, soi-même, vaguement adultère pendant quelques heures.»

Mais les réalités «vécues» sont trop puissantes pour ne pas susciter la sympathie qui nous empêche de percevoir les relations esthétiques dans leur «pureté objective», elles doivent donc être écartées en tant que contenu de l'art moderniste.

«La musique devait être débarrassée du sentiment. Debussy s'en est chargé. Grâce à lui, on a pu écouter la musique sereinement, sans larmes ni pâmoisons».

Le contraste entre ces deux attitudes est tout à fait évident dans le cinéma d'aujourd'hui, où art moderniste et art populaire continuent de coexister. Le cinéma populaire nous oblige, par des techniques coercitives d'illusionnisme, à éprouver la peur ou la joie, presque involontairement. Pour le cinéma moderniste de Stan Brackage, Hollis

Frampton ou Jean-Luc Godard, nous sommes confrontés à une «algèbre de métaphores» qui peut nous «surprendre, nous émerveiller», des conditions qui «placent toujours l'intellectuel dans l'extase perpétuelle du visionnaire».

Ortega déclare que «l'art devrait être pure clarté, pure intelligence. Les larmes et le rire sont, esthétiquement, des escroqueries. La beauté ne doit pas passer par le sourire, la mélancolie ou la joie». Le doute et la réflexion ne sont possibles que dans cette atmosphère. Et dans le modernisme d'Ortega, cette réflexion a un objectif élevé qui la rattache au courant de la pensée phénoménologique du XXe siècle.

Nous utilisons nos idées d'une façon «humaine» quand nous les utilisons pour penser à telle ou telle chose. Quand nous pensons à Napoléon, par exemple, nous nous intéressons naturellement au grand homme qui porte ce nom. Un psychologue, au contraire, adopte une attitude inhabituelle et «inhumaine» quand il oublie Napoléon et s'efforce d'analyser l'idée qu'il a de Napoléon en tant qu'idée. Sa perspective est à l'opposé de celle qui prévaut spontanément. L'idée, au lieu de fonctionner comme moyen pour penser l'objet, devient elle-même l'objet et le but de la pensée.

De cette façon, Ortega relie le modernisme davantage aux positions de la phénoménologie husserlienne du XXe siècle qu'au marxisme positiviste et déterministe du XIXe. Ortega insiste sur les limites de l'idéation humaine : «Nous ne connaissons de la réalité, au sens strict, que les idées que nous sommes parvenus à formuler à son sujet, et rien d'autre.» Mais selon Ortega, ce phénomène n'est pas pris en considération. «C'est grâce aux idées que nous percevons le monde, mais une disposition d'esprit naturelle nous empêche de voir les idées elles-mêmes... Le mouvement spontané de l'esprit l'incline à partir des concepts pour appréhender le monde.» Il démontre que l'art traditionnel se contentait de considérer les idées comme des synonymes de la réalité ; la réalité était «idéalisée, même s'il s'agissait d'une falsification innocente». Le moderniste, qui aspire à la «réalisation scrupuleuse», inverse ce processus : «... si nous tournons le dos à la prétendue réalité, et que nous prenons les idées pour ce qu'elles sont – de simples schémas subjectifs – et en les faisant vivre comme tels, minces et angulaires, mais purs et transparents ; en bref, si nous proposons délibérément de «réaliser» nos idées, alors nous les aurons déshumanisées, et, chemin faisant, déréalisées.»

L'artiste moderniste inverse le mouvement «spontané» du monde à l'esprit. «Nous donnons une existence tridimensionnelle à de simples schémas, nous objectivons le subjectif, nous «mondifions» l'imminent». Comme il écrit cela dans les années vingt, il trouve cette tendance à des «degrés divers» à la fois dans l'expressionnisme et le cubisme, réconciliant alors des approches que les formalistes considèrent comme antithétiques : «De la peinture des objets, l'artiste s'est tourné vers la peinture des idées. Il se concentre sur ses propres images subjectives.»

Les autres caractéristiques de la définition d'Ortega découlent de cette vision déréalisée de l'art. Le moderniste évite les «formes arrondies et douces des corps vivants», parce qu'elles sont fortement associées à la fois aux «réalités vécues», à l'art occidental traditionnel et ses aspirations au «salut de l'humanité», si puissantes dans l'atmosphère transcendantaliste du XIXe siècle.

Ortega déclare que, plongé dans le doute husserlien, le moderniste est «ironique», que «quelque soit son contenu, l'art lui-même est railleur. Rechercher la fiction en tant que telle... est une proposition qu'on ne peut exécuter qu'en plaisantant. Etre un artiste signifie cesser de prendre au sérieux la personne très sérieuse que nous sommes quand nous ne sommes pas un artiste». L'art moderniste fonctionne comme «un système de miroirs qui réfléchissent l'infini, [où] aucune forme n'est ultime, toutes étant éventuellement ridiculisées et révélées en tant qu'images pures».

De la même façon, il considère qu'il n'y a dans l'art «aucune transcendance», aucune prétention. «Le royaume de l'art commence là où l'air se fait plus léger et où les choses, débarrassées des entraves formelles, commencent à faire de malicieux entrechats». Ortega lie l'impulsion moderniste à l'idée de jeu et de jeunesse. En fait, le modernisme a été, de façon caractéristique, le cheval de bataille de jeunes artistes qui, en vieillissant, sont souvent retombés dans cette solennité qui rappelle l'artiste-héros au XIXe.

Pour apprécier la valeur de la définition du modernisme selon Ortega, il faut montrer à quel point elle s'applique aux événements artistiques de ce siècle, y compris les plus récents. Un panthéon moderniste pour Ortega est très différent de celui de formalistes comme Greenberg. Contrairement au choix de Greenberg, les modernistes proposés ici ne présentent pas d'unité formelle. C'est plutôt un mécanisme commun de signification qui unifie leur travail.

Dans la mesure où le modernisme selon Ortega est une théorie sur le comportement commun à tous les arts, il s'applique aussi bien à la musique qu'à la littérature. La quintessence des musiciens modernistes est représentée par des figures comme Eric Satie et John Cage ; chez les écrivains modernistes, on peut citer des dramaturges comme Pirandello, Samuel Beckett et Bertold Brecht, ou des romanciers comme James Joyce, Alain Robbe-Grillet et Thomas Pynchon.

Dans le domaine des arts visuels, on peut citer Picasso (de 1907 à 1914), Duchamp, Jasper Johns (de 1955 à 1960), Ad Reinhardt et Andy Warhol. Tous sont incontestablement engagés dans une démarche qui doit plus au relativisme du XXe siècle qu'à la «contagion psychique» du romantisme ou qu'au mécanisme de l'empirisme du XIXe siècle.

Dans les arts visuels, le modernisme naît bien entendu avec Picasso. Le cubisme analytique est une négation complète des postulats artistiques antérieurs. Avec le cubisme, on voit pour la première fois l'artiste se concentrer complètement sur ses schémas mentaux, et les «réaliser» sur la toile. C'est avec le cubisme que l'on voit pour la première fois l'artiste se contenter de considérer son travail comme une chose «sans conséquence transcendantale», une aventure avant tout ironique et ludique. (Voir les fréquents jeux de mots sur les lettres J.O.U qui transforment la réalité du *Journal* du XIXe siècle en jeu pictural.)

Chez Duchamp, ce point de vue moderniste est également bien défini. Le *ready-made* est une tentative de «réalisation scrupuleuse» dans laquelle la représentation de l'objet est en adéquation avec la présence (présumée) de l'objet lui-même. De la même façon, *Le Grand Verre*, selon la description de Duchamp, est «l'apparition d'une apparence». Duchamp était en plus passionné par le jeu (voir sa fascination pour les jeux de société, la roulette et les échecs). L'une de ses dernières pièces est un relief en plâtre, au titre digne d'Ortega : *With My Tongue In My Mouth, Torture – morte* (1959).

Chez Jasper Johns, on remarque aussi ce souci de la «réalisation scrupuleuse». Dans ses premiers travaux, il abandonne toute velléité de représenter des objets tridimensionnels sur un plan bidimensionnel, en préférant limiter scrupuleusement ses représentations sur des plans bidimensionnels à des motifs bidimensionnels (tels que les drapeaux, les cibles, ou les nombres), ou restituer des objets tridimensionnels, en utilisant le moulage (parties du corps, flashs, etc.). Le chevauchement est rendu par celui des toiles (comme dans *Three Flags,* 1958). A travers tout ceci Johns garde une attitude ironique (il a même intégré l'empreinte d'un fer à repasser dans certains de ses derniers tableaux). Le jeu est plus précisément évoqué, dans son travail, par la cible (objet utilisé dans un jeu d'adresse) ; par son utilisation des bandes dessinées (dans *Alley Oop*, 1958), et par des balles de caoutchouc (dans *Painting With Two Balls*, 1960). En faisant des signes le sujet même de son art, Johns a donné, comme le suggère Ortega, une «existence tridimensionnelle à de simples motifs». Johns a lui-même déclaré qu'il peignait «des choses que l'esprit connaissait déjà. Ce qui me donnait toute latitude de travailler à d'autres niveaux [3].»

Il y a chez Reinhardt une approche à la Ortega de l'abstraction. Dans son «L'Art en tant qu'art», il déclare que «L'Art en tant qu'art est une réflexion sur l'essence de l'art». Reinhardt affirme que : «La prochaine révolution artistique sonnera le glas des vieilles rengaines sur «l'art et la vie» que les vieux artistes ratés aiment chanter en chœur avec les vieux amateurs sur le retour et un public nouveau, riche et avide [4].»

Les déclarations de Reinhardt rejoignent tout à fait les idées d'Ortega : «Non seulement la douleur et la joie devant les destins qu'une œuvre d'art montre ou raconte sont aux antipodes du vrai plaisir artistique, mais l'intérêt pour le contenu humain de l'œuvre est *a priori* incompatible avec la jouissance esthétique proprement dite.»

Pour réaliser cela, Reinhardt souhaite libérer radicalement

son travail de tout sujet autre que les schémas mentaux et les processus intellectuels. Dans une autre diatribe, il écrit : «...Pas de représentations, pas d'associations, pas de distorsions, pas de caricatures, pas d'effets de pâtes, pas de *drippings,* pas de voyages délirants, pas de sadisme, ou de déchirures, pas de thérapie, pas de destruction d'idoles... pas d'empâtement, pas de plasticité, pas de relations, pas d'expériences...»

A la place, il préconise «la symétrie absolue, la raison pure, la rigueur... Une peinture centrale, frontale, régulière, répétitive... Pour la couleur, le noir, le vide... La verticalité et l'horizontalité, le rectiligne, le parallélisme, la stase». Reinhardt illustre la revendication d'Ortega : «L'art moderne ne doit pas procéder par contagion psychique, la contagion psychique étant un phénomène inconscient, alors que l'art doit être pure clarté, pure intelligence.» On peut aussi constater que l'esthétique de Reinhardt s'est constituée à partir d'une démarche ironique dans son travail : «Tout ce que les artistes [abstraits] se sont vus reprocher de mauvais, je l'ai volontairement choisi, et j'en ai fait quelque chose de positif. Des mots comme inhumain, stérile, froid sont devenus *cool*... Et les autres – académique, dogmatique, absolu – je les ai eux aussi choisis et j'ai dit : «Eh bien ? Pourquoi pas académique ?»

Mais c'est peut-être Andy Warhol qui pousse les principes d'Ortega sur le modernisme à leurs plus extrêmes limites. Warhol applique «l'inversion» de la déshumanisation moderniste non seulement à son art mais à sa vie elle-même. Il ne se contente pas d'accomplir la «réalisation» de ses idées dans son œuvre, mais, plus encore que Duchamp, il les réalise également dans sa vie de tous les jours. Il abandonne sa vie «humaine» dans son art, et dans sa vie quotidienne. Comme Warhol le dit lui-même : «Je crois qu'une fois qu'on a vu les émotions sous un certain angle, on ne peut plus les considérer comme réelles. C'est plus ou moins ce qui m'est arrivé [5].»

Grâce aux instruments d'enregistrement électroniques, Warhol a pu abandonner les «réalités vécues» pour se concentrer sur le «pan de verre» de la perception : «L'acquisition de mon magnétophone a mis fin définitivement à ce qui me restait de vie émotionnelle, mais j'étais tout à fait heureux qu'il en soit ainsi. Plus rien ne m'a jamais posé de problème, car un problème signifiait un bon enregistrement, et quand un problème se transforme en bon enregistrement, ce n'est plus un problème.»

Ceci répond à la description de l'artiste par Ortega : «Le peintre n'est pas concerné, il ne fait que garder les yeux ouverts. Ce qui se produit ici ne le regarde pas ; il est en quelque sorte à des centaines de kilomètres. Son attitude est une attitude entièrement perceptive ; en fait, il ne peut percevoir l'événement dans toutes ses implications. Le sens profond de celui-ci échappe à son attention, entièrement concentrée sur le visuel... Nous trouvons chez le peintre un maximum de distanciation et un minimum d'investissement émotionnel.»

Warhol était fasciné par ceux dont les médias avaient «déshumanisé» la vie, les stars de cinéma, les célébrités, les travestis. Selon Warhol, le cinéma offrait le meilleur exemple de cette inversion : «La meilleure atmosphère à laquelle je puisse penser est celle du film, car il est physiquement tridimensionnel et émotionnellement bidimensionnel.»

En même temps, Warhol partage avec Ortega cette conscience du caractère ludique de toute la tradition moderniste. Ortega précise à ce sujet : «Pour l'artiste d'aujourd'hui, le royaume de l'art commence là où l'air se fait plus léger et où les choses, débarrassées des entraves formelles, commencent à faire de malicieux entrechats... Le symbole de l'art redevient alors le dieu Pan faisant cabrioler les chevreaux à l'orée du bois.»

Warhol se fait l'écho de ce point de vue : «Dans certains cercles où des gens très importants pensent avoir des cerveaux importants, des mots comme «charmant», «agréable», «joli» sont tous rejetés, et tout ce qu'il y a de plus léger dans la vie, ce qui est le plus important, est rejeté.»

Aujourd'hui, les critiques post-modernistes prétendent que les jeunes artistes ne travaillent plus en fonction des paramètres du modernisme. C'est vrai – et ce le fut pendant longtemps – si on définit le modernisme selon l'approche formaliste de Greenberg.

Cependant, si on adopte la thèse d'Ortega, on constate que bon nombre de jeunes artistes, surtout ceux qui sont défendus par la critique post-moderniste, travaillent dans la même direction que cette théorie vieille de cinquante ans. R.M. Fischer, Steven Keister, Cindy Sherman et Richard Prince sont les noms qui viennent à l'esprit quand on songe à des artistes pouvant aspirer à l'idée de modernisme proposée par Ortega.

D'autre part, une certaine partie de la production artistique aujourd'hui n'a effectivement rien à voir avec l'idée de modernisme. Mais la qualifier de post-moderniste est sans doute une erreur dans la mesure où elle présente toutes les caractéristiques d'un «pré-modernisme». Le retour à la perspective, à l'unité de l'objet d'art, à l'expression humaine, à la «sensibilité» ne sont qu'un retour aux stratégies du XIXe siècle, exploitées par les artistes rétrogrades, comme le précise H. D. Buchloh dans son récent essai sur la «nouvelle image [6].»

Il y a toujours eu un art rétrograde dans notre culture, mais le phénomène nouveau, aujourd'hui, c'est que ce travail puisse être considéré comme majeur. Ceci est la conséquence des changements intervenus dans notre société depuis dix ans.

Des années cinquante aux années soixante-dix, c'est la classe des entrepreneurs qui, en période de prospérité économique, a soutenu le modernisme dans le domaine qui lui est le plus souvent associé : les arts visuels. Cette classe a aujourd'hui largement abandonné son intérêt pour l'idée de modernisme (comme elle a abandonné ses aspirations au libéralisme). Elle cherche au contraire à se rassurer en se réfugiant dans l'historicisme, le romantisme et une parodie d'individualisme.

Aujourd'hui, le modernisme s'est en grande partie déplacé dans une autre sphère, où il est soutenu par une classe différente. Il est aussi vivant en musique qu'il est attaqué dans les arts visuels. Des groupes comme les *Talking Heads*, les *Clash*, les *Gang of Four* et *Public Image Limited*, ont tous pris une position fondamentalement moderniste. David Byrne, des *Talking Heads*, par exemple, chante que «les faits sont inutiles en temps de crise», que :

«Les faits sont simples, les faits sont directs
Les faits sont paresseux, les faits sont en retard
Les faits ont tous des points de vue
Les faits ne font pas ce que je veux
Les faits trafiquent la vérité
Les faits sont vivants et réversibles [7].»

Il reflète ici la position d'Ortega sur les limites de l'idéation. Les *Clash* chantent la confrontation, dans un dessin animé, entre le *G.I. Joe* et *Ivan*, un «ours russe», en retournant ironiquement contre eux les étiquettes chauvinistes. Les

Gang of Four chantent :

«Le problème du loisir
Que faire pour le plaisir
L'amour idéal, un nouvel achat
Un marché des sens [8].»

Ils transforment les procédés publicitaires en une «algèbre des métaphores» et neutralisent ainsi la «contagion» de la culture populaire. De la même façon, le leader du groupe les *Dead Kennedys* utilise le nom de plume moderniste de Jello Biafra (candidat à la mairie de San Francisco, avec ce slogan : «Il y a toujours de la place pour Jello»).

Dans l'instrumentation, ces groupes parodient constamment le phrasé des débuts de la pop-music. Le jeu permet aux *B-52s* de transformer le bourdon un peu vide de la musique du début des années soixante en autre chose. Beaucoup de ces musiciens ont aussi adopté une attitude clairement moderniste pour leurs personnages publics. John Lydon, de *Public Image Limited*, a déclaré lors d'un entretien pour le magazine canadien *Mac Lean's* : «J'en ai assez du passé, et le futur commence également à être répétitif. Je ne sais pas vraiment quoi dire. Je dis tout le temps des conneries. Je suis un menteur, un hypocrite, un vrai salaud. On devrait me jeter...»

Le modernisme de ces musiciens est particulièrement significatif, parce qu'il s'attaque au principal bastion d'un art populaire ancré dans le XIXe siècle : la musique électronique rock. Parce qu'ils appliquent l'attitude moderniste de l'ironie et du doute à des problèmes politiques et sociaux, leur travail finit par servir le propos qui, selon Ortega, était l'objectif du modernisme – préserver la possibilité de la démocratie libérale. Leur volonté de traiter des événements majeurs de notre culture fait de ces musiciens des successeurs importants des modernistes les plus audacieux du passé.

cieux du passé.

Dans les périodes d'incertitude et de crises économiques, comme la nôtre, les riches se réfugient toujours dans la peur et la réaction.

D'autre part, pendant ces périodes défavorables, il y a des petits groupes, parmi ceux qui n'ont pas trouvé de statu quo, qui seront amenés à la réflexion et au doute les plus intenses. Ces musiciens ne sont pas soutenus par la classe aisée des entrepreneurs (comme l'ont été les artistes modernistes), mais par une minorité d'individus qui réfléchissent, qui doutent et qui possèdent les quelques dollars nécessaires à l'achat d'un album.

Cette structure de marché a permis l'éclosion du modernisme dans le domaine musical aujourd'hui. Elle pourrait donner l'impulsion nécessaire à sa résurgence dans les arts visuels.

Publié pour la première fois dans *Arts Magazine,* (New York) vol. 56, n° 3, novembre 1981.

Ross Bleckner : la peinture à la fin de l'Histoire

Finis les arbres et les espaces clos. Finies les habiles compositions d'entrelacs. Finies les descriptions d'objets, l'éclectique représentation du cubisme synthétique qui liait le travail de Ross Bleckner à des artistes comme Jennifer Bartlett et Elizabeth Murray.

Seule demeure la lumière – une lumière qui naît d'une dialectique des oppositions, le noir et le blanc, l'optique et le pictural – la lumière naît d'un «art mauvais», du souvenir adolescent de l'*Op' Art*, de Cap Canaveral, de la «*New York's World Fair*», de l'âge d'or américain. Les pensées tourbillonnent sans fin d'arrière en avant. Et la lumière repousse. L'œil ne peut se fixer sur les bandes floues et mouvantes. La lumière se métamorphose alors en barres qui empêchent d'entrer dans la peinture.

Une grande partie de la production récente a choisi pour sujet des images qui sont d'une certaine façon emblématiques de l'ère moderniste. Pour Sherrie Levine, cette imagerie est la photographie du XXe siècle. Pour Cindy Sherman, ce sont les photographies de films, où sa propre image remplace celle du «produit-célébrité». Pour Ross

Bleckner, dans son travail récent, le sujet du discours, c'est l'*Op' Art*.

L'*Op' Art* est choisi comme symbole éloquent de l'échec complet du positivisme après la guerre, de la transformation des impératifs technologiques et formels introduits par le Bauhaus dans la modernité impitoyable préconisée et pratiquée par l'Amérique après la guerre, de la transformation de l'esthétique de Mies et de Gropius en hoola hoop, en arrière de Cadillac, en Tang et en *Op' Art*. Comment et pourquoi cela s'est-il produit ? Comment, a-t-on pu en arriver par exemple à ce que Coca-Cola choisisse Josef Albers comme consultant pour décider quelle nuance de rouge devait être utilisée dans son logo ?

Le positivisme du Bauhaus soutenait qu'il était possible de se débarrasser de l'Histoire, des fidélités ethniques ou régionalistes, de la sensiblerie destructrice, de l'adhésion irrationnelle à la tradition, pour se tourner vers des solutions rationnelles et formelles, basées sur la connaissance scientifique et le savoir-faire technique. Dans l'Europe d'avant-guerre, ce modernisme positiviste servait les objectifs des idéaux socio-démocrates qui avaient, à l'origine, suscité sa création. Dans l'Amérique d'après-guerre, il s'est détaché de ce programme social et, aidé en cela par la prédilection américaine pour le fonctionnalisme, il est devenu la modernité, cette vision du monde proposée par l'Amérique.

Mais l'attrait de la modernité, pour l'Amérique, ne reposait pas sur des possibilités de production plus efficaces, offertes par la réflexion formelle et technologique. La modernité était devenue utile parce qu'elle permettait de dire à la communauté que les valeurs technologiques étaient des valeurs modernes ; que le consommateur devait abandonner ses habitudes alimentaires, vestimentaires, ses loisirs traditionnels, pour qu'on puisse lui proposer des alternatives plus compétitives financièrement donc plus intéressantes ; que les communautés devaient abandonner leurs coutumes, leurs modes de production et leurs organisations sociales pour qu'on puisse transformer la société, afin d'exploiter plus efficacement les ressources naturelles et d'ouvrir de nouveaux marchés. La modernité devint alors un moyen de stimuler les ventes et les profits du marché tout entier, grâce au concept d'obsolescence planifiée, qui persuadait le consommateur de se débarrasser de ses appareils ménagers ou de son automobile en parfait état de marche et de les remplacer par un nouveau modèle répondant aux nouveaux critères de l'esthétique industrielle : une plus grande efficacité formelle et technologique.

L'*Op' Art* fut l'expression de cette stratégie. Ignorant l'Histoire, ignorant les savoir-faire artistiques traditionnels, l'*Op' Art* a représenté cette énergie pulsative, presque électrique qui était censée faire fonctionner les marchés de la société industrielle. Pour créer ses effets, il n'a utilisé que les règles scientifiques de l'interaction optique, les couleurs et les pigments synthétiques les plus récents. L'*Op' Art* est apparu en 1965, en plein âge d'or de l'expansion américaine, la même année que la grande exposition de la modernité américaine, la «*New York's World Fair*». Il est apparu avant la prise de conscience d'un possible éclatement des valeurs du progrès moderne, avant le Viêt-Nam, avant 1968, avant l'O.P.E.P. Et plus que tout autre mouvement artistique contemporain, l'*Op' Art* obéissait parfaitement au principe d'obsolescence planifiée de la modernité sur lequel il était construit et au bout d'une saison seulement il avait disparu.

*

«La Tour de Lumière. La Tour de Lumière était très isolée. Très peu de gens y allaient. C'était un si bon *emplacement.* Près de la Cour de l'Univers, pratiquement au cœur des choses. Près de General Electrics, pas loin de Coca-Cola, qui était si célèbre, près de *Clairol,* du Pavillon *Clairol* où les femmes faisaient la queue pendant des heures afin d'être conseillées sur leurs cheveux, sur la façon de les coiffer. C'était un bon emplacement, mais il était isolé [1].»

Pour toute une génération d'artistes d'aujourd'hui, ces années, symboles de la toute puissance américaine, ont une signification précise. Le rêve américain était la réalité de leur adolescence. Approfondir sa signification, faire revivre sa syntaxe a, pour eux, un sens psychologique et sociologique, tout comme pour les surréalistes, l'imagerie de la Belle Epoque, période de leur adolescence, a eu des conséquences iconographiques particulières. Dans son récent essai, cité plus haut, *Within the Context of No Context*, George W.S. Trow Jr. évoque ses souvenirs d'adolescent à la «*New York's World Fair*», en 1964-1965. Des artistes comme David Salle et Steve Keister, des groupes musicaux comme les *B-52s* et les *Modern Lovers* ont aussi exprimé dans leur travail le besoin de faire revivre et de créer à partir de la sociologie du milieu des années soixante. Ross Bleckner reconnaît que pour lui aussi l'*Op' Art* était alors le nec plus ultra de l'art moderne.

Dans ses premiers travaux, comme *Photo-Synthesis* et *The First Morning of the Second World* (tous les deux de 1980), Bleckner avait déjà commencé à traiter ce problème du positivisme. Dans *Photo-Synthesis*, quatre panneaux avec des figures – d'inspiration non occidentale, symboliste et du début de la Renaissance, suggérant une certaine compréhension non rationnelle du processus de croissance végétale – cachent un plan noir grossièrement quadrillé d'un réseau de lignes blanches. On a alors l'impression que l'iconographie intuitive obscurcit et nie la rationalité suggérée par le titre et la grille cartésienne de l'arrière-plan.

Dans son nouveau travail, *The Forest,* Bleckner s'est concentré sur l'échec du positivisme, non comme vérité philosophique, mais comme credo social. Il nous offre non sans ironie un exemple de l'esthétique de la modernité même, montrant ainsi non les possibilités du positivisme mais son échec et ses limites. (Ces toiles sont alors proches des images de Warhol, des chaises électriques et des émeutes raciales en particulier.)

L'ironie inhérente à ces tableaux s'applique aussi au processus pictural lui-même. Bleckner prend une distance ironique par rapport à la stratégie de «l'art sur l'art» qu'il utilise lui-même. Alors que des artistes comme Bill Jensen, Gregory Amenoff, ou les nouveaux peintres italiens ou allemands, utilisent comme modèles certains aspects largement reconnus des débuts de l'art moderne, Bleckner préfère choisir ses citations dans un style que la critique n'a pas légitimé. Il a créé quelque chose qui ne relève pas de «l'art sur l'art» mais de «l'art sur l'art mauvais». Par ailleurs sa stratégie est encore plus complexe que celle d'autres artistes récents trouvant leur inspiration «d'art mauvais» dans l'art populaire, commercial ou fantastique qui n'ont jamais été pris en considération par la critique. Bleckner travaille à partir d'un art aujourd'hui considéré comme sans intérêt, mais qui a été, même très peu de temps, important.

*

Mais les tableaux de Bleckner ne sont pas seulement une critique de la culture américaine d'après-guerre, car il a retrouvé une autre clef importante : cette conscience inhérente à l'*Op' Art*, inhérente à l'univers de vibrations et d'abstraction qu'il suggère, c'est le psychédélisme et la transcendance. En fait, les années soixante ont pleinement exploité ce potentiel. La syntaxe de l'*Op' Art*, les bandes ondulantes claires et sombres, a été déplacée de son contexte technocratique et adoptée comme symbole du psychédélisme, cette quête visionnaire de l'âge post- industriel.

Bleckner a mis en valeur cette prise de conscience dans une série de stratégies qui insiste sur la transcendance implicite de ses bandes blanches. Quand on fixe son attention sur les vibrations des surfaces, on commence à remarquer la présence des gouttes et des coups de pinceau. L'échelle éléphantesque des tableaux évoque davantage les murs de lumière de l'expressionnisme que les objets discrets, portables et esthétiques que proposait l'*Op' Art*. (Le plus grand mesure 6 x 2,50 mètres-format du *Vir Heroicus Sublimis* de Barnett Newman.) Bleckner a réduit le vocabulaire de l'*Op'Art* à des bandes verticales parallèles, remettant de manière provocante, à l'ordre du jour le concept apparemment caduc de la composition *All-Over* où la distribution de l'énergie dans la toile répond à la toute puissance du transcendantal dans l'univers. Ainsi on est confronté à un malaise engendré par la coexistence du transcendantal et de l'ironique dans la même œuvre.

Aujourd'hui, le modernisme est appréhendé de deux façons différentes par deux camps opposés, les relativistes et les transcendantalistes. Les transcendantalistes ont attribué au modernisme la qualité première de la présence. Pour eux, le modernisme est idéaliste et jungien. Ils considèrent Matisse, Mondrian et Kandinsky comme exemplaires et recherchent les racines du modernisme chez les symbolistes français et chez Emerson. Ils estiment que le travail de Pollock, de Rothko et de Newman répond radicalement à cette exigence de présence. Cette position transcendantaliste, défendue par la très convaincante et non moins réactionnaire Barbara Rose, est tombée en désuétude.

Il y a d'autre part les relativistes. Ebauché chez Manet, pleinement exprimé chez Picasso et Duchamp, puis Rauschenberg et Johns, le relativisme nous considère comme prisonniers de notre propre système de signes et donc incapables d'appréhender le monde qui nous entoure. Puisant ses sources dans la phénoménologie, chez Freud et dans l'incertitude heisenbergienne, ce modernisme s'exprime par l'ironie et le doute, l'humour et le jeu.

Dans les tableaux de Bleckner, le fossé entre ces deux modernismes est comblé. Ils sont ironiques et indiquent la présence dans le même temps ; ils sont blancs et noirs. L'image qui nous est proposée est à la fois métaphysique et moqueuse : c'est celle d'un dieu hilare. Mais la divinité que crée Bleckner n'a plus rien à voir avec la sévérité et le tragique des divinités du panthéon judéo-chrétien ou grec. Bleckner a créé, à l'inverse, une image transcendantale dans la tradition de la pensée orientale, du bouddhisme et de l'hindouisme, avec leurs divinités joyeuses et ironiques.

Si on étudie les religions orientales, on peut retrouver une trace de ce type de pensée dans le travail de Bleckner. C'est une reminiscence du transcendantalisme ironique des écrivains de la période *beat* :

«Je reste assis chez moi pendant des jours
    à regarder les roses dans les cabinets
Quand je vais à Chinatown je me saoûle
    et ne me fais jamais sauter.

Je me suis fait à l'idée qu'il allait y avoir
des problèmes.
Vous auriez du me voir lire Marx.
Mon psychanalyste pense que je vais
très bien
J'ai des visions mystiques et éprouve des
vibrations cosmiques.
Amérique, je ne t'ai pas encore dit
ce que tu as fait à l'oncle Max
quand il est arrivé de Russie [2].»

Dans ce passage d'*America*, Allen Ginsberg propose une idée très proche de celle que Bleckner a élaborée dans ses travaux récents. Les deux derniers vers, où s'expriment simultanément les «visions mystiques» et la désillusion ironique, renvoient tout spécialement au contenu à la fois ironique et transcendantal de Bleckner. On trouve un état d'esprit similaire chez Ferlinghetti, Kerouac et Gregory Corso.

*

Mais pourquoi le transcendantalisme s'est-il constamment réaffirmé dans l'atmosphère laïque de l'après-guerre ? Pourquoi est-il un facteur si important pour l'art des années cinquante et pour un travail comme celui de Bleckner aujourd'hui ? Il est évident que la construction et l'utilisation de la bombe atomique à la fin de la Seconde Guerre mondiale puis celle de la bombe H au début des années cinquante, ont eu un effet déterminant sur les thèmes de l'expressionnisme abstrait et de la littérature *beat*. Quand il parle de son travail, Bleckner désigne lui aussi la terreur nucléaire comme le principal facteur qui lui a permis d'introduire un contenu transcendantal dans son travail aujourd'hui.

Ce phénomène historique qu'est l'armement nucléaire a joué de plusieurs façons sur le retour du transcendantalisme dans l'art. La force destructrice des armes nucléaires – leur pouvoir d'anéantir notre civilisation tout entière – rend caducs les élégants jeux syntaxiques des relativistes. De la même façon, l'armement nucléaire a transformé la relation des êtres humains avec l'absolu. Nous avons de bonnes raisons de penser qu'il nous est possible de rayer l'espèce humaine de la surface de la planète, que nous pouvons transcender notre existence par la destruction : nous avons apparemment acquis un pouvoir qui était attribué traditionnellement à des êtres surnaturels.

La puissance et la méthodologie même de la destruction nucléaire ont aussi renforcé l'idée que l'être humain peut pénétrer la structure *a priori* de l'univers, qu'il existe un code du savoir super-humain que l'on commence à peine à pénétrer. Tout porte à croire que, en concevant l'armement nucléaire, l'humanité a pénétré à la fois la structure de l'atome, constituant de base de la matière, et celle du soleil, source d'énergie vitale dans notre univers. L'armement nucléaire a renforcé l'hypothèse de base du point de vue transcendantal : la nature est structure et on peut, d'une façon ou d'une autre, connaître cette structure.

La peinture de Bleckner semble réaffirmer en grande partie ce point de vue transcendantal. Son incandescence vibratoire crée une analogie avec la base rythmique d'une nature connaissable. Simultanément, Bleckner est ému par des événements historiques plus sombres. Son travail est une réaction à l'échec du positivisme, à son dévoiement commercial d'après-guerre, et à la folie qu'il a finalement contribué à susciter – la terreur nucléaire. Son travail est une forme de questionnement, dans le sillage de cette Histoire troublée, et une prise de conscience, assez récente, dans la civilisation occidentale, que le savoir peut être doute et que le doute peut apporter la lumière, que la réalité de la désillusion peut elle aussi mener à la transcendance.

Publié pour la première fois dans *Arts Magazine,* (New York), vol. 56, nº 9, mai 1982.

Nature et culture

Il y a une dizaine d'années, on pensait qu'avoir du *soul* était un remède à l'aliénation de la conscience dans le monde industriel. Dans un univers bourgeois, répressif et mécanisé, disait-on, les gens avaient perdu vitalité, spontanéité et émotion. Donc, toute manifestation ayant du *soul*, de la spiritualité, pouvait aider l'humanité à retrouver son unité avec la nature, son «essence».

Aujourd'hui, cependant, cette façon de voir les choses a changé, tout au moins dans le monde de l'art. Des idées comme le *soul* et la spiritualité sont souvent considérées comme le moyen utilisé par la culture bourgeoise pour consolider sa position en niant son historicité. Dire d'une œuvre d'art qu'elle est spirituelle, c'est lui attribuer une valeur universelle et intemporelle. Cela suggère également que la société qui encourage et cautionne ces travaux est elle-même universelle et intemporelle.

Le changement radical et soudain de l'opinion elle-même appelle la réflexion. Il est le résultat du changement intellectuel qui s'est abattu comme un raz de marée sur le monde de l'art au cours de cette dernière décennie. La pratique artistique qui domine depuis la Seconde Guerre mondiale a été complètement balayée et remplacée par une autre.

De la Seconde Guerre mondiale à la fin de la dernière décennie, l'activité artistique était dominée par des idées issues de la phénoménologie, de l'existentialisme et du transcendantalisme jungien. L'après-guerre a attribué au modernisme un rôle avant-gardiste et héroïque, non pas dans un sens politique, mais dans la mesure où on pensait que l'art pouvait aider les hommes à retrouver leur essence perdue et libérer des potentialités jusqu'à présent cachées chez l'être humain.

Une histoire de l'art a été écrite autour de cette idée. Elle a confirmé la portée trans-historique du travail de «maîtres» appartenant à d'autres cultures ou à d'autres périodes historiques, non seulement pour valider un standard de valeurs formelles, mais parce que la qualité formelle elle-même était le signe qui donnait accès au caractère transcendantal de la conscience de chaque maître. On élabora aussi un canon pour les maîtres modernes. Matisse et Brancusi étaient admirés pour la magie de leurs gestes subjectifs, pour leur façon de personnifier la patience et la transcendance de l'artisan ; Mondrian était vénéré pour la pureté de son investigation phénoménologique ; Klee pour l'ingéniosité et la sincérité de sa quête visionnaire.

Parallèlement à cette recherche de l'harmonie et du spirituel dans l'art européen, on établit aussi un canon pour les primitifs à partir du modernisme européen. Cet intérêt pour le primitif reposait sur l'idée que les sociétés tribales sont la preuve que l'homme peut vivre en harmonie avec la nature.

Cette attitude devant le primitif apparaît tout d'abord dans l'expressionnisme abstrait, dans le sentiment de la terreur primitive chez Barnett Newman, dans l'influence des cultures américaines autochtones chez Still et Pollock.

On trouve ensuite chez Pollock l'idée que l'objet peut être remplacé par l'action en «temps réel», suggestion récupérée dix ans plus tard par toute une génération d'artistes que ce soit dans l'art conceptuel, la performance ou le *Process*, pour qui l'expérience tribale de «l'art en temps réel» était une clef pour annuler l'effet mortifiant de l'objet d'art bourgeois.

L'après-guerre fut aussi l'époque d'un art de la nature, une époque où l'artiste voulait renouer avec des absolus perdus ou cachés, que ce soit par la sérénité de la méditation, l'exploration de l'inconscient universel jungien, ou par des actes de réunification avec la terre elle-même.

C'est l'époque du paysage, celui qui établit l'imagerie de l'expressionnisme abstrait, puis des peintres de la *Color-Field* (Caro, Noland, Olitski, etc...) jusqu'à son apogée avec le *Land Art*, dont l'objectif est de restituer, littéralement, la conscience à sa mère originelle, la Terre.

Les manifestations qui, à première vue, contredisent cette interprétation, ne font que la confirmer si on les étudie attentivement. Le *Pop Art,* par exemple, qui aurait pu changer radicalement le cours de cette histoire, s'est finalement contenté de la tourner en dérision. A l'époque, les artistes du *Pop* étaient isolés, sans successeurs. Le *Pop Art* commence seulement aujourd'hui à influencer une autre génération d'artistes. Les efforts des artistes formalistes ont été eux aussi mal interprétés, à cause des besoins dominants du moment. En attribuant de la «présence» au travail d'artistes réellement formalistes comme Stella ou Judd, on le rendait transcendant. Mais beaucoup d'autres artistes, soi-disant formalistes, étaient en fait autant influencés par le mysticisme oriental que par les idées formalistes proprement dites.

Cette époque est entièrement dominée par les principes

philosophiques de la phénoménologie et de l'existentialisme. L'art est alors entièrement dévolu à la position de l'individu comme entité perceptive et décidante. Mais avant de réduire la production de cette époque, qui voit la fin de l'ère industrielle, à la volonté de préserver l'importance mythique de l'individu et celle d'une nature absolue sur laquelle celui-ci peut agir, il faut ne pas oublier que cette époque a été constituée et déterminée par un autre événement historique, un événement dont l'influence doit être appréhendée indépendamment de la lente évolution du capital.

Si on peut dire que l'art de cette époque énonce la relation entre l'homme et la nature, c'est peut-être parce que la Seconde Guerre mondiale est un événement qui a pu agir sur ceux qui l'avaient vécu comme phénomène naturel. Cet événement monstrueux, bien qu'évidemment provoqué par des forces sociales, fut considéré par une grande partie de la population mondiale comme un phénomène proche du fléau, le déluge ou l'incendie. La Seconde Guerre mondiale fut une «catastrophe naturelle» dans la mesure où elle a complètement détruit le réseau de signes qui constitue la civilisation occidentale. Elle a laissé un nombre incalculable d'individus dans une situation où ils étaient confrontés non plus aux codes inventés pour eux par leur société, mais au gouffre inattendu de l'«empire des signes».

Il suffit de regarder l'importance de l'existentialisme sartrien, qui défend le plus souvent les mêmes valeurs que l'expressionnisme abstrait, pour comprendre l'impact de la Seconde Guerre mondiale sur cette époque. Pour Sartre, comme pour les expressionnistes abstraits, la responsabilité, l'action, «l'engagement», et la volonté de trouver du sens et d'établir une morale, constituaient la base de leur problématique. Comme pour dire que dans ce monde sans code engendré par une guerre à une si grande échelle, un monde où les lois habituelles du marché et des classes – le fonctionnement normal de l'univers bourgeois – étaient en suspens, la philosophie et l'art ne pouvaient s'intéresser qu'à la marge de manœuvre et à la capacité de décision dont un individu, privé de son rôle social, disposait.

Dans ce cas, pourquoi, à la fin des années soixante-dix, cette approche à la fois transcendantaliste et phénoménologique, qui avait prévalu pendant trente ans, a-t-elle brusquement disparu pour être remplacée par une nouvelle pratique, prenant son répertoire d'images dans les mass media, rejetant la phénoménologie de la création artistique à cause de son côté prétentieux et mandarin et interprétant le langage comme une entité coupée de la réalité extra-humaine ? Pourquoi une nouvelle pratique a-t-elle émergé, substituant à l'étude phénoménologique une fascination pour la réalité politique et sociologique, rejetant à la fois le positivisme des sciences humaines et physiques, et remplaçant le culte de l'originalité par de multiples variations sur le thème de la répétition ?

Comment et pourquoi, vers 1980, un ensemble de textes français, vaguement considérés comme post-structuralistes ou structuralistes, où on trouve des oeuvres écrites dix ou vingt ans plus tôt par Roland Barthes, Michel Foucault, Jacques Derrida et Jean Baudrillard, a-t-il soudain trouvé grâce dans le climat intellectuel du monde de l'art, en influençant à la fois les artistes et les théoriciens, signant par là-même l'obsolescence de l'idée de nature dans ce monde de culture ?

Pour commencer, il est impossible de passer sous silence le fait que la génération d'artistes responsables de ce bouleversement est la première à être née après la guerre et que, vice versa, les figures significatives dont le travail était forgé par l'expérience de la guerre ont disparu progressivement. Par conséquent, les valeurs existentialistes de la génération de la Seconde Guerre mondiale se sont évanouies pendant que la nouvelle génération (en tout cas en Occident), qui n'avait jamais vécu cette situation où toutes les règles s'avèrent inapplicables, s'est précisément fixée sur les règles, c'est-à-dire sur le langage.

Cette interprétation pourrait suggérer que l'Europe, beaucoup plus touchée par la guerre que les Etats-Unis, en garderait plus longtemps les traces intellectuellement, alors que dix ans à peine après la fin de la guerre apparaissait déjà le mouvement structuraliste. Ceci ne fait peut-être que montrer quelle force intellectuelle prédominante était le marxisme en Europe pour que le structuralisme, qui en est proche, évolue si rapidement, si peu de temps après l'expérience de la guerre.

Ou peut-être, à moins de chercher une explication dans une théorie formaliste, qui ferait le lien entre l'évolution des tendances intellectuelles et le décalage inévitable dû à la traduction des textes fondamentaux, ou qui expliquerait les changements artistiques par l'entropie inhérente aux mouvements artistiques, on doit revenir à l'étude des facteurs socio-économiques qui subordonnent le changement culturel au développement de la société industrielle et capitaliste. De ce point de vue, le structuralisme et la nouvelle forme d'art montrent tous les deux le passage d'une société industrielle à une société post-industrielle ; d'une société de marché en expansion au marasme économique, où la richesse est plus redistribuée que créée ; d'une société où production, innovation, individualisme seraient mythifiés au nom de la créativité à une société mettant l'accent sur la manipulation de ce qui existe déjà, que les signes en soient économiques ou culturels. Il s'agit de la culture décrite par le structuralisme ou dont on peut dire aussi qu'elle crée le structuralisme. Les ferments de cette société post-industrielle existaient en Europe depuis la fin de la Seconde Guerre mondiale, dès la publication des premiers textes structuralistes. Aux Etats-Unis, ils ne sont apparus que ces dernières années, après le Viêt-Nam (qui freine les ambitions coloniales américaines) et les chocs pétroliers des années soixante-dix, qui ont effectivement mis fin à l'expansion économique américaine. Avec l'émergence de l'ère post-industrielle, une nouvelle pratique artistique structuraliste est apparue aux Etats-Unis.

L'avènement de l'ère post-industrielle semble aussi rendre obsolète le concept même de nature, suscitant une critique du règne de la nature dans l'art. Si la période industrielle représente le moment où la nature était considérée comme réelle, on peut aujourd'hui estimer que la société entre dans une ère où la culture bourgeoise renforce son lien avec la nature et poursuit le processus qui lui a permis d'imposer comme référent son mode de pensée et sa conscience. De plus en plus, l'importance des «autres» durant la période industrielle a été éliminée, la sauvagerie est jugulée par la loi, alors que les modes d'organisation sociale, tribaux ou folkloriques, ont été pratiquement assimilés (il ne reste plus que la question difficile de l'inconscient).

Baudrillard, en particulier, a défendu une historicisation de l'idée de nature. Il décrit le «triomphe de la nature» à l'époque industrielle comme un événement historique : «La Nature n'apparaît véritablement comme essence, dans toute sa gloire, que sous le signe du *principe de production*. Cette séparation en recoupe une autre : celle du *principe de signification*. Sous la découpe objective de la Science, de la Technique et de la Production, la Nature devient le grand Signifié, le grand Référent, elle se charge idéalement de «réalité», elle devient *la* Réalité... [1]»

La culture bourgeoise a de plus en plus souvent l'occasion de «simuler» (selon la terminologie de Baudrillard) les pouvoirs cruciaux qui appartenaient jadis à la nature –le pouvoir de la pensée, reproduit par l'ordinateur, qui «réalise» la dualité bourgeoise ; la capacité de créer la vie, chimiquement et mécaniquement ; la capacité de créer l'espace lui-même grâce aux circuits binaires de l'animation électronique. Ainsi, le cercle de la pensée bourgeoise se referme ; l'univers bourgeois ne peut plus se référer qu'à lui-même. Récemment, même le cœur humain, sans doute le plus naturel des objets dans l'ordre ancien, a été reconstitué selon les processus de pensée de la conscience bourgeoise.

La récente appropriation du vocabulaire de la nature et du modernisme d'après-guerre par la publicité montre l'étendue de ce changement, victoire du marché sur la nature. Que la bière, la lessive ou le maquillage soient maintenant qualifiés de «naturels» est significatif. Aujourd'hui, l'appellation «*Nature Valley*» désigne des céréales pour le petit déjeuner ; des cigarettes reçoivent des qualificatifs aussi transcendantaux que «Vraie», «Légère» et «Nouvelle»...

Pourtant la pratique artistique structuraliste la plus récente soulève un certain nombre de questions troublantes. D'abord, comment les artistes peuvent-il s'adresser au monde du simulacre ? Si l'ère post-industrielle est caractérisée par des signes qui simulent plus qu'ils ne représentent, comment un artiste peut-il rendre cette situation ? Est-il possible de représenter une simulation ? Dans la négative, c'est à l'artiste de s'investir dans la pratique de la simulation. Ce qui crée alors une situation problématique. On peut considérer que la pratique de la simulation par l'artiste est une acceptation de la culture du simulacre. Et on se demande si cette appropriation est souhaitable, si, comme les critiques marxistes le pensent, la culture post-industrielle constitue une étape supplémentaire dans l'aliénation sociale ? Certains artistes, engagés dans une pratique structuraliste sérieuse, sont apparemment sur le point de répondre à cette question. Mais comme l'a montré Hal Foster, les artistes néo-expressionnistes cautionnent clairement les nouvelles conditions sociales en simulant la notion moderniste de chef-d'œuvre [2].

Frederic Jameson a fait remarquer que l'analyse culturelle est aujourd'hui dominée par deux tendances différentes. Il y a d'une part la théorie du simulacre selon Baudrillard. Nous trouvons, de l'autre, l'œuvre de Michel Foucault qui considère la culture contemporaine non comme une surface miroitante de signes autonomes, mais comme le lieu où les techniques de surveillance, de normalisation et de catégorisation ont un pouvoir toujours plus grand sur la vie sociale [3]. Là où Baudrillard voit des signifiants autonomes, Foucault discerne, derrière les différents signifiants de la société contemporaine, le signifié voilé du pouvoir à travers la consolidation de la position de classe. On se demande pourquoi les artistes et les théoriciens de l'art sont aujourd'hui si exclusivement attirés par l'interprétation des relations sociales de Baudrillard, plutôt que celle de Foucault. On se demande si le monde brillant de surface de Baudrillard n'est pas plus séduisant que la froide répartition des espaces disciplinaires de Michel Foucault. Et on se demande si l'artiste et le public, séduits par ce monde miroitant, n'ont pas été détournés d'une analyse sérieuse des problèmes fondamentaux de la structure sociale.

Finalement on se détourne à contre-cœur de la promesse du post-structuralisme – sa capacité à balayer les mythologies de tant d'humanismes décevants – au profit d'une prise en compte des résultats négatifs qu'il peut engendrer. Car le structuralisme, que ce soit celui de Barthes, de Foucault ou de Baudrillard, ne peut être séparé de certains contresens qu'il engendre naturellement. Mal interpréter le structuralisme, c'est parvenir à une seule réalité, la réalité du pouvoir, non pas le pouvoir d'une classe sur une autre, mais le seul et unique pouvoir de comprendre et de manipuler les codes.

On voit souvent à la télévision une publicité pour une compagnie d'investissements qui avertit le téléspectateur que «certains investissements exigent de la discipline, d'autres du courage». Cette publicité demande clairement à l'«investisseur» potentiel d'être sur le pied de guerre. Ici, comme dans tellement de secteurs de la société contemporaine – y compris sans doute le monde de l'art actuel – , la manipulation remarquable des codes pour s'imposer dans l'échelle sociale est traitée comme s'il s'agissait d'une question de vie ou de mort. Le fait de reconnaître uniquement l'existence du langage a ainsi fâcheusement limité la portée des actions conçues pour faire sens.

L'image finale que suscite ces réflexions est l'image de la destruction. On pense alors à la Seconde Guerre mondiale, cette «catastrophe naturelle» provoquée par les acteurs sociaux, et on frémit en imaginant quel torrent de destruction pourraient involontairement provoquer les habitants de notre propre empire de signes si, dans leur lutte pour dominer les codes, ils libéraient des forces que personne ne peut contrôler.

Publié pour la première fois dans *Arts Magazine*, (New York), vol. 58, nº 1, septembre 1983.

La crise de la géométrie

Là où autrefois la géométrie était un signe de stabilité, d'ordre et de proportion, il n'y a plus aujourd'hui qu'étalage de signifiés fluctuants, qu'images d'enfermement et de dissuasion.

Le projet formaliste en géométrie est discrédité. Il ne semble plus possible d'explorer la forme pour la forme (dans le domaine géométrique), comme cela pouvait l'être pour les constructivistes et les néo-plasticiens, ni de vider la forme géométrique de sa fonction signifiante, comme l'ont proposé les minimalistes. D'une certaine façon, la viabilité de ces idées formalistes s'est simplement atrophiée avec le temps. Elles ont aussi été déformées pour se conformer à l'idéal académique bourgeois auquel se sont référées des générations de classiques géométriques.

Mais la crise que traverse depuis deux décennies l'art géométrique est comparable à celle de tous les formalismes depuis l'après-guerre ; celles qui ont précipité la transition du formalisme littéraire au structuralisme, et du structuralisme aux relectures post-structuralistes que l'on peut trouver dans les œuvres de personnalités comme Barthes [1] et Foucault [2].

Car à l'instar de ces crises, la crise de la géométrie est celle du signifié. Il ne semble plus possible d'accepter la forme géométrique comme un ordre transcendantal, comme un signifiant autonome, ni la *Gestalt* comme base de la perception visuelle (comme chez Arnheim). On est bien plutôt entraîné dans une quête structuraliste des signifiés cachés que peut revêtir le signe géométrique. Telles sont alors les questions soulevées : quelle mission remplit le signe géométrique dans notre culture ? Pourquoi la société moderne est-elle obsédée par la forme géométrique au point que nous nous soyons efforcés au cours des deux derniers siècles de construire et de vivre dans des environnements géométriques toujours plus complexes et exclusifs ? Pourquoi l'art géométrique a-t-il été si largement accepté par notre siècle, et pourquoi son imagerie a-t-elle pris une si grande importance dans l'iconographie publique ?

Pour répondre à ces questions, il faut examiner la sociologie de la géométrie durant l'ère moderne, littéralement une sociologie du formalisme. La géométrie sera ici étudiée en fonction de son rôle dans l'histoire culturelle, et non comme idéal *a priori* du processus mental.

Cet essai sera axé sur l'analyse de deux textes pertinents sur ces questions, textes qui ont tous les deux influencé la production de l'art géométrique, et qui pourront être utiles au décodage des travaux géométriques produits lors de ces années de «crise». Il s'agit de *Surveiller et Punir* de Michel Foucault [3] et de *Simulacres et simulation* de Jean Baudrillard [4]. L'ouvrage de Foucault est d'une grande pertinence pour l'art géométrique produit pendant les années soixante-dix, alors que le texte de Baudrillard, qui se refère souvent à celui de Foucault, est fondamental si on veut comprendre l'art géométrique de cette décennie.

Surveiller et Punir démontre les grandes ordonnances

géométriques de la société industrielle. Le déploiement omniprésent de structures géométriques dans les villes, les usines et les écoles, dans le logement, les transports et les hôpitaux, est montré comme un mécanisme qui permet de canaliser, de mesurer et de normaliser l'action et le mouvement (et tout comportement), et comme un moyen de contrôler la population grandissante de l'ère industrielle naissante, et de maximiser sa productivité.

Foucault décrit comment ce processus s'est mis en place dans le déploiement du géométrique. L'espace a été géométriquement différencié et cloisonné. Des couloirs de circulation, les lignes droites omniprésentes du paysage industriel, ont été créés pour faciliter un mouvement ordonné. Le panoptisme associé à la sérialité est apparu comme le principe fondamental grâce auquel les corps et les lieux pouvaient être le plus efficacement surveillés et contrôlés dans des lieux clefs comme la prison, l'hôpital, l'usine et l'école.

En outre, cette géométrisation du social fut étendue de l'environnement physique jusqu'aux schémas d'organisation. Le cadran, la carte et le graphique, permettant de mesurer et de classer par catégories les corps et leurs mouvements, sont alors apparus comme techniques omniprésentes de l'ordre industriel.

Les artistes du XXe siècle ont souvent voulu légitimer leur utilisation de la géométrie en prenant comme référence des sources antiques et religieuses. Ironiquement, ces sources sont justement celles que désigne Foucault comme véritables modèles des schémas géométriques d'enfermement et de surveillance générés par la société industrielle.

Premièrement, la Rome antique offrait au capitalisme naissant non seulement un modèle de gouvernement républicain comme on le dit souvent, mais aussi un modèle de discipline idéale, basée sur la technologie militaire romaine. Deuxièmement, à la naissance de l'ordre industriel, l'organisation de la vie monastique traditionnelle, avec son contrôle rigide du temps et de l'activité, fut soudainement adoptée par le corps social dans son ensemble.

On trouve là une analyse qui permet de réinterpréter l'obsession moderne pour la géométrie (une obsession que tous ceux qui vivent dans la société industrielle peuvent vérifier en sortant jeter un coup d'œil dans la rue). Mais, cette réinterprétation change radicalement notre appréhension du mysticisme géométrique de Mondrian, Malevitch, Rothko et Newman, et remet en question ce présupposé curieux qui consiste à croire en la neutralité de la géométrie, et dont se réclamaient le minimalisme et le formalisme des années soixante.

A partir de cette analyse, on peut en fait voir dans le travail de ces transcendantalistes géométriques un mécanisme classicisant où l'objet même du malaise, la géométrie, est transformé en objet d'adulation. On peut de la même façon considérer la revendication formaliste d'une neutralité de la géométrie comme une tentative pour normaliser et accepter comme telle l'omniprésence de ces signes géométriques.

Cette critique de Foucault pourra également servir de base à la réinterprétation de l'art géométrique des deux dernières décennies. On peut déjà considérer le minimalisme comme le début de la crise de la géométrie. Le minimalisme prétendait avoir atteint la neutralité intellectuelle, la clarté cartésienne et même l'intégrité marxiste. Mais malgré les imperfections de ce discours, l'objet minimaliste lui-même peut être lié à la critique de Foucault, même si les intentions de ses créateurs étaient d'un autre ordre. Le minimalisme a d'abord rattaché idéologiquement la géométrie à la production matérielle de l'industrie contemporaine en utilisant des matériaux et des déchets industriels sans les revendiquer (comme le fit le Bauhaus). Le minimalisme a également abandonné l'idée de la Renaissance sur la composition au profit d'une organisation conforme aux principes de sérialité (voir les œuvres de Stella et de Judd) et de centralité (comme les agencements panoptiques de Noland et Irwin) qui sont propres à la géométrie industrielle.

Le meilleur du post-minimalisme a porté cette critique à un niveau plus conscient. Dans les *Earthworks* de Robert Smithson, par exemple, il y a une confrontation entre la géométrie idéaliste et les géométries réelles du paysage industriel. Les figures géométriques, emblématiques de la tradition idéaliste (les cercles, les spirales...), s'inscrivaient presque arbitrairement dans le paysage industriel ravagé, attirant l'attention sur le violent contraste entre les deux.

De façon beaucoup plus catégorique, les deux essais «*A Tour of the Monument of Passaic, N.J.*» et «*What is a Museum*» ?, où des photographies d'architecture et d'intérieurs modernes et idéalistes sont juxtaposées à des images d'usines et autres sites industriels, ridiculisent l'utilisation d'un art géométrique idéal en tant que support idéologique de l'organisation sociale géométrique contemporaine [5].

Les derniers dessins de Smithson représentent des environnements insulaires infernaux, hérissés de fortifications, jonchés d'instruments de mort, brûlants et fumants, la plupart du temps de simples formes géométriques comme des cônes, des cylindres et des cubes. C'est dans ces travaux que Smithson s'approche le plus d'une vraie critique à la Foucault : les monuments géométriques de la tradition des lumières deviennent ici des instruments de l'enfermement et de la torture sado-masochistes.

Le travail de Richard Serra, à la fin des années soixante, utilise lui aussi la géométrie comme menace. Dans *Corner Prop*, un cube de plomb, à la fois polygone cartésien et produit industriel, est suspendu de façon précaire au-dessus de la tête du spectateur. Mais tout en suggérant l'anxiété et la menace les plus immédiates, inhérentes à certaines caractéristiques de la forme géométrique, les pièces de Serra n'en sont pas moins ambiguës, dans la mesure où elles (ou il) insistent sur leur «matérialité». Cette affirmation constante de la matérialité renforce l'idée que ces formes et ces procédés représentent une réalité immuable et transcendante.

Les pièces d'Alice Aycock, de façon caractéristique, contiennent toutes sortes d'espaces impénétrables et de chemins inutiles décrivant une sorte d'impasse du géométrique. L'introduction, à la fin des années soixante-dix, de figures géométriques tortueuses et absurdes met encore davantage l'accent sur la séparation entre le géométrique et son rapport avec la raison. De façon très significative, son travail, qui suggérait en permanence des signifiés architecturaux et narratifs, rejetait l'idée que la forme géométrique puisse fonctionner comme signifiant autonome. Enfin, en insistant continuellement sur le lien entre ses constructions et ses propres programmes idéologiques imaginaires, Aycock attire l'attention sur la présence de l'idéologie dans le géométrique, partout où il apparaît.

A la fin des années soixante-dix, un certain nombre d'artistes avait commencé à travailler sur les questions soulevées par *Surveiller et Punir*, traduit en anglais en 1977.

Le travail de Robert Morris illustre bien le processus. Pendant les années soixante-dix, Morris a, semble-t-il, reconsidéré la signification implicite d'œuvres comme

Untitled, de 1967, où un compartimentage métallique crée une succession de couloirs et d'espaces sans issue. Exécuté dans le courant de la pensée formaliste et phénoménologique, ce travail se rapproche néanmoins énormément des structures cloisonnées utilisées pour les hôpitaux et les bureaux, surtout quand ils sont vus du dessus (d'un point de vue panoptique).

La photographie de Morris pour l'affiche d'une exposition en 1974, où on le voit en tenue sado-maso en règle, avec chaînes, collier et casque allemand, est à la fois une réponse aux dessins de Smithson évoqués plus haut et l'annonce de sa prise de conscience des relations de pouvoir et même de violence implicites dans sa propre production.

En 1978, dans sa série de dessins, *In the Realm of the Carceral*, Morris réagissait directement aux idées développées dans *Surveiller et Punir*. Dans ces dessins, une ligne précieuse et mécanique sert à dépeindre un environnement dénaturé où l'enfermement est total, la discipline implacable. (Depuis cette date, alors qu'il prête à la forme des signifiés toujours plus complexes, le travail de Morris s'est résolument rallié aux ambitions métaphoriques du libéralisme.)

C'est également à la fin des années soixante-dix que l'architecte Bernard Tschumi a commencé une série de dessins, *The Manhattan Transcripts*, explorant les thèmes de Foucault. Le but de ces dessins, est de dépister toutes les difficultés du mouvement humain dans la typographie architecturale de New York. Les dessins de Tschumi mettent en évidence l'omniprésence de la grille à la fois en section et en plan, et la relation entre une activité humaine enrégimentée, comme le sport par exemple, et la structure quadrillée de la ville industrielle. Dans ce dessin, le mouvement humain le plus précisément contrôlé (le match de football) est transformé en diagramme géométrique qui, à son tour, devient une forme tridimensionnelle sortant du plan. Ces transformations mettent en parallèle la façon dont le mouvement humain réel est limité dans le domaine industriel, où le mouvement est constamment canalisé à partir des rues ou des couloirs, vers les appartements, les bureaux ou les zones où on ne peut entrer et sortir qu'à des heures et à des vitesses réglementaires.

L'installation de Lauren Ewing, *Auto Plastique : The Prison*, montre à quel point les idées sur la géométrie ont changé depuis la position abstraite du minimalisme. Ewing conserve le vocabulaire formel du minimalisme – ses structures géométriques simples, ses techniques de constructions industrielles et son programme d'interaction spatiale avec le spectateur – mais ici le vocabulaire minimaliste est cependant aménagé pour établir un constat explicitement foucaldien.

L'installation de Ewing définit les conditions de l'espace panoptique telles que Foucault les décrit dans le domaine carcéral : «Par l'effet du contre-jour, on peut saisir de la tour, se découpant exactement sur la lumière, les petites silhouettes captives dans les cellules de la périphérie. Autant de cages, autant de petits théâtres, où chaque acteur est seul, parfaitement individualisé et constamment visible [6].» Dans la tour, au contraire, la pénombre créée par l'épaisseur des murs fait que le gardien n'est plus visible.

Cette disposition permet d'indiquer une transformation du social, dont la signification va bien au-delà de l'exemple spécifique de la prison : «La foule, masse compacte, lieu d'échanges multiples, individualités qui se fondent, effet collectif, est abolie au profit d'une collection d'individualités séparées. Du point de vue du gardien, elle est remplacée par une multiplicité dénombrable et contrôlable ; du point de vue des détenus, par une solitude séquestrée et regardée [7].»

Ewing a ajouté à son analyse de cette situation, une invention de son cru, «l'orateur parfait», un mur à angle droit derrière lequel on peut parler dans un haut-parleur, une réponse à la situation panoptique, sans voir ni être vu. Cet orateur peut être considéré comme paradigme de l'individualisme, comme position contestataire parfaitement détachée. Mais la position de l'orateur remonte aussi à une étape beaucoup plus ancienne dans l'histoire des prisons, le donjon où le prisonnier est caché plus qu'observé, d'où le prisonnier crie sans être entendu de son geôlier.

Depuis 1980, une nouvelle génération de travaux géométriques est apparue, qui doivent moins aux textes de Foucault qu'à ceux de Baudrillard. Cette génération d'artistes ne se réclame plus de l'expérience industrielle (voir l'insistance de Serra sur son travail préparatoire en aciérie, ou l'utilisation de bois de charpente chez Aycock). Ce groupe d'artistes est bien plutôt le produit d'un environnement post-industriel où l'expérience n'est plus celle de l'usine, mais celle des subdivisions, plus celle de la production, mais celle de la consommation.

Ces artistes décrivent un environnement où le système panoptique ne fonctionne plus, où, pour reprendre les termes de Baudrillard, «la distinction de la cause et de l'effet, de l'actif et du passif, du sujet et de l'objet» n'existe plus [8]. C'est un environnement où l'enfermement selon Foucault a été transformé en dissuasion selon Baudrillard, où la géométrie *hard* de l'hôpital, de la prison et de l'usine, laisse place aux géométries *soft* des réseaux autoroutiers, des ordinateurs et des jeux électroniques [9].

De plus, cette génération n'attribue plus à l'art le rôle d'expérience privilégiée, comme Serra a pu le faire, par exemple, en affirmant que l'art pouvait transformer la société. L'art géométrique des années quatre-vingt ridiculise les mécanismes de cette attitude. Pour ces artistes, il ne peut y avoir qu'un simulacre, avec la «récurrence orbitale des modèles» (la nostalgie) et la «génération simulée de la différence» (les styles).

L'un des premiers artistes à exprimer ce point de vue est R.M. Fischer. La sculpture de Fischer joue sur l'idée de lampes et de meubles, illustrant ainsi sa propre désillusion envers l'idée de l'art comme objet privilégié, coupé des réalités du commerce et de l'idéologie. Il y a quelques années, Fischer recherchait toutes les occasions d'exposer dans les vitrines de grands magasins ou des boutiques à la mode comme Fiorucci, plaçant ainsi son travail – qui lui-même traite de la façon dont on signifie le style – au beau milieu du contexte de la mode et du commerce, à son niveau le plus sophistiqué, et donc rejetant l'illusion de neutralité entretenue par l'atmosphère de la galerie [10].

Les sculptures elles-mêmes participent de cette critique. Elles prennent la forme soit de lampes (compromis de sculpture domestique), soit de fontaines (compromis de sculpture publique). A l'intérieur de ces signes, elles réunissent et aménagent tant de signes contradictoires que la fonction signifiante elle-même devient circulaire et s'annule. Dans *Half Past Ten*, une sculpture-fontaine de 1982, l'eau coule d'une boîte métallique rectangulaire (qui représente peut-être une boîte à fusible ou même, comme la source de lumière est cachée, une boîte à fusible futuriste), à travers un tube métallique (qui représente une conduite de gaz et donc, une fois de plus, l'industrie, à travers un cylindre de verre translucide, décoré d'un motif ressemblant à des coulures de cire de bougie (qui représente le kitsch, les intérieurs privés, la banlieue), puis dans un ustensile de cuisine en acier inoxydable (qui représente le travail, l'absence de décoration signifiante). Sont ajoutés à cela deux bras faits d'éléments de luminaires, enrichissant encore ce mélange de signifiants et transformant le signe-fontaine en signe-pendule. Fischer démontre ainsi le degré de complexité atteint par le signe géométrique contemporain.

Dans ces sculptures, le signe emprunte une circularité, que Baudrillard décrit comme caractéristique de la société contemporaine : «Alors tout le système passe en apesanteur, il n'est plus lui-même qu'un gigantesque simulacre – non pas irréel, mais simulacre, c'est-à-dire ne s'échangeant plus jamais contre du réel, mais s'échangeant en lui-même, dans un circuit ininterrompu dont ni la référence ni la circonférence ne sont nulle part.»

Le travail de Jeff Koons traite lui aussi de l'état des choses à l'intérieur de ce simulacre. Le travail de Koons, *New Wet / Dry Triple Decker*, par exemple, prend pour modèle certaines caractéristiques du minimalisme, jouant ainsi sur la nostalgie du style, sur la circularité des signes définissant le simulacre. Mais dans le travail de Koons, les signifiés du minimalisme, orientés vers la production (l'acier, les peintures industrielles, etc.) sont remplacés par des éléments (les appareils ménagers, les boîtes de plexiglass apparentées à des vitrines d'exposition) attirant l'attention sur la consommation. Alors que le minimalisme cherchait à révéler la structure, Koons expose des appareils dont les mécanismes sont cachés derrière des surfaces lisses en plastique ou en émail.

A l'intérieur de ces «vitrines d'exposition», Koons a créé un environnement répondant presque parfaitement à l'idée d'ordre et de propreté. Les aspirateurs eux-mêmes sont «nickel», et chaque surface de plexiglass est parfaitement nettoyée et polie. Il n'y a aucune traces de doigts, de poussière, ou autre signe d'utilisation. Les pièces de Koons excercent sur le spectateur un effet identique à celui, décrit par Baudrillard, des missions spatiales sur le grand public. Koons, comme la NASA, a créé un «univers expurgé de toute menace de sens, en état d'asepsie et d'apesanteur», un univers de «fascination par la norme maximale et la maîtrise de la probabilité», alors que dans l'organisation sociale contemporaine, «rien ne peut être laissé au hasard».

La vision de ce travail est une expérience intense du simulacre. Les aspirateurs ne semblent pas réels mais «hyperréels» . Ils sont totalement «nickel» (le hasard du réel n'a pas prise sur eux) ; ils sont présentés en série (sans l'original), et font partie d'un univers «étrangement ressemblant à l'original», où «les choses sont dupliquées par leur propre scénario».

Mon propre travail, depuis cinq ans, met l'accent sur le rôle du modèle à l'intérieur du simulacre. Baudrillard constate que «la simulation se caractérise par une *précession du modèle*, de tous les modèles sur le moindre fait». Le simulacre est un lieu où «le réel se confond avec le modèle» ; c'est un «univers total de la norme», un «espace digital», un «champ lumineux du code» . Dans mon travail, l'espace est justement considéré comme un champ digital où sont localisées des «cellules» en imitation stuc d'où irradient des «conduits». Cet espace ressemble à l'espace simulé du jeu vidéo, du microprocesseur et de la tour de bureaux, un espace qui n'est pas une réalité spécifique, mais plutôt un modèle de l'«espace cellulaire» sur lequel s'établit «l'échange social "cybernétisé", qui irradie le corps social de ses circuits opérationnels». Se définit alors un système où les bâtiments ressemblent aux «colonnes d'un graphique statistique», un système dont la représentation «s'est déplacée de la pyramide à la carte perforée».

En outre, mes peintures font appel à différentes techniques empruntées aux styles *Hard-Edge* et *Color-Field*. Car avec la simulation, «nous n'avons plus droit qu'au rétro, à la nostalgie, réhabilitation fantomatique, parodique de tous les référentiels perdus». Pour moi, les styles, utilisés comme référence à une certaine idée de l'abstraction et à une idéologie du progrès technique, remplacent la référence au réel.

Mais c'est dans les récents travaux de Sherrie Levine que cette fascination du simulacre pour la nostalgie est la mieux rendue. Dans ses aquarelles récentes, Levine a systématiquement épuisé, une à une, les images reconnues du modernisme au XXe siècle. Dans des travaux tels que *After Stuart Davis*, la géométrie moderniste est vidée de tout contenu autre que celui de sa propre nostalgie.

Comme le contenu est nié, l'acte productif est purifié. Levine a produit des œuvres géométriques où la géométrie a à nouveau été débarrassée de tout signifiant, comme à l'époque du formalisme. Dans le travail de Levine, on voit la production entrer dans une phase de «reduplication esthétique... quand, évacuant tout contenu et toute finalité, elle trouve le moyen de devenir abstraite et non figurative». Le travail de Levine «exprime alors la forme pure de la production ; il assume, en tant qu'art, la valeur d'une finalité sans objectif».

Dans quelle mesure ce travail, utilisant la forme géométrique, garde-t-il son importance comparé à celui, idéologique, des artistes qui décodent les images de la publicité, de la télévision et du cinéma ? Si une analyse des thèmes inhérents aux mass media est sans nulle doute significative, une exploration idéologique de la géométrie pourra l'être encore plus, car malgré la profusion des images de médias dans la culture contemporaine, les signes géométriques restent les plus ambigus et les plus importants de notre société. Nous sommes presque à chaque instant confrontés à des signes géométriques innombrables, même dans les environnements libres de tout signe.

De plus, s'il faut toujours croire en la distinction entre le capital et le travail, le dirigeant et l'ouvrier, on remarquera que si les signes des médias s'adressent au départ à la masse, au consommateur et au travailleur, ce sont les signes géométriques de l'art, de l'architecture et des analyses statistiques, que se réservent les classes dirigeantes pour communiquer entre elles. Utiliser cette idéologie est davantage pour l'artiste un acte d'autocritique qu'une forme de condescendance.

Enfin, il y a de nombreux artistes aujourd'hui qui ignorent à la fois la critique de la géométrie et des médias, et qui semblent convaincus que grâce à l'intuition, au subconscient et aux techniques traditionnelles de la peinture à l'huile, ils pourront réintroduire la «vie» dans cet univers sans vie. Baudrillard décrit cet effort désespéré : «Surenchère des mythes d'origine et des signes de la réalité. Surenchère de vérité, d'objectivité et d'authenticités secondes. Escalade du vrai, du vécu, résurrection du figuratif là où l'objet et la substance ont disparu.»

Ces artistes, et les œuvres qu'ils produisent, ignorent la complexité des changements qui sont intervenus dans le champ du social. Et ils oublient le prix de ce retour romantique qu'ils préconisent et que Baudrillard énonce là aussi : «Si nous commençons à rêver à nouveau, surtout aujourd'hui, d'un monde de signes sûrs, d'un "ordre symbolique" fort, ne nous méprenons pas : cet ordre a existé et c'était celui d'une hiérarchie féroce, car, chez les signes transparence et cruauté vont de pair.»

Publié pour la première fois dans *Arts Magazine*, (New York), vol. 58, nº 10, juin / été 1984.

Après l'art

La mort de Dieu a entraîné celle de l'art. L'art s'est constitué à partir du même ordre symbolique dont l'idée de Dieu est issue, ordre qui a commencé à mourir avec la Renaissance. Jusqu'à la Renaissance, l'art avait servi à relier la matière d'ici bas au sens caché et à l'unité du cosmos. L'art avait permis à l'homme de s'approcher de l'infini. C'était une technique qui donnait à l'homme mortel la possibilité d'établir une relation symbolique avec l'univers éternel. De cette façon, l'art maîtrisait la mort ; il avait vaincu le vide, en lui conférant un sens.

La mort de Dieu correspond à la naissance du capital. L'ordre symbolique a commencé à s'atrophier ; il a été remplacé par la loi du surplus, de la raison et de l'Histoire. Mais Dieu ne s'est pas contenté de mourir, comme l'avait décrété le modernisme.

Au lieu de cela, Dieu est entré dans une agonie interminable qui se poursuit encore de nos jours. Avant, Dieu était la condition nécessaire de la pensée. Après, Dieu est devenu une voix possible dans un concert polyphonique de sens et de non sens. De plus, l'ordre moderne – celui du capital, du marché et de l'Etat – a découvert qu'on pouvait conférer à l'idée de Dieu de nouveaux rôles. D'une part, l'idée de Dieu corrobore l'unité phallocentrique de l'idéalisme bourgeois. D'autre part, elle alimente les tentatives de retour au transcendantal, faites périodiquement par les unitariens, les rosicruciens et les jungiens.

L'art est dans la même situation : toujours mourant, jamais mort, ressuscité par les pré-raphaélites, les post-impressionnistes, les expressionnistes abstraits et les post-minimalistes, sans mentionner les historiens d'art et les aquarellistes. Mais la magie n'opère plus.

Fac-similés et transgression

Alors après l'art, après Dieu ? Un paysage de mort, un paysage privé de sens. Qu'est-ce qui pourrait jouer ce rôle, jadis assuré par l'art, de vainqueur de la mort, de phare au sein du vide ? Après l'art, deux approches ont vu le jour.

Quitte à surprendre, nous oserons proposer une structure bipartite après Greenberg : nous voyons une scission entre la pratique populaire et la pratique avant-gardiste. Depuis la Renaissance, mais de façon plus dramatique encore depuis une centaine d'années, la culture moderne a tenté d'appliquer deux solutions (alors que l'art n'en finissait pas de mourir...) pour combler le vide que l'art illuminait autrefois : premièrement, les fac-similés de vie éternelle fournis par la culture populaire ; deuxièmement, la transgression utilisée par l'avant-garde, pour créer une étincelle de vie dans un univers sans vie.

Il y a, dans la culture de masse, une image figée de la vie éternelle. N'ayant pas de place dans l'univers symbolique, la culture populaire s'est efforcée de créer des images de la vie triomphant sur le temps, de représenter l'arrêt des processus implacables de mort et de déclin, en bref, de créer un simulacre d'éternité vivante. Ce projet commence à la Renaissance avec la perspective, le portrait et le monument funéraire. Il s'intensifie au XIXe siècle avec l'avènement du réalisme. Au cours des cent dernières années, les progrès technologiques ont foisonné : d'abord la photographie, puis le phonographe, le cinéma, la photographie couleur et ensuite, peut-être, les hologrammes. Grâce à ces technologies, les images des morts ne meurent plus – on en conserve la netteté, la vivacité des couleurs et le mouvement. Dans les images produites par ces machines, la jeunesse éphémère ne vieillit plus. Le temps y est figé sur un plan bidimensionnel.

Dans un monde d'après Dieu, d'après l'art, «Walt Disney attend sa résurrection par moins 180 degrés centigrades» (Baudrillard). Car entre temps, il a enregistré des centaines de messages sur cassettes vidéo afin qu'on les projette aux réunions annuelles de son conseil d'administration pendant cette période d'«arrêt momentané de ses fonctions vitales».

A la télévision, Steve Allen monte un spectacle où des acteurs, interprétant le rôle de «personnages historiques» de différentes époques, discutent actualité ou philosophie. Le temps est aboli. Les morts de tous les temps se rencontrent. Les ancêtres peuvent vivre pour nous parler.

Les enregistrements phonographiques sont ainsi nommés parce qu'ils enregistrent cette activité humaine la plus précaire, la production de sons. Dans les années soixante, ces enregistrements sont soudain devenus la forme artistique la plus populaire. La promesse d'immortalité que l'enregistrement offrait était si directe que les plus grandes stars de l'époque ont semblé vouloir précipiter la fin de leur existence réelle pour commencer leur vie éternelle exclusivement sur disque.

Qui est la vraie Greta Garbo ? L'image de celluloïd des années trente qu'on voit sur grand écran ou cette vieille femme qui vit à New York ?

On pense à Andy Warhol : «Un de ces jours vous êtes capables d'aller à une soirée et de vous retrouver seul.»

On parvient à ces effets non seulement dans la vie, mais aussi dans les moyens d'enregistrement. Nous assistons à un événement sportif : un match de football ou de baseball. Les athlètes apparaissent, jeunes, bien proportionnés, en bonne condition physique, dans des uniformes qui mettent tout cela en valeur. Des dieux grecs. Mais ce qui est plus important encore que la santé et la vigueur des hommes eux-mêmes, c'est la façon de les présenter. Ils sont cadrés sur fond d'immensités incroyablement vertes (la plupart du temps une pelouse synthétique), un signe, hyperréel, par la couleur, de la vie elle-même – et un moyen efficace de mettre en valeur la peau bronzée et saine des athlètes (selon le principe de contraste simultané des couleurs). Mais l'élément le plus puissant dans cette situation est l'éclairage rayonnant, blanc, sans aucune ombre, sans aucun mouvement, diffusé par les centaines de lampes qui entourent le stade (l'attrait de cette lumière, qui est aussi utilisée dans les productions télévisées, explique la popularité sans cesse croissante des événements sportifs nocturnes ou en stades couverts). Jadis, les événements sportifs se déroulaient à la lumière changeante du soleil. Mais aujourd'hui, «sous les spots», pendant deux heures ou plus, le temps s'arrête pour ces demi-dieux à la fleur de l'âge. Le soleil ne parcourt plus le ciel. La mort est bannie par cette lumière hors du temps, immobile et sans ombre, qui illumine ces corps parfaits.

Dans ce grand spectacle de l'obsession de la mort, et peut-être en réaction, l'avant-garde a suivi une autre piste : la transgression. Ne considérant aucune réalité en dehors des codes, l'avant-garde n'a vu dans la mort qu'une invention du langage. L'avant-garde a pensé que pour revitaliser les codes, il fallait transgresser leurs mécanismes ; que cette transgression offrait un moment de vie dans le paysage de mort de l'univers post-symbolique. De Courbet à la Seconde Guerre mondiale, tel était le paradigme de l'activité avant-gardiste, cette recherche du moment de vie malgré l'omniprésence de la mort.

Après après l'art – La fascination et la mort de l'avant-garde

Après l'art, la culture de la transgression et du fac-similé. Alors que la culture du fac-similé demeure, la transgression et l'avant-garde disparaissent rapidement ou plutôt se transforment. C'est la crise que connaît l'avant-garde actuellement. Aujourd'hui la transgression essaie de s'imiter elle-même ; mais le moment de vie créé par la transgression est finalement remplacé par le regard stupéfié de la fascination.

Ce changement est intervenu après la Seconde Guerre mondiale. Soudain, on voit Picasso, le grand maître de la transgression, transformé en icône photo-journalistique, en idole photographique de la culture de la vie simulée. Son âge ajoutait encore à ses qualités photogéniques ; son image était une représentation de jeunesse figée, aussi forte que celle des jeunes et beaux acteurs ou actrices. (Il faut pourtant examiner ses derniers travaux à partir de sa propre position sur les questions de simulation et de nostalgie.)

Au même moment, les artistes d'après-guerre perdaient le pouvoir de s'engager spontanément dans des actes de transgression. Selon le livre récent de Serge Guilbaut sur l'expressionnisme abstrait, *Comment New York vola l'idée d'art moderne,* les expressionnistes abstraits et leurs partisans ont sciemment créé l'impression d'une activité d'avant-garde en écrivant des lettres de protestation, en organisant des manifestations et en défendant l'art non-occidental, en sachant que ces actions obéissaient au modèle constitué par la transgression avant-gardiste en Europe. La transgression devient un événement médiatique. Etre d'avant-garde devient une stratégie de médiatisation. Le dernier acte spontanément transgressif de l'expressionnisme abstrait a été son utilisation originale de la transgression comme stratégie médiatique.

L'aliénation est remplacée par la fascination. L'artiste ne peut plus se retirer dans un dédain hautain, dans une position où il pourrait voir les codes sans être impliqué. Il est au contraire attiré par eux, enchanté, hypnotisé. Il trouve dans son sujet un plaisir acide, répétitif et monotone, comme celui d'un narcotique synthétique. Le moment-clef de ce changement intervient quand Andy Warhol fait la sérigraphie de la chaise électrique avec des couleurs *Day-Glo*.

La fascination est une chute libre. On ne peut ni lui échapper, ni la détourner. La carrière de l'artiste se réduit à une période de cinq ans peut-être avant qu'il ne soit digéré par les médias et que la critique s'arrête. L'artiste fasciné devient rapidement un objet de fascination. C'est ce qui est arrivé en premier aux expressionnistes abstraits, dont beaucoup ont eu le malheur de mettre brutalement fin à leurs jours avec un mépris de bon ton pour ce destin. (Ou était-il plus rapide d'abdiquer au profit de leur propre image, comme l'ont fait les stars du rock ?) Plus tard, les artistes ont su rester plus sereins devant cette éventualité et ont su simplement profiter de la production de masse quand l'opportunité se présentait.

De l'aliénation à la fascination. C'est le passage d'une culture de l'isolement et de la coercition à une culture de la prévention et de la séduction. Nous ne sommes plus isolés, assis dans une pièce éclairée par une petite ampoule électrique, dans un appartement, rongés par l'angoisse et torturés (comme Beckett a pu le décrire). Ces temps sont révolus. La torture de l'industrialisme a laissé place à la séduction du paysage post-industriel. Nous n'avons plus aucun désir de quitter nos foyers. La petite ampoule électrique est supplantée par le merveilleux tube qui offre des mouvements, des sports, des paroles. Des conduits de toutes sortes entrent et sortent, amenant à domicile la conversation, l'air pur, la lumière, l'eau fraîche, la musique. Cette transformation est l'événement majeur des trente dernières années.

Alors que la transgression devient impossible, la demande qu'elle suscite s'accroît. Depuis au moins les années soixante, la culture de la fascination est telle qu'elle a absorbé tous les actes de transgression que l'on a seulement osé envisager. Les criminels et les extrémistes politiques écrivent des best-sellers. Les artistes d'«avant-garde» participent au journal télévisé de 20 heures, alors que les transsexuels sont interviewés par le maître du *talk-show*, Phil Donahue.

La forme créée par la transgression est pleine de nostalgie. L'exigence d'une transgression devenue impossible est satisfaite par des recours plus ou moins érudits à la nostalgie. Quand le moment fut venu de transgresser les structures vacillantes du formalisme, les artistes italiens et allemands ont simulé la transgression en faisant appel à une figuration du début du XXe siècle. Quand les architectes ont voulu transgresser le langage du style international, ils n'ont pu utiliser qu'une panoplie de références historiques.

Qu'advient-il alors de l'artiste et de l'intellectuel dans une telle situation ? Sommes-nous des «animateurs» jouant un rôle qui n'existe plus, sauf dans la parodie ? Baudrillard et d'autres insistent sur le fait que la fascination s'exerce avant tout sur le grand public. Pourtant, personne n'est plus fasciné que l'artiste et l'intellectuel. Warhol, Baudrillard, Jonathan Borofsky et Richard Prince se délectent bien plus de leur fascination que ne le font n'importe quel producteur de télévision, employé de bureau ou retraité. Le rôle de l'artiste et de l'intellectuel réside-t-il maintenant dans cette «conscience» post-marxiste de leur situation qu'implique leur fascination ?

Mais ce phénomène de fascination semble être plus proche d'un autre modèle. Dans notre univers post-moderne du simulacre, nous avons abandonné les objectifs du Discours et de l'Ecrit. Nous sommes entrés dans une ère du Commentaire, tel que Foucault définit la pratique de l'érudition dans le monde de la Renaissance. Mais à présent, artistes et intellectuels créent un commentaire sur un univers de simulation, sur un univers sans Texte. Il s'agit d'un commentaire sur la «superposition sans fin des signes» qui constituait autrefois le monde renaissant et qui constitue aujourd'hui le simulacre. Il y a là une exégèse sans fin, ni vraie, ni fausse. C'est un commentaire sur un univers de sables mouvants et de chimères où rien n'est solide, où rien n'est vrai.

Publié pour la première fois dans *New Observations*, (New York), n° 23, 1985.

La terre de glace

Car la Mort, dans une société, il faut bien qu'elle soit quelque part ; si elle n'est plus (ou est moins) dans le religieux, elle doit être ailleurs : peut-être dans cette image qui produit la Mort en voulant conserver la vie.

Roland Barthes, *La Chambre claire.*

Nous assistons à un spectacle étrange et macabre. Les morts ne reposent plus, oubliés, dans leurs tombes. Ils se lèvent devant nous, en grand nombre, dans des chambres sombres : ils resplendissent de lumière. A un endroit, ils font des discours politiques, ailleurs, ils racontent des bonnes blagues. Ici ils parlent entre eux, là ils s'adressent aux vivants. Ils dansent et chantent, parfois sérieusement, parfois gaiement. Mais, et c'est là le miracle, ils ne présentent aucune trace d'âge ou de déclin. Ils sont jeunes, au sommet de leur force et de leur beauté. Les vivants les contemplent, à la fois effrayés et fascinés, buvant chacune de leurs paroles. Leurs images apparaissent partout, aussi bien en public que dans les recoins les plus intimes des maisons des vivants.

Nous voyons alors que les vivants habitent un univers qui n'a plus de sens. Pour les vivants, la vie est devenue un spectacle de marionnettes, grotesque, alors que la mort est un vide prêt à tout engloutir. Pourtant, cet étrange spectacle des morts constitue une sorte de fac-similé d'espoir, un semblant de réconfort contre la peur éternelle. Suivant en cela l'exemple des morts, les vivants les plus puissants consacrent beaucoup de temps et d'énergie à préserver et à enregistrer leur propre apparence. Les moins fortunés font la même chose, selon leurs moyens. Quand ils vieillissent, de nombreux vivants se font remodeler le visage et le corps, à l'image d'une jeunesse idéale, en croyant que cette mascarade les protègera des assauts de la mort et du temps.

Cette scène macabre n'est pas la description d'un rituel primitif, elle n'est pas non plus le produit d'un scénario affreux de science-fiction. C'est la vie, ou tout au moins ce qu'il en reste, dans le paysage glacé du XXe siècle. C'est la vie dans une culture coupée du symbolique, mais qui pourtant, comme lui, n'en est pas moins obsédée par la mort. Mais ici la mort n'est pas synonyme de fusion avec l'universel, ni de retour aux origines. Elle n'est qu'un vide éternel, un destin à éviter à tout prix.

Et le prix est considérable. C'est ce que coûte la construction de la grande façade figée de la pseudo-vie, où la vie éphémère semble merveilleusement statique et immatérielle, où la jeunesse ne semble devoir jamais finir, où le mouvement et le discours, phénomènes par essence éphémères, sont conçus pour sembler éternels. Nous vivons aujourd'hui dans une culture qui nie la mort, comme on l'entend souvent, mais qui en plus s'efforce de transformer la vie en un simulacre, gelé et sans fin, d'elle-même.

Tous les moyens dont nous disposons sont utilisés pour atteindre cet objectif. Dans la scène macabre décrite plus haut, la chambre sombre est bien sûr la salle de cinéma, et les personnages lumineux sont ceux du film ou de la télévision. On a dit que les films et la télévision détachaient la réalité de «l'expérience vécue». Mais leur rôle, dans la création d'une toundra gelée de pseudo-vie, n'est pas moins important. Ces médias ne représentent en fait que l'état actuel de l'art, dans une série d'inventions technologiques et idéologiques faites pour créer un simulacre de vie gelée. C'est une série qui remonte à la Renaissance, quand le monde symbolique a commencé à s'effondrer.

Si nous nous basons sur les découvertes de nos historiens, nous constatons que, jusqu'à la Renaissance, hommes et femmes se préparaient consciemment à la mort. Ils acceptaient que leur heure puisse arriver ; ils pouvaient se préparer, un peu résignés bien sûr, à se fondre à nouveau dans l'ordre universel. Au moment de la mort, on trouvait le repos après les épreuves du monde temporel : on allait être jugé par Dieu. La mort était l'événement le plus important de la vie. C'était le temps de la réunification, du jugement, de la récompense ou de la damnation.

La Renaissance marque le début du déclin de cet ordre. On voit alors apparaître les premiers fac-similés de vie, à côté et même étroitement mêlés à l'ordre symbolique sur lequel reposait jusqu'ici l'appréhension de la mort. Depuis la Renaissance, le rôle de ces fac-similés n'a cessé de prendre de l'importance, alors que l'ordre symbolique n'a cessé de s'effacer.

Trois inventions majeures, apparues à la Renaissance, servent de base à la création de cette façade de vie simulée : le portrait, le concept d'art et celui de célébrité.

Le portrait est généralement appréhendé comme illustrant l'émergence de l'individu à la Renaissance : les traits du commanditaire sont généralement très distincts de ceux des autres personnages du même sexe et du même rang.

Mais on peut aussi y voir la première utilisation d'une technologie visant à arrêter le cours du temps et à se jouer de la mort.

Le portrait isole l'âge du sujet de la même façon qu'il insiste sur les caractères particuliers de ses traits. Il devient une horloge humaine dont l'âge est figé par la peinture à un moment précis. L'arrêt du temps est aussi explicite dans le traitement de la lumière. L'utilisation du clair-obscur donne l'impression qu'on a voulu restituer la lumière naturelle à un moment particulier. Et cette lumière en suspens est bien synonyme d'arrêt du temps, d'autant plus qu'à la Renaissance le passage du temps et le mouvement de la lumière allaient de pair.

Le portrait devient alors un équivalent portable et statique, de l'apparence de l'individu. Avec le portrait, l'image d'un individu échappe au temps, transcende la mort. Le simulacre intemporel commence à remplacer la personne vivante.

C'est le talent des artistes, leur art, qui a permis au portrait de jouer ce rôle extraordinaire. A la Renaissance, l'art cessa d'être une pratique au service du symbolique. Il n'y a plus alors de crucifixions ou de cathédrales anonymes. L'art est maintenant chargé d'«immortaliser» les humains eux-mêmes. L'artiste de la Renaissance défend ardemment cette idée : Alberti, par exemple, soutenait que la peinture rendait «présents les absents et semblait presque redonner vie aux morts».

L'artiste devint le grand prêtre du culte de la vie simulée. Non seulement l'œuvre d'art immortalise le sujet en préservant son apparence spécifique, mais elle attire aussi, grâce à la beauté de l'œuvre, l'attention des générations futures, assurant alors encore davantage «l'immortalité» de son sujet.

L'idée d'immortalité s'exprimait aussi à travers le concept de célébrité. La culture européenne ne se contentait plus d'assurer la vie éternelle en rendant grâce à Dieu. Le concept religieux de vie éternelle commença à laisser place à une autre idée : on pouvait gagner cette vie éternelle en inscrivant ses hauts faits dans l'esprit des générations à venir – en étant célèbre. La préservation du nom et de la réputation remplaça alors celle du corps et celle de l'âme. Nous pouvons pourtant aujourd'hui trouver maints exemples de la puissance de cette idée. Des rues, des places et des bâtiments portent les noms de générations d'hommes d'Etat, de révolutionnaires et de généraux.

Le portrait, l'art et la célébrité suffirent à repousser la mort pendant trois cents ans ; mais au XIXe siècle, de nouvelles inventions vinrent remplacer les structures déjà atrophiées du symbolisme. Ces nouvelles inventions –l'Histoire, le réalisme et la photographie – rendirent possible la pleine réalisation de l'idéal d'une vie hors du temps.

L'Histoire parvint à établir un discours entre les morts et les vivants, qui allait bien au-delà du concept de célébrité. Elle permit à l'ensemble d'une ère donnée – à ses structures économiques, à ses conflits, à ses styles – d'aller et venir dans le temps. Grâce à l'Histoire, la conscience put remonter des centaines d'années en arrière. Les générations du présent purent discourir avec celles du passé. Grâce à l'Histoire, nous pouvons croire que le futur participera un jour aux débats et aux crises du présent.

Le XIXe siècle a aussi inventé le réalisme qui, d'une certaine façon, a étendu le concept de vie figée de l'individu à la scène collective. Chez Courbet, par exemple, la spécificité du portrait s'étend aux vêtements des paysannes, au paysage poussiéreux et même au bétail décharné. Le réalisme élargissait d'une part la portion de vie que l'on pouvait simuler, il permettait d'autre part d'établir une nouvelle confiance en la «réalité» du simulacre.

C'est au sein de ce même mouvement qu'est apparue la photographie. Techniquement l'appareil photo permettait de figer instantanément le temps, sans avoir recours aux techniques laborieuses de la peinture. Le temps imprimé sur l'image et celui nécessaire à la constitution de cette dernière était identiques.

L'invention de ce processus mécanique rapide contribua aussi à banaliser la création de l'image figée. L'intermédiaire n'étant plus nécessaire, la photographie finit par être considérée comme aussi vraie que son modèle vivant.

Avec l'avènement de la photographie, ce n'était plus seulement les images du riche et du puissant qui étaient préservées. On fit des photographies de tout le monde. Grâce à cette popularisation, l'image figée prit de plus en plus d'importance au sein de la cellule familiale, là où justement l'idée de mort était de plus en plus honnie. Les familles devinrent alors dépositaires de clichés de leurs proches, morts ou vivants.

La famille possédait des témoignages de la vie de chacun étape par étape. Il existe des photographies de l'enfance et des différentes étapes de l'âge adulte. Ainsi, ces étapes ne disparaissent plus complètement après avoir été vécues ; elles deviennent des monuments figés s'opposant au flux inexorable de l'existence temporelle. Le temps lui-même commence alors à perdre son sens. Dans *La Chambre claire*, Barthes examine une photographie de sa mère à l'âge de cinq ans, après la mort de cette dernière : «J'étudiai la petite fille et enfin retrouvai ma mère.» L'homme mûr rencontre sa mère enfant.

L'accumulation de toutes ces inventions technologiques et idéologiques depuis quatre cents ans a préparé le terrain des événements du XXe siècle. On ne peut plus aujourd'hui distinguer les morts des vivants, et le temps ne semble plus suivre son cours. La machinerie, qui nous permet de tourner radicalement le dos à la mort, est en place maintenant.

Il y a eu prolifération de moyens d'enregistrement. Soudain, avec le film, non seulement l'image de l'homme est enregistrée mais aussi le mouvement – ce signe qui très précisément fait la différence entre la vie et la mort. L'enregistrement de la voix humaine est mis au point à la même époque. Le discours, la chanson, les signifiants les plus poignants du passage du temps, peuvent maintenant être préservés à jamais.

Il existe un véritable culte des médias – le cinéma, les disques, la télévision. Des budgets énormes, des ressources incroyables leur sont consacrés. L'importance du tournage d'un film est telle que, partout dans le monde, les autorités n'hésiteront pas à interrompre la circulation et la vie quotidienne pour qu'il puisse être réalisé : et il y a toujours un attroupement de badauds subjugués par le spectacle de la vie transformée en une image plus permanente qu'elle-même.

Les médias ont créé une culture propre, complexe, dont l'objet est de poursuivre plus avant la simulation d'une vie hors du temps. Les figures clefs de cette culture sont les stars du cinéma, du disque et de la télévision. La star est ce personnage superréel avec lequel nous nous identifions, et dont la vie figée permet à la nôtre de le devenir tout autant. (Pour quelle autre raison des millions de gens vieillissants passent-ils des dimanches entiers à regarder les images d'athlètes éternellement forts, éternellement jeunes ?)

Mais la tâche-clef de la culture des médias est la destruction finale de la vieille idée du déroulement chronologique.

Ceci est fait en rapprochant la technologie de l'enregistrement et l'idée de l'Histoire. La culture des médias procède de deux façons. Elle enregistre des simulations du passé (et du futur) comme s'il s'agissait du présent et, en même temps, présente les enregistrements effectivement réalisés dans le passé comme s'ils appartenaient au présent. D'une part, on invente le film historique et, de l'autre, le culte des vieux films. D'une part, on enregistre les symphonies de compositeurs disparus et, de l'autre, on distribue les disques des stars du rock, elles aussi disparues.

Tout finit par appartenir à un présent asynchronique où le temps se trouve condensé, sans ordre, sans signification. Les paradoxes sont légion dans cette nécropole. Shirley Temple est-elle une femme ou une enfant ? Lauren Bacall a-t-elle vingt ou soixante ans ? John Wayne est-il mort ou vivant ? Dans *Naissance d'une nation,* la guerre de Sécession, qui a eu lieu il y a longtemps, est interprétée par des acteurs qui sont morts depuis longtemps. La mort est ici niée deux fois.

Nos vies sont si pleines de ces images fantastiques créées par les médias, qu'il nous est très difficile de nous concentrer sur la mort. Cependant, il est vrai qu'à un moment donné, nous mourrons tous. Mais des brèches commencent à se creuser dans le mur de la mort. On arrache les mourants à la mort pour les maintenir en vie avec des organes artificiels. La génétique devient capable de cloner la vie à partir de la vie. Pendant ce temps, Walt Disney, le grand maître du temps, «attend sa résurrection par moins 180 degrés centigrades». Si cette ère de modernité se poursuit, si nous continuons à fuir la mort avec horreur, alors peut-être d'autres inventions permettront-elles au mort de marcher à nouveau ; notre «scène macabre» sera rejouée à un niveau encore supérieur de «vérisimilitude».

Et Walt Disney se lèvera un jour pour parler à ceux qui ne sont pas encore nés. Il s'éveillera alors peut-être dans un futur dont il avait rêvé dans un passé lointain.

Publié pour la première fois dans *ZG,* (New York), n° 12, novembre 1984.

Le déploiement du géométrique (1984)

Le déploiement du géométrique domine le paysage. L'espace est divisé en cellules discrètes, isolées, conçues pour se multiplier et fonctionner. On les atteint par un réseau complexe de couloirs et de routes qui doivent être empruntés à des vitesses précises et à des moments précis. L'augmentation constante de la complexité et de l'échelle de ces géométries transforme continuellement le paysage.

Des conduits alimentent les cellules. L'électricité, l'eau, le gaz, les lignes de communications et parfois l'air lui-même, y sont amenés par eux. Ils sont presque toujours enterrés, invisibles. Les grands réseaux de transport donnent l'illusion de mouvement et d'interaction perpétuels. Mais le réseau de conduits réduit au minimum le besoin de quitter les cellules.

L'enrégimentation du mouvement humain, de l'activité et de la perception, accompagne la division géométrique de l'espace. Elle est gouvernée par les systèmes de contrôle du temps, l'application de standards de normalisation et l'appareil policier. A l'usine, le mouvement doit se conformer à des géométries spatiales et temporelles rigoureuses. Au bureau, l'enregistrement sans fin des chiffres et des statistiques est présidé par les employés.

Parallèlement à la géométrisation du paysage apparaît la géométrisation de la pensée. La réalité spécifique laisse place à la primauté du modèle. Et celui-ci est à son tour imposé au paysage, déplaçant ainsi la réalité selon un processus de circularité croissante.

L'art, ou ce qu'il en reste, a été également géométrisé. Mais il a été curieusement associé au transcendantal. Chez Mondrian, Newman et même Noland, il devient le blason de l'intemporel, de l'héroïque et du religieux. La géométrie, ironiquement, devient le lien privilégié avec la nature dont pourtant elle s'écarte.

L'art géométrique a ainsi été utilisé pour justifier le déploiement du géométrique. Il a lié celui-ci à la sagesse des anciens, à la tradition de la vérité religieuse et aux pratiques ésotériques de méditation des civilisations non-occidentales. L'art géométrique a été utilisé pour cacher le fait que le déploiement moderne du géométrique était plus étrange encore que les mythes étranges des sociétés traditionnelles. L'art géométrique a cherché à nous convaincre, malgré l'évidence du contraire, que le progrès de la géométrie est un progrès humaniste, qu'il fait partie de la «marche de la civilisation», qu'il s'inscrit dans une continuité historique. Et l'art géométrique a pleinement rempli son objectif. Il a ainsi permis la seconde phase de la géométrisation (coïncidant avec l'après-guerre) où la coercition a été remplacée par la fascination.

Nous sommes convaincus. Nous sommes volontaires. L'enfermement décrit par Foucault est aujourd'hui remplacé par la dissuasion décrite par Baudrillard. Nul besoin aujourd'hui d'enfermer le travailleur dans l'usine. Nous nous inscrivons tout seul dans un club de body-building. Nul besoin d'enfermer le prisonnier dans une prison. Nous investissons dans des lotissements. Le fou n'a plus à errer dans les couloirs de l'asile. Nous circulons sur les autoroutes.

Nous nous investissons aujourd'hui pleinement dans les géométries qui symbolisaient autrefois la discipline coercitive. Les enfants sont fascinés par les géométries *Day-Glo* des jeux vidéo. Les adolescents sont enchantés par les mystères arithmétiques de leurs ordinateurs. Adultes, nous finissons enfin par prendre directement part à l'univers cybernétique hyperréel grâce aux cartes de crédit, aux répondeurs téléphoniques et aux hiérarchies professionnelles. Nous pouvons maintenant vivre dans des «banlieues spectrales» ou des villes simulées. Il nous est possible de jouer tous les jeux, corporatifs, économiques et même artistiques.

Maintenant que la géométrie domine, l'art géométrique a disparu. Marden ou Ryman n'ont plus de raison d'être, n'ont plus besoin de nous convaincre de la beauté essentielle du géométrique concrétisée aujourd'hui par l'image lumineuse du téléviseur. Nous investissons au contraire dans «l'art figuratif», afin de nous persuader que le vieux corps humaniste n'a pas totalement disparu – même si cela est faux. C'est seulement maintenant, au moment où l'art géométrique a disparu, qu'il peut justement prendre part à la description du déploiement du géométrique.

Publié pour la première fois dans *Effects,*(New York), n° 3, hiver 1986.

Notes sur la nostalgie

« La simulation est maîtresse,
et nous n'avons plus droit qu'au rétro,
à la nostalgie, réhabilitation fantomatique,
parodique de tous les référentiels perdus.

Baudrillard

1. La nostalgie n'est pas un phénomène passager induit par le «conservatisme» des années quatre-vingt. C'est bien plutôt une «réalité» structurelle : tout est affecté – les médias, la politique et l'art.

2. La nostalgie a remplacé la nature en tant que référent dans la culture post-industrielle. Elle résulte de la «réalisation» massive du concept d'Histoire, qui est intervenue dans tous les secteurs de la pensée ; elle est aussi paradoxalement issue du nivelage de l'Histoire accompagnant cette prédominance de la pensée historique. L'image de l'Histoire n'est plus cette route ardue, bien définie, serpentant le long du flanc de la montagne. Elle est au contraire devenue un marais, un bourbier parcouru de myriades de chemins boueux qui ne mènent nulle part et qui disparaissent dans un horizon éternellement brumeux.

3. Chaque aspect du social est réglementé par cette Histoire sans déterminisme. Dans les journaux télévisés, le présent devient historique : les événements sont sélectionnés de façon à ce qu'ils puissent chaque jour se conformer au système de l'Histoire. A la radio, l'Histoire est écrite heure après heure. Mais les révolutions nationales, les accidents de voiture et les commentaires sur les stars du cinéma sont tous traités de la même façon par cette historicité nivelée.

4. L'Histoire devient divertissement et le divertissement devient Histoire. Il y a des dramatiques historiques à la télévision, et il y a les *Academy Awards*. Il y a *60 minutes* et le *Baseball Hall of Fame* *. Il y a l'année 1984, selon le calendrier chrétien traditionnel, et il y a le *Super Bowl XVIII* **».

5. En politique, la nostalgie promet le retour d'une réalité qui était elle-même un idéal abstrait. Les politiciens se drappent dans le manteau de la nostalgie. Gary Hart est Kennedy, John Glenn est Ike, et Mondale, Hubert Humphrey. Mais Reagan gagne car il se présente comme John Wayne. Reagan nous propose un retour à l'époque où les hommes étaient à cheval, coupaient du bois et possédaient des ranchs (bien que dans ce cas précis le ranch soit situé en Californie du Sud). La question est la suivante : la simulation de cette réalité peut-elle entraîner une vraie catastrophe ? Ou le système de dissuasion caractéristique du simulacre continue-t-il à contenir ces approximations

* Musée du baseball.
** Finale de football américain, en janvier.

du réel ? (L'époque de la réalité et celle de la guerre totale étaient, bien entendu, les mêmes.)

6. Dans le domaine de l'art, la nostalgie est partout. Il existe une nostalgie du début du siècle. Il existe une nostalgie du romantisme. Il existe une nostalgie des années cinquante et une nostalgie du *Pop*. Baudrillard nous dit que tout est appelé à une seconde vie en tant que référence nostalgique. Les artistes d'aujourd'hui peignent les années cinquante comme les impressionnistes peignaient des meules de foin au crépuscule.

7. Dans la mesure où l'Histoire a perdu son pouvoir, cette nostalgie ne peut plus être celle de l'artiste moderne quand il se référait à un style antérieur. Picasso citait Cézanne car celui-ci représentait un jalon dans la progression historique. Il ne subsiste aujourd'hui qu'un commentaire sur le réseau entrecroisé des styles historiques. (Ou l'Histoire était-elle déjà nivelée quand Picasso citait Cézanne ?)

8. La nostalgie a aussi remplacé la transgression, ou plutôt elle simule maintenant la transgression. Les expressionnistes abstraits simulaient la transgression par leur utilisation nostalgique des stratégies du modernisme européen. Les néo-expressionnistes simulent la transgression en «réhabilitant parodiquement» le début du siècle ; les architectes post-modernes ont fait la même chose en réhabilitant un vocabulaire architectural pré-moderniste.

9. C'est la fin de l'art «tel que nous le connaissons». C'est la fin de l'art de l'histoire de l'art. C'est la fin de l'art urbain avec ses luttes dialectiques. Cet art simulé existe

aujourd'hui dans des villes qui sont aussi les doubles d'elles-mêmes, des villes qui n'existent que comme références nostalgiques de l'idée de ville et de communication sociale. Ces villes simulées sont plus ou moins localisées à l'emplacement des cités anciennes, mais elles ne remplissent plus la même fonction. Ce ne sont plus des centres, elles servent seulement à simuler l'idée de centre. Et c'est à l'intérieur de ces centres simulés, en plein cœur en général, que se déroule l'activité artistique simulée, une activité elle-même nostalgique d'une activité artistique réelle.

Publié pour la première fois dans *New Obervations,* (New York), n° 27, 1985.

Frank Stella... et le simulacre

Voici le temps venu de la grande culture de
la communication tactile,
dans l'espace cinématique du théâtre
spatio-dynamique total.

Baudrillard

La critique du travail de Frank Stella a toujours été articulée autour de deux pôles. D'une part, son travail a été salué comme l'apothéose de la peinture moderniste la plus rigoureuse. On a dit qu'elle était matérialiste dans ses effets, implacable dans sa logique et hermétique dans sa conception. D'autre part, il a été tourné en dérision et considéré comme un cul-de-sac déshumanisé de la peinture. On a estimé que toute complexité picturale avait été évacuée et que les images n'étaient plus que des «graphiques». On considère que la subtilité humaniste est absente de son travail où il ne reste qu'un réaménagement «bureaucratique» et une gestion «administrative» du processus artistique.

Ironiquement, c'est la synthèse de ces deux points de vue qui autorise une critique convaincante du travail de Stella. Nous verrons alors que l'art de Stella est à la fois matérialiste et bureaucratique, et à la fois hermétique et graphique. Mais pour réunir ces différentes qualités, il faudra nécessairement passer par un autre point de vue critique. Et nous découvririons que Stella n'est ni moderniste, ni bureaucrate, mais que son travail est très proche d'un post-modernisme dominé par les idées d'hyperréalisation, de simulation, de clôture et de fascination.

On doit d'abord se demander comment le travail de Stella peut être post-moderne, dans la mesure où la critique n'utilise l'idée de post-modernisme que dans les années quatre-vingt. La réponse est que la formulation et la diffusion, par la critique, de l'idée de post-modernisme suit de très loin son apparition dans les domaines artistiques et culturels. C'est en fait au début des années soixante, quand Frank Stella s'impose en tant qu'artiste, que les éléments du post-moderne et son corollaire, le post-industriel, commencent à se mettre en place.

Le début des années soixante voit l'émergence de la culture de l'informatique, avec l'ordinateur et l'électronique. Les voyages internationaux en jet se sont développés à une échelle commerciale, en entraînant un bouleversement des relations spatio-temporelles et culturelles. C'est dans les années soixante qu'est mis en place un réseau d'autoroutes, l'*Interstate Highway System*, et que sont créées parallèlement les villes décentrées du *Sun Belt*, conçues en fonction de la circulation automobile. C'est l'époque des missiles inter-continentaux, des missions spatiales, de l'observation par satellite, qui tous inscrivent la réalité à l'intérieur de leurs orbites circulaires et leurs trajectoires paraboliques.

Si les années soixante faisaient la jonction entre les mondes industriels et post-industriels, entre le réel et le simulé, l'art des années soixante était une réponse à cette situation. D'une part, il y a dans les années soixante une nostalgie intense du traditionnel et de l'industriel. Les musiciens de rock étaient fascinés par le blues acoustique de la culture *Hobo* des années vingt et par la musique indienne du sitar. La mode mélangeait les textiles du Guatémala et les vêtements de l'ouest américain du XIXe siècle. Mais il y a en même temps une fascination du technologique, du simulé et du futuriste, illustrée par les meubles en plastique moulé, la guitare électrique et le dôme géodésique.

On peut considérer que Stella, vers 1960, réagissait précisément à cette situation. Une transition cruciale s'est opérée dans son travail entre les *Black Paintings*, où on trouve encore une nostalgie de l'industriel et du traditionnel, et les *Aluminium Paintings* qui proposaient franchement des éléments du monde hyperréel et post-industriel.

Les *Black Paintings* étaient encore d'inspiration moderniste. L'application de la peinture, bien que mécanique, est irrégulière – et elle brille d'une sensibilité à la lumière que l'on trouve, par exemple, chez un Rothko. Les bandes sont peut-être répétitives, mais leur qualité symétrique, hiératique, et l'utilisation fréquente de motifs en diagonale, rattachent les images à l'utilisation des structures ornementales dans l'art traditionnel non-occidental. Les configurations peuvent rappeler le travail de la terre cuite islamique ou peut-être encore les tapis kurdes. Finalement, cette couleur noire, omniprésente et mélancolique, rattache les peintures au nihilisme et à l'existentialisme des années cinquante.

C'est d'une conscience radicalement différente dont il s'agit dans les *Aluminium Paintings*. La peinture est appliquée de façon égale et les bandes sont séparées par une ligne définie. L'effet est froid, presque science-fictionnel. La peinture ne se contente plus de briller – il s'agit d'aluminium, métal contemporain, technologique, lié à l'idée de légèreté, d'efficacité et d'utilité commerciale. Plus important encore, les configurations ont complètement perdu leurs associations traditionnelles. L'introduction du *jog* * semble soudainement les rendre mouvantes : elles ressemblent aux allées autoroutières, accentuant le mouvement de la circulation. De plus les bandes sont sans variations ni inflexions. Elles emplissent l'espace, de façon régulière et neutre, devenant alors des succédanés de l'activité dans la peinture, et des substituts à l'incident et à l'imagerie.

Les zones entre les bandes des *Aluminium Paintings* ont elles aussi une fonction importante. Les couloirs de mouvement et de circulation ne sont plus visibles sur un fond comme elles le sont, par exemple, chez Mondrian. Chez Stella, le fond, et donc la nature, est occulté. La circulation et le mouvement abstraits demeurent la seule réalité.

Le propos des *Aluminium Paintings* est poursuivi et élargi dans les diverses séries de peintures à bandes des cinq années suivantes. Les *Copper Paintings* sont intéressantes dans la mesure où les changements et les intersections à angle droit explicitent encore davantage le propos circulatoire de Stella. La série *Purple* introduit un niveau supplémentaire d'intensité simulée par l'utilisation d'un pigment métallique pourpre. Leurs configurations – triangles, parallélogrammes et pentagones, où les bandes forment un circuit continu – définissent aussi une situation de clôture et de circularité où les lignes se poursuivent, sans début ni fin.

Dans la série *Running V*, les bandes semblent acquérir une vélocité supplémentaire, plus proche de l'électricité dans un microprocesseur que de simples automobiles sur une autoroute. Dans la série *Moroccan*, la peinture *Day-Glo* est utilisée. La couleur elle-même est maintenant

* Impression visuelle d'oscillation.

remplacée par son équivalent hyperréel et simulé. Et les thèmes issus des cultures non-occidentales réapparaissent, mais sous l'angle post-moderne. Une sensibilité non-occidentale ne peut en aucun cas avoir une quelconque influence ici. Ou plutôt, dans ces peintures comme dans les *Super Graphics*, la culture marocaine est complètement déracinée et réduite à ses signes les plus faciles à reproduire. Une culture tout entière est rendue par des diagonales répétitives, aux couleurs vives. L'emprise de l'hyperréel sur toutes les autres réalités est totale.

L'évolution de Stella, pendant ces années, est intéressante, non seulement par les thèmes visuels qui apparaissent dans ses tableaux, mais aussi par sa façon de gérer la production de ses toiles. Pendant cette période, Stella hyperréalisait les moyens qu'il employait. Il n'utilisait que des pigments artificiels issus des recherches de pointe. Ses châssis épais, ses formats façonnés et l'échelle extra-humaine semblent aussi hyperréaliser les peintures en tant qu'objets : elles se dégagent plus du mur qu'une peinture «réelle» ; elles sont plus grandes et leur forme est plus agressive.

L'utilisation que fait Stella de la série (en passant d'un ensemble de peintures à un autre) est elle aussi très importante. Les artistes ont souvent travaillé à des séries, mais chez Stella il n'y a pas cette évolution progressive d'une toile à l'autre qui fait qu'une nouvelle série naît de la précédente. Plutôt, les séries se suivent presque annuellement, comme les nouveaux modèles de voitures à Détroit. De plus, il n'existe pas, à l'intérieur de chaque série, un original moderniste qui serve de base aux autres tableaux. Au lieu de cela, la configuration de la série tout entière est en fait décidée à l'avance. L'identité de chaque peinture repose sur son appartenance à l'ensemble.

L'exposition de ces peintures en tant que série complète

hyperréalisait l'idée moderniste d'exposition. On ne pouvait discerner aucune évolution dans une exposition de Stella au cours de ces années. Il n'y avait pas de grands formats à côté de formats plus petits, plus intimes. Mais la simple présentation des séries, associée aux autres procédés d'hyperréalité et de simulation que Stella utilisait, donnait à ces expositions une qualité science-fictionnelle.

En 1967, avec la série *Proctractor* (rapporteur), Stella va encore plus loin dans l'univers de la simulation. Jusque-là, on avait pu lire les tableaux de Stella littéralement, comme des surfaces planes sur lesquelles de la peinture avait été apposée, sans illusion ni ambiguïté. Mais dans la série *Proctractor*, l'espace est conçu de telle façon qu'il devient triple et contradictoire. Premièrement, il y a l'espace physique de la peinture en tant qu'objet, dramatisé par les dimensions de l'œuvre, sa découpe inhabituelle, son relief profond. Ce qui est encore accentué par la façon dont la toile est apparemment grossièrement tendue sur l'énorme châssis, les coups de crayon fortuits et les zones alternées de peinture uniformément appliquée et de toile vierge. Deuxièmement, il y a l'espace du dessin lui-même, qui accentue à la fois l'entrelac des bandes qui s'entrecroisent et les rapports d'emboîtement entre les bandes en éventail et les bandes d'encadrement. Troisièmement, il y a l'espace créé par la combinaison de couleurs *Day-Glo* et d'acryliques très vives. Elles entrent en pulsation avec un étrange effet *push-pull* qui crée cet espace coloré. Ainsi, ce sont donc trois systèmes spatiaux indépendants qui, combinés, créent un espace de théâtralité et de fascination. Il n'y a là aucune tentative d'unifier ces différents éléments. Tout au contraire, les signes spatiaux s'additionnent les uns aux autres – ils se combinent afin de produire l'effet visuel le plus intense possible. Nous avons alors quitté l'espace moderne unifié de la raison pour pénétrer un espace post-moderne dont le premier objectif est la séduction.

Dans la série *Proctractor*, Stella approfondit aussi la problématique de la multiplicité et du modèle. Les peintures ne sont plus seulement basées sur une série de motifs pré-existants, mais chaque variante est maintenant traitée de trois façons différentes, les «entrelacs», les «arc-en-ciel» et les «éventails». Le choix du rapporteur (*Proctractor*) comme base de la série est lui aussi significatif. Avant, les formes utilisées par Stella étaient basées sur des formes géométriques simples – carrés, triangles, pentagones, etc. – des formes qui sont toujours en relation avec la tradition classique et idéaliste de la géométrie. Avec le rapporteur, Stella choisit un outil, celui du dessinateur et de l'ingénieur. Le rapporteur est lui-même à la fois un modèle et un outil pour faire des modèles. Avec la série *Proctractor*, Stella passe définitivement du monde moderne idéaliste au monde post-moderne, où le modèle prédomine.

Dans le travail de Stella, la série *Proctractor* était à la fois une fin et un début : la fin de peintures simplement constituées de pigments sur toile, le début de l'utilisation d'effets, par l'ajout, la couleur et l'espace, pour créer une surcharge visuelle, caractéristique de son travail de reliefs métalliques jusqu'à aujourd'hui.

Les diverses séries de peintures en reliefs métalliques représentent une intensification de l'approche initiée avec la série *Proctractor*. Des formes massives d'aluminium en nid d'abeilles sont assemblées avec une facilité déroutante. Elles se superposent de façon si complexe que toute appréhension de leurs véritables relations spatiales devient presque impossible. La figure et le fond sont eux aussi obscurcis dans la mesure où les espaces vacants sont remplis par des formes qui pointent de l'arrière. Chaque panneau est ensuite couvert d'une profusion de textures, peintures et coups de pinceau, qui compliquent encore davantage l'espace et créent une impression de scintillement. Avec cette œuvre, nous sommes dans un monde où l'espace est dramatique mais ne fait plus sens, où tout est agencé pour produire l'effet maximal. Comme à Disneyworld, à Las Vegas ou dans une galerie marchande, tout est agencé pour attirer, séduire et éblouir.

Il s'agit aussi d'un monde où tout signe est admis, mais où tous perdent leur signification réelle. Dans ces œuvres le coup de pinceau des expressionnistes abstraits est réduit à un signe vide, neutre. Les couleurs, brillantes et complexes, n'ont d'autre objectif que simplement produire l'effet coloré. De la même façon, la composition ne vise qu'à établir les idées de mouvements et d'attraction. Les œuvres ne sont plus alors qu'une simulation neutre, hyperréelle, de la peinture elle-même.

Les seules références extérieures au travail appartiennent au monde du simulacre. L'aluminium en nid d'abeilles et le magnésium gravé nous rappellent le monde post-industriel des métaux ultra-légers et des circuits imprimés. Les «cônes et piliers» illusionnistes des travaux les plus récents rappellent les simulations spatiales des dessins sur ordinateur. Et, bien sûr, tout se réfère à l'univers du modèle – les différentes parties produites en série, à l'imagerie répétitive, sont assemblées dans des tableaux qui sont eux-mêmes des multiples.

Si nous avons pu définir le travail de Frank Stella comme post-moderne, il faut finalement nous demander comment cela est possible puisque Stella lui-même en a une appréhension radicalement différente. Peut-être simplement parce que dans la situation post-moderne, l'artiste n'a pas le même degré de conscience qu'à l'époque de l'idéal moderniste. En fait, nous pouvons considérer que Stella joue le rôle de l'artiste moderniste pour un public post-moderne, et nous pouvons voir dans son travail une hyperréalisation du modernisme. Ou il est à ce point enfermé dans le simulacre qu'il n'a plus conscience de son existence (contrairement à Warhol qui, dans les années soixante, faisait sans cesse allusion à la conscience qu'il en avait, bien que ce soit peut-être justement cela qui l'ait rendu incapable de soutenir sa critique). Par exemple, Stella a déclaré récemment qu'il voulait donner à son travail la même réalité intense que celle inhérente au travail du Caravage. Mais si nous transformons ce désir de réalité intense en désir d'hyperréalité intense, nous aurons alors une idée de sa position vis-à-vis du simulacre.

Le certificat de modernité de Stella est finalement souvent étayé par des références à son éducation : en tant que produit de l'école préparatoire et de l'université, il est indubitablement le représentant type de la tradition moderniste. C'est très précisément cette formation qui explique pourquoi on peut le situer dans le concept du simulacre. Car celui-ci n'a pas été inventé par les masses, par ceux qui boivent du Pepsi ou qui regardent les *Super Bowls*. Il a été inventé par les entreprises, les agences de courtage et de publicité, les médias, c'est-à-dire toutes ces institutions qui vont chercher leurs leaders dans ces machines à transformer la connaissance moderniste en information post-moderne, les universités d'élite.

Publié pour la première fois dans *Flash Art*, (Milan), n° 126, janvier 1986.

De la ligne

Soudain, dans les années soixante, les cercles ont commencé à faire leur apparition. Il y eut les cibles de Noland, les organisations circulaires de Smithson, les configurations en forme d'anneaux de Morris et de Serra. L'époque a vu dans cet engouement pour le cercle un désir d'unité – le cercle, c'était l'orbe, l'image de la plénitude, un signe d'unité. Ces motifs circulaires avaient pourtant des implications plus complexes. Dans presque tous les cas, le centre était vide. Il s'agissait finalement d'images linéaires et non de ronds pleins. Cet art annonçait que, désormais, la ligne devait revenir sur elle-même, qu'elle avait fini de se frayer une trajectoire dans les sous-bois de la Nature, que la boucle était bouclée, que, dorénavant, la ligne allait couler dans la ligne en un cercle éternel.

Les autoroutes fédérales. Elles serpentent majestueusement à travers les villes – surélevées comme malgré elles par de fades piliers de béton. Elles parcourent le pays, franchissent les abîmes, aplanissent les collines, glissent sur les marais. Le long de ces routes, toute publicité est interdite, et les constructions avoisinantes ont été démolies. Le vaste chemin prioritaire est bordé de pelouses bien entretenues et d'harmonieuses rangées d'arbres, comme se doit de l'être tout lieu de cérémonie.

Elles couvrent la nation entière selon des axes nord-sud et est-ouest régulièrement répartis. Les routes nord-sud sont répertoriées de I-5 à I-95 par intervalles de dix, et celles d'est-ouest de I-I0 à I-90. Un troisième chiffre s'ajoute lorsqu'il y a interaction entre l'autoroute et une ville (par une voie de ceinture, une rocade ou une zone industrielle). Le pays est totalement quadrillé par cette grille cartésienne. C'est notre plus grand monument à la ligne.

A partir de 1860 et jusqu'à 1920 environ, l'art annonçait plutot l'avènement d'un univers linéaire. D'abord Manet, puis Gauguin, et enfin Matisse, ont libéré le dessin des limites du clair-obscur. Le dessin était libre et la ligne pouvait devenir une force picturale dont le rôle allait vite s'étendre dans le domaine social. Quand s'épanouirent le cubisme et le néo-plasticisme, l'univers linéaire fut considéré comme bien établi : pour le cubisme, l'ordre du réel laissait la place au vecteur et au schéma. Le néo-plasticisme a ensuite célébré l'apothéose de l'univers linéaire dans toute sa gloire.

Derrière le volant. Sur l'autel de la ligne. Les mains agrippées au plastique glacé de l'objet linéaire devenu circulaire. Les yeux sur la route. Les yeux fixés sur cette route mais aussi sur la froide géométrie des lignes qui divisent la voie en différentes files. Au crépuscule, le paysage et la route elle-même disparaissent progressivement et il ne reste plus qu'une composition fluorescente de signes linéaires luisant dans la clarté des phares. Sur la route. Il paraît que c'est la plus grande sensation de liberté. C'est davantage un sentiment de complétude. Sur la route, au volant, dévorant la distance, il y a un sentiment de communion avec la puissance de la forme linéaire. C'est notre scène philosophique.

Dans la ville, en revanche, on est submergé par la complexité des réseaux de lignes. La rue, bien sûr, est également une artère de circulation. Son efficacité en tant que telle est améliorée par le système de feux qui utilisent des signes de couleur pour arrêter ou guider le flot de voitures. Mais la rue est aussi le toit qui recouvre l'énorme tissu de conduits fonctionnant au-dessous d'elle. Les canalisations d'eau, les égouts, le gaz. Les fils électriques, les lignes de téléphone, les cables de télévision. Les tunnels de métro, les passages souterrains pour les automobiles. Ce sont ces entrelacs de lignes, cette élaboration de systèmes parallèles de circulation, qui caractérisent la modernité.

Ce système formel s'est développé sur un mode universel. C'est le mode de la cellule et du conduit, le formalisme de la «prise de courant». Le 747 vient s'arrêter devant la porte qui lui a été réservée et immédiatement des techniciens apparaissent avec des tuyaux, des fils électriques et des rampes d'accès qui relient l'avion aux conduits d'où s'écoulent le fuel, le courant électrique, les bagages et les passagers. Le malade à l'hôpital est branché sur l'arrivée d'oxygène ou sur l'intra-veineuse, tandis que l'employé de bureau est branché sur son terminal d'ordinateur. A la maison, on branche tout ce qui, auparavant, était naturel, qu'il s'agisse du vent, de la lumière, de la chaleur ou de l'eau.

La cellule. L'ubiquité du concept reflète l'atrophie de l'échange social et le règne de l'interconnexion. En même temps que l'arrivée de «commodités» canalisées nous épargne la nécessité de quitter la cellule, elle nous y confine. On se trouve coincé chez soi dans l'attente d'un coup de fil ; au lieu de rejoindre le monde social, on est obligé de rester dans sa cellule pour communiquer avec l'autre. Ou bien on reste tout simplement chez soi pour regarder quelque chose à la télévision ; pour être informé ou amusé par d'autres à la télévision, on renonce à leur présence et à leur compagnie. On entre dans une autre cellule, l'automobile, pour quitter sa cellule et l'automobile aussi est de plus en plus équipée de matériel de communication qui en font un lieu où l'on désire rester.

Le mécanisme de la cellule et du conduit, bien qu'universel, reste caché. L'automobile se déplace d'une destination à une autre le long de divers axes de circulation, mais c'est seulement lorsqu'elle s'arrête à une station-service qu'elle se branche sur le réseau. Le plein, cette tâche subalterne, n'a pas vraiment de rôle essentiel dans le système. De la même façon, chez soi, la tuyauterie est cachée, ignorée, anodine. La plomberie est scellée dans les murs, les prises électriques sont dissimulées dans les plinthes, les systèmes de chauffage sont au sous-sol. C'est un royaume sans absolu. Les réseaux linéaires contiennent des cellules, et les cellules contiennent à leur tour des réseaux linéaires en progression constante. L'avion de ligne est une cellule, mais il comprend également des kilomètres de fils et de tuyaux. La maison est une cellule, mais elle est pleine de machines comportant leurs propres circuits.

Dans les années vingt, l'abstraction linéaire était à son zénith. La linéarité était encore un but, un idéal que l'on ne pouvait exprimer pleinement que dans une œuvre d'art, qu'il s'agisse de peinture, de sculpture ou d'architecture. Or aujourd'hui, l'occlusion de l'univers linéaire est parachevée depuis longtemps. La linéarité a quitté le domaine de l'abstraction pour celui du diagramme. Elle opère un retour en arrière et essaie de s'appproprier les pièges de la réalité dans sa spécificité ; d'où le graphisme des jeux vidéo, des cadrans informatiques, des signaux d'aéroport et du symbole des années soixante-dix représentant un visage fendu d'un large sourire commercial vous souhaitant une bonne journée.

New York est la ville représentative par excellence de l'époque héroïque de la conquête de la ligne. Avec sa grille rigoureuse de rues numérotées, elle rappelle constamment la qualité cartésienne de son plan. Les lignes de ses gigantesques gratte-ciel surgissent dans le ciel dans un défi aux lois de la gravité. Des réseaux de conduits souterrains creusés profondément s'élèvent jusqu'à des hauteurs vertigineuses. (L'ascenseur, cette route verticale, est un élément-clef de son organisation spatiale.) La ligne de base de la terre est ignorée. Les structures linéaires s'étendent en trois dimensions avec une frénésie dionysiaque.

A Los Angeles, comme dans d'autres villes de l'âge d'or de la banlieue résidentielle, la perspective linéaire ne cherche plus à s'imposer à tout prix en dépit des forces de la gravité et de la topographie. La grille s'étend simplement horizontalement, en deux dimensions, sans accroc, presque naturellement – comme le plan idéal de Borges (selon Baudrillard) qui recouvrait le paysage entier.

Le semi-conducteur est tout à fait conforme à ce modèle de circulation bidimensionnelle. Petit à petit, en même temps que le monde social s'adaptait à un schéma d'autoroutes et de centres commerciaux, la mémoire et la connaissance étaient transposées sur circuits miniatures.

Les stimuli du monde moderne – le son et l'image – sont également reproduits et distribués par des systèmes infinis de technologie linéaire. (Les sens les plus intimes étaient autrefois exclus de ce registre.) La stéréo et la vidéo sont enregistrées sur bande, cette substance opaque et noirâtre qui symbolise l'ordre temporel linéaire et intransigeant de notre univers. Les ordinateurs et les chaînes hi-fi utilisent des disques plats dont les sillons reflètent le contenu circulaire. Toute l'information visuelle et orale – la conversation téléphonique, l'image télévisée, les données informatiques – est encodée en circuits électroniques. La linéarité devient langage. La science absconse de l'électronique garde maintenant la porte des sens.

La prolifération de l'ordinateur est l'élément du système qui en favorise le plus l'occlusion. Par le biais de l'ordinateur, on a la confirmation matérielle, comme issue d'une source indépendante, de toutes les hypothèses émises par la pensée linéaire. En revanche, l'ordinateur ne reçoit pas ce qui est émis en dehors des règles de son propre code linéaire. Le petit ordinateur personnel, de plus en plus répandu, devient un véritable oracle des structures linéaires. Il donne des instructions sur comment écrire ou conduire ses affaires, mais selon ses propres règles linéaires. Il est même employé pour endoctriner les enfants sur le même mode. Ajouté à cela que dans la mesure où une part de plus en plus importante de l'information nécessaire à la société est stockée dans des ordinateurs, les plus réticents sont finalement contraints d'en passer par eux et par le système de pensée qu'ils introduisent.

La couleur et le dessin. Ce sont les mots d'ordre d'une certaine forme de formalisme dans les arts visuels. L'accent mis sur le dessin reflète bien l'omniprésence du mode linéaire, mais l'importance donnée au rôle de la couleur a aussi une signification. La couleur dans le modernisme est parfois perçue comme un moyen de mettre en action un idéal d'expression hédoniste – de libérer la sensibilité bourgeoise de ses contraintes morales et symbolistes. Mais cette importance de la couleur reflète le rôle crucial qu'elle joue dans la structure linéaire. Dans l'univers plan, seule la couleur peut donner un sens à la ligne. Les tracés colorés sur les cartes différencient les catégories de routes.

Les fils sont de diverses couleurs selon leur fonction. Dans les hôpitaux, on peut se repérer dans le dédale des couloirs jusqu'à sa destination en suivant des bandes colorées sur le sol.

Dans les années soixante, le seul but des astronautes était de se mettre en orbite autour de la terre et d'inscrire dans les cieux un cercle qui entourerait la planète. Ce fut à la fois un grand spectable et un événement d'une haute signification rituelle. Dans leurs combinaisons argent réfléchissantes et leur capsule luisante (l'archétype de la cellule avec son peu d'espace vital et sa toute petite fenêtre), ils ont annoncé par leurs vols épiques l'occlusion du mode linéaire de sorte que l'humanité entière y assiste (à la télévision) : la linéarité et l'abstraction allaient désormais circonvenir la nature. La tradition spéculative de Descartes, Kant et Hegel avait refait le monde. C'est comme si la magie des Chamans s'était révélée toute puissante et que les recettes chamaniques avaient banni pour toujours les mystères de la Nature. La ligne pouvait maintenant se retourner sur elle-même. Le système s'était refermé, était devenu une vaste machine à reproduire ses postulats, avait enfin atteint, sur le modèle orbital, un état statique.

Publié pour la première fois dans *L.A.I.C.A. Journal*, (Los Angeles), décembre 1985.

Première publication en français dans *Peter Halley,* (cat. d'exp.), Paris, Galerie Daniel Templon, 1986. Traduction de Ann Hindry.

Essence et modèle (1986)

Qu'on le qualifie de post-modernisme ou de néo-modernisme, ce qui caractérise cet ordre, c'est son hyperréalisation des éléments du modernisme. Ceux-ci sont réduits à des formes pures et débarrassés de tout vestige de vie ou de signification. Ils sont redéployés dans un système auto-référentiel qui est lui même une hyperréalisation de l'auto-référentialité moderniste – bien qu'elle soit maintenant détachée du rêve moderniste de renouveau révolutionnaire. Dans le post- ou néo-modernisme, les éléments syntaxiques ne changent pas. Le vocabulaire du modernisme demeure, mais ses éléments, déjà abstraits, sont complètement et définitivement coupés de toute référence au réel.

Dans cet hypermodernisme, le moderne n'est jamais rejeté. Il est simplement remplacé par son double formel. La transformation de la ville moderne illustre bien ce processus. Paris, Boston et New York ne changent pas. (C'est la caractéristique du modernisme que de précipiter le changement – élargissement des rues, remplissage des terrains vagues, construction de monuments). Les villes deviennent simplement leur double formel. Enfermées dans l'univers post-industriel, transformées en parcs thématiques du moderne, on s'y rend pour contempler les vestiges du public, comme le métro ou les parcs, et du social, comme par exemple dans les cafés ou les théâtres. De la même façon, l'art est remplacé par son double, par des objets et des images dupliquant «l'effet d'art».

On atteint à l'univers du double en transformant chaque élément en modèle de lui-même. Le concept moderniste d'essence, dont le référent est la nature, est encore davantage réduit à l'état de modèle, où seule la forme, débarrassée de toute signification, demeure. L'univers du modèle devient ainsi la réalisation finale et brutale de l'impulsion moderniste vers l'idéalisme. Notamment, l'abstrait devient le réel, et l'environnement dans son ensemble devient un modèle de l'environnement. Toutes les autres réalités, et tout spécialement celles de la spécificité et de la transcendance, sont soit exclues, soit englobées par le modèle et transformées en modèles d'elles-mêmes. Il n'y a donc pas seulement la réalité du modèle, il n'y a plus d'autre réalité que celle du modèle. Par conséquent les promoteurs construisent des villes qui sont des modèles de villes, les architectes des bâtiments qui sont des modèles d'architectures, et les artistes des œuvres d'art qui sont des modèles de l'idée d'œuvre d'art. De la même façon, dans cet univers, grâce à la psychologie et à la physiologie, les êtres humains ne peuvent être que des modèles d'êtres humains, alors que les sondages d'opinion, les tests à choix multiples et les répondeurs téléphoniques établissent que la communication ne peut être qu'un modèle de communication.

La force opératoire qui gouverne la constitution de ce monde du double et du modèle, c'est le pouvoir du principe de communication. Les vestiges du déplacement physique s'inscrivent dans les systèmes de circulation, qu'il s'agisse des automobiles, des piétons ou des marchandises. Le savoir moderniste devient information ; celle-ci est véhiculée par la télévision, les hebdomadaires et les circuits électroniques des ordinateurs. La métaphysique devient cette circulation sans fin de signes à travers les conduits d'un espace mental irréel.

L'hypermodernisme se définit finalement par la clôture et la circularité. La nature moderniste est enfermée dans la réserve naturelle et dans le parc d'attractions. La ville moderne est ceinturée par les autoroutes, nichée à l'intérieur du réseau circulatoire de la subdivision. Et la terre elle-même, définie à l'origine en tant que globe par le modernisme, est encerclée, à l'ère hypermoderne, par les orbites des satellites artificiels et leurs détecteurs électroniques.

Dans le modernisme, le signifiant était détaché du signifié – mais cela procédait d'une volonté de conférer du pouvoir et de redonner vie au signifiant. Dans l'hypermodernisme, le signifiant n'est pas seulement donné au signifié, il peut s'attacher à une séquence infinie de signifiés. Mais cette situation hypermoderne définit un hermétisme encore plus total que celui du modernisme. Aucune signification n'est finale, et les signifiés se perdent les uns les autres dans un cercle sans fin. Le cercle est le métasigne de l'hypermoderne.

Publié pour la première fois dans *Peter Halley, Collected Essays, op. cit.*

Réponse au :
« Le sublime, c'est maintenant »
de Barnett Newman

Le quadrillage n'a pas de mémoire. Il n'y a là que des positions définies numériquement et des vitesses temporairement calculées. Quand un événement disparaît du quadrillage, la structure implacable de ce dernier l'avale et ne laisse aucune trace de son existence. Sur le quadrillage, il n'y a pas de monuments. Le quadrillage lui-même est un monument à l'infini de sa propre nature circulatoire.

Quand la New York moderne fut planifiée au début du XIXe siècle, des lois imposaient aux propriétaires le nivellement des collines dépassant une certaine hauteur. On servait ainsi deux objectifs : premièrement, aucune pente, aucune colline ne devait gêner la circulation ; deuxièmement, aucune caractéristique du terrain ne devait provoquer la mémoire. S'il n'y a pas de collines, il ne peut y avoir d'endroit où tel ou tel événement a pu se produire telle ou telle nuit : pas de *Bunker Hills*, pas de Montmartre. Tous les référents naturels devaient systématiquement disparaître du paysage. (De la même façon, plusieurs cours d'eau et même le lac en-dessous de Canal Street furent supprimés).

Il n'y a sur le quadrillage que la présence du mouvement sans fin, le flux abstrait des marchandises, du capital et de l'information. Tout est interchangeable. On ne peut se souvenir de rien dans la mesure où tout peut être remplacé. L'existence ne se définit qu'en termes de position. Si celle-ci est perdue, l'existence disparaît.

La mémoire devient information quand elle s'intègre aux quadrillages des enregistrements électroniques et photo-chimiques. Ici, le temps passé et le temps futur sont pulvérisés par les mécanismes ésotériques de la culture du divertissement. Nous regardons une photographie de cinéma, tirée l'année dernière d'un film de 1932, dont l'histoire se déroule dans un futur appartenant déjà au passé. Les jeunes acteurs sont vieux ou sont morts, les costumes du futur sont démodés. Le passé et le futur s'annulent dans cette équation temporelle qui ne laisse subsister que le présent.

Finalement, c'est la mort qui disparaît. Les corps sont escamotés. Les définitions de la vie et de la mort deviennent floues. Des éléments de remplacement prolongent la vie alors que la reproduction des médias étend sa visibilité. Mais la vie elle-même est simultanément remplacée par les exigences du quadrillage : vitesse, circulation et échange.

Voici l'origine du «Maintenant» de Newman. C'est aussi le «Maintenant» de l'existentialisme et des diverses psychologies expérimentales américaines des années cinquante et soixante. C'est le même «Maintenant» que celui de la présence chaotique de la poésie *beat* et du *free jazz*.

Après la mort de Newman, Warhol a dit que Newman était la seule personne qui allait à plus de réceptions que lui. Warhol pensait que, dans la mesure où Newman peignait si peu de lignes, il avait le temps de sortir le soir. Warhol lui aussi est prisonnier du présent. Comme il n'a aucune mémoire, il passe son temps à prendre des photographies.

Michel Foucault, lui aussi, atteste cette coupure avec la mémoire. Son travail reconstituant une Histoire amnésique, une Histoire consacrée uniquement au moderne, qui, dans sa méthodologie, dépendait de ces obscurs enregistrements d'archives, substituts de la mémoire à l'ère moderniste. Son travail était dramatiquement coupé de tout passé antérieur à l'ère moderne. Son Histoire ne débute qu'à la Renaissance, au moment où l'information enregistrée commence à remplacer la mémoire, et exclut toute approche des cultures orientales, tribales ou pré-modernes.

C'est à la fin que s'opère le changement. Foucault redécouvrit la mémoire lors de sa méditation finale sur la sexualité dans la Grèce antique. L'extase torturée du présent, qui avait été prédominante dans tout son travail jusque-là, est alors remplacée par l'extase de la mémoire des temps anciens, du cortège de la vie organique. Foucault aurait-il fait volte-face au dernier moment ?

Publié pour la première fois dans *Arts Magazine*, (New York), vol. 60, n° 7, mars 1986.

Notes sur l'abstraction

Il y avait les grands, Euclide, etc.,
mais aujourd'hui
tout le monde doit essayer d'interpréter
l'énigme de la technologie.

Paul Virilio

Le temps est venu de cesser de faire sens – de remplacer l'Histoire par une myriade de théories échevelées sur le post-, le para-, le quasi- et le super-. L'Histoire a été vaincue par les déterminismes du marché et des chiffres, par les processus de réification et d'abstraction. Ceux-ci constituent le maelström de la modernité qui a détruit l'Histoire en l'absorbant, en transformant chaque concept indépendant de l'Histoire afin de servir son propre propos. Il faut faire appel à un autre type de réponses. Des idées qui elles-mêmes changent ou se dissipent quand elles sont absorbées, qui sont formulées avec la conscience de leur réification imminente. Seul est possible un repli stratégique basé sur les idées de la guerilla qui permettent de retourner dans la jungle de la pensée et de réapparaître sous d'autres déguisements ; des idées fantastiques et excentriques, apparemment inoffensives et donc admises, échappant à la vigilance des médias ; des idées de doute se moquant de leur propre vérité et qui ne sont alors pas détruites quand on les manipule ; des idées nihilistes, rejetées car trop déprimantes.

*

«C'est comme si les «bébés de la guerre», ceux qui sont nés après 1937-1938, étaient «nés morts» pour employer une expression chère aux *Hell's Angels*. La philosophie de la «réalité» a pris fin peu après le largage des bombes sur Hiroshima et Nagasaki, et les esprits se sont alors refroidis[1]».

*

La pensée marxiste a toujours supposé que la destruction des prétentions de la culture humaniste favoriserait une réalité plus sensible et plus cohérente que celle de l'illusionnisme humaniste. Ce ne sont cependant pas les vérités du matérialisme qui se cachaient derrière le masque de l'humanisme, mais les scénarios cauchemardesques de la logique et du déterminisme. Emerge alors un monde cristallin qui n'est plus sensible qu'aux impératifs numériques, à la manipulation formelle et au contrôle financier.

*

«Prenons par exemple les deux cents agents travaillant à la réservation générale pour *Pacific Southwest Airlines* à San Diego. La compagnie aérienne avertit ses agents qu'ils sont assujettis au «contrôle électronique de la productivité et à l'écoute téléphonique». En clair, cela signifie que les agents sont surveillés par ordinateur à partir du moment où ils branchent leur casque jusqu'au moment où ils quittent leur travail. Chaque appel est censé durer 109 secondes, en moyenne, avec une interruption de 11 secondes environ, entre chaque appel, qui doit être consacrée au travail de bureau. L'ordinateur surveille aussi les pauses et le temps imparti au déjeuner. Les agents encourrent un blâme s'ils sont «débranchés» pendant plus de 12 minutes d'affilée [2]».

*

Le capital s'est toujours présenté comme une culture du flux, basée sur les idées de changement, d'évolution et de développement. Mais le capital est, en fait, un univers statique, gouverné par des principes immuables se perpétuant eux-mêmes, repoussant graduellement mais inéluctablement toute autre réalité dans un processus de purification sans cesse croissant. Ironiquement l'univers du capital pur, caractérisé par le modèle, la vérité numérologique et les relations abstraites, est une sorte d'accomplissement de la philosophie idéaliste. Mais il se trouve que le monde de l'essence n'est pas dominé par l'Esprit mais par le produit. Le monde abstrait ne relève pas de l'utopie, mais de l'aliénation et de la banalité.

*

Telle est peut-être la signification réelle de la culture américaine : l'image de l'immigration par delà l'océan, du voyage au-dessus du plan de l'eau. Le voyage a entamé un processus d'abrasement grâce auquel, par le passage au-dessous d'un plan abstrait, la spécificité de l'Europe pouvait être désengagée, laissant toute latitude aux lois du capital.

*

Cela ne veut pas dire pour autant que l'Amérique est le futur. Au contraire, l'Europe est aujourd'hui, le véritable lieu de la science-fiction. C'est l'évidence : les voitures y sont plus rapides, la conception des biens est plus rationnelle, les marchés financiers sont plus souples. Même l'Europe en tant que site nostalgique de l'authenticité accuse sa dimension science-fictionnelle, comme si le temps avait oublié le continent. La Seconde Guerre mondiale a entraîné un autre type de coupure avec le passé.

*

«Des programmes intitulés «vers de terre» peuvent modifier les opérations fondamentales d'un système ou le mettre complètement hors fonction. Ils effacent certaines portions précises de la mémoire d'un ordinateur, créant ainsi un trou dans l'information. Un autre type de démon informatique, le «virus», demande à la machine-hôte de restituer ses programmes. Chaque fois que la machine s'exécute, le programme se copie lui-même sur le logiciel. La mémoire de l'ordinateur peut vite atteindre la confusion totale [3]».

*

Valeur d'usage et valeur d'échange. L'idée de changement dans le capitalisme est basée sur l'idée que la conscience, à l'intérieur du capital, peut changer qualitativement. Ce changement repose sur l'idée qu'on est passé d'une société dominée par la valeur d'usage (où les hommes étaient des hommes et les chevaux des chevaux) à une société dominée par la valeur d'échange, dominée par l'illusion et la manipulation. Mais à quand remonte cet âge d'or de la valeur d'usage ? Ne peut-on pas considérer qu'il y a là une simple invention idéologique du XIXe siècle ? Après tout, la naissance du capitalisme moderne à la Renaissance était basée sur le commerce des produits de luxe, de la soie et des épices. Elle était basée sur l'invention des lettres de change. Les premiers objets produits en série furent les livres.

*

«Les manufactures alignent l'une après l'autre leurs briques salies, leurs façades nues, leurs fenêtres sans volets, comme des prisons économiques et colossales... C'est là que sous la lumière du gaz, au roulement assourdissant des métiers, des milliers d'ouvriers, parqués, enrégimentés, immobiles, tous les jours, tout le jour, poussent machinalement leur machine [4]».

*

Dès la Renaissance, certaines caractéristiques structurelles du capital apparaissent qui demeurent inchangées jusqu'à aujourd'hui, même si elles n'ont jamais cessé de s'intensifier. Ces outils se basent sur le principe d'une cassure des limites inhérentes au temps et à l'espace, et leur remplacement par des définitions plus malléables. L'un des paradigmes de ces outils est la lettre de change qui permet à un marchand d'acheter ou de vendre des marchandises dans une ville, en l'assurant que le paiement peut avoir lieu ailleurs et plus tard. Au même moment se forment les premières compagnies commerciales dont les membres sont liés par les intérêts économiques plus que par les relations familiales. C'est aussi le moment où les réseaux de transport se développent, pour diminuer la durée des voyages et du déplacement des denrées d'un endroit à un autre. La constante a été de faciliter la manipulation du temps, les espaces spécifiques étant devenus plus interchangeables. Le principe directeur a été le remplacement de toutes les autres instances par le pouvoir du marché.

*

«Qu'un sauvage américain vienne au Palais-Royal, en une demi-heure, il serait magnifiquement paré, aurait une maison richement meublée, un attelage, de nombreux serviteurs, vingt couverts sur sa table, et, s'il le souhaitait, une Lais resplendissante mourant à tout moment d'amour pour lui. Là sont assemblés tous les remèdes à l'ennui et tous les divins poisons pour la santé spirituelle et physique, tous les moyens pour escroquer ceux qui ont de l'argent et tourmenter ceux qui en sont dépourvus, tous les moyens pour jouir de et tuer le temps. On pourrait passer sa vie entière au Palais-Royal et, comme dans un rêve enchanteur, dire avant de mourir : «J'ai tout vu, tout connu [5]».

*

Si le capital est statique, comment peut-on justifier l'apparition du changement à l'intérieur du capital ? Alors que les forces de base du capital demeurent statiques et cherchent à asseoir leur pure hégémonie, l'économie des valeurs, quant à elle, change. Le niveau d'aliénation s'intensifie en même temps que s'affirme, chaque fois davantage, la domination du capital. La notion d'un capitalisme classique, qui aurait existé au XVIIe siècle, appelle aussi un examen minutieux. L'idée d'un capitalisme classique deviendrait ainsi un capital épuré du futur plutôt qu'un capitalisme rudimentaire du passé.

*

«Le modèle biologique n'était pas le mieux approprié pour tracer l'histoire des choses. Un système métaphorique, issu des sciences physiques, aurait peut-être mieux couvert la situation de l'art que les métaphores biologiques qui lui furent préférées : ceci tout spécialement si nous traitons d'un art basé sur la transmission d'une certaine énergie ; avec des impulsions, des centres générateurs et des points de relais ; avec des augmentations et des pertes en transit ; avec des résistances et des transformateurs dans le circuit. En bref, le langage de l'électrodynamique aurait pu être un meilleur mentor que Linnaeus en ce qui concerne l'étude de la culture matérielle [6]».

*

L'apparition du changement dans le capitalisme est due à deux facteurs. En premier lieu, l'augmentation des recettes provoque un changement dans la physionomie des institutions. Ainsi, un ensemble de maison du XVIIe siècle à Amsterdam diffère de la *Co-op City* à New York. La Florence de la Renaissance diffère du Tokyo de la fin de ce siècle. La vitesse d'une diligence n'est pas la même que celle du Concorde. Mais sur le plan structurel, chacun de ces phénomènes reste cohérent avec son prédécesseur. En second lieu, chaque étape du développement technologique et social représente un pas supplémentaire dans l'abstraction : une consolidation des liens entre le but à atteindre et la nature matérielle, un renforcement du lien entre la technologie et l'abstraction de la pensée rationnelle.

*

En restant à l'intérieur des exemples fournis par l'évolution des moyens de transport, on observe une progression qui va du voilier au bateau à vapeur et au sous-marin nucléaire. Dans le domaine de l'argent, on passe de la pièce en métal précieux (avec l'effigie du roi) au papier monnaie (portant les symboles de l'Etat) et à la carte de crédit en plastique (portant le logo de l'entreprise).

*

«Chez Ed Debevic» est un petit restaurant loufoque des années cinquante où les cuisiniers se penchent au-dessus de la viande hachée, où les serveuses portent des chaussures à éperons ; un signe bigarré y annonce, «*Ed Chili Dog : the Cadillac of Chili Dogs*». A un demi mile au sud se trouve «*Shaw's Crab House*», un entrepôt de fruits de mer mal éclairé rappelant les vieux bâtiments fréquentés par les gangsters dans les années quarante. Au nord de la ville, un «Grand Café», avec sa décoration de cuivre et ses peintures, recrée la gaieté fin de siècle d'un bistro parisien. Bien que très différents, ces restaurants hauts en couleurs ont deux choses en commun : les gens font généralement la queue pour y entrer, et leur propriétaire est Richard Melman, un impresario irrévérencieux de quarante quatre ans... Afin d'obtenir la bonne atmosphère, M. Melman décrit chaque restaurant comme si chacun d'entre eux était un film. «Chez Ed Debevic», nous sommes en 1952, année où l'adolescence n'est pas encore sauvage, où Elvis Presley n'est pas encore un géant. Ed, personnage de fiction, était polonais et a ouvert son restaurant après avoir fait la Corée [7]».

*

Cette idée d'abstraction progressive combinée à l'augmentation numérique progressive peut être caractérisée par le terme hyperréalisation. Ce terme est généralement utilisé pour décrire le bond entre la culture industrielle (le réel) et la culture post-industrielle (qui est hyperréelle). On pourra cependant dégager de cette chaîne d'événements une séquence qui montre de façon globale la progression des époques dans l'histoire du capital. Chaque époque devient une hyperréalisation de la précédente, à qui on confère alors la valeur de réalité.

*

Le processus d'hyperréalisation peut être parfaitement compris dans un simple paysage urbain – comme par exemple celui de New York. La rangée de maisons où les étages sont desservis par un escalier est hyperréalisée quand elle devient un grand immeuble avec ascenseurs. Les couloirs, les installations de plomberie et les systèmes électriques des immeubles d'habitation se multiplient et créent de nouvelles configurations à l'image de nouvelles hyperréalités de la population, de l'économie et de la technologie. De la même façon, les immeubles de bureaux sont transfigurés. L'échelle passe de l'immeuble commercial à quatre ou cinq étages aux premiers gratte-ciel, comme le *Woolworth Building* ou le gigantesque *World Trade Center*. On passe de matériaux, comme la brique, le bois, la pierre, à l'acier, au verre et aux panneaux synthétiques. Les premières tours de bureaux accentuaient le relief de leurs façades – permettant à la lumière et à l'ombre de jouer dramatiquement sur leurs surfaces. Après la guerre, les murs-rideaux deviennent de plus en plus plats, de plus en plus réfléchissants et glacés. Le passage de la lumière a moins d'importance et l'intérieur des bâtiments est caché à la vue (par la surface réfléchissante) : à un niveau symbolique, la tour de bureaux devient une réalité autonome.

*

Cette idée d'hyperréalisation est particulièrement utile quand il s'agit d'analyser l'art du XXe siècle. On peut considérer le cubisme comme une hyperréalisation de Cézanne, ou Cézanne, de la même façon, comme une hyperréalisation de Courbet. De même, on peut comprendre l'expressionnisme abstrait comme une hyperréalisation du modernisme européen d'avant-guerre, ou Frank Stella comme une hyperréalisation de l'expressionnisme abstrait. Chaque transition reflète un mouvement vers une abstraction, au sens social du terme, de la forme antérieure. Ainsi, à chaque étape, la forme devient à la fois plus vide et plus générique. Dans certains cas, comme l'expressionnisme abstrait, l'augmentation de l'échelle est même conçue pour suivre celle, évidente, du paysage social.

*

«La conception moderne de l'homme en tant que machine possède un accent plus économique que biologique. Elle fait davantage référence au robot humain qu'à l'animal humain et suggére un contrôle efficace des mouvements trop coûteux du corps, une soumission à quelque objectif externe auquel l'individu est indifférent... [8]»

*

L'hyperréalisation offre aussi une alternative utile aux concepts polaires d'influence et d'appropriation. Si l'idée d'influence implique une relation historique consciente entre une génération d'artistes et la suivante, et si l'appropriation nie justement ces idées basées sur la hiérarchisation historique et la possibilité de transgression, l'hyperréalisation, quant à elle, implique bien l'avènement du changement dans le domaine culturel. Cependant, ces changements ne dépendent pas de la volonté de l'artiste, mais du mouvement social. L'hyperréalisation différerait, d'ailleurs, de l'idée psychanalytique «d'interprétation erronée» selon laquelle une lutte œdipienne entre générations peut être source de changements. Sans tenir compte de l'existence possible de tels conflits œdipiens, l'hyperréalisation suggère que le changement culturel d'une génération à l'autre dépend de forces sociales, déterministes et extra-individuelles.

*

L'hyperréalisation permet aussi d'expliquer l'obsession du «nouveau» qui caractérise cette culture. On dit parfois que le «nouveau» est lié au concept d'originalité. Mais le «nouveau» est plus profondément lié (comme peut-être le culte de l'originalité lui-même) au processus d'hyperréalisation. Le «nouveau» représente l'état hyperréalisé de ce qui précédait. Ainsi, les produits de consommation sont souvent présentés comme «nouveaux» pour leur donner l'aura d'hyperréalisation. Périodiquement, on dit de certains mouvements culturels qu'ils sont «nouveaux» ou nouvelle vague – dans les domaines de la musique, de la danse, de la littérature (il y a même un nouvel humanisme). De telles étiquettes annoncent la venue d'un phénomène qui se veut l'hyperréalisation de la norme culturelle antérieure. Le préfixe *pop* (comme dans *pop-culture*) fonctionne de la même façon.

*

«Les grands héros et héroïnes du mythe de la modernité appartenaient à la petite bourgeoisie. Ils ont semblé à bien des égards n'appartenir à aucune classe, comme exclus de la bourgeoisie et du prolétariat pour cependant profiter de cette absence d'appartenance. C'étaient des décalés de la société de classes, ceux qui connaissaient ses limites et ses friches. Ils furent ainsi pour un temps les alter-ego de l'avant-garde, traités avec ironie, bien sûr, et condescendance, on se moquait d'eux, mais on en dépendait quand il s'agissait de s'insérer dans une vie moderne [9]».

*

Alors que le processus d'hyperréalisation mène inéluctablement à la fin du système capitaliste, toutes les anciennes catégories organiques commencent à perdre leur signification. Les dualités traditionnelles vie-mort, homme-femme, s'évanouissent. Il n'y a plus aujourd'hui d'hommes et de femmes, en dépit du renouveau apparent de ces catégories lors de cette dernière décennie. En fait, Sylvester Stallone n'est pas un mâle, il n'est que le signe générique de l'idée de mâle, alors que Madonna n'est qu'une séquence des diverses représentations nostalgiques de la femme.

*

De la même façon, les pôles vie-mort basculent dans la non-vie et la non-mort. Plus personne ne vit ou ne meurt. La possibilité de vie est niée par la contrainte du temps mécanique et de l'enrégimentation, à la fois physique et temporelle. La mort, quant à elle, est remplacée par la disparition et niée par la manipulation du temps dans les médias.

*

En ce qui concerne les arts visuels, l'idée prédominante du début des années soixante-dix était le développement d'une culture post-capitaliste. On pensait que le produit et l'état d'esprit qui y était lié seraient remplacés par la performance et les interventions sur des sites spécifiques. L'artiste travaillerait en temps réel, proposant alors l'exemple d'un travail non-aliénant. L'artiste jouerait jusqu'au bout le rôle du sujet libre, qui devrait alors faire des émules partout ailleurs dans le champ du social. Mais les années soixante-dix ne représentaient pas l'apparition d'une nouvelle conscience, mais bien plutôt la dernière expression incandescente du vieil idéalisme de l'autonomie. Par la suite, le temps ne serait plus réel, aucun travail ne relèverait de la vie, aucune expression culturelle ne pourrait échapper au système de production.

*

Les artistes des années soixante-dix cessèrent de vivre dans les environnements urbains traditionnels pour investir des espaces industriels sous utilisés comme Soho à New York. Ce faisant, ils rejetaient tous les problèmes de l'ordre urbain capitaliste et s'inventaient une nouvelle culture dans des bâtiments où personne jusqu'ici n'avait vécu. Il n'y avait plus là d'appartements bourgeois, seulement des «espaces» ouverts. La nourriture américaine commerciale, dangereuse, serait remplacée par la cuisine macrobiotique, génératrice de vie. Mais ce type de «rénovation», ignorant la fonction commerciale des vieux bâtiments de lofts pour seulement en changer l'appréhension formelle, fut en fait un facteur déterminant dans la transformation de la ville en son double, vide. La banlieue, qui avant entourait la vieille ville «moderne», commençait alors à prendre racine, comme un virus né en son centre, alors que ces espaces se transformaient en cités-dortoirs.

*

«[Howard Hugues] fut le premier à fermer le cercle vide, dans les années trente, avec son «*Lockhead Cyclone*», il faut noter qu'il ne s'agit pas d'un mystère ou d'un fantôme, mais d'un cyclone... Il revenait au même endroit : New York. Howard Hugues fut le Linbergh de la fin du monde, un héros du post-modernisme. Après s'être énormément investi dans l'aviation, il monta des studios de cinéma. Il était impliqué dans tout ce qui, à cette époque, avait un rapport avec la vitesse : l'avion et le cinéma. Il essaya de jouir de son omniprésence dans le monde. D'abord, il avait plusieurs appartements dans le monde entier, tous décorés de la même façon. Tous les jours on lui servait le même repas, en lui apportant le même journal.

Puis la situation devint insupportable et quand il finit moine technologique dans le désert de Las Vegas, il ne quittait plus son lit. Il a passé les quinze dernières années de sa vie enfermé dans un hôtel, à regarder des films, toujours les mêmes, surtout un vieux film américain sur la vie d'une équipe bloquée dans le «*Ice Station Zebra*» au Pôle Nord. Il l'a vu cent soixante quatre fois [10]».

*

Le crédit à la consommation avait acquis une banque d'investissement et une maison de courtage. Les besoins de la maison de courtage nécessitaient la construction d'un nouveau bâtiment pour le système informatique. L'entreprise avait tout d'abord songé à le construire en banlieue, où les coûts étaient moindres, mais un emplacement fut choisi en centre ville après l'offre gratuite de la municipalité. Le bâtiment fut nommé le Centre des Services Financiers. Il était près de l'autoroute, pour faciliter l'accès automobile. Des escaliers roulants doubles permettaient d'accéder à l'ascenseur du premier étage. Le soir, des files de taxis attendaient les employés qui travaillaient tard. Mais ce centre informatique était aussi situé dans une zone où des bâtiments industriels avaient été transformés en immeubles résidentiels. Ainsi, des «aménagements agréables» furent requis pour la «communauté». Près du bâtiment, de style moderne, recouvert de plaques de béton préfabriquées, face à l'ère de stationnement, on aménagea un petit parc, avec pelouses, lampadaires du XIXe et un petit pavillon en treillage appuyé sur des colonnes néo-classiques blanches. Plusieurs poteaux métalliques furent disposés autour du parc, au design fonctionnel, sans décoration historique, surmontés d'une caméra vidéo de surveillance, dans un boitier en émail beige à l'épreuve des balles.

*

Il y a un certain effondrement des deux pôles constitués par le capital et le travail. Le chef d'entreprise est prisonnier de la situation des bénéfices et de la cote en bourse. Les titres de l'entreprise peuvent être gérés par de nombreuses institutions dont, peut-être, les fonds de retraite, représentant théoriquement le monde du travail. De la même façon, pour le travail, dans la mesure où il est lié à l'idée de consommateur, on observe une tendance au nivellement des hiérarchies. Andy Warhol disait : «Vous voyez Coca-Cola en regardant la télévision et vous savez alors que le président boit du Coca, que Liz Taylor boit du Coca, et vous vous dites qu'après tout, vous pouvez aussi boire du Coca.»

*

Il y a également un certain écroulement dans les hiérarchies du travail. La volonté de pouvoir est remplacée par la volonté de «glamour». Comme Warhol l'expliquait aussi en 1975 (avant la dérégulation des transports aériens) : «Les hôtesses de l'air ont une excellente image publique... En réalité, elles font le même travail que les servantes de Bickford avec quelques devoirs en plus... La différence, c'est qu'il sagit là d'un travail du Nouveau Monde, où ne subsistent plus aucuns stigmates du syndrome aristocratique et paysan du Vieux Monde.» Mais plus important encore, ceux qui sont à la tête du système – les «capitaines d'industrie», les producteurs de divertissements populaires, les leaders politiques – n'opèrent plus, eux-mêmes, en champ libre. Eux aussi sont prisonniers de la démographie, de l'électronique et des forces du marché.

*

La vie a été remplacée par ce que Debord appelle le «non-vivant». C'est l'espace du travail mort où la vie ne suit plus son cours normal et s'aliène d'elle-même. Le rôle du vivant est confié aux célébrités qui incarnent l'idée d'autonomie avec son libre champ d'action. La vie n'est alors plus qu'une image des médias. Les archéologues pensent que la société aztèque choisissait certains jeunes dans la noblesse, les choyant pendant une année avant de les sacrifier sur l'autel des dieux. Mais les pratiques de la société contemporaine ne sont pas moins sauvages. Quand quelqu'un devient une célébrité, sa vie n'en est pas moins littéralement balayée. Le temps organique de la célébrité ne sert plus qu'à créer l'image générique exigée par les médias. La star «renonce à toute autonomie afin de s'identifier à la loi générale d'obéissance au cours des choses».

*

L'idée même de temps organique est annulée et remplacée par un temps mécanisé, segmentarisé, digital (correspondant à l'espace du système). La mesure chronologique standard est celle de la vibration du cristal de quartz. L'existence est transférée à des moyens d'expression séquentiels, segmentarisés et linéaires : les enregistrements audio et visuels. D'abord le film remplace le temps organique par ses images séquentielles, au rythme mécanique.

La bande vidéo remplace le film, enfermant encore un peu plus la vie dans les lignes d'information magnétiques et codées. Pour l'enregistrement sonore, on passe du phonographe, où le son est lu mécaniquement par une pointe de lecture, à l'enregistrement sur bande magnétique et finalement au disque compact, où un rayon laser lit l'information codée digitalement. La constante purification du système lui confère une qualité paraspirituelle : le son vivant devient un amalgame alchimique de rayons lumineux et de chiffres.

*

Le même système, qui remplace la vie, remplace la mort. L'inscription du temps sur ces pistes linéaires permet de le stopper, de le répéter ou de le modifier à volonté. Grâce au cinéma et à la télévision, on peut présenter n'importe où et n'importe quand une scène du Londres des années trente. L'«action» ne meurt jamais, mais elle perd sa spécificité par rapport au temps et à l'espace. Warhol avait particulièrement bien compris ce processus. C'est ce qui l'a conduit à photographier, enregistrer et filmer en permanence. Ce faisant, il a repris à son compte le fonctionnement des médias, la transformation du moment organique en moment médiatique. Il est vrai cependant que, pour l'instant, nous sommes toujours conscients de la mort organique du corps physique. Mais cela est devenu un événement sans signification, une gêne. On espère que très vite, les corps se contenteront de disparaître, pour ne pas gêner la réalité du temps médiatique.

*

La vie et la mort perdent aussi toute signification métaphorique dans le champ culturel. Parler de la mort du modernisme revient à parler d'une fin organique dans une culture où la construction de l'organique s'est à la fois dispersée et cristallisée, où les concepts de fin se transforment en continuités séquentielles. La mort est remplacée par le processus d'hyperréalisation. L'art classique ne meurt pas. Il est hyperréalisé à l'intérieur du modernisme. A chacune de ses étapes, le modernisme, est à son tour hyperréalisé en quelque chose d'autre.

*

«Sur le Sony, une guerre de l'espace bidimensionnelle s'effaça derrière une forêt de formes générées mathématiquement, démontrant les possibilités spatiales des spirales logarythmiques ; séquence militaire bleu-acier brûlé, animaux de laboratoire branchés sur testeurs, casques se nourrissant sur les circuits de contrôle de tanks et d'avions de guerre. L'espace cybernétique... représentation graphique de données dérobées à toutes les banques de tous les ordinateurs de l'humanité. Complexité inimaginable. Traits de lumière agencés dans le non espace du cerveau, amas et constellations de données [11]».

*

Il y a des sous-entendus religieux dans ces exemples. Les systèmes numériques deviennent en tant que tels les garants d'une signification possible de notre culture. Il y a ainsi trois grands centres religieux aux Etats-Unis : Los Angeles, la nouvelle ville éternelle, la nouvelle Rome des médias, puis Las Vegas et Atlantic City, lieux de pélerinage où la populace part en quête de la vérité numérique. Los Angeles est la Rome des représentations des médias. A Beverly Hills, on a donné aux maisons des stars la splendeur figée des palais des cardinaux dans la Rome baroque. Les foules se pressent aux Studios Universal et à Disneyland pour rendre hommage à ces splendeurs de la réalité médiatique. Las Vegas et Atlantic City sont les hauts lieux de cette vision. Le peuple se teste face aux jeux numériques dans des casinos hors de l'espace et du temps. C'est là qu'on apprend la métaphysique, que les présages se révèlent et que les destins sont scellés.

*

«Retrouvez-vous en prenant un «*Kohler Masterbath*». Votre univers personnel consiste maintenant en six sensations climatiques (le sauna, le tourbillon, le soleil, la vapeur, le vent, la pluie), que vous appelez ou rejetez à volonté. Programmez votre climat à l'avance ou changez le au fur et à mesure [12]».

*

Parallèlement à la vie et à la mort, aux hommes et aux femmes, la sexualité cesse elle aussi d'être un facteur. Les années soixante et soixante-dix n'étaient pas tant une période de révolution sexuelle qu'une dernière démonstration de l'idée de sexualité avant que celle-ci ne s'effondre dans l'extase des chiffres. Foucault prétendait que l'Ancien Régime était une société de sang où le courage guerrier, la volonté de mourir au champ d'honneur, étaient les passions dominantes. Il affirmait que la culture bourgeoise avait inventé la sexualité, en mettant l'accent sur la procréation, la cohésion familiale et le plaisir sensuel. Si l'ère du sexuel débute à un moment de l'Histoire bien défini, il se pourrait bien qu'il en soit de même pour sa fin. Les passions charnelles ont aujourd'hui laissé place à des obsessions plus abstraites. L'érotisme de la vitesse, de l'automobile et de l'avion ; l'érotisme des chiffres, des marchés financiers, de l'ordinateur domestique ; et l'érotisme des médias, du walkman et de la télévision couleur.

*

«Ce qui semblait si mal venu dans l'environnement avait en fait créé un nouveau type de monde interne – un théâtre empêchant toute distraction et fixant l'attention sur ce que l'industrie appelle «le drame du détail». Parce qu'elle est coupée du rythme planétaire des jours et des saisons, parce que la direction exige que tout sans cesse paraisse nouveau, la galerie marchande est intemporelle, parce qu'elle est coupée de tout, la galerie marchande peut se trouver n'importe où. C'est un espace malléable dans un pays qui n'existe pas où se rejoignent l'idée d'approvisionnement et l'idée de divertissement [13]».

*

Tout au long du siècle, les artistes ont décrit la transformation du corps organique en machine. Les cubistes, les futuristes et Duchamp (dans *Le Grand Verre*) ont tous traité de ce problème. Les premiers travaux de Robert Smithson illustrent l'obsession de la chair comme armure, avec des accessoires organiques devenant des tubes rivetés. Warhol, bien sûr, disait qu'il voulait être une machine. Les artistes conceptuels sont allés plus loin, en créant un art dont le processus s'apparentait à celui de la machine. Hanne Darboven se transforme en ordinateur perdu dans ses propres calculs, Roman Opalka en horloge digitale humaine. Sol LeWitt a devancé le marché des programmes informatiques, à Wall Street, avec ses sculptures programmées.

*

Tout ceci reflète bien la disparition littérale du corps humain au cours de ce siècle. La figure humaine devient la figure statistique. La chaîne de production substitue le mouvement mécanique au mouvement organique. En médecine, les organes humains sont remplacés par des organes électro-mécaniques. On absorbe des pillules, dont l'aspect relève toujours du symbolisme le plus pur, tant dans la géométrie que dans les couleurs, pour changer les fonctions métaboliques ou l'humeur. La génétique, bien sûr, va encore plus loin. Non seulement la vie s'explique en tant que données numériques, mais elle est sujette à des manipulations techno-mécaniques par lesquelles les lois de la production remplacent finalement la reproduction. Chaque vie humaine devient une statistique, dont l'utilité démographique servira à déterminer la politique des gouvernements, les stratégies commerciales et le tarif des assurances. C'était auparavant l'apanage de l'ouvrier que d'être soumis à la machine. C'est aujourd'hui le corps social dans son ensemble qui se soumet volontairement au même type d'enrégimentation. Il y a l'acier chromé des machines du club de gymnastique, les espaces géométriques et fermés de l'automobile et le fonctionalisme du style international.

*

Sol Yurick, dans son livre *Metatron*, a écrit sur ce système d'un point de vue que l'on pourrait qualifier de structuralisme à l'envers. Selon lui, ce ne sont pas les archétypes anciens, naturels, qui influencent le système actuel, mais ce serait le capital lui-même, en tant qu'archétype formel parfait, qui opérerait seul dans les structures de pouvoir traditionnelles. Le présent se résume alors, au libre jeu des systèmes électroniques et financiers, débarrassé à jamais des mythologies et du symbolisme traditionnels.

*

En dépit de Baudrillard, il convient de noter que la signification de la simulation est davantage la somme des recherches des années soixante que la conclusion de découvertes originales. Dans le domaine critique, la simulation est une synthèse du spectacle de Debord et des recherches sémiotiques de Roland Barthes. Mais ses précédents dans les arts des années soixante n'en sont pas moins clairs : Les Beatles, après tout, chantaient: «Des champs de fraises, rien n'est réel, rien à quoi se raccrocher». Warhol disait : «Plus rien ne faisait problème, car un problème ne signifiait rien d'autre qu'un bon enregistrement, et quand un problème se transforme en bon enregistrement, ce n'est plus un problème.» La contribution-clef de Baudrillard, c'est sa description détaillée du conditionnement d'un système sémiotique sans référent.

*

«La combinaison d'obscurité et de clôture dans la salle de jeux et de ses espaces annexes favorise l'intimité, la sécurité, la concentration et le contrôle. Le complexe labyrinthique avec son plafond bas ne reçoit jamais de lumière extérieure et ne donne pas sur l'espace au-dehors. Ceci désoriente l'occupant : il y perd la notion de l'espace et du temps. Le temps semble sans limites parce que la lumière de midi et celle de minuit sont exactement les mêmes. L'espace paraît sans limites parce que l'éclairage artificiel obscurcit plus qu'il ne définit les contours [14]».

*

L'ensemble du corps social est progressivement intégré aux grilles électromagnétiques de l'ordinateur. Du téléphone au contrôle aérien en passant par la banque, tout le flux des communications, des mouvements et des échanges est canalisé dans les circuits digitaux. Le micro-processeur devient le passage obligé de toute chose. Grâce aux graphiques informatiques, à la musique et aux voix synthétisées, l'ordinateur se permet même de reconstituer une réalité spécifique selon ses propres lois digitales.

*

On ne sait pas vraiment jusqu'à quel point chaque individu se trouve lié au réseau de la communication informatique. Le téléphone est cependant l'un des éléments de l'énorme réseau électronique qui couvre le monde entier. Plus important encore, les cartes de crédit, remplaçant l'autonomie relative de l'argent liquide, soumet une immense partie de la population à un esclavage de la dette informatique. La possiblité de crédit, de payer n'importe où et n'importe quand, attire la clientèle. Mais si les paiements n'ont pas lieu, une espèce de colère passive s'abat sur l'usager qui est alors exclu du système. Il se retrouve dans une détresse aussi grande que celle du chrétien excommunié au Moyen Age.

*

Le social devient ainsi le lieu de la «pure abstraction». L'individu n'est plus seulement un nombre, mais un ensemble de nombres, chacun le liant à une matrice différente de l'information. Il y a le numéro de téléphone, le numéro de sécurité sociale et le numéro de la carte de crédit. Les marchés financiers, ces arènes gigantesques de la guerre abstraite, se sont complètement détachés du monde matériel. Les frontières nationales s'écroulent. Les marchés sont gouvernés par des impératifs techniques, par le commerce informatiquement contrôlé. Le héros du marché n'est plus l'ingénieur, toujours engagé dans la technologie pratique, mais le magicien de la finance, le «broyeur de chiffres», le manipulateur des forces purement abstraites.

*

C'est aussi au niveau de l'expérience que le social se meut sur les grilles de circulation, encastrées les unes dans les autres. Chaque jour, le «banlieusard» se déplace de son domicile à sa voiture, à son bureau. Le voyageur passe du réseau urbain au réseau autoroutier transcontinental et au réseau aérien – et vice versa. Le plaisir sensuel est remplacé par le plaisir abstrait. L'ambiance remplace la nourriture. L'espace est remplacé par des «aménagements agréables».

*

L'histoire de l'art abstrait reflète l'histoire de cette transformation. Avec Cézanne, la matérialité de l'objet prend fin, de façon poignante. Le cubisme transforme la culture naissante du produit, dans ce nouveau XXe siècle, ainsi que ses habitants, en un monde gris de plans et de vecteurs abstraits. Mondrian, une décennie plus tard, écarte toute référence à la spécificité et voit le monde comme une grille utopique de forces et de flux abstraits, l'expressionnisme abstrait met quant à lui l'accent sur l'aliénation générée par le système. L'espace systémisé est révélé comme vide de sens. C'est, par exemple, cette réalité qui emplit les espaces vides de Rothko. Ainsi, l'histoire de l'art abstrait est l'histoire d'une progression effective dans le social. C'est l'histoire de l'organisation des espaces compartimentés et des systèmes formels constituant l'univers abstrait.

Publié pour la première fois dans *Arts Magazine*, (New York), vol. 61, nº 10, juin / été 1987.

Notes

Le mouvement beat, le minimalisme, le New Wave et Robert Smithson

1. Jeffrey Deitch, «Report from Times Square», *Art in America*, vol. 68, n° 7, septembre 1980.
2. John Berger a utilisé le terme de «normalisation» pour définir le processus de retranchement social et politique qui a eu lieu, après 1968, dans le monde occidental. John Berger, «Beetween Two Colmars», *About Looking*, New York, Pantheon Books, 1980.
3. Robert Smithson, «Entropy and the New Monuments», *Artforum*, juin 1966. *The Writings of Robert Smithson*, Nancy Holt ed, New York, New York University Press, 1979.
4. *Ibid.*
5. Ronny Cohen, «Energism», *Artforum*, septembre 1980.
6. «Entropy and the New Monuments», *op. cit.*
7. *Ibid.*
8. Smithson, «Interview with Robert Smithson for the Archives of American Art, Smithsonian Institute» (entretien avec Paul Cummings, 14 et 19 juillet 1972), dans *The Writings of Robert Smithson, op. cit.*
9. Allen Ginsberg, *Howl and Other Poems*, San Francisco, City Lights Books, 1956.
10. *Ibid.*
11. «Interview», *op. cit.*
12. William Burroughs, *The Soft Machine*, New York, Grove Press, 1961.
13. Smithson, «Conversation with Robert Smithson on April 22, 1972 (entretien avec Bruce Kurtz»), *op. cit.* Toutes les citations qui suivent sont tirées de cet entretien.

Contre le post-modernisme : une relecture d'Ortega

1. Clement Greenberg, «Modernist Painting», *The New Art*, Gregory Battcock ed., New York, E.P. Dutton, 1973.
2. Les citations d'Ortega proviennent de deux sources : *The Dehumanization of Art*, (1925), Princeton, Princeton University Press, 1968 et *The Revolt of the Masses*, (1930), New York, W.W. Norton and Co., 1932. (à paraître aux éditions Klingsieck).
3. Leo Steinberg, *Other Criteria*, Oxford University Press, 1972.

4. Les citations de Ad Reinhardt sont extraites de *Art-as-Art : The Selected Writings of Ad Reinhardt*, Barbara Rose ed., New York, Viking Press, 1975.
5. Les citations de Warhol sont extraites de *Andy Warhol, ma philosophie de A à B,* Paris, Flammarion, 1977.
6. Benjamin D. Buchloh, «Figures of Authority, Ciphers of Regression», *October*, nº 16, printemps 1981.
7. The Talking Heads, «Crosseyed and Painless», *Remain in Light*, New York, Sire Records, 1980.
8. Gang of Four, «Natural's Not in It», *Solid Gold*, New York, Warner Brothers Records, 1981.

Ross Bleckner : La peinture à la fin de l'Histoire

1. George W.S. Trow Jr., «Within the Context of No Context», *The New Yorker*, 17 novembre 1980.
2. Allen Ginsberg, «America», *Howl and Other Poems*, *op. cit.*

Nature et Culture

1. Jean Baudrillard, *Le miroir de la production*, Paris, Galilée, 1985.
2. Hal Foster, «Between Modernism and the Media», *Art in America*, vol. 70, nº 6, juin 1982.
3. Frederic Jameson, *The Political Unconscious*, Ithaca, New York, Cornell University Press, 1981.

La crise de la géométrie

1. Voir Michael Halley, «Argo Sum», *Diacritics*, vol. 12, nº 4, hiver 1982.
2. Voir John Rajchman, «Foucault, or the Ends of Modernism», *October*, nº 24, printemps 1983, sur le fossé entre le premier et le dernier Foucault.
3. Michel Foucault, *Surveiller et punir : naissance de la prison, Paris*, Gallimard, 1975.
4. Jean Baudrillard, *Simulacres et Simulation*, Paris, Galilée, 1981.
5. *The Writings of Robert Smithson, op. cit.*
6. Foucault, *op. cit.*

7. *Ibid.*
8. Baudrillard, *op. cit.*, pour cette citation et les suivantes.
9. On peut considérer que ces deux systèmes ont un fonctionnement simultané, la dissuasion étant réservée aux classes moyennes alors que l'enfermement demeurerait la règle pour les classes inférieures, aussi bien dans les pays industriels que dans ceux du tiers monde.
10. Plusieurs artistes des années quatre-vingt ont recherché des «sites» plutôt en milieu urbain qu'en milieu «naturel». Fischer «installait» son travail dans les grands magasins «Bloomingdale», alors que Keith Haring choisissait ses «sites» dans le métro new-yorkais.

Notes sur l'abstraction

1. Robert Smithson, «A Museum of Language in the Vicinity of Art», *Art International*, mars 1968.
2. Harley Shaiken, «When the Computer Runs the Office», *The New York Times*, 22 mars 1987.
3. Jamie Murphy, «A Threat from Malicious Software», *Time*, 4 novembre 1985.
4. Hippolyte Taine, *Notes sur l'Angleterre*, Paris, 1872.
5. Nicolaï Mikhaïlovitch Karamzin, *Voyage en France, 1789-1790*, Paris, Hachette, 1885.
6. George Kubler, *The Shape of Time*, 1962.
7. Steven Greenhouse, «Eateries Aim to Entertain», *The New York Times*, 21 août 1986.
8. Meyer Schapiro, «The Nature of Abstract Art», *The Marxist Quaterly*, janvier-mars 1937.
9. T.J. Clark, *The Paintings of Modern Life*, New York, Alfred A. Knopf, 1985.
10. Paul Virilio, *Pure War* (entretien avec Sylvère Lotringer, trad. Mark Polizotti), New York, Columbia University, Semiotext(e), 1983.
11. William Gibson, *Neuromancer*, New York, Berkley Publishing Group, 1984.
12. Publicité pour les salles de bains Kohler dans la presse, 1987.
13. William Severini Kowinski, «Main Street in a Spaceship : The Covered Mall», *Smithsonian*, décembre 1986.
14. Robert Venturi, Denise Scott Brown, Steven Izenour, *L'enseignement de Las Vegas, ou le symbolisme oublié de la forme architecturale* (1972), Bruxelles, Pierre Mardaga, 1978.

Table

Maquette de la collection :
Sophie Costamagna
Réalisation : Pascale Georget

Photocomposition (Times roman), photogravure et impression
réalisées par l'École nationale supérieure des Beaux-Arts
17 quai Malaquais Paris 6e

Dépôt légal : avril 1992
No d'Imprimeur : 266